CW00501554

Omega Teacher's Baby

ANNA WINEHEART

ISBN: 1977681743
ISBN-13: 978-1977681744

For two guys who deserve all the good things
in the world.

1
Dale

DALE KINNEY leaned into his seat, holding a cup of Colombian brew to his lips.

It smelled heavenly, rolling hot and bitter over his tongue. The coffee needed powdered milk and a ton more sugar—the jars were eight steps away, next to the coffee machine in his office.

But his chair was so comfortable right now, all smooth leather, and Dale would much rather relax before his heat arrived next week.

Rows of ring folders sat along the office shelves, ten full years of lab paperwork. Gold-framed academic plaques were crammed behind those folders, hidden from sight. Dale had thought about displaying them, just so he had something to prove his worth, but part of him still felt like he didn't deserve those awards.

In the other corner of the room, a soft red couch was tucked against two walls, the sheet he'd slept on folded and hidden, so it looked as though Dale spent barely any time in his office.

He pushed thoughts of his empty apartment away, glancing at his email inbox.

Meadowfall Lions Trounced Highton Beasts. Greg

Hastings named this season's MVP! the first email subject screamed in bold, black words.

Dale's stomach flopped. *Why does he have to be in my email, too?* But he clicked on the email title, holding his breath as he waited for the message to load. *Surely there are pictures.*

And there were.

On the very top of the email, right after the Meadowfall Lions' logo, there was a full-color photo of Greg Hastings on the court, feet apart, basketball in hand, his black eyes fixed on something beyond the camera. He was probably about to shoot.

In that picture, sweat glistened on the tendons of his neck, highlighted the contours of his biceps. His jersey clung damply to his broad chest, his tanned skin gleaming, and Dale followed the lines of his body down to his powerful thighs, his toned, scarred calves.

Greg was twenty-two, a magnificent alpha, and the college president's firstborn. And Dale couldn't tear his eyes from Greg's spiked brown hair, the intensity of his eyes, the full lips that pulled so easily into a smirk.

Dale gulped. He knew that mouth too well.

He shouldn't be staring at pictures of his employer's son. Especially when Greg was a student in his chemistry classes, and Dale was twenty years older than him.

But the damp valley of Greg's pecs dipped past his jersey, and Dale remembered other pictures, when Greg had pulled his shirt up to wipe sweat off his face. His abs were beautiful, too, and so was the V at his hips disappearing behind his waistband.

Dale's cock twitched—it was probably his hormones preparing for his heat.

Or maybe not, his mind whispered. *Greg's been trying to ask you out all semester.*

Before he had time to mull on that, someone knocked on the office door. Dale scrolled further down the email, sliding the pictures off the screen. Then the door opened, and June poked her head in.

"Have a moment?" his TA asked, smiling sweetly like she wanted a favor.

Dale sighed. Since she studied under him six years ago, June had become his closest friend; she could ask him for ten cars, and he'd probably take a loan so he could buy them for her. "Sure. What is it?"

June eased into his office and shut the door. Her eyes darted over the piles of homework assignments and his cup of coffee, then the striped origami sheet Dale slid off his stack. "This is kind of last-minute," she said. "But Cher just got laid off from her job. I want to take her on a whirlwind vacation and propose."

Dale looked up from folding a crane. That was sudden. "Okay, and...? When is this?"

"Tomorrow. For the next two weeks." June smiled sheepishly, running a hand through her hair. "Please? I'm sure you can handle everything just fine without me."

He froze, glancing back at the basketball team's email.

For the past two months, ever since Greg Hastings started asking him out for coffee, Dale had been borrowing June's birch scent, pretending he was bonded to an alpha. It never seemed to deter Greg; Greg stepped up to his lecture hall podium every other week, asking if Dale wanted coffee, his dark eyes trailing down Dale's chest. Dale's instincts always responded with an answering roar.

Gods, Dale wanted to say yes to him.

Except Greg Hastings was his student. And Dale was an omega who had been discarded, who had no use to an alpha.

He was infertile, and he'd been divorced for it.

"You know I need you around," Dale said, giving June his most pathetic look. He didn't know how else to decline Greg. Not when his own self-control was nonexistent.

June pushed her lips into a pout. "Come on, Dale, you can borrow another alpha's scent. There's plenty around here. About fifty on the campus field right now."

"Most of whom would sue me for an inappropriate proposition." Dale winced. He had no desire to deal with students, or his fellow professors. Which omega would ask a random alpha to mark them? It would invite trouble, or rumors, and Dale was far too close to tenure to risk it.

He looked at his screen again. June followed his gaze, grinning. "Basketball newsletter just got in?"

His cheeks burned. "I wish I'd never told you."

"You're glad you did," June said, wandering around his desk. "Come on, let's see it. I passed by

4

Greg one floor down."

Greg was here? Dale's stomach flipped. He didn't need to be distracted, especially not with Greg hovering so close. "Did he say anything?"

"Nope. Just stared at me like he was jealous. He's one hundred percent possessive, I'll tell you that." June stopped by him in a rush of birch, scooping up the mouse. Then she scrolled up the email, back to the photo of Greg on the court. She whistled.

Dale stared at Greg's biceps, his fierce gaze, and a slow heat burned down his body.

"You know, you should just tell him. He'd be the first to mark you. Take your virginity and all that."

Dale frowned. "I'm not a virgin! And I can't believe you're saying that to me."

"You know what I mean. Greg would probably time-travel just to have your untouched butt." June laughed, bumping Dale's shoulder with her hip. "Let him mark you. It'll be a win-win situation, right? He wants you. You want him. Better still if he marks you in bed."

"His dad's the college president, June. Bernard will fire me before sunset."

"You want Greg's knot."

Dale stared up at June, his cock twitching, his face scorching with the heat of ten thousand suns. "You did not just say that."

"Yes, I did." June winked. "Should I tell him?"

"No!" Dale covered his eyes. Greg *knowing* what he wanted? That would be the worst day of Dale's career. Probably the day he locked himself up forever. "Oh, gods, no. It would be a train wreck if he found out."

"So start thinking up some new plans. Because I'm taking Cher up north to Oregon and asking her to marry me. And you owe me enough to let me go on this sabbatical."

Dale groaned, planting his face on his desk. Three times a week, before he went to his classes, June brushed her wrists over his face, marking him with her alpha scent. No one questioned it. The students who frequented his lab thought he and June were a thing, but June was a post-doc, and aiming for an Assistant Professor status.

Perfectly safe, compared to any connection with Greg.

June patted Dale on the shoulder, looking kindly down at him. "He'll find out sooner or later, you know. I heard he'll be staying on in Chem. You'll have him for the next two years."

Two years of Greg asking him out, his eyes promising sex? Dale groaned, his pants tight. "I need to look for some birch perfume," he muttered. "Just to get through next week. Thanks for copping out right before my heat starts."

June sighed. "I'm really sorry. I mean, I would've stayed, but this trip is important to me."

"I know." Dale didn't have the heart to say no. June had been with her girlfriend nearly five years, and he'd listened to her through the ups and downs of their relationship. "Fine, take the two weeks off. I'll deal with this."

"Really?" June's voice lifted, and Dale glanced at her from the corner of his eye. She squirmed excitedly. "I already have the rings, you know."

She pulled them out of her pocket, two silvery bands that glinted in the light. They were sleek, smooth like satin, and Dale's heart ached with yearning. He had had a ring, nineteen years ago. Then his alpha had wanted it back, and he'd left Dale alone and mateless, his clothes shoved into a suitcase by the door.

Dale smiled weakly, standing to give June a hug. "Go grab that vacation—you deserve it. And I'm sure Cher would love to be your bondmate. You'll make a really happy couple."

She hugged him back, leaving a faint whiff of birch on his clothes. She was taller than him by an inch, more muscular, whereas he was thin, weak for his age. "Thanks so much, Dale. I'm just hoping she'll feel better, you know? Her job's the one thing she was really proud of."

I know that feeling. He patted June's shoulder, looking down at the photo on his laptop screen.

Greg Hastings, the star of the court. The college president's son. The only person who had asked, *Want to grab some coffee with me?* as though none of Dale's past mattered. As though it was okay for him to be infertile, for him to be *a waste of my time.* Charles had said that, and Dale had believed it. And Greg knew about none of that.

If there was an alpha Dale wanted, it was Greg.

And more than anything, Dale wished he was younger. That he was fertile. So he wouldn't be a pervert, hiding behind his screen, jerking off to pictures of Greg.

Who else wanted him that way? No one. If

7

Dale ever said yes to Greg, he could lose his chance at tenure, and it would be ten years of wasted effort.

"It'll be okay," June whispered in his ear. "You'll get through your heat just fine."

Dale watched as she left his office, a spring in her step. Alone with Greg? Fine?

He didn't think so.

2
Greg

GREG STRODE along the chemistry building corridors, glowering down at his phone.

On the screen, a voicemail awaited: one minute and thirty seconds of a message from his father, the president of Meadowfall College. Greg hadn't listened to it yet, and he didn't want to. Half of it would be about his future. The other half would be about finding a good omega, like Greg hadn't heard it a hundred times over.

He wove between the students, nodding at the people who waved. Then he stepped into an empty spot between a potted plant and a pillar, glancing down at his phone.

On the lock screen, there was an old photo of himself and Tony, back when they were still in high school. In that picture, he and Tony had been dicking around on a rowboat at the Salton Sea, back on that camping trip four years ago. Before the fire.

Greg swallowed, tapping the passcode to unlock the screen.

He probably shouldn't still be using that photo. But his grief had faded with time, and the picture was a reminder of his mistakes. He needed to remember not to make promises, not to stupidly think the future would always be there for him.

Greg scrolled through his email, glancing briefly at the basketball team's newsletter. They'd named him MVP. Kind of cool, really.

He wished he had someone he could tell outside of the basketball team. Maybe his mom.

It was three minutes before the lecture when he glanced around, waiting for Professor Kinney to show up. Kinney was almost always late, and Greg didn't expect him to appear until a minute before the bell rang. His stomach flipped anyway.

Since he spotted Dale Kinney last semester, rushing out of a lecture hall in a fluster, Greg had developed a bit of a crush. But the professor wasn't here yet, and he might as well get the voicemail over with.

"Haven't heard from you lately, Greg," his father said in the recording, his voice tinny. *"I hope you're doing well with your classes."*

As the college president, Bernard Hastings was one of the highest-ranked alphas in Meadowfall, rubbing shoulders frequently with the mayor, the police chief, and other important alphas. Greg understood why his father placed such importance on education.

But Greg didn't want to hear him talk about the future. His dad hadn't been there when the vacation cabin burned down. Bernard hadn't seen Tony gasp for breath, hadn't seen Greg carry him out of the fire, pumping his chest, trying desperately to make him breathe.

Four years ago, Bernard Hastings had found

his son at the hospital, burns on his calves. He'd taken Greg to the morgue. He knew Greg no longer believed in a future, but he'd been pushing Greg to find an omega anyway.

As though Greg could promise an omega his future, when he couldn't even save his best friend.

"*You'll have to decide on a major soon, Gregory,*" his father said on the voicemail. "*You need to focus. Make the most of your life. You'll get nowhere if all you do is finish Year One of ten different majors.*"

Yeah, well. It wasn't like Greg knew what he wanted to do right now. He hadn't been able to concentrate in med school. Then he'd tried law, and it was damn boring. So he'd switched to chemistry last year, and it had seemed interesting. Quiet. Not quite as rigorous with the schoolwork.

"*Your mother and I have discussed it. If you don't find an omega by the end of this year, we'll match you up with someone.*"

Greg pulled the phone away from his ear, his pulse thudding. His dad had said the same thing through his previous course change. But this time, Greg wasn't planning on jumping ship.

Not with Dale Kinney as his professor.

He hit Delete on the voicemail, then shoved the phone into his pocket, looking up. And there, on the other end of the atrium, Dale Kinney hurried out from a stairwell, a harried frown on his face.

For an instant, Greg forgot to breathe.

Professor Kinney was a lithe man, his auburn hair threaded with gray, his eyes striking green. He was half a head shorter than Greg, with a pair of steel-rimmed glasses perched on his nose, his lab coat fluttering around his thighs.

11

But what Greg liked about him was how easily he could read this man, how Kinney's lips pursed when he frowned, how his hibiscus scent teased when Kinney brushed by. He was pretty. He seemed lonely. With him around, Greg didn't have to think about his dad, or Tony.

Kinney stopped by the lecture doors, rubbing his nose.

Greg had been in Kinney's office twice. Unlike his father's office, there had been no plaques in it, only a mess of paperwork, some picture frames, and Kinney's laptop. And that plush red couch in the corner that smelled like hibiscus, even though it looked like no one had spent any time on it.

Greg would bet a hundred bucks Kinney slept over in his office, all curled up on that couch, and he woke with his hair mussed and his shirt rumpled, and none of his thoughts were about how to get rich, or rank higher, or any of that crap.

And unlike all the other omegas Greg's age, Dale Kinney had no idea how to react when Greg asked him out for coffee. He fumbled and stuttered and always said no, but Greg's instincts said Dale was interested.

Except the professor also smelled like birch, like that alpha TA in his lab, and gods fucking damnit, Greg was jealous of that woman. He wanted Kinney. Wanted this omega as his own, wanted to pin him and kiss him and taste those lips.

The professor frowned up at the lit *In Progress* sign above the double doors. The students from the previous lecture were starting to trickle

12

out. And this always happened to Kinney's classes, somehow. The other professors seemed to know he always ran late, and *they* held their own students back in their godawful long lectures.

Kinney rustled his papers in irritation. Gods, he was adorable. Greg wanted to hug him.

As though he could feel Greg's stare, the professor glanced around the crowded atrium, eyes landing on him. His throat worked. Greg didn't look away. And for five heart-thumping seconds, Kinney held his stare, his tongue darting over his lips, his eyes dragging down Greg's T-shirt, over his jeans, all the way to his basketball shoes.

Kinney himself was wearing a neat button-down, its lines following his chest, his black pants clinging to his thighs. And he always wore those oxford shoes, brown leather with black laces, and they were always polished.

The professor tore his gaze away, glancing around them as though he was afraid he'd been found out. Greg looked around, too, half-wondering if someone would notice the knife-edge tension that stretched between himself and his professor. But no one noticed, and it felt as though there were only the two of them in the atrium, him and Kinney, each stripping the other in his mind.

For a moment, Greg wondered what the consequences were, if he walked over right now and kissed his professor. He wondered if Kinney would kiss back, if Kinney would open for him. If Kinney would taste like the coffee he sometimes brought along.

And whether Kinney would get hard for him, bonded or otherwise.

The bell rang shrilly overhead. Kinney jumped, looking up. Greg felt sorry for him sometimes. Whereas the students had grouped themselves into little cliques around the atrium, Dale Kinney stood alone, looking down at his notes, sneaking glances at Greg every few seconds.

So Greg walked over, smooth as he could, trying to impress an omega who had probably seen all the slickest moves.

Kinney met his eyes, gulped, and turned just as the lecture hall doors burst open. A swarm of students streamed out past him, trapping him against the wall.

Greg stepped aside to avoid the human traffic, approaching his professor from behind. And Kinney knew he was close, too, from the way he stiffened, trying to look over his shoulder. Then he looked at his papers, ignoring Greg.

Two steps from him, Greg caught his hibiscus scent, mingled with that telltale birch. He scowled. Kinney was spoken for. He'd seen the professor's TA walking along the chemistry building corridors, Kinney's hibiscus scent a faint whiff on her clothes. For two months, Greg had only seen Kinney with June's scent, had watched as they chatted with each other in the lab.

Why, then, did Dale Kinney always look at Greg like he wanted something more?

"Hey," Greg said, tapping him on the arm. Kinney tensed, and Greg pulled his hand away. "Sorry."

"No, don't worry about it," Kinney said, looking at his feet.

Inches away, Greg stared at the silvery scar

on Kinney's neck, right over his scent gland. Someone had bonded with him and left that mark. Probably the TA, June. Hot dislike surged through Greg's veins again. He wished he'd been there first, wished he could've stood a chance against anyone else his professor had been with. They were at least twenty years apart.

So yeah, maybe Greg was no longer your typical twenty-two-year-old.

"Can I talk to you in private?" Greg asked quietly, glancing at the students striding past.

Kinney sighed, turning around to face him. In the bright daylight of the atrium, his eyes were forest-green, intelligent, and his lips glistened. Greg wanted to know what they felt like against his own. Wanted to feel Dale's mouth part against him. Brush over his skin.

"Do you need help with the assignments?" Kinney asked, his nostrils flaring like he was smelling Greg.

A thrill shot up Greg's spine. *He likes my scent.* "If I said yes?"

"You're going to have to shower first. I don't need your sweat clogging up my office," Kinney said. Except a dusting of red spread up his pale neck, like he was flustered. Like all the other times Greg had asked him out for coffee. And maybe this was something he wanted, Greg's sweat in his office.

Greg swallowed, fighting the urge to step closer. "Can I drop by your office today?"

Kinney glanced at the students waiting to enter the lecture hall. "Maybe in two weeks. I'm rather busy at the moment."

"Fine."

When neither of them spoke, Kinney turned toward the lecture hall doors.

"Hey," Greg said.

Kinney paused, looking over his shoulder. And Greg was almost distracted by the sharp point of his nose, the curl of his eyelashes, the soft hair falling over his forehead.

"I know a great coffee place," Greg said.

Kinney's gaze snapped away, his tongue darting over his lips. "I-I'm sure you'll find plenty of friends to have coffee with."

"If I want to have coffee with you?"

The professor froze for a heartbeat. Then he kept walking, disappearing into the lecture hall, and the dusting of red spread all the way up to his ears.

Greg's heart thudded. Was Kinney flustered because he wanted Greg, or because he wanted Greg to stop with the flirting? Or did he want out of his relationship, and he couldn't?

So Greg took a seat right in front of the podium, at eye-level with the professor. Dale Kinney plugged his flash drive into the laptop, pointedly avoiding Greg's stare. He smelled faintly like musk, like arousal. Greg closed his eyes, desire humming through his body. *Who's the one making you hard? Is it me?*

He didn't know anyone with a relationship like that, an alpha bonded to an omega twice his age. It was something his father would disapprove of. *You won't have a future with him, Gregory. He's old. Pregnancy past forty bears a risk.*

Screw my future, Greg thought, pulling his

lecture notes out of his backpack.

Kinney started the lecture when most of the hall was filled. He talked about nanoparticles, their various applications in biochemistry, and their existing production methods.

Greg had already read the textbook chapters for this lecture. So he spent his time half-listening to Kinney, half-watching the way Kinney moved: rubbing his nose, pulling his shirt sleeve over his wrist, his eyes darting over the audience to make sure they were following.

Twice through the lecture, while Kinney was doing his visual scan, his eyes locked with Greg's. "Current methods of producing silver... silver nanoparticles include..."

Kinney paused.

The first time, Greg let him glance at his lecture slides to remember his sentence. The second time, Greg raised his hand, stopping Kinney halfway through an awkward pause. "Professor. Most of the procedures involve aqueous solutions. Are there nanoparticles synthesized in solid state?"

Kinney froze, and a slow smile crept over his lips. "There are, actually. Carbon nanotubes are an excellent example of solid-state synthesis. Several studies have reported..."

He's smiling because of me. Greg's cheeks burned. He glanced down at his lecture notes, then back up when Kinney went on a tangent about the nanotubes. Kinney wasn't looking at him, of course, but his smile lingered, and Greg couldn't stop looking at it.

For a fifty-minute lecture, time whizzed by like a basketball game. Except all Greg had done was remain seated, his heart jumping through hoops in his chest.

At the end of the lecture, Kinney said, "Your homework is the assignment I've uploaded on the intranet. Please submit last week's homework on the podium according to your classes."

Greg waited until the lecture hall cleared. When a few people remained, Kinney unplugged his flash drive, stacking the assignments together, his movements hurried.

He was fleeing from Greg, as usual. Greg stepped off the stairs, striding to the podium just as the professor turned to leave.

"Hey," Greg said, lightly catching Kinney's wrist. It was thin in his hand, warm.

Kinney looked up, his breath hitching, his eyes flying to the empty seats.

If Kinney had pulled away, or looked at him with revulsion, Greg would've let him go. But he stayed, his eyes raking down Greg's chest, his nostrils flaring.

The doors slammed shut. There was no more movement in the empty room, no more people, save for Greg and Kinney. Kinney's chest heaved.

"You keep running," Greg said, watching his professor. Kinney smelled like a mix of alpha and omega and musk, and Greg wanted to lean closer, breathe Kinney's scent right off his skin.

"This isn't appropriate," Kinney murmured, but he didn't pull his hand away. "You know that."

"You forgot my homework." Greg held his assignment out. Kinney made to accept it, but Greg held on to his hand, sliding his assignment between Kinney's chest and the stack in his arm. The end of the sheet scraped against Kinney's shirt all the way down, catching on the buttons. When he'd gotten the homework almost aligned with the rest, Greg stepped closer, raising Kinney's trapped hand to his lips.

Kinney's throat worked, and he couldn't look away.

Greg turned Kinney's wrist toward himself, dragging his nose over smooth skin, to where Kinney's hibiscus scent was the strongest on his wrist. There wasn't a trace of birch here, no silvery scar. On this wrist, there was no marking from an alpha.

Something in Greg's chest roared. *What if he's mine?*

"You aren't stepping away," Greg whispered. His grip was feather-light.

"I would if you'd let me," the professor breathed, but Greg felt the flutter of his pulse. Faint musk curled into his nostrils, like he'd gotten Kinney hot, just by smelling his wrist.

"You want me," Greg said.

Kinney's throat worked. "No."

But his eyes read *I need,* and Greg parted his lips, dragging his tongue over Kinney's scent gland. Then he sucked lightly on it, two short, firm tugs, and musk rolled through the air between them, heady and sweet, distinctly omega.

Greg glanced down. There was a telling line in Kinney's black pants now, and Greg's blood surged between his legs. Then he looked up.

Kinney's pupils had blown wide, his lower lip bitten red. He yanked his hand out of Greg's, striding away to hide his erection. But the sight of it had burned into Greg's mind, and he couldn't think about anything else.

Kinney had stayed. Kinney had gotten hard for him, and maybe he didn't actually want that relationship with his TA, after all.

A spark of hope lit in Greg's chest, tiny and bright, like the candle he used to keep by his window.

The professor didn't look back at him as he left, but Greg was fine with that. He had a chance with Kinney. Now he needed not to fuck everything up.

3
Dale

A WEEK later, Dale stared at the ungraded assignments on his desk, his body aching.

His heat had begun yesterday, taking him by surprise—it was supposed to be milder now that he was forty-two, except his hormones were acting up. He'd spent his weekend preparing for this week's classes, adjusting the syllabus.

Then his hormones had swollen like the tide and torn through his body, sending a throbbing ache through his limbs.

Dale *wanted.*

All of yesterday, Dale had locked himself up in his apartment with his hands down his pants, trying to work off the ravenous desire in his body. He'd thought about last week over and over, Greg's large hand around his wrist, Greg's nose dragging along his skin.

The thought of Greg's tongue on his wrist had ripped an orgasm through him, and there'd been no refractory period before he was hard again. Dale had groaned, sliding a plug up his ass, pretending it was Greg's knot.

He'd gone through three pairs of briefs

before he'd given up on clothes, stroking himself until he'd barely had any cum left. His body had given him a two-hour break. Then lust had crawled through his limbs, and Dale had gone back to stroking himself sore. He was still a little tender, his foreskin pinkish, sensitive to touch.

To force those thoughts from his mind, he'd dragged himself to work, popping a suppressant so he wouldn't be distracted.

Except the suppressant didn't seem to be helping, and he was faintly damp, a vague restlessness whispering through his mind.

Stop thinking about him. He's your student.

The assignments stared up at him, accusing. They were due in an hour. Dale had promised to return them to his class today, so he could go over the questions and explain them in detail.

And just because the world hated him, Greg's assignment sat on the very top of the pile, smelling faintly like aspen. Greg would be in Dale's classroom an hour from now.

Dale groaned, closing his eyes. They were fortunate that no one had been in that lecture hall last week. Greg was the college president's son; there'd be eyes on him everywhere he went. And if his scent lingered on Dale... who knew what sort of rumors would spread? The president would fire his sorry ass.

Class in an hour. Get to work.

Dale cracked his eyes open, sipping some coffee. He'd added extra milk and sugar today, and it was sinfully creamy, rolling over his tongue in a burst of flavor.

He swallowed, making a decision.

He wouldn't grade Greg's assignment first. He'd save it for last, grade it if he had time. And if he didn't, well. That was that.

Dale slid Greg's homework to the bottom of the pile. Then he pulled his red pen from his white-knight pen holder, and started on the first assignment.

FIFTY MINUTES later and still aching, Dale stepped into the undergrad classroom corridor. Students crowded the hallways, waiting for the classrooms to empty out.

Dale hugged the assignments to himself. He'd managed to grade all of them. Well, *most* of them. By the time he'd reached Greg's, it was four minutes to class, and he'd shoved it back to the bottom of the pile.

Greg could probably wait. Dale would return everyone else's first.

He wove between the chattering students, searching out his classroom. Then his neck prickled like someone was watching him.

Dale didn't have to guess who it was; the same alpha eyed him every time. He looked up anyway.

Past the twenty-odd students between them, Greg met his eyes, his expression watchful. Dale's pulse missed a beat. He should've grown used to this by now, after two months of Greg Hastings in his classes, but Dale still couldn't believe Greg was interested.

His body hummed, needing touch. The

suppressant he'd swallowed right before class still hadn't kicked in; he wasn't sure it would now. And it was pointless, anyway, because Greg would be able to smell his heat.

Dale wished June was still in California. She'd been posting photos of her Oregon vacation on Facebook, sipping margaritas with her fiancée, and Dale should've tried to tag along.

A thousand miles away from Portland, Dale was in heat, the alpha of his choice five yards away.

Greg wasn't someone he could take home.

Dale strode past the students, past Greg, hoping none of them would pay attention to his scent. Except Greg's eyes never left him. Dale's insides squeezed. He still had no idea why Greg paid attention to him. Why Greg would watch him this closely, asking him out every two weeks.

He slowed down when he approached his classroom, waiting for the previous class to vacate. They were running late, too, and he needed a teacher's desk to hide behind. Right now, he was defenseless against twenty-two-year-old alphas. Like the one prowling toward him.

His breath snagged in his throat.

Paces away, Greg's nostrils flared, his tongue darting over his lips. Like he was sniffing at Dale. Like he wanted to drag his tongue down Dale's chest, all the way to his cock. Maybe suck on it.

An answering heat flooded through Dale's veins. *Climb him,* his body whispered. *Take his cock. Fuck him.*

Dale clenched his hole so he wouldn't drip, but Greg's lips curled in a smile. As though he could smell Dale anyway. Smell Dale's slick, and how ready he was for Greg. Greg's gaze dropped right to his hips, and Dale fought the urge to cover up even though he wasn't hard.

But he was half-hard, and Greg's smile widened.

Greg stopped inches away, his gaze raking down Dale's body, from his throat to his hips to his shoes. He was shameless. He ogled Dale just like Dale ogled his basketball photos, so maybe that was fair.

Dale squirmed, needing more of his attention. Needing to spread for him.

With June gossiping in the lab, Dale had learned a few things about this alpha: the college president paid for his tuition and board. He scored As in his schoolwork. He played basketball thrice a week. He didn't have a bondmate.

"Where's your alpha?" Greg muttered, meeting his eyes. His voice sounded like rumbling thunder, and Dale wanted it growling in his ear. Against his skin.

"Alpha?" Dale blurted.

Greg's stare sharpened.

Belatedly, Dale remembered June, how she'd dab her wrists over his face, hug him during his heats. Through the jerk-off fest over the weekend, he'd clean forgotten to buy some birch perfume. *Crap.* "I'm your professor. That question is hardly appropriate."

"You're in heat," Greg said, his voice barely audible. His gaze dropped to the bonding scar on Dale's neck, and Dale knew there wasn't a trace of alpha scent on him. "You broke up with June? I haven't seen her around."

"Oh." Dale gulped. "She's on a vacation. She'll be back soon if you need her."

"Do *you* need her?" Greg's eyes bored into his. His scent coiled into Dale's nose, heady and musky, like loamy aspen, and Dale wanted Greg pressed up against him. Fucking him up against the wall.

The bell screamed above his head.

Dale jumped, his heart crashing into his ribs. Time for class. He was a professor, and all it took was one student to upset his life. He still had this last class to get through. Then he was done for today, and he'd be free to lock himself away and jerk off. Rinse and repeat for the rest of the week.

Gods, he hated being in heat.

He eased away from Greg, watching as students from the previous class streamed out of his classroom. The air filled with the floral scents of omegas, the grassy scents of betas, the woodsy scents of alphas.

Behind, Greg touched his wrist to Dale's elbow. The leaving students shielded them from the rest of his class, and Greg dragged his scent gland down Dale's forearm, to his wrist.

He was leaving his scent on Dale. Marking him.

Blood surged down Dale's body, right to his cock. The thought of being Greg's omega... His body sang with that idea, a throbbing hum through his limbs. *I can't believe I want this. I'm a professor.* Cheeks scalding, he squeezed past the leaving students, calling out, "You guys take a seat first! I'll be back for class!"

Greg's stare clung to his back the entire way

down the corridor.

The moment he rounded a corner, Dale breathed a sigh. Then he raised his wrist to his nose, sniffing at the new aspen scent. Greg had marked him. Just a little, but it lingered, enough to set his cheeks burning.

Aside from June, Dale hadn't been marked in years. He'd slept with alphas, worn their scents, but this... It was different. Greg wanted him. And it felt a little like belonging, a little like acceptance. Greg knew nothing about Dale's infertility. He was too young.

But more than a family, Dale craved being needed. He hadn't realized this until now.

Maybe Greg was just after him for a notch in his belt.

Dale sucked in a deep breath, then released it. That was okay. It was nice having someone want him, and Dale... didn't want to give in. If he did, maybe Greg would fuck him and leave. And being wanted was better than being left behind.

When Dale returned to the classroom, he was calmer, in control of his aching body. He breezed into the classroom with a smile. "Sorry I'm late—a slight issue came up. Let's get started with class."

The students looked questioningly at him. Dale shrugged, handing the stack of graded assignments to the closest student. He avoided Greg's stare and set his class schedule in front of his seat.

"I'll be explaining questions from two assignments today," Dale said, drawing the answers from the first assignment on the board. "You should have completed the homework on nanoparticles."

The lesson built momentum as time ticked by. Greg didn't ask questions—he usually scored full marks on his assignments. Not that Dale was paying special attention to him, or anything like that.

Dale breezed through questions on nano dots and iron particles, the various synthesis methods in current research, and included a short segment about his lab's nanoparticle projects. He knew some professors vigorously promoted their own research groups, hoping to attract the brightest minds to their stable.

All he wanted were students who loved chemistry, who would be willing to learn. It made his research lab a less competitive place, so everyone could afford to joke around a little.

Dale kept talking, sometimes going on tangents with the questions, sometimes breezing through others. Greg kept watching him, and Dale kept talking. If he stopped thinking about his work, he'd start imagining what he looked like to Greg instead, thin and awkward in front of his students. He wasn't attractive, or special. He had nothing to offer a rich young alpha.

The stack of assignments drifted along the rows of students. Dale lost track of where it went.

Twenty minutes before the end of class, he started to explain the first question from the graded assignment, the one he'd distributed to the class. Greg raised his hand.

Dale's stomach squeezed. *What do you want?*

For a second, Dale considered ignoring him. If he turned and explained the next few questions,

28

Greg would probably put his hand down.

Except the other students would notice, and Dale didn't need them drawing conclusions about him and Greg, when a trace of Greg's scent was already on him. "Yes, Greg?"

"You didn't grade my assignment," Greg said.

Dale's stomach sank. Of course he'd forgotten, when he'd been rushing through the assignments, trying not to be distracted by his heat. He'd shoved Greg's homework under the pile and had no time to grade it, and now it had come back to bite him.

Acutely aware of the students' stares, Dale nodded. "I'll grade it after class. Could you hang on to it for now?"

"I'll come by your office."

"Sure." The moment it left his lips, Dale knew it was the worst thing he could've said. He was in heat. And Greg would be alone with him.

Greg's eyes dropped to Dale's hips, like he had plans for a private viewing. Visceral need tore through Dale's body. He spun on his feet, lifting his marker to the whiteboard, hoping no one saw the strain of his cock in his pants. He needed to calm down. Needed to stop thinking about Greg's gaze on his naked ass. Or Greg spreading him open, touching his hole. Licking it.

It was 10:45 AM on a Wednesday, and Dale wanted Greg Hastings to fill him with potent seed.

His skin flushed hot. The marker trembled in his hand. *Stop thinking. Focus on the assignment.*

Dale spoke over his shoulder, raising his voice. He explained question after question on semiconducting solids, blathering about electrons and band gaps. Everything he said was something he'd memorized ages ago, and he couldn't think. His pants were tight.

If he turned around, the class would see the outline of his cock. He couldn't let that happen, couldn't let *Greg* see it, let him realize how much Dale wanted him.

Except he was a little wet, too, and maybe Greg could smell that.

By the time he got to the last question, his skin was damp with sweat. Dale probably reeked of musk, and everyone in class had probably figured he was in heat. And the only alpha scent he had on him was a light touch on his arm, indiscernible to anyone else but Greg.

How embarrassing.

"That's all for today's class," Dale said, his legs trembling. "Please email me if you have any questions. I won't be in my office this afternoon, but feel free to come by tomorrow."

He scooped up the loose sheets of paper on his desk. In those seconds, Greg's gaze scalded his skin, hot and hungry. And Dale's heat throbbed along his limbs, intensified the ache in his body.

He needed to get away. Needed Greg's body pressed up against him. Inside him.

Dale swept out of class, not thinking about the students, or the musk, or Greg. His cheeks burned. He needed to pull out that plug in his bottom drawer, the one he'd hidden away in a cardboard box. His body ached to be filled.

Because he'd ended class earlier than usual, the hallways were empty. Dale hurried through the whitewashed corridors, his shoes clicking on the floor tiles. Disgust roiled in his stomach. Which professor fled from his students? Which professor secretly hoped for a student to spread him open?

Halfway to the office, Greg said from somewhere behind, "Professor."

Dale's heart stumbled, and his cock was so hard he thought it would spear through his pants. Dale slid his papers over his hips, lengthening his strides.

"Professor!"

Dale kept up his pace. Who was he fooling, trying to run? Greg was the star on his basketball team. Dale could never outrun him. Except he tried anyway, climbing the stairs, striding down the hallways until he reached the sanctuary of his office.

Two paces from the door, Greg closed the distance between them, snagging his arm.

"Professor."

Greg spun him around in a dizzying whirl, meeting his eyes. He smelled like musk, like arousal, and his warmth burned through the space between their chests. Then Greg looked down, and Dale realized that his sheets of papers had slipped, that the line in his pants stood tellingly between them. Greg licked his lips, his eyes boring into Dale's. Like he meant *I want to taste you.*

Dale's throat went completely dry.

"W-What?" he gasped. They were leaving their scents in the hallway. A telltale mix of hibiscus and aspen and musk, and anyone sharp would identify that as sex.

And Dale knew they weren't stopping here,

not right now.

"I need to—to get into my office. Please," he said.

Greg released his arm. Dale fumbled with the key from his pocket, his fingers shaking. He needed Greg. Needed Greg pressing him down on his desk. Needed Greg shoving his legs open, pushing his cock inside.

The key turned in the lock. Dale swung the door open, and he was four steps into the room when Greg followed him in. Then Greg shut the door, turned the lock, and the click rang through the air like a deadbolt sliding home.

Dale leaked through his briefs, his body throbbing. He couldn't refuse Greg. He didn't want to.

"Your alpha isn't taking care of you," Greg said behind him. And he stepped closer, so his chest was inches from Dale's back, his heat brushing through Dale's shirt.

Dale dropped his papers on his desk, leaving them to flutter across the floor. Their hips were so close. All Greg had to do was to slide his cock out, rub it up against Dale. Push it between Dale's legs. Dale's heart pattered. "My—my alpha. Um."

He chanced a glance over his shoulder. Greg's nostrils flared. Then Greg looked over the photo frames on his desk, the photos on the wall, and sniffed at Dale again. "Where's June?"

The question hung between them: *Where is your alpha when you need someone?*

Dale closed his eyes. He knew he could lie, or tell the truth and forever hold his peace. His heat sluiced through his veins, whispering, *Tell him the truth, and you'll get what you want.*

More than anything else, Dale wanted this alpha, wanted Greg's touch on him. Wanted Greg to look at him like he mattered.

"She's on vacation," Dale mumbled. "She's proposing to her girlfriend."

Greg sucked in a sharp breath. "Her girlfriend? So your bonding marks..."

"I'm divorced," Dale said, closing his eyes. He had no wish for Greg to scrutinize him, asking why he'd been discarded.

"You've been smelling like June."

"I asked her to mark me."

Greg growled, stepping closer, his shoes bumping into Dale's. "You don't have an alpha?" he asked, his voice rumbling, his fingertips trailing lightly along Dale's waist.

"No," Dale choked. Shame scorched through his face.

And Greg moaned softly, his warm breath rushing out across Dale's neck, his fingers twitching against Dale's hip. "Damn it."

"What?" Dale turned, and a wall of musk crashed into his nose, smelling like aspen and Greg and *need.*

Dale's cock throbbed so hard it hurt, and his hole quivered.

"My rut," Greg muttered, reaching down with his other hand, grinding his palm against his bulge. He panted. "Just—just triggered."

4
Dale

FOR A moment, Dale stared, trying to figure how Greg's rut had begun. It had to be a coincidence that it happened here. Or maybe it was because of Dale's heat.

But Greg met his eyes, his gaze burning into Dale's, and Dale realized Greg wanted him. And Dale's lack of an alpha had sent Greg into a rut.

His body throbbed, slick soaking through his clothes, his hole squeezing. He needed Greg inside.

"I'm your professor," Dale whispered. His pants gripped his hips, and his cock was still a little tender from the weekend. Every movement sent a little tendril of pleasure-pain down his nerves. "I can't—can't possibly—"

Greg leaned in, brushing his soft lips over Dale's. Dale tensed, and Greg pulled away slightly, watching him.

But every instinct in Dale's body said to grab Greg's collar, yank him close. Dale whimpered, tipping his face toward Greg's, offering him his lips.

Greg's eyes glinted in triumph. He leaned in, caught Dale's lips with his own, and kissed him hard, nipping on his lower lip. Greg felt good. Inviting. Better than Dale had dreamed, with his broad chest and hungry lips. Dale moaned, parting for him, a primal need shooting through his veins. He needed Greg closer. Needed Greg devouring him, plunging inside him.

Greg slid his tongue into Dale's mouth, forceful and hungry, stroking Dale's tongue like Dale was his. And Dale opened wider for him, leaning into his alpha, completely pliant. Greg walked Dale backward, grasping his hips. Then he pinned Dale to the desk, ground their hips together, his cock on Dale's, separated by layers of clothing. Pleasure whispered through Dale's body.

"Fuck," Greg muttered, pushing their cocks together. Dale throbbed, a dark thrill shooting up his spine. He'd dreamed of this, jerked off to this, and he wanted Greg to touch him everywhere. So he pushed back, hungry, his cock aching in his pants.

Greg tangled his tongue with Dale's, sliding out of his mouth, thrusting in again, pressing into Dale's space like he was his bondmate, and Dale's instincts said, *Obey.*

He ground up against Greg, chasing the damp warmth of Greg's tongue. Greg tasted like blueberry — it came from the sports drinks he brought with him to classes. He was Dale's *student,* and Dale was honor-bound not to sleep with him.

Guilt slithered through his gut.

Despite the heat throbbing through his body. Dale flattened his hands on Greg's chest, shoving him off. "You can't," he rasped. "I'm your teacher."

Greg licked his lips, his eyes glinting. "You

want my cock."

Dale's cheeks burned. "I can't answer that."

"But you know what you want."

Yes, Dale did.

Greg smirked. Then he caught Dale's wrist, pressing Dale's hand to the hard line of his jeans. Behind the denim, Greg's cock was thick, solid, a ravenous length Dale wanted inside him. Heat shot down his spine, and a moan tore from his throat.

"I'm this hard for you," Greg whispered, rolling his hips, his cock straining against Dale's palm. "Want to slide this inside you."

Dale's breath punched out of his chest. For long seconds, he could only think about Greg's cock rubbing against his hole, fucking in. He needed to see it. Feel it against his skin, all hot and smooth and slippery.

"Gods," Dale groaned, squirming.

Greg leaned in, licking along the shell of his ear. "I want you as my omega," he whispered, releasing Dale's hand, curving his own palm around Dale's side. "Want you to be mine."

Dale shivered, hardly daring to move. He wanted it all. Wanted to belong. Wanted to be Greg's.

Then Greg trailed his hand down Dale's cock, stroking it lightly with his fingers, following the taut fabric of his pants.

"You're so damn hard," Greg murmured.

His fingers whispered all the way to Dale's tip, squeezed him there, and pleasure jolted up Dale's nerves. Dale gasped, his hips bucking up, his face burning like he'd been set ablaze. He wanted his student's touch, wanted Greg kissing down his belly. This was wrong.

All Greg had to do was ask, and Dale would spread for him.

Greg stepped closer, his foot easing between Dale's shoes, his knee nudging Dale's thighs apart. Dale whimpered, leaning back into his desk. Then he parted his legs, and a low growl rumbled in Greg's chest. He stepped between Dale's feet, his hard thighs pressing against Dale's, keeping them open.

Dale could no longer hide how much he wanted this alpha. After two months of yearning for him, allowing Greg to know felt like a weight had slipped off his shoulders.

"Greg," Dale whispered, lifting his hips, inviting touch.

And Greg growled, planting his hands on the desk, on either side of Dale, caging him in. Then he caught Dale's earlobe between his teeth, dragging his tongue along Dale's skin. "Say my name again."

"Greg." Dale ducked his head, embarrassed.

Greg bared his teeth, sliding them off Dale's earlobe, pressing damp kisses down Dale's neck, licking at his pulse point, all the way to his scent gland. Then he nipped at the sensitive skin there, his breath puffing heavy on it. Dale shivered, knowing Greg could bite him now, and mark him for life. His cock jerked in his pants.

"Not gonna bite," Greg murmured. Then he dragged his hot, wet tongue over Dale's scent gland, an intimate touch, and Dale shuddered against him, gasping, his fingers curling into Greg's shirt. His body hummed with pleasure.

"You're just teasing me," Dale hissed,

grabbing Greg's hand. Then he pushed it down against his cock, rocking up at him, and Greg chuckled darkly, squeezing Dale, tracing him from base to tip. Dale gasped. Greg was touching him. It shouldn't feel so sinfully good.

"What do you want me to do?" Greg whispered, sliding his fingers down, stroking Dale's balls through his clothes. His touch was firm, careful, like he knew exactly what he was doing. How exactly he was affecting Dale.

Dale bucked into his hand, his thighs trembling. "We shouldn't be doing this."

Greg kissed up his neck, nipped along his jaw, and met his lips. And Dale moaned into his mouth, sliding against Greg's tongue, tasting him again. Greg's touch promised sex, promised pleasure. And Dale was so wet he had probably soaked through his pants.

He sucked on Greg's lip, then his tongue. Greg groaned, sliding his hands under Dale, lifting him off the desk, hefting Dale against his own hips. Then he stroked his fingers down Dale's spine, all the way to his ass. Firm fingers dipped between Dale's cheeks. They pushed the soaked fabric of his pants up against his hole, cloth rubbing over his sensitive skin.

Dale panted, pushing back against Greg's fingers. He was beyond ready.

"You're so damn wet," Greg murmured, groaning. "Wet for me."

Dale couldn't deny it, not when his body ached, needing to be shoved down, held open, pierced with a thick, hard cock. "I—I..."

Greg crooked his fingers, and the cotton of

Dale's briefs caught against his entrance. Greg pressed harder, and Dale's hole parted slightly, taking him in. Greg's breath rushed over his cheek, his finger dipping a little further in, his covered cock pressed snug against Dale's.

Dale wanted him all the way inside.

"Want you," Greg murmured, "Professor."

Dale flushed. He didn't need that reminder right now, when all he wanted was to be pinned beneath Greg. "Stop calling me Professor," he breathed. "My name's Dale."

"Dale," Greg whispered against Dale's lips, working his fingertip in, slick fabric dragging against the rim of Dale's entrance.

Dale writhed, his cock throbbing. Greg was inside him.

In that heartbeat, he forgot who he was, who Greg was. He only knew he was omega, and Greg was alpha, and Greg was prepping Dale for his knot. And Dale's nerves were wound so tight it would take a hard fucking to relax them.

Greg shoved their hips together, heaving Dale against him. Then he rutted up, his bulge sliding hard against Dale's. Dale's voice broke. "Greg, please!"

"Please what?" Greg slipped his finger out of Dale, leaving his hole neglected. He eased his hand between them, ground his palm down on Dale's cock, and Dale was only aware of him, of this alpha who pleasured him, made him *need.*

Greg's touch was so much better than his own. It was hotter. Heavier.

"Need—need you," Dale gasped, shoving his hips at Greg.

Greg smirked, pulling open Dale's belt. He undid Dale's pants, slid his zipper open, and pushed his briefs down. And Dale's cock finally slid free into the cool office air, pink and glistening, accompanied by a surge of musk. The pressure at his groin eased a little. Greg inhaled deeply, sliding his fingers down Dale's length, inspecting it. Dale hissed, pulling back.

"What's wrong?" Greg asked, pausing.

"Friction burns." Dale's cheeks prickled. "I was... busy over the weekend."

A slow smile crept along Greg's lips. He trailed his fingers down Dale's cock, then up to his tip, avoiding the pinker splotches of sensitive skin. Then he rubbed Dale's tip through his foreskin, sending a ribbon of pleasure through his nerves. "Who were you thinking of?"

Warmth swept through Dale's face. It was bad enough that he was doing this with Greg. To have Greg know... "It's none of your business."

"You were jerking off to me," Greg said, watching him carefully.

And Dale's face burned like the fires of hell, condemning and traitorous.

Greg's smile grew wider. He eased Dale's foreskin away from his tip, exposing him, and Dale shivered, squirming.

"Does it hurt here?" He rubbed a callused finger right over Dale's tip, sending a spark of pleasure through his body.

Dale's hips jerked up. "No."

"What about here?" Greg flicked his finger right under his head. Pleasure shot through his body.

Dale choked, gasping. Somehow, Greg knew where exactly to touch him. Where he wanted to be touched. This wasn't what his heats were like. It was a thousand times better. "Greg, stop teasing."

"You want me to fuck you," Greg murmured, curling his fingers around Dale's cock, and Dale thrust up into his hand, his cock pushing thick and ruddy past the circle of his fingers, unabashedly hungry. "You want me to knot inside you."

Dale couldn't look at him. "Yes," he muttered, rocking into Greg's touch.

And Greg smiled, hooking his hands into Dale's waistbands, pushing his pants and briefs down his thighs. Then he slid his hand between Dale's legs, rubbing his tight balls, before stroking behind them, touching Dale's hole.

Dale hissed, relaxing for him. Greg worked his callused finger around Dale's hole, drawing circles around it, sliding over it, his finger smearing with slick.

"Want something?" Greg whispered, his finger rubbing slow and hot against Dale's entrance, tempting. One well-angled push, and he'd be inside.

Dale whined. "Fuck."

"Fuck you here?" Greg stroked him, teasing, and sank his fingertip inside Dale.

Dale shuddered. He curled his hand around Greg's wrist, trying to push him deeper. "Don't stop there."

Greg smirked, sliding the rest of his finger in. Dale's body stretched around the welcome intrusion, and his face burned. He shouldn't be this needy for his student.

"So fucking wet," Greg murmured, swirling his finger inside, probing, exploring Dale's body. Dale's spine arched; he tried to breathe through the pleasure, all his thoughts fleeing his mind. "So ready for my cock."

Dale's cheeks burned. This was wrong, his pants down, his student between his legs. Greg's finger inside him, finding out just how much Dale needed to be fucked.

"This—this will get us in so much trouble," Dale breathed the moment he could speak. "I—I'm not—You're my student."

Greg crooked his finger against Dale's prostate, and Dale's cock jumped, his body thrumming. Greg licked his lips. "And yet you need me," Greg whispered, sliding his finger out. "Look."

Under the fluorescent lights of Dale's office, Greg's finger glistened between them, covered in Dale's slick.

Dale's face burned. Greg had touched him *inside*.

"This is wrong," Dale moaned.

"Not if it stays a secret."

Greg slid his thumb down Dale's balls, a light, warm touch, and Dale's fingers curled around the edge of his desk. Slick trickled down his thighs. But Greg didn't touch him inside.

"That's all?" Dale whispered.

"That was prepping you," Greg said, rubbing Dale's tip, watching as it jerked out of his hand. "Before you take my cock."

Dale's breath tore out of him. And Greg slid his arm around Dale's waist, pulling Dale away from the desk. He turned Dale around, pressed his chest to Dale's back, the hard line in his jeans pushing against Dale's spine.

"I'm gonna fuck you so hard," Greg whispered in Dale's ear, his breath rushing hot on his skin. "Split you open with my cock."

Dale throbbed, and Greg bent him over the desk, hooked his hand against Dale's hip, angling Dale's ass into the air. Dale groaned, spreading his legs wider, his cock dripping. The entire office smelled like musk, like sex, and Dale ached, needing more.

"Gonna give you a good pounding," Greg murmured. Dale bit his lip, trying not to groan.

Past the rush of his breathing, he heard Greg's button snap, his zipper rasp. There was a rustle of clothing, and he looked over his shoulder.

Greg's cock pushed out of his pants, big, damp at the tip, and Dale's entire body clenched with need.

Greg pressed his cock down against Dale's ass, let its heat soak into Dale's skin. Then he rocked it between Dale's cheeks, sinking closer to his hole, spreading his cheeks open. Dale couldn't think past the heft of it. Part of him said he shouldn't have waited this long. He should've had Greg's cock up his ass the very first day they met.

Dale reached down, needing to hold Greg so he could sit back on it. But Greg caught his wrist, held it down against Dale's back, and slid his cock between Dale's cheeks.

"Feel my cock," he whispered, pressing right against Dale's hole. "Gonna sink this inside you."

It was heavy, hot, and Dale whined, his own

cock dripping onto the floor. Greg slapped his ass lightly, sending a jolt of pain and pleasure down Dale's body. But Greg lifted his cock away, sliding his fingers between Dale's cheeks, spreading him open. Dale's face prickled with embarrassment. He hadn't had anyone look at his hole in a while.

Then Greg rubbed his fingertip over Dale's entrance, teasing him, slipping just his fingertip inside. Dale panted, the papers on his desk rustling under his breath.

"Leg up," Greg said, tapping on Dale's thigh.

Dale squirmed, kicking off his shoe, shoving his pants down, sliding his leg out so he could hike it up on the desk. And this left his ass spread wider, his balls and hole exposed. Cool air brushed against his skin.

"Very nice," Greg murmured, squeezing Dale's balls, rolling them against his palm. Then he reached further between Dale's legs, grasping his cock, trailing it to its sensitive tip, his touch feather-light. Dale whimpered, rutting against his hand, his cock so hard he needed to come.

"Inside," he whispered.

Greg continued to stroke Dale's cock, his eyes darting around the office. "Need a condom. You have one?"

Dale squirmed, his hole squeezing. Greg was going to fuck him. "Test status?"

"Negative," Greg said. "Haven't—haven't slept with anyone since."

Dale stared. "You haven't?"

A light tint of pink swept through Greg's cheeks. "Didn't wanna. I was waiting for you."

Dale's heart skipped. Greg had been waiting

for him. Greg wanted him. And his body ached harder, needing Greg inside, needing Greg's knot filling him. Gods, this heat had to be his worst. Or his best, when Greg stood waiting, his cock thick and ready.

"Go bareback," Dale said, lifting his hips. He reached down to spread his cheeks, showing Greg his hole. "I won't get pregnant."

Greg moaned, his eyes flickering between Dale's face, and his hole. Then he rubbed his fingers over Dale's entrance. Pushed two fingers in. Dale arched, gasping, rolling his hips. And Greg slid his fingers in to their knuckles, crooking them up against Dale's prostate.

Pleasure shot through him like wildfire. Dale whimpered, his sweaty fingers slipping against his ass. "Greg, more. Please."

"You're so damn pushy," Greg muttered, but he slid his fingers out, wiping Dale's slick onto his cock. Then he angled his cock down, rubbing his blunt tip over Dale's hole. "Gonna take my knot too?"

"Fuck yes," Dale hissed, pushing his hips up.

Greg pressed down on his hole, slowly stretching him open. His tip slipped in. Then he eased the rest of his cock inside, thick and hot, and Dale trembled. "Greg," he gasped, his body snug around his alpha. Greg was *big*.

"Fuck," Greg said, sliding in completely, until his balls bumped into Dale's ass, and he was inside, he was fucking inside, and Dale needed him to *move*. Greg squeezed his ass. "You're so damn tight."

Dave shoved his hips at Greg, trying to take

him deeper. "Fuck me. Please."

Greg slid out, thrust back in, his cock sinking home. Then he slid out again pausing, and Dale glanced over his shoulder. Greg was looking down at where they joined, sliding in slowly, and Dale could imagine the sight: his pink hole spread around Greg's cock, taking in his entire length.

Then Greg looked up, meeting Dale's eyes, and he slid all the way in, his cock grinding against Dale's prostate. Dale writhed.

"Feel it?" Greg whispered, sliding out, fucking back in, and Dale couldn't think past that thick cock inside him, stretching his body open.

"Yes," he hissed.

Greg smirked, and his next thrust jerked Dale forward, skidding over his desk, his papers caught under him. Dale's cock leaked onto his class worksheets.

"Gonna ruin you for anyone else," Greg said, pumping harder, shoving hard against Dale's prostate. For a blinding moment, Dale couldn't breathe, could only hang on to his desk, taking the vicious shove of Greg's cock inside him.

"More," Dale gasped.

Greg gave him more. He held on tight to Dale's hips, his own snapping forward, thrusting deep and fast into Dale. The tension in Dale's body wound tighter. He groaned, pushing back, and Greg pounded into him, their hips slapping, his cock a thick, unyielding presence inside Dale's body.

Dale dripped, surrendering his body and his control. All of it belonged to his alpha now, when all he wanted was for Greg to make him come.

"Hard enough?" Greg asked, pumping in.

"No," Dale panted, and Greg's next stroke slid deep, sent hot pleasure sizzling through his nerves. He fucked Dale, steady and unrelenting, and Dale forgot everything but this alpha inside him, Greg's cock massaging his body, swelling bigger, about to fill him with his seed. Dale's fingers crushed his papers, moans ripping from his throat.

"I'm gonna come," Greg growled, anchoring his arm around Dale's hips, holding him down so he slid home, hard and hot, jerking Dale's entire body with his thrusts.

Then he slid his hand down to Dale's cock, stroking him carefully like he remembered Dale was sore, and Dale shuddered. *He cares.* The dam burst. Pleasure slammed through his body, arching his spine, tensing his limbs, and Dale only knew the heat of Greg's body around him, hard and careful and *safe,* and he was gasping, clutching the edge of his desk, trying to hang on as he spilled.

Behind, Greg snarled, fucking Dale through his pleasure. He sank in deep, over and over, until his cock jerked inside Dale, and his fingertips pressed heavy into Dale's hip, his cock filling Dale with spurts of heat.

He's coming inside me, Dale thought, panting as he pushed his ass firm against Greg's hips, needing to catch every drop of his come. *I want his babies.*

Greg's arms tightened around him. He held on to Dale, his chest heaving, his cock pulsing, and a primal instinct in Dale relaxed. He had Greg's seed. It sat potent inside him, and the thought made his cock twitch.

Dale caught his breath, relaxing into Greg's warmth, the sturdy wall of his body. It felt like he belonged somewhere, and this was good. Safe.

Then Greg leaned back to pull out, and Dale's pulse stuttered.

"No," he blurted, curling his fingers around Greg's forearm. Greg was withdrawing before his knot grew, and Dale understood that. It was a courtesy. But Greg had also helped him through his heat, had done Dale a kindness, and Dale didn't want him to leave just yet. "I—I mean, if you'd like to stay."

Greg met his eyes, hesitating. Then he drew closer, easing his knot back inside.

Greg's knot stretched his body, sat wide and heavy in him. Dale moaned, panted until he grew used to the width of it, a whimper caught in his throat. This felt right, him and Greg locked together, Greg's knot pulling inside him every time either of them moved.

It was intimate. And it was probably a hundred sorts of wrong, Dale taking his student's knot. He was old enough to be Greg's father.

Dale looked down at his desk. Droplets of come had scattered over his papers, leading back to his still-flushed cock. Greg's knot pulled lightly inside Dale's body, an incriminating, delightful presence.

"You regret this?" Greg asked when Dale didn't speak.

Dale bit his lip. The last time anyone had knotted inside him... he couldn't remember.

"I don't know," he said. Greg had come

inside him. He was still inside, and he was twenty-two years old, someone Dale was supposed to mentor. Not fuck.

Dale didn't know how this would read to someone else, a student fucking his professor. Bernard Hastings would find Dale a horrifying embarrassment. And proceed to fire him.

Dale's chest squeezed. He folded the corner of a receipt, scratching the fold into its fibers. "I'm twenty years older than you. I'm your professor. This shouldn't have happened."

"You wanted it." Greg held Dale's hips, pushing further in, sending a whisper of pleasure through his body. Dale moaned. Greg traced his finger down Dale's spine. "You've been watching me for the past two months."

Dale's cheeks burned. So Greg had noticed. "You were the one who looked first."

Greg shrugged. "But after that, you looked back. I read it in your eyes, Professor. You wanted me."

Dale stared at his papers, a sick feeling in his stomach. If he had been obvious to Greg, had he been obvious to anyone else?

"This won't happen again," he said. "I hope you know that."

Greg didn't answer, but he worked his thumb up along Dale's back, working out the kinks in his muscles. "I didn't know you had condoms in here."

Dale winced. "I didn't say I did."

"You weren't even panicking about test statuses. It's like you fuck students in here regularly or something."

"I don't! I haven't—I've never..." *You're the first,* he wanted to say, but that was far too incriminating as it was.

Dale pushed away from the desk, thinking of scrambling off, pulling away. Greg was reading too much into him. He could find out everything else Dale was uncertain about, and then he'd have all the power over Dale.

"Then you fuck yourself in here?" Greg murmured, leaning in, sliding his arms around Dale's hips. Dale froze, Greg's biceps pressing into his sides. He felt good. Greg stroked his warm palm down Dale's belly, over his sensitive cock, squeezing his balls. "Your condoms are for use with a toy."

Greg caressed his balls, and Dale moaned. *How did you even figure that out?* But Greg wasn't stupid, and he'd read Dale correctly so far.

"It's none of your business," Dale said.

And Greg squeezed his cock, a smirk in his voice. "How many times do you fuck yourself in here? Do you wear a plug around all day?"

He rolled his hips, his knot pushing deeper into Dale. Dale gasped, his body thrumming with pleasure. He needed to leave before he somehow got hard again. Before he decided to take Greg home and fuck him all night.

Except he was still locked around Greg, his cock twitching against Greg's palm. Greg smiled against his shoulder, his breath warm. "I want to see you wear a plug all day, Professor. Stretch yourself open for me."

Dale shivered, heat winding through his body. Behind him, Greg growled, sniffing at his scent gland.

"You like that."

Shit, Dale thought, looking down at his body. *Stop betraying me.* Out loud, he said, "You should leave. There's nothing left here for you."

Greg pressed a kiss to his skin. "I want to keep on seeing you."

And Dale's heart missed a beat. "What?"

"That wasn't clear enough?"

Dale turned, biting his lip when Greg's knot pulled inside him. *He can't be serious.* "Weren't you going to look for the next omega professor? I can give you a list. Go hunt them down and fuck them. Stop bothering me."

Greg narrowed his eyes. "I'm not looking for other professors."

"Surely you are."

Greg's fingers tightened around his waist. "I like you."

His words rushed by Dale's ears. Greg couldn't possibly want him. "I'm old, and you're probably confused. Please see a counselor."

"I've been waiting to do this for months." Greg leaned in so their lips were inches apart. His eyes bore into Dale's, intent. "I don't care if you're my professor."

"Your dad will fire me if he finds out."

"It's none of his business who I fuck."

Greg pushed his lower lip out, his nostrils flaring. Watching him, Dale's heart thumped. Greg was beautiful. He was the perfect alpha, and he had a whole future ahead of him. He should be looking for a fertile young omega, not someone like Dale.

Through the last two months, Dale had thought about this over and over; he'd never understood why Greg wanted him. They weren't even in love. Dale had made countless mistakes in front of Greg's father — the lab fire, the declining course signups, the messed-up presentation.

The moment Greg's knot receded, Dale squirmed out of his arms, stepping back into his clothes. It was only after his pants were fastened, when he'd regained some semblance of his composure, that he relaxed slightly.

"You're sure you won't get pregnant," Greg said, watching him.

Unexpectedly, Dale's chest squeezed, so tight he couldn't breathe. To admit to his infertility was one thing. To tell Greg about it, this handsome boy, the only person who seemed to want Dale... Even if he was too young, Greg had to ask, didn't he?

Dale looked at his feet, wishing the floor would swallow him. "I'm infertile. It's why I'm divorced."

He didn't mention the doctor's explanations, the continued hospital visits when he and Charles tried to find out what was wrong with him. *Your ovum tubes are almost completely sealed,* the doctor had said. *The chances of a baby are less than one in a thousand.*

It had been an arranged marriage, and with a signed statement from the doctor, Charles had brought their marriage certificate to the Drakestown registrar and annulled their union.

Dale didn't blame him; Charles had been insistent from the start that he wanted heirs. When the years passed and Dale failed to bear him children, Charles had lost his patience with Dale. *I should have ordered some fertility tests,* Charles had said. *I need a functioning omega. I've lost so much time in this marriage trying to conceive a child.*

Charles' parents had been worse with their insults, but there had been nothing Dale could do. He'd wanted a family, too. Wanted someone he could share a child with.

"I don't care about kids," Greg said, his forehead wrinkling. He stepped closer. "Are you okay?"

Dale flinched, his heart heavy. At some point, Greg would want children. He was an alpha. He belonged to a high-ranking family. Dale was too old, and he was Greg's professor. Nothing could happen between them.

"No," he said, backing away. "We're done here. Please leave."

Greg opened his mouth, as though he wanted to protest. But he studied Dale's face, and Dale looked away, refusing to meet his eyes.

After a moment, Greg turned. He picked up the backpack he'd left on the floor, pulled his assignment out, and set it on Dale's desk. Then he straightened his clothes, nodded at Dale, and left.

The door clicked shut behind him.

Dale looked around his office, at the mess on his desk, the paper cranes motionless on the walls. The room smelled like musk and aspen, like stolen moments that would come back to haunt him.

Greg was a student. Dale had slept with him, had told him the things he hated most about himself. And then he'd chased Greg away. Who knew what the basketball team would hear about him now?

Dale returned to his desk, his eyes hot, his gut swimming with unease.

None of this should have happened.

5
Greg

GREG STOPPED in front of his apartment door, fishing his keys out of his pocket.

The decision to drive home hadn't been easy. Several times on the road, he'd wanted to turn around and head back to the college, knock on Kinney's door. Step into his office and pull him into a hug.

Kinney — Dale — had looked crestfallen, a little terrified, like he was about to cry. And Greg was kicking himself for leaving Dale behind.

It wasn't the sex that had upset him — Dale had moaned through it all. It was the mention of children, the infertility, that had shaken him, and Greg had watched him, baffled, trying to figure why fertility was so important to his professor. Everyone knew omegas weren't so great with fertility when they were in their forties.

Thing was, Dale wasn't going to end up pregnant. That was fantastic. Greg had no wish to knock his professor up. But he liked the thought of his cum inside Dale, his scent clinging to Dale's clothes.

Dale hadn't noticed, but when they'd

knotted, Greg had dragged his wrists along Dale's sides, over his hips, his chest. The entire time he'd marked Dale, Greg had thought, *Mine,* and something in his chest had rumbled with satisfaction.

Best of all, June wasn't Dale's alpha. And Greg wanted more of his professor.

For now, he wondered if Dale was going to catch crap for having Greg's scent on him. If anyone even recognized it. Maybe that was what Dale had been worried about.

It was typical of people to have similar scents. Greg's aspen scent was commonplace, much to his father's annoyance. In this case, it helped. Especially when Dale and he were teacher and student, and Dale seemed to think it was wrong.

Well, it probably was. Greg's dad would flay them both if he found out. Even though it was none of his business—a mate was a mate. Greg's choice, not his dad's.

He ran his thumb over the silver keys, thinking about Dale's office. The hunger in Dale's eyes, the curiosity, the admiration. He'd looked at Greg like he'd never seen someone so hot, and Greg had wanted to pin him down, kiss him, worship his body.

Dale had been damp and ready beneath him, spreading for Greg, musk rolling off his skin. He'd been everything Greg had dreamed about, and then some. And Greg had sunken right into him, slid into his heat like he was always meant to be there.

He wanted more, wanted a slower second time, wanted to savor every bit of Dale's body instead of chasing their release.

Greg smiled, sliding his key into the front door. He was probably going to get into the shower and jerk off again. Once in the Porsche hadn't been enough.

When he turned the key, the door lock didn't click. Greg frowned.

He remembered locking the door when he left this morning, so this was... odd. The only times he found his door unlocked, well. It wasn't pleasant.

Greg held his breath, pushing the door open.

On the leather couch, Bernard and Henrietta Hastings sat primly, drink glasses in their hands. Their eyes flickered up when he stepped into the apartment.

"Hey Mom, Dad," Greg said, cringing inwardly. They could've given him a heads-up before they dropped by. He still smelled like sex. "How're things going?"

Henrietta leaped up from the couch, hurrying over in a rush of morning glory scent. In his starched suit, Bernard scrutinized him, comparing Greg to his own standards. Greg would always be two points short of his father's expectations.

"I've missed you so much," Mom said, tiptoeing to comb her fingers through Greg's hair. "We haven't seen you in a month!" She came up to his chest, short and plump with curly brown hair, and she wore her favorite rose-print dress. "How has my Gregory been? You smell different today."

She leveled a hopeful, knowing look at him, and Greg swallowed. Not the right time to tell them about Dale.

"Found someone special?" she whispered, her eyes gleaming. "It's all right, you know. I won't tell your father."

Greg eyed her. She always said that, and he mostly trusted her. Except for the time he'd wanted to go out with a fellow alpha to prom night. Dad hadn't been happy when Mom told him about it. "Yeah, well," Greg said. "Maybe another time."

Her shoulders sagged. Greg pulled her into a hug, careful to keep his hands off her—the same hands he'd touched Dale with. "The basketball team voted me as their MVP last week."

Henrietta's eyes lit up. Bernard stepped over to clap Greg on the shoulder. He was tall and tanned, muscular like Greg, and Greg liked to think their similarities ended there.

"Very good," his dad said, looking down his pointed nose at Greg. "I expected no less from you."

Bernard Hastings was ambitious, goal-oriented. The sort of person you'd find at shareholder meetings, raising shrewd questions about business expenditures, demanding answers when company profits didn't meet their targets.

Three decades ago, Bernard had scraped together money to put himself through school, crawling up the social ladders so he could emerge as a leader. Then he'd started his own college, built it up into a respectable institution, and earned a place as one of the top-ranking alphas in Meadowfall.

Greg was proud of his father for that. But Bernard would also cast Dale aside because he'd think Dale wasn't a good enough omega, and Greg didn't want to subject Dale to that.

Whatever he grew up to be, it wasn't the head of Meadowfall College.

"The omega scent smells familiar," his dad said, eyes narrowing. "I seem to have encountered it recently."

Greg froze. The college president held quarterly meetings with his faculty staff. Of course he'd have smelled Dale at one of those. And his father would terminate Dale's employment the moment he found out they'd slept together. *Shit.*

"Lots of people around with that scent," Greg said, shrugging. His heart thumped.

"Who was it?" Bernard leveled a look at him. "It's one of those I've smelled time and again. I should have a name to match to it."

"You must've remembered wrong," Greg said. "Guy on the basketball team. Ivan."

There was no Ivan on the team, but his father didn't know that. Bernard nodded and turned away. Henrietta eyed Greg speculatively, as though she wanted to know more. Greg swallowed the whisper of guilt in his throat. He didn't like lying to her.

Greg stepped away from his parents, grabbing a bottle of deodorant to mask Dale's scent. It sprayed light and cool on him, minty, and he discreetly spritzed more into the surrounding air. The more he hid Dale's scent, the better. "Why are you guys here, anyway? Could've told me you were coming."

Of course, it would be nice if they didn't have a key to his apartment, but they were the ones paying for his lodging.

"You'll be graduating in two years," his father said, eyeing the basketball posters on the living room walls. "I've been expecting news about a bondmate. You're aware that your job prospects improve greatly with an omega at your side."

Greg shrugged. "Lots of alphas get jobs without being bonded."

"I don't care for the majority of alphas, Gregory. I'm concerned for you. Why present yourself as a common alpha when you can be better?"

Not this again.

Four years ago, Greg had wanted all that his status could offer him—fast cars, his own house, money to travel the world. He'd made plans with his best friend: they'd go on hot air balloon rides, buy neighboring houses, and visit all the comic conventions around the world.

"I don't care about being better than everyone else," Greg said.

"Is this about Tony again?" his father asked, eyes narrowing. "He wasn't even your bondmate."

"He was my best friend!" Greg snapped. So what if he and Tony knew they'd never be mates? They'd still been best friends. They'd cosplayed for years, and they'd talked about how their lawns would bleed into each other's, and they'd have a fence around both their houses.

Greg wasn't ready for that kind of relationship again, not when he couldn't save his best friend. He'd brought his candle to the vacation cabin, lit it by the window, and a stray breeze had pushed the curtain right into the candle flame.

In one night, Greg's dreams for his future

had burned down to ashes.

"Regardless, he wasn't your bonded omega. You should have drawn a line in that friendship. There's no point spending so much time with a person if they aren't of use to you," Bernard said.

Rage bubbled in Greg's chest. He looked to his mom, but Henrietta shrugged and glanced away, her lips thinning. She'd never stood up for him in front of his dad.

Greg loved his mom, but *gods,* if his parents could understand him, maybe even sympathize with him for once. His mom had, back when Tony died. His dad had told him to move on.

"Your mother and I have raised and clothed you." Bernard studied him coolly. "We expect to see you succeed with the education we've provided. Don't let our efforts go to waste."

Greg thought about a professor huddled in his lab coat, Dale Kinney with regret in his eyes, and said nothing.

His mom stepped closer, slipping her arm around his back. "If you've been pursuing an omega, you should think about bonding, dear," she said kindly. "Or your father will bring out the list he's prepared."

He frowned. "What list?"

"Potential bondmates. Omegas. Brightest students in the college," Bernard said. "I've contacted the professors to come up with lists of candidates."

The idea hovered around Greg's mind, not sinking in. "Okay, and?"

"If you haven't found one, we'll match you up with an omega we think is best," Bernard

Hastings said. "That is, if you and Ivan decide not to pair off."

What? "You've never said that before. You said I can choose my own."

"You're taking too long to decide, Greg," his mother said, holding his elbow. "We're concerned for you."

Had Dale put together a list as well? His best omega students, all in a tidy list going to the college president? "I can't believe this," he said, betrayal snarling in his chest. He was supposed to have at least five more years to decide. "I'm not even graduating yet."

"It will be a work in progress," his father said. "You'll graduate in two years, but we'll prefer for you to be bonded in one."

"What if I find someone else and he doesn't fit your criteria?"

Bernard narrowed his eyes. "Then we'll evaluate him."

Greg thought about Dale pressed against him, his lips bitten red, a flush crawling up his neck. His memories of Dale still made his heart skip, and if they'd fucked and he still had a crush... then the crush would probably never leave.

He looked back at his parents, his father in his austere suit, his mother smiling jovially at him. They waited expectantly for his answer.

If Greg said anything about sleeping with Dale, then Dale would lose his job the moment it left his lips. He wasn't going to put Dale through that crap.

"I'll look into it," Greg said, his thoughts churning.

His father nodded gravely, and his mom hugged him again. "It'll work out," she whispered in his ear. "I'm sure you'll find a good one."

He'd already found an omega. But Dale had sent Greg away, and it wasn't as though they'd *be* in a relationship. Greg wasn't looking for a partner. Dale didn't want to see him again.

Greg hugged his mother, dread pressing down on his heart. He probably shouldn't keep pursuing his professor.

The thing was, he couldn't stop.

6
Dale

A WEEK later, Dale's heat had ebbed away. His body had calmed over the weekend. Even though thoughts of Greg sent his blood rushing south, his desire was no longer quite so urgent.

Instead, he was uncomfortable. His skin had turned sensitive to touch, itching from the inner seams of his socks. The stale air in his apartment had become more musty. Daylight seemed too bright when he stared out the windows.

I haven't turned into a vampire, he thought. *Maybe I'm sick.*

It didn't stop him from thinking about Greg.

Over the past week, Dale had been avoiding him. He'd hidden behind his lecture hall podium, pointedly scanning the other students. He'd arrived early to work and left late, hoping not to bump into Greg.

And after his lectures, Greg had stopped coming up to ask him out.

It was obvious—Greg had had his fill of Dale. Why stay when he could have his selection of other people? An MVP like him would surely want the best. Sample everyone before he decided on one omega, maybe two.

After two months of Greg pursuing him, that thought hurt.

He shouldn't have allowed Greg to come to his office, shouldn't have fucked him. Greg had moved his attention elsewhere, and Dale missed being wanted. Missed feeling attractive. Missed the days where he stopped remembering *You aren't worthy as an omega.*

Dale breathed in, focusing on the paper cranes tucked into little corners of his office. He cradled his mug, steam fogging up his glasses. The milk smoothed out the Colombian brew, and sugary sweetness burst across his taste buds.

Greg probably likes his coffee black, Dale thought. Then he yanked his mind back to his research notes, before it nudged up Greg's body.

There was nothing else between them. They had had a fling, and that was it.

"Work," Dale told himself. "June's coming back."

She'd texted last night saying she'd be on time today—which meant she'd be in the lab in five minutes. It would be another hour before the students showed up, and Dale needed June to mark him again, mask the lingering traces of aspen that had clung to his skin. No matter how hard he'd scrubbed, his soap didn't remove Greg's scent.

And maybe his skin was starting to smell a little different, a little sweeter, but he thought it might've been all the sugar he'd been drinking. Funny—he was a scientist, yet he believed in little nonsensical things like that.

Dale tucked his papers under his arm,

grabbed his coffee, and headed out of his office.

In the mornings, he liked to spend his time in the quiet lab verifying the students' results. They performed experiments that the post-docs created, preparing nanoparticle solutions with varying reagents and concentrations. Whenever anyone came up with a particularly fascinating discovery, Dale liked to carry out the experiment himself, watch as the results came alive at his hands.

Today's experiment would be to test the fluorescence of enzyme-bonded gold nanoparticles —if the test results worked, they could expand into biochemistry research, perhaps land research grants from large medical corporations. It would add reputation points to Meadowfall College, give Dale a better standing in the faculty. Maybe trim a couple months off his time to tenure.

Dale unlocked the lab, flicking on the lights and equipment on the bench tops. He set his coffee by the general-use computers, then spread his papers down on the counters, grabbing a fresh pair of nitrile gloves.

Two minutes in, the door squeaked open, accompanied by a familiar birch scent. "Dale!"

Dale glanced up from the bottles of chemicals, smiling at his friend. "June! Congrats! How was your trip?"

She breezed in with a smile. "Thanks! It was awesome—Cher said yes! I mean, you've seen it on Facebook. I thought she might not, you know, with her losing her job and all. But we went out to the bars and quaint bookstores in Portland, and she was thrilled. So I dropped the ring in a shot of tequila and handed it to her. You should've seen her face—her eyes grew so wide, I thought they might fall out."

June dropped her purse in front of her computer, a ring glinting on her finger.

Dale fought down the coil of envy in his chest. *She's young. She deserves a chance at happiness. Don't make this about yourself.*

"I saw the rings on Facebook," he said, bringing the bottles of chemicals to the weighing scale. "You could say I'm jealous."

"Aww, no, don't be. I mean, I'd been waiting for that moment forever." June turned on her computer, then wandered over, her gray eyes sparkling. "So, what about you? What mischief have you been up to? How are you and Greg?"

He knew she meant that as a joke, but he couldn't help remembering Greg's hot body against his, pressing him down against his desk, Dale's thighs spread for that alpha.

While June was away, Dale had gone and fucked his student, and he'd thoroughly enjoyed it.

He looked down to hide the burn creeping up his cheeks.

"No way," June said, slowing down. "Don't tell me..."

"Nothing happened," Dale said tightly, unscrewing the first bottle. He set a filmy sheet onto the weighing scale to hold the oxidase powder. *Concentrate on your experiment. You're too old for a family. Gre—An alpha wouldn't want you.* "I'll need you to mark me later."

"Something *did* happen." June stopped next to him, watching as he dipped a spatula into the bottle. Her nostrils flared. "I can smell—wait. You smell different."

Dale tapped a minuscule amount of powder onto the reagent sheet, watching as the numbers on the digital scale flickered. *I know I smell like him. You don't have to dig it in.*

"It's not just Greg," June said, her eyes growing wide. "Merciful gods, Dale, you smell sweet. And I know that smell. My neighbor's been pregnant thrice."

"What?"

"You smell like my neighbor."

"I don't even know your neighbor."

"*No.* I mean, you smell pregnant, Dale." She looked him over, breathing deep. "Please don't tell me you slept with Greg. I mean, anyone else would be fine."

Pregnant? How in the world could he smell pregnant? It had been something he'd wished for countless times. All it had given him was loneliness.

Dale blinked at June, his heart sore. She knew not to talk about his infertility, especially when she'd just gotten engaged. "You know I can't do the pregnant thing."

"I *know* you can't, and I'm sorry." June winced. "But you smell different, Dale. I'm serious. I'll go out and buy you tests if it'll convince you."

"I can't be pregnant," he said in a tiny voice.

He'd been over this with Charles, with the doctors in Arizona. He remembered the marriage certificate, with *ANNULLED* stamped across it in big red letters. He remembered Charles' parents and their snide remarks. *Drop him, Charles, his body has rotted like a bad egg.*

Hearing June talk about this... It felt as though a spotlight had been cast on the ugliest part of himself. "I'm just... not feeling well."

"You smell like honey." June frowned, setting a hand on her hip. "Look, did something happen with Greg? 'Cause this is... not good. I'm two hundred percent sure you smell like pregnant omega."

His hand trembled. Dale swallowed past the lump in his throat. He'd waited years to be told that. Surely June knew not to make a pregnancy joke. "I—I'm not pregnant."

He put the spatula back into the bottle, and June's gaze snapped to it. She looked back at him, horror darting through her eyes. "You aren't starting a nanoparticle experiment, are you?"

"I'm *not* pregnant, June. The toxicity won't affect me."

"No, put that down immediately," June said, her voice sharp. "Whatever experiment it is, I'll do it for you."

He didn't believe her reasoning, but her tone forced his hand. Dale set the bottle on the counter, his heart thudding in his chest. This joke was getting old. He'd gone out of his way to give June a two-week break.

June pulled on a pair of gloves, shutting the clear box around the measuring scale, capping the bottles. She glanced at the experiment procedure, tugged all their gloves off, then held Dale by the shoulders, gently pushing him back to the computers. "Sit. I'm going out right now, and I don't want you to move an inch."

"I can't be pregnant," Dale said, miserable.

69

He sat stiffly in the office chair next to hers.

June eyed the scent gland at his neck, then his wrists, her expression completely serious. It wasn't like her at all, and a faint unease slid through Dale's gut. "Did you sleep with Greg? While you were in heat?"

He didn't want to lie to her. So he nodded, looking down at his hands. June's stare burned through his skin.

June knew. Dale sleeping with Greg was no longer a secret, and June could judge him for it. Dale's cheeks scorched. This was worse than the time the iron nanoparticles had caught fire in front of the college president.

"Oh, gods." June grabbed her car keys and purse. Then she gave him a quick hug, enveloping him in her birch scent. "I'm running out. Be back in ten."

The door slammed shut. Dale stared at the computer with its log-in screen, the vertical bar blinking patiently at him. He couldn't be pregnant. It was impossible. He and Charles had tried a hundred times, maybe a thousand, and he always went into heat the next month.

He didn't have the energy to convince June of his failures right now.

Instead of thinking about June, or Greg, Dale thought about the omega list Bernard Hastings had asked for two weeks ago.

Bernard had emailed him again, asking for more detail on Penny Fleming, the second-best student in his class. Greg was his top student. Why Bernard wanted omegas... Well, it was simple, now that Dale thought about it. He was looking for omegas for his son.

Penny would suit Greg, Dale thought. She was pleasant, bubbly, smiling whenever she talked to him. And she was, very likely, fertile.

His heart squeezed.

Unwilling to think further, he slid a square filter paper from June's workspace, folding it into halves lengthwise. Then he flipped it over and folded it along the diagonals, scratching in the creases so they became permanent.

Sometime later, the door burst open. Dale jumped in his seat, the paper crane falling out of his hands.

"I got you five tests," June said, brandishing the colorful boxes at him. "Sorry, bags cost extra. Blame that new California law. Anyway, Sam looked at me like I'd gotten a harem pregnant."

Dale cracked a smile. June waited until he took the test kits from her, before leaning in. Then she slid her hands under his arms and hefted him to his feet. Dale squawked.

"Off you go," June said, nudging him to the door. "Do you want me to accompany you?"

It was just a pregnancy test. He knew he couldn't get pregnant, so it wasn't like he needed her babying him. Dale shook his head. "I'll be fine."

"You're sure?"

"I don't need you staring at pee-drenched sticks. It's not even your pee." Dale smiled weakly. "Work on that experiment you kicked me off."

"Yes, professor," June said, squeezing his shoulder. "And if it's bad, call me, okay? I'll come fetch you."

"Sure."

71

Dale stepped out of the lab, looking at the gleaming test kits. The boxes were pink, or white, or blue—all different brands. June had tried to get him a wide variety to minimize the error margin, and he appreciated it.

It wasn't as though he'd need them, though.

He trudged through the corridor, looking at the floor tiles. There wasn't a baby involved. If there were, he'd have gotten pregnant years ago, and he'd still have an intact marriage and an alpha to belong to.

He shoved those thoughts out of his head, tucking his chin down further. He'd do the tests, see that they were all negative, and show them to June. And hopefully, that would be the last mention of Greg for a while.

Dale walked faster down the corridor, reading the fine print on the boxes. *Hold the end of the kit under your urine stream for 5 seconds. Then, leave the kit on a level surface for 5 minutes.*

Did he have twenty-five seconds of pee? Maybe. He had had coffee.

He rounded a corner. Crashed into a solid chest. The boxes in his hands scattered across the floor. Dale wobbled, trying to find his balance. "Ah!"

The person grabbed his arm, and Dale sucked in a breath, recognizing aspen. His heart thudded.

Inches away, Greg stared back at him, his fingers tightening around Dale's arm.

For a long moment, neither of them moved. Dale couldn't help looking into Greg's dark eyes, at his full lips, the flare of his nostrils as he breathed. Greg's eyes narrowed. "June's back?"

"Uh. June?" Dale blinked. Then he remembered he was supposed to fake that relationship with his post-doc. He'd been distracted by the test kits, then Greg. And Greg's chest rose and fell, a sturdy, inviting wall. "I, uh. Yes. She's back."

"She's not your alpha," Greg said. Then he glanced down at the test kits, and froze.

I told him about the infertility. What if he thinks I lied?

"June wants me to do the tests," Dale said, his stomach twisting. "I don't see why I should."

Greg narrowed his eyes. "Why would she want you to?"

"It's none of your business."

But a flicker of hurt flashed through Greg's eyes. Dale remembered last week, remembered Greg hesitating when he asked about condoms.

Dale shrugged awkwardly. "She thinks I'm pregnant."

"You said you can't get pregnant," Greg said, but he dipped his head closer, sniffing.

"I really can't. Please release me."

Greg watched him, doubtful. He slid his callused fingers off Dale's arm, then crouched to pick up the test kits. "You need that many?"

"I guess June's trying to convince me."

Greg glanced down the empty corridors. "Because of last week?"

"I guess."

"C'mon, let's go." Greg adjusted his backpack on his shoulder, dragging Dale down a quiet corridor. They stopped by a common-use bathroom, one of the wider ones that would fit wheelchairs, and Greg held the door open for Dale.

"You don't have to be this polite," Dale said, ducking inside. "I can do this by myself."

"Five tests? I've seen people do a couple at a time, and it's tedious." Greg pulled the door shut, locking them in. "Can't believe you'd try to do five at a go."

Dale shrugged, looking around. There was a toilet, a sink, and a paper towel dispenser. No privacy at all.

"You're going to watch me pee?" he asked, disbelieving.

Greg raised an eyebrow. "You're worried about privacy now?"

The memories from last week rose in his mind; Greg's hand down Dale's pants, his fingers rubbing over Dale's hole. Greg's knot inside him, stretching his body open.

Dale gulped. "I guess not."

Greg smiled, and Dale tried not to stare. There was nothing going on between them. Greg had stumbled upon Dale in heat. They'd fucked. And now they were back to being teacher and student.

He lined the pregnancy tests along the sink, opening the boxes one at a time. Greg stepped up to help, his arm brushing warm against Dale's.

"You really don't have to," Dale said.

Greg angled a look at him. "What if I want to?"

I don't believe you. Dale picked open the next box, pulling the thin plastic kit out. "This is... personal. I'm your professor."

"You keep saying that."

"I don't understand why you're still around."

Greg sighed. "I told you, I like you."

"Even though you shouldn't."

Greg's throat worked; he glanced away. "Yeah."

He understood, then, that any deeper relationship between them was futile.

They opened the rest of the kits in silence, five sticks of plastic with absorbent strips at their ends. Greg read the instructions on each kit, rearranging them according to the instructions.

Dale breathed in, then out. The furrows on June's forehead had been deep. She'd never pulled serious jokes on him, and her dash to the college bookstore had made his pulse stumble. He couldn't be pregnant. "I don't smell like a pregnant person, do I?"

"I don't know." Greg looked up from the test kits. "I've never been around pregnant people."

"You said you've seen people do pregnancy tests before."

"My friends, yeah. And the time I almost knocked my — my best friend up." Greg winced. "I was a stupid kid."

"You're still not much older than a kid," Dale said, watching him. Why wasn't Greg with his best friend, if they'd almost conceived? Was he pursuing omega professors, only to go home to someone else at night? June had said he was unbonded.

"I'm an adult," Greg said.

And even though he was twenty-two, Greg's eyes were old, shadowed. Dale wasn't sure what to make of it. Greg was half his age. He had a bright future ahead of him. And here they were in a college bathroom, Greg trying to help him with his pregnancy tests. "You're young enough to be my son."

Greg sighed. "Are you going to piss, or not?"

"I guess. I hope I have enough pee for this."

He pushed his pants down, pulling his cock out. The entire time, Greg watched him. Dale flushed. Sex was one thing, but peeing was... a little more private than that.

"Maybe you shouldn't be looking," Dale said.

"You've memorized the instructions on the kits? The timing and all?"

Dale patted over his pockets, realizing he'd left his phone somewhere. Maybe in the office. He groaned, his heart sinking. "I don't have a timer. Gods damn it."

"Glad I'm here now?" Greg pulled his phone out, and Dale didn't know if he wanted to hug this man. Greg was... nice. Adorable. Dale shouldn't want to breathe him in.

"I guess," he said.

"You *guess*." Greg rolled his eyes. "You're happy that I'm here."

"Brat."

"Shut up."

But Greg smiled, and Dale relaxed. He wasn't alone. He had someone doing these tests with him, and it was... nice. So unlike the silent bathrooms years ago, when he'd been trying to conceive.

Greg handed him the first stick. "Five seconds of piss on this one. Ready when you are."

Dale peed. It felt weird, having Greg's eyes on him, even though he knew Greg was waiting for the kit. It wasn't anything sexual. His cheeks prickled with warmth anyway.

At five seconds, Dale stopped the stream, looking around for a spot to set the stick down. *I should've been more prepared with this.*

Greg took the test from him, handing him another one. "Ten seconds on this."

"I don't think I'll have enough if they all need ten seconds."

"Just keep going." Greg set the stick down on its box, rereading the instructions on the third test.

Dale did the second and third tests in silence, and by the time he reached the fourth, there was no more pressure in his abdomen. "I don't think I have enough pee for the last one."

Greg took the fourth stick, checking the timer on his phone. "Can you hold the rest in? We'll see how the tests go. Three minutes left on the first one."

Dale sighed. "I suppose I'd have to."

It was mildly uncomfortable, holding in pee now that he'd gotten it going. The timer ticked away, and Dale had nothing to say to Greg. Not *You're doing very well in this class,* and certainly not *I'm impressed by your assignments.* Especially when his pants were down around his thighs, and Greg had just watched him urinate all over the pregnancy test kits.

Dale was a professor, but in front of Greg, he didn't feel like one.

"You've been avoiding me," Greg said.

Well, there was that, too. Dale swallowed. "I doubt we have much to talk about outside of class."

"Aside from last week?" Greg glanced at the

timer, then met his eyes. And Dale couldn't look away from him. A week after Dale's heat, Greg still looked magnificent, his T-shirt stretched over his pecs, his biceps twice the size of Dale's.

"Nothing happened last week," Dale said.

"I'd have stayed if you'd let me."

Dale looked down at the toilet, at their shoes almost touching. They belonged to two social circles—Dale with the professors, and Greg with his schoolmates. "Your father asked me for a list of omegas."

Greg rolled his eyes. "And you sent him a list."

"I didn't realize it was a list for you until the day after."

"Do you regret it?"

Dale breathed in the faint aspen scent rolling off Greg, stared at the lines of his full lips. "I don't know. Should I?"

Greg opened his mouth to answer.

The timer went off then, a jarring tune in the tiny bathroom, and Dale jumped. Greg looked down at his phone. Then he glanced over at the pregnancy tests, and frowned. "You might wanna look at this."

7

Dale

DALE'S BREATH snagged. He hurried over to the sink, staring down at the test kits.

On the first test, two blue lines ran through the little window. There were two lines on the second kit, too.

"About twenty seconds until the third one's ready," Greg said, but Dale wasn't sure if he heard that right.

"What — what does it mean?" he asked, even though he knew. His heart was thumping too hard. The tests had to be wrong.

"Two lines is a positive. I checked."

"I..." Dale blinked at the kits again, pressing his hand to his chest. His heart crashed against his ribs like it was trying to escape. "I can't be pregnant."

Greg glanced at his phone, then at Dale. "Third test is ready."

Dale didn't want to look, but he did. Two lines. One fainter than the other. "I... I can't believe it. I'm not... I can't be pregnant."

He remembered the suitcase, and Charles dropping him off at the train station, their annulled marriage certificate tucked away in his pocket. Nineteen years ago, Dale had wished desperately that he could've borne a child, if only so he could stop Charles' parents from saying those hurtful things. He'd spent hours staring at single lines on pregnancy tests, hoping they were wrong.

"Whose is it?" Greg asked, his eyes locked on Dale.

Dale swallowed. "I... I can't..."

He looked down at his flat belly, smoothing his hand over it. It felt normal. A little soft where he'd put on a bit of weight, but it didn't read *pregnant.*

The tests stared up at him, and the fourth test showed a single line through the window. That, Dale was more inclined to believe. "That one is right," he said, pointing.

Greg snorted. "Three positives, and you're saying the one negative result is right."

Dale nodded. "Yeah. I'm... I—I can't be pregnant."

For a long moment, Greg studied him. "Do the fifth test. It'll tell you."

"I doubt it will." But Dale dragged his feet back to the toilet, numbly taking the last test from Greg. It took a while for him to start peeing again. The absorbent material darkened with urine, and Greg took it from his hand seconds later.

"Sit down when you're done," Greg said, his eyes burning into Dale. "I'll start the timer for this."

When he'd zipped up his pants, Dale sat down on the toilet, his hands shaking. "I still don't believe it."

"Did you sleep with anyone else?" Greg

asked. "This week?"

Dale shook his head, staring at the tiled bathroom walls.

"In the past two months?"

He shook his head again.

"Four months?"

Still no.

"Fuck," Greg said, leaning against the sink. He stared at Dale, running his hand through his hair. "The baby's mine?"

"We're still waiting on the last test," Dale said. "The other three are probably flukes."

A beat of silence.

"You're a professor," Greg said, studying him. "You know how well these things work."

Pain hissed through Dale's chest, sharp and unwelcome. His throat tightened. "Don't you think I *know*," he muttered, and his voice cracked.

Nineteen years ago, Charles had brought home a case of pregnancy tests. Every week, Dale would sit in the bathroom, stopwatch in hand, waiting for the minutes to pass. Charles had begged. Then he'd threatened, and his parents had stared sourly at Dale, scorn on their faces.

Dale hadn't been prepared for it. His parents had bartered him off, and he'd never wondered why he was their only child.

The first year into the marriage, he'd taken bottle after bottle of supplements. The second year, Charles' parents had begun their whispering. The third, they'd dropped all attempt to be polite, and even Charles had started to question Dale's ability to bear children.

Dale had grown fond of Charles, had hoped

that Charles would keep him, maybe get a second omega. But Charles had handed him the annulled certificate and five hundred dollars, and Dale had felt like a ship unmoored in a storm, drifting through the choppy waves.

He'd hidden himself away in a small Californian town, hoping no one recognized him there.

In Meadowfall, the shame that had haunted him had faded with his history. Dale had studied for his PhD, worked his way through a lab, setting and meeting goals until he found worth in himself again.

Someone stepped in front of him. Dale looked up from the bathroom walls, his cheeks itchy.

"Sorry. I didn't think it would hit you this bad," Greg murmured. He crouched in front of Dale, reaching up to cup his cheeks. Then his thumbs brushed along Dale's eyes, damp and apple-scented like he'd just washed them with soap.

Greg wiped the tears off Dale's cheeks — Dale hadn't even realized he'd been crying.

"It can't be real," Dale said.

"Why not?"

"I would — would still have a family if I did," Dale said. He turned his wrist up, exposing the silvery bonding mark on his wrist. "I tried for three years straight. The doctor said I'm infertile."

Greg glanced past Dale's shoulder, at the sink, and Dale didn't have any words for this.

"So I'm going to be a dad," Greg said. His face was blank, too, and Dale hadn't even started to think what this meant for Greg.

"I won't—if the tests are accurate—I won't hold you responsible," Dale said. It was his fault. He'd told Greg to skip the condom. After Greg left his office last week, Dale had rolled a condom over his plug, slid it in, and savored the thought of Greg's cum inside him.

Years ago, he'd tried it with Charles, but it had never resulted in a pregnancy. It shouldn't be working now.

Greg stood and bent awkwardly, pulling Dale into a hug. "Sorry. I should've used a condom."

Why would you even...? "No, it's not your fault," Dale said, gulping. Greg's arms tightened around him, sturdy and strong, and Dale wanted to lean in and forget everything else.

The stopwatch beeped. Dale jumped again, his heart crashing into his ribs.

"Gods, I don't think I'll make it through today," he mumbled, sinking his face into Greg's shoulder. "I'm not... This is all a dream."

Greg shifted, shutting off the alarm. Then he eased Dale off his chest. "C'mon, at least let me grab the kit."

"I don't know if I want to see it," Dale said.

Greg leaned away, picking up the fifth test from the sink. Then he handed it to Dale, and two blue lines stared up at him.

He was pregnant. He was two years from tenure, and... and the child was Greg's.

"Oh, gods. This is fucked up."

"No shit," Greg said. "You want a photo of the results as proof?"

Dale bit his lip. That would be incriminating in itself. He shook his head. "No. I don't... I don't think I'll need it."

He leaned back on the toilet, turning the kit around in his hands. He was pregnant. The child was Greg's. And Dale didn't know where he'd go from here.

"Are you keeping it?" Greg asked.

"Yes." Dale rubbed his thumb over the test kit. He still couldn't believe he was pregnant. But if he was... If he really *was*... Then he wanted this child.

Especially when Greg had wanted Dale when they'd mated. It hadn't been sex for the sake of a baby. Greg had held him like he'd *mattered,* and the child was a reminder of that.

At twenty-two, Dale couldn't imagine Greg wanting a baby. "Sorry," Dale said, his throat tight. "This is my fault. I won't need you to share in the parenting, or anything like that. You're too young—"

Someone called out in the hallway outside, a muffled voice, and they both froze. Stared at each other. They were still in the college, one door away from the public.

"I'm not too young, damn it," Greg muttered, glancing at the door. He stepped closer. "That kid's also mine."

"What do you want with it?" Dale shrank away from him, sliding his hand over his belly.

"I don't know. I want to help." Greg sank to his knees in front of Dale, curling his warm fingers into Dale's palms. He was a basketball star. He had intelligent eyes, a well-to-do family, and he could do so much without the hindrance of a baby.

"You have other things to focus on," Dale said. "You have schoolwork. Your basketball."

"You know about the basketball?" Greg raised his eyebrows.

A traitorous heat crept up Dale's cheeks. "I've heard about it," Dale said. "I get emails from the team."

Greg studied him carefully. "You get the newsletter because of me."

"It's presumptuous to assume things," Dale said, looking at Greg's collarbones instead. But from the corner of his eye, he caught the growing smile on Greg's lips. Greg's hands were large around his, comforting, and he wanted to lean closer. "Especially about your professor."

"What if you were my omega?" Greg asked. Then he lifted Dale's hand, dragging his lips over Dale's knuckles, down his palm, to his wrist. Where the unmarked scent gland was.

Dale's heart kicked. Greg still wanted to mark him. And his instincts bellowed, *Yes.* "I'm two decades older than you."

"I don't care." Greg kissed his scent gland. Dale's face burned.

Turned out, he wasn't over this alpha yet.

"I'm too old for you," Dale said. "You know that."

"Fuck what everyone else thinks."

"You're saying that to your professor?"

Greg met his eyes. "You're Dale to me now."

He'd told Greg his name last week, when Greg had been pressed against him, their cocks sliding together. Right now, Dale's skin felt three sizes too tight, and he couldn't look away. "You haven't found another omega?"

"No. I wasn't looking."

Greg pressed another kiss to Dale's scent gland, his lips damp and soft. For a moment, Dale thought he might bite. His heart tripped.

He wanted Greg to mark him. It was ridiculous.

"Why me?" Dale croaked. "I'm just... I'm just another professor. I don't know what the pregnancy risks are, but I'm sure they're bad."

"Stop that." Greg frowned, biting down on the side of Dale's palm. Dale yelped. "I've told you before—I like you. You're different from the other profs."

"You mean, I'm not as strict and competitive."

"That too." Greg pressed kisses onto Dale's hand, his warmth soaking into Dale's skin. "You're nothing like my dad. You don't care about the achievements. Or rankings. Or results. I don't have to keep meeting someone else's expectations with you. You're all easy-going and you have that couch in your office, and those ink stains on your shirt, and you always wear the same clothes—"

Greg bit his words off, his glance cutting away. His cheeks turned ruddy.

Dale stared, his heart thumping slow and loud. "You have a crush on me," he murmured. This, he didn't know. He'd never had a student who was this fond of him.

Greg narrowed his eyes. "Don't call it a crush. Sounds godawful."

"You don't even know me."

"Then let me know you," Greg whispered, his breath hot on Dale's palm. Dale wanted to say yes. Gods, Greg's eyes held so much *want.* Dale felt safe with him. He wanted to curl up with Greg, and it was wrong. They belonged on opposite sides of the lecture hall podium.

Dale gulped, pulling his hand away. "I'll think about it," he said. "We may be rushing into decisions."

He rolled forward onto his feet, his limbs stiff and uncooperative. Greg slipped his hand into the crook of Dale's elbow, steadying him.

"You really don't have to," Dale said.

"I'll treat you as mine." Greg glanced down at Dale's belly, his gaze possessive, and a slow warmth bloomed in Dale's gut, unfurling through his limbs.

He hadn't realized how desperately he wanted to belong to someone.

Dale swallowed. Greg scooped up the test kits and boxes, dumping them all into the trash can. Then he turned to the sink, washing his hands. Dale stopped a foot away.

"I'm really not holding you to this," Dale said. Greg met his eyes. "If at any point, you want out, all you have to do is—"

Greg stepped forward and kissed him, his mouth hot against Dale's. He pulled Dale flush against his chest, dragged his wrists down Dale's arms, down his back, rubbing right over his ass, and a thrill of pleasure shot through Dale's nerves. He sank against Greg, trying to fill his lungs with that aspen scent.

Gods, he was insane. They weren't even in

love. This was just... chemistry. Instincts.

"Mine," Greg whispered, sliding his tongue into Dale's mouth. Dale moaned, pressing up against him, his body flooding with warmth. So maybe he still wanted this man. Wanted to follow Greg home.

Greg's phone rang, a quick burst of dance music shooting through Dale's ears. Dale jumped. Greg leaned away, frowning. "Damn it."

When Greg pulled his phone out, Dale glanced at the screen. It read *Dad*, and his stomach hardened like a rock. Greg was Bernard Hastings' son.

"He's going to fire me," Dale whispered, thinking about the presentation he'd done in front of Bernard Hastings four months back. He'd showcased his research group's ongoing projects, and midway through, he'd discovered that half his slides were blank.

He'd excused himself, looked through his flash drive, and realized he'd brought along a draft copy of the presentation.

It hadn't just been Bernard Hastings at the presentation. The school's Board of Directors had been there, too; it had been a performance evaluation. Bernard Hastings had stared hard at Dale, and Dale had felt his tenure slip out of his grasp.

If Bernard Hastings heard about this pregnancy... Dale would lose his job, and everything he'd worked so hard for would go to waste.

Greg rejected the call, glancing back at him. "I'm not answering that right now."

"Oh," Dale said, his heart pattering. He needed to sit down. Take a break from his life.

"I'm not gonna tell my dad," Greg said. "Or anyone else."

"But your scent is all over me."

"If you're carrying my baby, then you can be damn sure I'll mark you," Greg said, narrowing his eyes. "People will leave you alone if you smell like alpha."

"I've been smelling like a different alpha for two months!"

"You're not even with her," Greg said.

Dale looked at his hands, remembering June and her omega. There had been speculation among the lab students, and Dale had ignored it—better they thought he was with June, than with Greg. "People will talk."

"You're going to start looking pregnant," Greg said. "And I want you to be mine."

A thrill skidded down Dale's spine. "It's too soon to talk about that."

"Then when are we going to talk about it? Class starts in twenty minutes."

Dale sighed. "At the end of today. My classes end at four."

"I have basketball practice until six. You want to meet for dinner?"

It wasn't a bad idea, especially if it would keep Greg from leaving his scent in Dale's office. "Somewhere off-campus, I guess. I know a quiet place."

"Fine. Here, text yourself. I'll get in touch." Greg tapped on his phone.

The lock screen was an older photo—Greg

with a blond boy, their arms around each other's shoulders. Laughter sparkled in Greg's eyes. He was younger, less built than he was now, and in the background, sunlight glinted off a calm sea.

Greg tapped in the pass code, unlocking the phone without a word. Then he opened the contacts page, handing the phone to Dale.

Was that your best friend? Why would you have a picture of him, and pursue me instead?

Dale tapped his number into the phone, saving himself as a contact. *Dale.* So no one would know Greg was texting his professor. Dale handed the phone back, eyeing the bathroom door. It was quiet outside.

Greg read his expression. "I'll leave first."

Dale followed him to the door, scanning the bathroom. No incriminating pieces of evidence. Just his hibiscus scent, and Greg's aspen.

"Hey," Greg said, meeting his eyes. "Whatever happens, I promise I'll help with the baby. Just tell me how."

Dale's throat tightened. "You really don't have to."

"I want to."

He sucked in a deep breath, relaxing a little. Greg cared. And Dale was suddenly very glad that he wasn't in this alone.

Greg flashed a quick smile. He cracked the door open, peeked down the corridor. "No one here. See you later."

He slipped out. Dale pushed the door shut, locking it. Then he wadded up sheets of TP and tossed them into the trash, covering up the boxes. It still didn't erase the double blue lines razed into his mind.

Gods, he was pregnant. After all those years with Charles... All it had taken was one afternoon with his student. This shouldn't have happened at all.

Five minutes later, Dale stepped out of the bathroom, returning to the lab.

June looked up the moment he stepped in, her nostrils flaring. Then her eyes widened, and Dale's cheeks scorched. He smelled like Greg. And now it was futile to pretend they weren't involved.

"Not what I expected," June said, watching him. "I tried calling, but you weren't picking up."

"I left my phone in the office." Dale looked at the computers, ignoring the rest of the post-docs and research students in the lab. "You were right."

June winced, glancing over her shoulder. He knew who she was looking at; he could smell Greg from here, and he didn't know how to address this right now, Greg's child in his belly. Greg's gaze prickled his skin.

"Gods, I'm sorry," June murmured, pulling Dale into a hug. They didn't usually do this in front of the other students, but Dale didn't care right now. They probably assumed he was dating June. And if he wore another alpha's scent on him, June hugging him meant she accepted it. Nothing to gossip about. "What are your plans?"

"I'm keeping it." Saying it made it more real. Dale was pregnant. He was carrying a baby. Greg's baby. His stomach flipped.

Dale knew he didn't *need* a child. But his parents had always said *Omegas were built for babies*, and Dale had grown up looking forward to his own.

"Greg's serious about staying with you?" June whispered.

Dale nodded, his stomach flipping. He still hadn't processed that yet.

"Whatever happens, I'll cover your back," June said, her brow crinkled. "You can count on me, too."

"Thanks," Dale said, hugging her. It didn't give him any relief.

A week or a month from now, he'd probably be happy about the child. Right now, he could only think about the wrongness of it, and his heart ached.

But he had a class to teach, a role to play. Regardless of what happened in his life, Dale was still a professor.

He pulled on his lab coat, then stepped up to start the class.

8
Greg

AN HOUR ago, Greg had begun his day thinking he'd stop by Dale's office.

He didn't need help with the coursework, but he'd been increasingly mulling over the career options in this field. What he wanted to do when he graduated. He wasn't going into politics, and maybe he might pursue basketball instead. But he couldn't spend his entire life on the court, either — players grew old and retired in their thirties, and Greg figured a backup plan would come in handy.

Instead of having a discussion about his career, he'd bumped into Dale along the chemistry building corridors. Scattered Dale's pregnancy test kits all over the floor.

With a sinking feeling in his gut, he'd steered Dale into a bathroom on a quieter hallway, shutting them in.

The tests had come out positive. When Greg had first seen the results, he'd assumed Dale had slept with someone else, maybe even June. Greg was a student. Dale was pretty, and intelligent, and Greg figured Dale would have no shortage of alphas wanting to leap into his bed.

Except Dale had looked utterly miserable when he'd shaken his head, saying he'd slept with no one else.

If he'd known this would happen, Greg would've insisted on the condom, regardless of what Dale insisted.

How fucked up was it, that he'd gotten his professor pregnant?

He looked down at the lab bench, at the vial he'd set on the magnetic stirrer. At the bottom of the glass, in 10.0 ML of water, a little rice-shaped magnet spun, mixing the solution.

Greg slid a waxy sheet over, holding oxidase powder measured out to 1.350g. He tapped it into the vial, watching as the powder slowly dissolved around the spinning magnet.

The other students moved around him, working on their own experiments, but Greg ignored them.

In the corner of the lab, Dale hugged June. Greg's instincts growled with envy. Through the two months of watching his professor, Greg had wanted him closer, wanted Dale to need him.

And last week, Dale had clung to him, his pupils blown, his legs trembling.

Greg looked back at his experiment procedure, adding aqueous gold to his vial.

Dale was pregnant. With Greg's baby. He didn't look pregnant, with his lab coat cinched neatly around his waist, but Greg was starting to recognize that honey-sweet scent. It hadn't been on Dale before. And Greg wanted to mark him all over now, even if part of him bristled about the baby. *It's not your fault*, the voice said. *You asked about condoms. Dale said no.*

He wanted to be angry. He hadn't consented to being a dad. He was twenty-two, for fuck's sake, and he hadn't factored in space for a kid in his life.

Except Dale had been close to breaking down in the washroom. He'd swayed on the toilet, huddling into himself, his eyes unfocused, and Greg hadn't thought *I'm infertile* would lead to this.

Dale hadn't expected it, either. If he'd been infertile for years, if he'd shut down right after that conversation last week, then it made sense that he badly wanted a child. And Greg had given him one.

Where do we go from here?

Dale turned to face the students in his lab, his palm on his belly, and Greg knew Dale would protect the child no matter what. Dale wasn't blaming him for the pregnancy. But Greg knew responsibility, and he sure as hell wasn't leaving Dale alone to raise that child.

Maybe that was what shook him. He wasn't even out of school yet. He didn't have a job. He was the alpha, and his instincts said *You need to support that child. You need to get a job and help pay for it.*

So yeah, between his schoolwork and basketball, he'd scrounge up some hours here and there. Maybe spend less time on school. Make some money, help Dale with the baby.

Across the lab, his eyes locked with Dale's. For a moment, Greg wondered if the students around would recognize their scents—aspen on Dale, hibiscus on Greg. Some of the students glanced up, but for the most part, they kept their heads down, busy with their own projects.

Dale looked away, walking by without acknowledging him.

It felt like a slap. Greg scowled. He knew Dale was trying to keep attention away from him.

But it rankled, and Greg's attention anchored on Dale as he pipetted the sodium hydroxide into the vial, then the buffer solution. Dale's scent wafted into his nose, layered over with Greg's aspen, then June's birch. Did Dale really think he needed a second alpha's scent? Dale was carrying Greg's child. He should be wearing Greg's scent alone.

Except if Greg's dad found out, both he and Dale would catch so much crap. Dale could lose his job.

Greg's chest squeezed; his hand twitched. The tip of his micropipette hooked on the vial's neck, knocking it sideways. In slow motion, the vial skidded off the magnetic stirrer, spilling gold solution across the counter. Greg grabbed the vial before it rolled off the edge. "Shit!"

Dale's gaze snapped over. He grabbed paper towels off a side counter, striding over in a breeze of hibiscus.

"No worries," Dale said, setting paper towels on the spill. "Just make sure not to hurt yourself."

"Dale!" June hurried through the lab, her eyes narrowed. When she reached Dale's side, she muttered, "I've told you—no more experiments. That includes cleanup."

"I'm not touching it," Dale said, showing her his bare hands. June's eyes narrowed further, and Greg watched them, unease whispering through his mind. What did June know that he didn't? She shouldn't be the one telling Dale what to do; he was the professor.

"What's wrong with the spill?" he asked.

June's gaze darted around the lab, landing on the other students. She waited until the students returned to their work, before she nodded at Dale. "Toxicity of gold nanoparticles," she muttered. "I'm not letting Dale work on experiments."

Greg froze, ignoring the possessive part of himself that wanted to growl at June. Dale's safety was more important.

At the start of the semester, he'd read the Material Safety Data Sheets for the project—it only occurred to him now that gold nanoparticles, in larger doses, were toxic to fetuses. He'd ignored that bit, thinking he wouldn't encounter a pregnant person in the lab.

Some assumption that had been.

A scarlet tint crept up Dale's throat. He frowned at June, glancing surreptitiously at Greg. "I'm telling you, I'll be fine."

"No," June said. "I'll do the experiments you need."

"Or me," Greg said, staring at Dale. That baby was also his. And he wasn't letting Dale be exposed to the nanoparticles. Especially not if June was the one dragging Dale away from the experiments.

Mine, he wanted to say. *You aren't June's omega. I won't let you get hurt.*

Dale closed his mouth, looking away. June turned to grab a pair of gloves, and Greg stepped between her and Dale, so he'd be closer to his professor. His omega.

June picked up the paper towels Dale had left, chuckling. She wiped down the spill, then looked up, meeting Greg's eyes. Greg tried not to scowl.

"All yours," she said. "But be careful next time."

She glanced at Dale, then back at Greg. Greg understood that she wasn't talking about the lab bench, but Dale.

"Yeah, I'll be careful," he said. "Can't do shit about spilled milk."

"There's damage control." June folded up the paper towels. "But make sure that's all the damage you do, or you'll have me to deal with."

Greg bristled. Of course he wasn't going to hurt anyone else, especially not Dale. "I know."

June stared him down, and Greg held her gaze until she passed him in a rush of birch-scented air.

Next to him, Dale smiled weakly. "Like June said, be careful with the experiments. I can't afford to waste all those reagents, you know."

Greg blinked. "Lab running out of grants?" he asked quietly.

"I was joking." Dale's smile grew wider, and Greg relaxed somewhat. "But you do have to watch your lab techniques. I'll be grading you."

"You can grade all my techniques," Greg murmured.

Dale's cheeks turned a light shade of rose. He lowered his gaze, his lips pulling up in a little smile, and Greg's heart missed a beat. Dale strode away without an answer, his lab coat fluttering.

So that kiss hadn't been an abnormality. Dale liked him. And June wasn't going to fight him over Dale.

Greg breathed a sigh. He rinsed out the glass vial, placing it back on the magnetic stirrer. Another two months of school, and the semester would be over.

For now, he just needed to get through the day, then meet Dale after school for dinner.

With news like Dale's pregnancy, it was easier said than done.

9

Greg

HOURS LATER, Greg pulled into the parking lot of a Mexican restaurant. The sky was growing a deep velvety blue, and against the backdrop of shadowy trees, orange light poured out of the windows of El Asado, its doorways strung with tiny red-and-yellow lanterns.

Greg parked, checking his phone. Earlier in the day, he'd texted Dale: *Where do you want to meet?*

El Asado, Dale had texted back. *On Walnut and Rose. 7pm. They have pulled pork to die for.*

Greg had looked up the place—it was a higher-end restaurant on the other side of town, with no malls or libraries nearby. College students wouldn't be as likely to show up there.

He'd driven back to his apartment after basketball practice, showering to rid all his sweat and grime. Then he'd dressed in a button-down shirt and jeans, so he'd at least fit into the establishment.

I'm here, Dale's newest text said. *Far corner, in a booth.*

Greg's stomach flipped. He hadn't seen Dale

outside the campus before—although it was nowhere the size of Highton, Meadowfall was a relatively large town with a few malls, a couple of libraries, and its own college. Time and again, he'd hoped to catch Dale around town, but their schedules somehow never meshed.

Until now. They were on a sort-of date, except it was to discuss the baby.

Greg still wasn't sure what to think of that.

Phone in hand, he locked the car and headed over to the restaurant. The tiny bells on the door jangled as it swung shut behind him. Greg picked Dale out easily, tucked away in a corner booth.

If he hadn't been looking, he'd probably miss his professor entirely. The restaurant was decked out in colorful retro-themed decorations—music posters on the walls, horse figurines on the booth dividers, and wide-brimmed hats hanging from the ceiling. The frosted glass dividers provided privacy —perfect for people who didn't want to be noticed.

Greg wove between tables and chairs, sliding into the booth just as Dale looked up from his menu.

Forest-green eyes anchored on Greg's face. Then they coasted down his chest, his abs, his hips, like Dale was slowly stripping him in his mind.

Greg let him look. He settled right across from Dale, raising his eyebrows. "I pass the inspection?"

Dale flushed, meeting his eyes again. "Uh, hello. I wasn't..."

"Wasn't...?

"Wasn't expecting you to dress up."

A shirt with nice buttons and trimmings

didn't count as dressing up, but maybe that was Dale's thing. "Should I be dressing up for class, too?"

Dale's mouth fell open in horror. "Gods, no."

"Why?"

"It would be distracting." Dale smiled wryly, dropping his gaze back to the menu. He hadn't changed out of his work clothes—his long-sleeved shirt clung to his chest, and his pants were still the same dark ones he'd worn that morning. But in the restaurant, under the soft golden lights, Dale looked less like a teacher, and more like an ordinary person. Greg's pulse skipped anyway.

"So if I were to wear my jersey to class, that'd be fine?"

Dale blinked, eyes darting down to Greg's chest again. Greg imagined him standing behind the teacher's desk, his gaze glued to all of Greg's exposed skin.

"Preferably before you get sweaty," Dale said. "I don't need the classroom smelling like you."

His eyes glimmered with humor, and Greg relaxed. "Had a good day?"

"Ha!" Dale chuckled, his laughter frayed at the edges, suppressed and a little hysterical. For a long while, he didn't stop laughing. "A good day? I don't even..."

He rubbed the tears from his eyes, the tension in his shoulders easing. Greg watched, and when Dale finally stopped, he sagged into his seat, a tiny smile on his face. "I guess it's not the end of the world," Dale said.

Greg wanted to hug him. With this

pregnancy, Dale was the one who bore the heaviest burden—his job, his body, his strength. And Greg didn't know what he could do about it, except promise his support, being there for Dale whenever he could.

The waitress came by to take their orders. Dale smiled politely at her. "Sweet raspberry tea," he said.

"Sprite," Greg said. When the waitress left, he asked, "Come here often?"

"Sometimes. When I'm not in the mood to cook." Dale leaned into his seat, flipping through the menu. "Want a recommendation?"

"Sure."

"The pulled pork is delicious," Dale said, turning his menu around to point it out. "It's slow-cooked and savory—I think they season it with oregano, garlic and onion—it falls apart in your mouth. They serve it with rice and sweet corn, and the soup is mainly beans, cilantro and chicken. I have it every time I come here."

As he spoke, the weary lines from his face fell away. He smiled, waving his hands like when he got excited talking about nanoparticles, and Greg watched, unable to stop smiling. After all that news today, Dale deserved to be happy.

"You like the sound of the pulled pork?" Dale asked.

"I like the sound of you," Greg blurted.

For a moment, Dale stared. Then a scarlet blush crept up his cheeks, and he looked down at the menu. "I... I'm not sure how to respond."

"You don't have to. I was just telling how I feel."

"Oh."

Greg didn't know how to react, Dale being all shy, clamming up even though he was secretly pleased. And Dale was pleased — he couldn't hide the little twitch of his lips, the glow of his eyes. And maybe Greg could hope that this was the beginning of something good between them.

The waitress came by to deliver their drinks, before taking their orders. Dale watched as she headed over to the next table, some of the excitement fading away from his eyes. And even though Greg didn't want to, they needed to start the conversation about the pregnancy.

"So, the baby," he said.

Dale sighed, glancing back at him. "The baby."

"I thought you'd be more excited."

With the way he'd been so upset by his infertility, Greg had expected Dale to be elated by the news. But Dale fiddled with his cutlery, tugging at the napkin wrapped around them.

"Maybe when I feel a little more secure about it." Dale twisted his fingers together, his shoulders hunched. Greg wanted to scoot over, give him a hug. "I mean... This is unexpected news. I had no plans for children. And I certainly didn't mean to implicate you — I'm sorry."

"You shouldn't be sorry," Greg said. "I should be the one apologizing."

"I shouldn't have stopped you when, you know." Dale glanced around them, lowering his voice. "You asked about contraceptives. I should've been more careful."

"There's no point regretting it, I guess." Greg

shrugged. "You're fine with it. I'm fine with it. We just gotta move forward."

"You're fine with this? The baby?"

"Yeah. I'm not gonna abandon you just because I'm not prepared." Greg laid his hand on the table between them, palm facing up, inviting Dale's touch.

Dale eyed it, his gaze sliding away. He glanced at the patrons around them, then at Greg's hand, as though he wanted to link their fingers together. "I've thought about it," he said, pulling out a notebook from his satchel. "We'll just have to straighten things out."

On the notebook, there was a list of bullet points: *Responsibilities, Finances, Scents, Misc.* Under each point, tinier writing made up a few paragraphs.

Trust him to think this over. Greg smiled, watching him. *Why am I not surprised?* Dale was a professor. Of course he would analyze all these things and put them together like a goddamn lab report. It was kind of cute.

Dale tapped his pen on the first bullet point. "To be honest, this is entirely my fault. I'm perfectly willing to take on a hundred percent of the responsibilities."

"No," Greg said. "I'm its father too. I'd rather do fifty-fifty, or something in that range."

Dale's lips twitched. "You just have to be my best student, don't you?"

I am? Greg's heart skipped. "I want to be the best. For you."

He hadn't meant it to be that cheesy. But back in the college washroom, Dale had looked up at

Greg, his eyes watery, and Greg had felt something in his stomach *tug*. Dale had been helpless, and Greg had needed to help him, protect him. Make him happy.

The more Greg thought about it, the more this didn't feel like a crush anymore. Where was the line between a crush, and whatever came *after* that?

For a moment, Dale stared, his throat working. "It would be so much simpler if you shirked your responsibilities. Your... status as Bernard's son complicates many things."

And it came back to his father again—Greg's status, Dale's employment. Greg could have so much power over Dale, just by his status alone, but he didn't want that. "I know. Tell me if I'm pushing too hard."

Dale smiled wistfully, turning the pen over in his fingers. "You'd make such a good alpha for someone else. I don't mind being the only parent listed on the birth certificate."

Greg's stomach knotted tight. "What?"

Even though the pregnancy was unexpected, and even though he couldn't imagine himself a father at twenty-two, Greg had never once thought about leaving Dale. Not when this omega was important to him. Not when he'd watched Dale over the past two months, learning his mannerisms, learning how to read him. Learning the ways Dale smiled when he thought he was alone.

"You're young, Greg. You have an entire life ahead of you. Don't waste all those possibilities." There was a telling shadow in Dale's eyes. Greg's thoughts whirled. *Does this have to do with the divorce? Which bastard alpha would mark you and then dump you?*

"I won't be wasting it," he said, frowning. "I don't care about my future."

"I care. There are so many things you can do—fulfill your dreams, go on to play in the national league. Continue school. Travel the world. *Anything.* Don't you see?" Dale looked earnestly at him. "You don't need a child holding you back."

Greg fought down the whisper of dread in his chest. Dale's words were like a sermon he'd heard too many times. "You sound like my dad."

Dale looked away. "And he's right."

"I want to court you. In case that's not obvious."

"I just—" Dale sighed. "We've been over this. I'm not good for you. There won't be anything positive coming from a relationship with me."

Dale made himself sound terrible. Like he didn't deserve a chance. After Tony's death four years ago, Greg had realized that the future couldn't be taken for granted. Hell, Tony had died at eighteen. To hear Dale decline a relationship just because of age... Greg bit back the snarl of anger in his veins. "You don't know. You haven't even tried."

Dale met his eyes then, and the defeat in his eyes silenced Greg's protests. "Look around us. Everyone is in a socially-accepted relationship. I am your professor," he said quietly. "And your father employs me. Can you tell me what he'll do if he finds out?"

Yeah, Greg had thought about it. His father

would force Dale to end the relationship, maybe terminate his employment. Maybe schedule him for an abortion. Greg swallowed, his heart aching.

"He can't do anything if we're bonded," Greg said.

Dale opened his mouth. Closed it. He curled his wrist toward himself, looking at the silvery scar there. A mark from someone who had deserted him.

Greg wouldn't leave.

"I don't love you," Dale finally said. "It would be a... waste for us to bond."

A waste? Greg quelled the ache in his chest. "I don't expect love. I just..."

"It's just a crush," Dale said, looking away. He ran his thumb down the silver clip on his pen, watching the other couples at their tables, the smiles on their faces. "It'll fade. You should know you'll never have a normal relationship with me. I don't want to cause you that pain."

"I don't care about 'normal'," Greg said, thinking about the way Dale had leaned into his chest this morning, trembling with the news. Dale had needed someone then. "If you're worried about my dad, we'll find a way around it."

"Very optimistic," Dale said, his eyes dull with resignation. "If I'm fired, I'm not sure where else I can go. I'm not... bonded. I'm sure my employment prospects will be miserable if I lose my job."

"You'll have better prospects if you're bonded to me," Greg said. Which was exactly what his father had been telling him. And it sucked that he was saying the same thing to Dale.

Dale chuckled, skeptical but amused. "I guess you have a point."

"Spend a week with me," Greg said. "Then decide where you want to go from there."

Dale swallowed. He rearranged his cutlery on the table, dragging his lip between his teeth. He was interested. And Greg wanted him closer, wanted Dale curled up in bed with him.

"What will I learn in a week?" Dale asked eventually, looking up at him. "You remember that I'm your teacher."

To be honest, Greg didn't know, either. Dale was in his forties. He'd know a lot more things than Greg at this point.

But Dale didn't think a relationship possible between them, and maybe Greg could change that. He had had enough of making decisions based on his future.

"You'll learn that you're not just a professor," Greg said, looking at the lines of Dale's throat, the slant of his collarbones. He remembered Dale pressed against him last week, when he'd come *alive* beneath Greg, and that was something Greg wanted to remind him of. "You'll learn that being old doesn't make you a bad omega."

Dale's throat worked. He looked down at his fingers, hope flickering in his eyes. "Why aren't you with someone else your age?"

Greg rolled his shoulders. After Tony, he hadn't wanted to commit. Not when the omegas his age talked about nice homes and skincare products and preparing for their futures. The future *couldn't* be trusted.

"I'm not interested in the things they're

interested in."

"You're on the basketball team," Dale said.

"Basketball's fun. Takes my mind off things." The urgency of the game distracted Greg from everything else—the split-seconds between snatching a ball and tearing off with it, the focus of shooting, the adrenaline pumping in his veins. And now that he thought about it, maybe he was using basketball as an escape.

The waitress came by, setting down large oval plates of food between them. Chunks of pork glistened on Greg's plate, drenched with onion-speckled gravy. Around it, fragrant rice sat in a pile, next to juicy corn and a bowl of steaming soup.

Dale lit up, staring at their plates. "Try some. Tell me if you think it's good."

Greg unwrapped his cutlery, popping a bite of pork into his mouth. It landed on his tongue in a juicy burst of heat—oregano and garlic and onion, held together by tender pork.

Dale's smile widened. "I could eat that forever," he said. "Sometimes, I drop an entire pork shoulder in my crock-pot and leave it to cook through the day. It smells so delicious by the time I get home."

"You should show me how you do that," Greg said, biting into another piece. Dale wasn't kidding when he said this was good. "I haven't really tried Mexican recipes."

"Maybe this week," Dale said, looking down at his plate. His cheeks darkened. "You know, we could turn it into a week-long cooking lesson."

Greg snorted. "Does everything have to be a

lesson?"

Dale blinked. "I... don't know. I guess I'm still seeing you as my student."

"I don't just want to be your student." Greg lowered his voice. "I want to press you down in bed and kiss you."

A darker flush crept up Dale's throat. His gaze dropped to Greg's shoulders, then his chest and arms, and his tongue darted across his lips. "That still doesn't make a relationship."

"We can be friends," Greg said, his heart racing. He wanted Dale. And whatever Dale wanted to call this, he'd roll with it. "Sounds better?"

"It does," Dale said, except his gaze lingered on Greg's body, flickering up to his lips. He was thinking about last week.

"It'll be better in bed," Greg murmured.

Dale's throat worked. He spooned soup into his mouth, that shade of crimson fanning all the way to his hairline. "I, um."

A faint coil of musk rolled through the air between them, followed by hibiscus, and a trace of honey. Greg wanted to worship him. Dale looked like he hadn't enjoyed himself in a while, with his shoulders hunched, his eyes jaded.

Maybe they could start exploring tonight.

Greg let silence lapse between them, not reaching over, not touching Dale. Dale squirmed under his stare, his gaze darting between his own food, and Greg's hands.

Dale wasn't leaving. He wasn't saying no. He was fighting his own desire, and in that moment, Greg saw the loneliness that surrounded him.

Dale had a couch in his office. He slept there sometimes. He didn't seem to have anyone to go home to, and Greg could've kicked himself for not noticing this earlier.

"We don't even need to fuck," Greg said. Sex didn't solve everything; he shouldn't be focusing so hard on that. "Go out with me. Watch a movie. Come watch my games. Stuff like that."

"And if I..." Dale bit his lip. "If I want to?"

"Want to what?" Greg smirked. "Watch my games?"

"That too." Dale folded a corner of his napkin. "All of those. I mean, it... doesn't hurt to try. If we're careful. I guess."

Greg polished off the last of his food, his body thrumming with anticipation. When he'd gotten dressed for dinner, he hadn't expected Dale to be open to a night with him, much less a whole week.

But Dale was agreeing now, cautiously, his expression a mix of hope and fear, and Greg wanted things to work out between them.

So he reached over, stroking his fingertip over the back of Dale's hand. Just to remind Dale of his promise, and the heat of his touch.

Dale swallowed, his nostrils flaring. He wanted more.

All Greg had to do was wait. Then they'd go to one of their homes, and Greg would treat Dale the way he deserved to be treated—carefully, and with spine-arching pleasure.

At some point after that, when they were both sated, they'd discuss the baby further.

10
Dale

WHEN DALE had dragged himself to El Asado an hour ago, he hadn't thought he'd be bringing Greg home.

He hadn't known what to expect, when his stomach had been twisted up into knots, his thoughts focused on the new life in his belly. He was pregnant. He was carrying his student's child, all because he'd given in to his heat last week.

A tiny part of him marveled at the baby. Nineteen years ago, the doctor had said, *It'll be best for you to adopt.* Charles hadn't wanted an adoption. He'd thought it beneath his status. His parents had said, *If Dale can't conceive, how can he even be a good father? How is he even a good omega?*

Haunted by their words long after he'd left Drakestown, Dale hadn't even dared to consider an adoption. Slowly, he'd stopped wishing for a baby.

And now that he'd finally conceived, the baby turned out to be his student's. A little voice in his head whispered, *You should be ashamed of yourself.*

Neck-deep in guilt, he'd found himself at his favorite restaurant, across the booth from Greg

Hastings. They'd talked a little about the baby. Then Greg had suggested they stay together for a week, and Dale's mind had flooded with the implications of that.

A week with Greg? In the privacy of his apartment? He wouldn't be able to keep his clothes on.

Dale gulped, heat curling through his belly. He wanted to be Greg's. Wanted Greg to taste him. All of him.

Greg traced circles on the back of Dale's hand. Then he slipped his fingers around to his wrist, rubbing right over his scent gland. Dale's throat went dry.

For two months, he'd begged June to mark him, so he had an excuse not to say yes. Now, Greg's fingers made love to Dale's wrist, a slow touch on sensitive skin, and Dale's self-control evaporated like water on desert sand.

"You shouldn't—shouldn't be doing that here," he breathed, his heart thudding. Any of the restaurant's patrons could look over, and maybe they'd be able to tell how old Dale was. How young Greg was. They'd think Dale was buying Greg's interest with money, or something equally terrible.

Greg glanced at the windows. "What if we do this outside?"

The sky had darkened, and Dale could barely make out the gleam of streetlamps on the parked cars. His stomach flipped. "It's still visible to the public."

"Then you want to continue in private," Greg murmured, massaging Dale's scent gland. He circled it, rubbed right over it, the ball of his thumb callused and firm. Pleasure hummed down Dale's nerves. He slid his hand away, biting down a moan. Greg smiled.

I need to stop this. It's not right. Dale signaled for the bill. The waitress gave him a thumbs-up.

"There are countless omegas waiting in line for you," Dale said, pushing his half-finished food away. It was his favorite dish, but tonight, he'd lost his appetite. He wasn't hungry for pulled pork right now.

He was hungry for Greg.

"You probably know their names better than I do," Greg said. "I don't know the other students all that well."

"I..." Dale's gaze fell on the forgotten notebook on the table. *Crap, we got distracted.* He rubbed his face, groaning. "We were supposed to talk about the baby."

"We'll talk about the baby after." Greg watched him with dark eyes; there was no question what the *before* would be. Dale swallowed.

The waitress breezed by with the bill. Dale tugged his wallet out, handing her his credit card before Greg could. The waitress thanked him, stepping away.

Greg frowned. "I was supposed to get that."

"Well, I'm your professor," Dale said.

"Stop that. I'm your alpha."

Dale's heart missed a beat. "You're not," he said, even though *I'm your alpha* sent a surge of heat down his body. "We're not bonded."

"We don't have to be bonded," Greg said, glancing at Dale's wrist.

Except Dale wanted to belong. Wanted an alpha. It was nice of Greg to offer to pay, nice of him to be concerned about the baby.

Dale said nothing, tucking the notebook back into his satchel. The waitress returned. Dale signed the receipt. Then they stood up to leave, Greg waiting by Dale's seat, offering his elbow.

"You really don't have to," Dale said, slipping his hand into the crook of Greg's arm. They weren't a couple.

But he appreciated the old-fashioned courtesy of that gesture, stepping alongside Greg as they left the restaurant. Greg wasn't an ordinary student. The shadows in his eyes never truly faded, and he seemed wise for his age. Seemed to desire Dale a lot more than Dale would give himself credit for.

As they left, Dale kept his head held high, expecting someone to recognize them, or sneer about this unusual pairing. Except no one did. They were safe here.

It was only when they stepped into the parking lot, the front door closing behind them with a jangle, that he let his breath out. The late March air brushed cool over his skin.

"That was surprisingly easy," he said, removing his hand from Greg's elbow.

Greg followed him to his car. "We're alpha and omega. No one will care."

"I'm older than you," Dale said.

Greg rounded on him, eyes flashing. "I've told you twenty damn times—age doesn't matter," he growled, inches between their lips.

Then he kissed Dale, hot and hard, and Dale

116

melted against him. Greg's mouth consumed his, sliding damp and silky, his teeth dragging lightly against Dale's skin. He smelled like aspen, like alpha, and Dale trembled, his body reacting with a visceral heat.

He wanted to spread for Greg. Wanted Greg to taste him. Wanted Greg's hands sliding down his bare skin.

When Greg pulled away, Dale's knees were weak. He slumped back against his car, his breathing shallow, his cock hard.

"I'm not gonna abandon you like your previous alpha," Greg murmured, dipping his face close so their foreheads brushed. "I care about you and the baby. I won't leave."

Dale gulped, Greg's words ringing in his ears. He wanted to lean close, sink into Greg's chest. But they were still in public, and the more time they spent here, the higher their chances were of being recognized. "We can't stay here."

"Your place. My parents have the key to mine."

Dale winced. "Definitely not your place."

"Address? I'll get in my car and follow you."

"Sure."

Greg slipped his phone out, that same photo of him and the other boy on his lock screen. Again, he said nothing about it. He turned on the GPS, opened up a map application, and handed his phone to Dale. Dale keyed his address in.

"Thanks," Greg said. Then he leaned in, pressing a kiss to Dale's forehead. "See you at your place."

Dale stared after him. Greg strode across the

parking lot, the headlights on a red sports car flashing as he approached. A Porsche, which probably cost twice as much as Dale's Volkswagen.

Greg was the college president's son. He'd kissed Dale maybe five times by now, and Dale didn't want it to stop.

He wobbled over to the driver's seat, slipping inside. Across the parking lot, the Porsche's headlights flashed on. Dale started his car, pulling out toward the street. Greg followed.

To steady his shaking hands, Dale put on some music. The notes of a country song twanged in his ears, and he took a deep breath, flipping his turn signal.

He was doing this. He was bringing Greg home.

His body ached with need.

The drive home usually took ten minutes. Today, there was construction along some of the roads, and Dale swore at himself for not checking this in advance. Greg might be starting to rethink this.

Dale couldn't see anything but the Porsche's headlights in his rearview mirror. As the minutes wore on, he realized this was a bad idea. He wasn't in heat. Greg wasn't in a rut, and he'd think more clearly. See Dale for who he was. Dale wasn't supple like his omega students; he didn't have the stamina they did.

By the time he pulled into his apartment complex, he was ready to apologize to Greg for wasting his time.

Greg pulled into the parking spot next to him. For a moment, Dale remained seated,

118

wondering if he should roll down the window and tell Greg to leave.

Except Greg slipped out of his car, rounding its hood to stand by Dale's door. He peered at Dale through the window, and Dale's breath caught in his chest. He would hate to disappoint Greg.

The car door opened. "Hey," Greg said, his aspen scent wafting through the air, layered with a trace of musk. "You okay?"

Dale met his eyes. "Are you sure about this?" He waved at himself. "I'm not twenty anymore—"

Greg sighed, leaning into the car. Then he kissed Dale again, firmly, his lips soft, and Dale's doubts melted away. "Are you going to keep saying that the rest of the week?" he murmured against Dale's mouth, his breath hot, heady.

"Yes," Dale said, and Greg squeezed his thigh, unbuckling his seat belt.

"I'm not gonna fuck you out here," Greg whispered in his ear. "Better get your ass out."

Dale's blood surged between his legs. "You're talking to me like that?"

Greg smirked. "You smell wet."

Dale blushed. He grabbed his satchel, locked the Volkswagen, then led the way to his first-story apartment. "I hate how my body betrays me."

"You mean, by giving you a baby?" Greg smiled wryly, and Dale groaned.

"Don't remind me about it."

"I thought you'd be happier about the pregnancy. Aren't you?"

"It still feels surreal right now, to be honest." Dale stopped at his apartment, fishing out his keys. "I don't *feel* pregnant."

He unlocked the door, flicking the lights on. Then he stood back, waiting for Greg to enter first.

"Nice place," Greg said when he stepped in, his gaze sweeping over the large windows, the plush couches in the living room, the kitchen with its granite counter tops. Pots of indoor plants stood in the corners, and stacks of origami paper on the coffee table. "It smells like you."

"'I guess it does." Dale shut the door behind them, kicking his shoes off. The blinds had to be shut—that was most important. Greg shucked his shoes and followed Dale through the kitchen, the study, the bedroom. The entire time, Greg's eyes lingered on Dale's skin, appreciative, hungry. Dale's body hummed.

"Even a professor's apartment can't distract you, huh?" Dale asked when the last of the blinds had been turned down. He looked over his shoulder, glancing at the alpha in his doorway.

"I've been thinking about last week," Greg admitted. "I don't think I did right by you."

Dale stared. What about last week wasn't good? "You mean, the condom?"

"I want to take more time," Greg said, crossing the bedroom. He didn't stop to admire the pink salt lamps in the corners, or the oval mirrors that lined the walls. Neither did he look at the dozens of paper cranes hanging from the ceiling. "Getting to know you."

With each step, Greg's scent grew stronger. The aspen and musk that had seeped into the car now flooded Dale's nostrils, smelling like alpha and *want*.

Greg stared down at him, his shoulders

broad, his biceps straining against his sleeves. There was a telling line in his pants, that had pressed against Dale's skin last week. To think about it sliding against him now... His hole quivered.

As though he could smell Dale's reaction, Greg's nostrils flared. He licked his lips, stopping inches from Dale, the heat of his body radiating through the space between them.

Dale swallowed dryly. "How would you get to know me?"

"Like this," Greg whispered, cupping Dale's cheeks with both his hands. Then he tipped Dale's face up to his, and kissed him softly on the lips.

Dale's breath snagged in his throat. He hadn't expected this gentleness from Greg, not when it told of care, of respect and adoration.

Last week had been heavy strokes and desperate kisses. Right now, Greg kissed him slowly, and Dale savored the silky friction between their lips, the careful brush of Greg's thumb on his cheek.

He moaned, parting for Greg, trying to lean closer. Except Greg held him where he was, dragging the seam of his mouth over Dale's lips, a soft, damp touch, his breath feathering hot on Dale's skin.

"I'm sorry I didn't treat you better," Greg said.

How much better could Greg treat him? Last week had been phenomenal, and to top that...? Dale's chest squeezed. Greg should save this for his future mate. Someone he truly cared about.

But Dale also wanted Greg to need him, and

Greg's desire was addicting.

"I'm curious to see more," Dale whispered. And Greg slid into his mouth, tasting a little like Sprite, a little like aspen. Dale moaned, sucking him deeper, tangling their tongues together.

Greg growled, backing him into the bed. Then he broke the kiss, sliding his hands under Dale's arms, lifting him further back onto the mattress. Dale landed somewhere in the middle with a thump, his breath rushing from his chest. They were doing this. He wasn't in heat, and... he was inviting Greg into his bed. And Dale couldn't bring himself to refuse Greg, not right now.

When Greg leaned over him, watching his face, Dale spread his legs. Locked gazes with Greg.

Greg swallowed, flicking his gaze down. His eyes raked over Dale's body, from his work-rumpled shirt to the belt at his hips, to the dark pants that barely hid his cock. "Ten minutes ago, you said you weren't good enough."

"I don't want to think about it," Dale mumbled. "Help me forget."

For a taut, exposed moment, Greg studied him, his eyes inscrutable. Then he settled on the bed next to Dale, sliding his hot palm up Dale's calf, squeezing his thigh. "You're good enough," Greg murmured, tugging Dale's shirt from his waistband. "You're more than just good, Dale."

Greg leaned closer, pressing a soft, damp kiss on his belly, right above his waistband. Dale watched him, admiring the curl of his lashes, the intensity of his eyes, the fullness of his lips.

Greg was his student, and he felt so irrationally good.

Greg unbuttoned Dale's shirt, kissing up his chest, until he exposed the pink discs of Dale's nipples. Then he flicked his tongue over them, and Dale gasped.

"Always wanted to do this," Greg said, watching him. He took Dale's nipple into his mouth, sucking lightly on it, the points of his teeth tracing over Dale's skin. A whisper of pleasure raced down Dale's nerves. "Wanted to touch you. Feel you under me."

"I didn't—didn't know." Dale squirmed, arching up, offering his chest. And Greg smiled, slipping his hand under Dale's back to hold him up.

"I was gonna do this after we go out for coffee," Greg murmured against his skin, dragging his teeth over the crest of Dale's nipple.

"Oh," Dale breathed. Greg's face was so close to his. His body curled over Dale's like a predatory animal, and Dale was so hard it hurt.

"You didn't know?" Greg smirked. He met Dale's eyes, pressing kisses over Dale's chest, before closing his lips around his other nipple. Then he sucked, and the pressure went straight down to Dale's cock, yanking a moan from his lips.

"I thought—I thought all you wanted was coffee," Dale breathed, his hips rocking up. He needed Greg's touch further down, needed Greg's body pressing him into the mattress. "Greg— more."

Greg's smile grew wider. Instead of stroking Dale's cock, he set his hand on Dale's hip, pressing his thumb down into the sensitive spot by his hipbone. The pressure was a bright point on Dale's body, stark through the layers of his clothes. "Feel this?"

"Yes," Dale hissed, bucking up.

Greg slid his thumb half an inch down, rubbing a firm circle a little further south. "This?"

"Yes."

He pressed his thumb closer, in increments of half inches, massaging slow circles along Dale's groin, closer and closer and closer to Dale's cock... but not touching it.

"Greg," Dale moaned, winding his fingers through Greg's hair, pulling him closer, trying to make him nuzzle his cock, lick it, anything.

Greg smirked. And kissed the taut fabric just by Dale's balls, blowing through it, his breath a hot touch caressing Dale's skin. It wasn't enough.

"Touch my cock," Dale said, lifting his hips.

"No," Greg said, shoving Dale's hips down onto the bed. Dale gasped. Greg pinned them down with his weight, and Dale couldn't lift them, couldn't move as Greg climbed between his legs, nudging them further open with his knees. "Want to see how hard you get for me."

Dale's cheeks burned. He was hard for Greg. That, he couldn't deny.

Before he could reach for his pants, Greg caught his wrist, pinning it down against the mattress.

"Your body is mine tonight," he whispered, releasing Dale's hip to trace his knuckle up his belly, up his chest to his throat, then his lips. "Your mouth, your nipples, your ass."

Dale trembled, his skin tingling, his body aching for Greg.

Greg rubbed his thumb along Dale's lower lip, pinching his nipple. Dale gasped, pain and pleasure twisting down his nerves. Greg smiled, cupping Dale's neck in his hand, sliding his palm down Dale's chest, to his belly, his groin. Except Greg lifted his palm, skimming his fingertips down around Dale's cock, leaving it neglected.

Dale groaned, rocking up, trying to push into Greg's palm.

Greg stroked his fingertips down Dale's balls, between his legs, pressing up against the damp fabric covering his ass. Right against his hole. Dale gasped, writhing, rolling his hips. *He knows what I want.*

And Greg pulled his touch away, sliding his fingertip down the line of Dale's cock, pausing where he'd soaked his pants through with precum. It wasn't enough touch. "All of you belongs to me tonight. But especially this."

Greg slid his wrist heavily down Dale's cock, dragging his scent gland over it. Dale shuddered, gasping for breath. He was Greg's. His cock was Greg's, and it shouldn't make him throb. Instead, his hips bucked up, inviting Greg's touch. Inviting Greg to mark the rest of him.

Gods, he was such a whore. Cheeks scorching, Dale said, "I really sh-shouldn't. You're my — my —"

"Don't even finish that sentence," Greg muttered, his eyes flashing. Then he straddling Dale's hips, leaned in, and kissed him hard, pushing his cock against Dale's. Dale arched.

Like last week, Greg's cock was thick in his pants, heavy, and it was a delicious weight promising to fill him.

Greg slid his tongue into Dale's mouth, his hips rocking hard against Dale's, shoving him into the mattress. Dale moaned, pleasure thrumming through his body, so wet he dripped.

"Next time you think of saying 'You're my student,'" Greg murmured, "say 'You're my alpha.'"

Dale's breath rushed out of him. Those words held too much weight. But to acknowledge Greg as his, to *belong* to Greg... Pleasure jolted through his cock.

"Greg, please—" Dale gasped, writhing.

"*Say it.*"

"You're my a-alpha," Dale moaned, his cock jerking in his pants. It sounded right. It felt right. Especially when Greg held him down like this, letting Dale feel how hard he was for him. "Gods, Greg. Please. I need you inside."

"Not yet," Greg growled. He leaned up, taking away some of the pressure on Dale's hips. Then he loosened Dale's belt, yanked it from his belt loops, and tossed it off the bed. It landed on the floorboards with a clatter. Greg tugged Dale's fly open, curled his fingers into Dale's pants and briefs, and pulled them out from under his hips.

Dale lifted his legs. Greg slid his clothes along his thighs, over his calves, off his feet. The pants and briefs hit the floor with a rustle. Dale parted his legs, and Greg's gaze burned down Dale's chest, to his flushed, straining cock.

Unlike last week, when Dale had been desperate and in heat, the tension between them built like the rising tide, steady and unyielding.

"I'm not like I was," Dale mumbled, covering his belly with his hand, his cock leaking onto his fingers. He'd put on a bit of weight over the years, and he wasn't as svelte as a younger omega could be. "I—"

"You're *fine,*" Greg said, tugging Dale's hand away. Then he leaned in, pressing a kiss to Dale's abdomen. "You look fine. Good. Like someone I wanna fuck through the night."

Dale's cheeks burned. "I might fall asleep after the first round," he said. "I can't—"

"Gods, stop putting yourself down." Greg leaned over him, planting one hand by Dale's cheek. He stared into Dale's eyes, his gaze hot and serious. "One round is fine, too. I don't care. I'm not here because you're my professor, and I'm not here expecting someone my age. I don't care about that."

Dale's chest squeezed. "That's—that's very kind of you."

Greg slid his fingers down to Dale's chest, rubbing over Dale's nipples. Pleasure stung through his nerves, and he gasped. And Greg reached down, caught the tip of Dale's cock, the barest touch sliding his foreskin down. Dale moaned, thrusting up, needing more. Greg circled his rough fingers loosely around his cock, looking down as Dale fucked into his hand. Then, as though Dale's pleas meant nothing, he brought his hand further down, stroking between Dale's cheeks, the barest brush of his finger.

"Greg," Dale moaned, spreading his legs, pushing up at him. "Don't tease."

And Greg met his eyes, pulling his fingers

away. "You see that?"

"See what?"

"The way you want me," Greg murmured, lowering his lips to Dale's. "You're not old or bad. Especially not when you beg me to fuck you."

Dale swallowed. "Oh."

Greg dragged his finger between Dale's cheeks, an intimate touch that kept just shy of his hole. "Now spread for me."

Dale groaned, reaching down to clasp his cheeks. Then he pulled them apart, exposing his damp hole, and Greg's nostrils flared.

"Very nice," Greg rumbled. He circled Dale's hole once with his fingertip, then sat back, catching Dale's ankle. Dale watched as Greg pressed soft kisses down his calf, his knee, his stubble scraping along Dale's sensitive inner thigh. Dale trembled, keeping himself spread, waiting for Greg to reach his cock.

But Greg nuzzled Dale's balls, dragging his tongue over them, his lips sliding damply against Dale's groin. Dale's cock jerked, needing touch.

"Greg," he moaned.

And Greg finally dragged his tongue up Dale's cock, a hot, wet touch, from his base to his tip, lapping at where his head had pushed out of his foreskin. Dale groaned, leaking onto his tongue, trying to rock into his mouth.

Greg kissed his tip, licking it, a thread of precum stretching between them when he pulled away. He caught Dale's knees, pushing them down against the bed, holding Dale exposed. Dale's face burned. Greg fucking him was one thing, but Greg looking closely at Dale's slick hole, at his tight balls? Greg's lips curled in a smile. "You're so damn wet for me."

"Yes," Dale hissed.

"Hold your position," Greg said, releasing him. Dale hooked his hands behind his knees, his pulse racing when Greg unbuttoned his shirt.

He'd never seen Greg shirtless in person, only in pictures on the basketball newsletters. He was so *young,* and Dale couldn't stop staring at the expanse of his pecs, the flat discs of his nipples, the grooves of his abs. He admired the V of Greg's hips, and Greg pulled his belt off, stepped out of his jeans. His thighs were strong, his calves muscled, their skin red with flame-streak scars.

He smelled like musk, like *alpha,* and when he slipped his boxers off, Dale's throat went dry.

At the apex of his thighs, jutting up from his hair, Greg's cock was thick, flushed, damp at the tip. It had been inside Dale last week, but looking at it now, and seeing just how big it was... Heat flooded through his body.

"Want it?" Greg asked, reaching down to stroke his cock. Dale moaned. Greg smiled, climbing onto the bed. He straddled Dale's chest, still kneeling. "Suck me."

Dale's cheeks scorched. He scrambled up, supporting himself on one arm as he curled his fingers around Greg's cock, breathing in the musk of it, its length hot against his fingers. Dale licked it first, dragging his tongue from base to tip like Greg had done for him, flicking just beneath Greg's sensitive head. Greg bared his teeth, leaking salty onto Dale's tongue.

Then Dale took him into his mouth, his lips

stretching around Greg's cock, and Greg's hips jerked, his breath staggering.

"Gods, you feel damn good," Greg hissed, his fingers curling into Dale's hair, guiding him closer. Dale moaned around his cock, sucking on it, his lips sliding against silky skin. It tasted good, like alpha, like Greg and sweat and skin."Want me inside?"

Gods, just thinking about Greg's cock stretching him open... Dale's hole squeezed, utterly ready for his alpha. "Yes."

Greg slid out of his mouth, his cock glistening. Dale squirmed, his slick smearing across the sheets.

"Spread for me," Greg said, easing backward until he was between Dale's thighs. Dale reached down, pulling his cheeks open, showing Greg his sensitive, vulnerable hole. Greg groaned. He pointed his tip down, trailing it over the underside of Dale's cock, sending a frisson of pleasure down his nerves. "Want a condom?"

Dale chuckled. "I think it's pointless to use one now, isn't it?"

"Thought I'd ask anyway," Greg murmured, meeting his eyes. Dale's heart thudded. It was considerate of Greg.

"Put it in," he breathed, spreading his cheeks apart wider, lifting his hips to temp Greg with his hole. "Now."

Greg smirked, dragging his cock over Dale's balls, over his taint, rubbing it over Dale's hole. Then he pushed inside, spreading Dale open, and Dale's breath punched out of his lungs.

Greg was his student, and he was sliding all

the way in, his cock thick inside Dale, filling him up inch after inch. And Dale's body stretched pleasantly around him, his own cock tellingly hard, his body screaming *yes, yes, yes.*

Then Greg's balls bumped against Dale's ass, and he was all the way inside, and Dale could only pant, his body adjusting to Greg's thickness. Greg's fingers pressed into Dale's hips, anchoring him to the bed, and he was building a rhythm, fucking deeper in, his eyes watching Dale, watching the way he opened Dale's hole.

Dale's face burned, but he needed more of this, of Greg moving inside him, his solid cock rocking inside his body, sending pleasure sizzling up his spine.

"More," Dale gasped, digging his nails into the sheets. "Greg, please."

"Harder?" Greg murmured, snapping his hips forward, grinding against his prostate. Dale cried out, his cock pulsing. He couldn't describe the pleasure that Greg fucked into him, over and over. His fingers dug into his knees, and he gasped for breath as Greg's cock sank into him, stroking his body inside.

Greg reached down to stroke Dale's cock, sliding his foreskin away from his head. Then he swirled his thumb around Dale's exposed tip, just the way Dale liked it, and pleasure crashed through his body.

His spine arched, his cock throbbed. He couldn't breathe, couldn't think. All he knew was Greg's touch, the heat of Greg's body, the way Greg murmured above him, his voice gravelly.

When he blinked himself back into his

bedroom, Greg hovered above him, his face inches away, his cock surging inside Dale. "I'm gonna come," he murmured between ragged breaths, his strokes forceful and deep.

"Yes," Dale whispered, cradling Greg's waist, pulling him closer. "Please."

A growl fell from Greg's lips; he thrust in harder, his cock swelling, sweat beading across his skin. Dale watched as he squeezed his eyes shut, fucking in a final time, his chest heaving.

For a moment, they breathed, Greg pressing their foreheads together, his body curled around Dale's, powerful and possessive. Dale watched the sweat trickling down his neck, the thick lashes lining his eyes, the muscles of his shoulders taut. He was beautiful.

Greg could've chosen anyone, and he chose to return to Dale.

When his breathing evened out, Greg kissed him on the lips. Then he kissed Dale on the cheeks, eyelids, nose, and Dale's heart pattered. "What are you doing?"

"Showing you I appreciate this," Greg whispered, trailing kisses along Dale's cheek, to his ear. "Showing you that I want you."

Dale watched him, speechless. When he'd brought Greg home, he'd expected sex, yes. But not Greg to treat him with such tenderness. Not someone like Dale, when this couldn't possibly last.

"Want my knot?" Greg asked, sliding his wrist over Dale's chest, leaving his scent on Dale's skin.

"Yes," Dale said, cautiously touching Greg's thigh. "I'm really pregnant, aren't I?"

Greg pressed his nose into Dale's hair, breathing in deep. "Yeah, I think so. You smell different from last week. It's kinda faint, but your scent is sweeter."

And in just one week, Dale's life had changed, for better or worse. He'd wanted a child too much to regret it.

As Greg's knot swelled inside him, Dale moaned, gazing up at this alpha, this man who had pursued him for two months. They weren't in love. But Greg had promised to commit, and Dale... felt safe in his arms. Felt wanted.

The corners of his eyes prickled. He couldn't remember the last time anyone had needed him this close.

"What's wrong?" Greg asked, kissing his temple.

"It's just funny," Dale said, his throat tight. "I've never... never had an alpha want me. Not until you."

"I thought you were married."

"It was arranged. He—" Dale swallowed, remembering harsh words and withering looks. "He annulled the union when I couldn't bear him heirs."

"Fucker," Greg muttered. "That's not what an alpha's supposed to do!"

Dale laughed dryly, shrugging. "It was in the contract. He'd given me three years instead of one. Thinking back on it, I don't think he should have."

He thought about Charles' parents, with their prying questions, their little snide comments. *Is he really spreading for you? Has that bitch been washing out your seed? Or is he so loose that he can't keep anything inside?*

Dale's cheeks burned. He closed his eyes, wishing he could burn those memories away.

"What did he do?" Greg's voice rumbled next to his ear, concerned.

He shook his head. "It's in the past. Don't worry about it."

"It's still bothering you, damn it. Tell me."

"It wasn't a pleasant marriage," Dale said. "I mean, it was fine at first. They treated me with respect. But when I failed to conceive after six months, Charles started taking me to the doctor. His parents were pushing hard. I think they must've influenced him somehow... He started doubting me."

"You were his goddamn husband. Did he...?" Greg sucked in a breath, horror flickering through his eyes.

"It wasn't anything like violence," Dale said, trying to ease the tension in Greg's body.

He hadn't wanted to tell Greg, not really. But he was risking his tenure, and he didn't have the heart to tell Greg to leave.

So Dale tried telling Greg the ugly words, in the hopes that Greg would think the same and abandon him.

"His parents started calling me a whore. A greedy bitch. They said I was withholding pregnancies so Charles would give me more money before I conceived." Dale looked away, his throat tight. He couldn't meet Greg's eyes. "They said I was a bad egg, that maybe my body was rotten and maybe they should've had Charles test me out before they sealed the marriage. And maybe they should have. I'm not... worthy. This pregnancy is a complete surprise to me, I swear."

"What the actual fuck," Greg said, his fingers pressing so hard into Dale's arms they hurt. Dale yelped, and Greg released him immediately. "Sorry. But what the hell," Greg snarled. "I can't believe they did that to you. They're goddamn scumbags! Your ex never told them to shut up?"

Dale shook his head. Greg's eyes flashed.

"You actually stayed in that marriage," Greg said, his voice low, dangerous. "You deserve better than that sort of crap."

Dale sighed, leaning back into the pillows. "I make all the wrong decisions. Like this."

When all was said and done, he was still a professor, and Greg was his student. And Greg was knotting inside him, stretching him open, their bodies locked together. Exactly what the first clause of his employment contract said *not* to do.

Greg was quiet for a moment. But his chest heaved, and Dale could feel the furious tension in his limbs, the way he looked as though he'd hunt down Charles and his parents, and rip them all up. It was very sweet of him.

"This isn't wrong," Greg said, his nostrils flared. "We're alpha and omega."

"And I'm also your teacher."

Greg glanced at the paper cranes on the ceiling, the rumpled sheets on the bed, the strewn clothes on the floor. Then he looked back at Dale, pressing his nose into Dale's neck. "No. Not here, you aren't. I don't need you to be my teacher in bed."

Dale's throat tightened. This, too, was new.

135

He'd only been this close to Greg for two days — once last week, and once today. And it was comfortable. Nonjudgmental. It felt like he belonged, even though they hardly knew each other.

"I'm not anything," Dale said. "There are so many better options for you out there."

Greg hugged him tighter. "Honestly, I can't see why anyone would annul a marriage with you. You're — you're good. Special."

Dale's cheeks heated. "Just special? After your tirade, I expected a better vocabulary from you."

"Damn you. You want more words?" Greg scowled and kissed him on the lips. "You're humble. Your lab lessons are kinda fun. You're not constantly advertising your research group like the other profs."

"That just means you like me as a teacher."

Greg leaned away, his brows drawing low. Dale couldn't fathom what Greg saw in him. "You need someone," Greg said slowly. "And you're so human. I've told you about the ink blotches on your shirt. That damn couch in your office. And if you saw yourself just now... You — you needed me."

The words settled between them, heavy. Staring into Greg's eyes, Dale knew he was serious. And maybe he could allow himself to believe in Greg. Believe that he could be loved.

"I won't treat you like your bastard ex did," Greg murmured. "You deserve better."

"Maybe," Dale said, sagging into the bed. Mostly, he wanted to be desired. He'd been watching Greg for months, admiring him. Thinking Greg deserved a better omega than himself. "But your father is still my employer, and there's no circumventing that."

Greg slid out when his knot receded, pulling Dale onto him as he rolled onto his back.

Dale's cum smeared between their stomachs, cool and sticky. Dale winced. Greg kissed him.

"We'll deal," Greg said. "Shower more. My scent's common, anyway. You could be sleeping with someone else who smells like me."

"But anyone in our classes would smell us on each other." Dale sighed, burrowing his face in Greg's shoulder. "Perhaps you should sit at the front of class. So our scents would be difficult to differentiate."

"Sounds good."

Dale yawned. Fatigue bore down on him; after the day's events, it was too much to handle all at once. The pregnancy, Greg, and the mind-blowing sex.

"Grab some sleep," Greg said. "I'll shower, then come join you in bed. Get you a towel to wipe down if you don't wanna come along."

Dale's pulse skipped. This, he wasn't used to. "That's generous of you. Very forward."

"Have I been not forward?" Greg smiled, kissing him again. "Leave some space for me in bed."

And as scandalous as it sounded, Dale wanted him here. Greg's presence calmed him more than anything else had done.

11
Dale

DALE AWOKE the next day to the tantalizing aroma of coffee and bacon. It smelled like a dream, and he rolled over in bed, trying to ignore his rumbling stomach.

Except he caught a telltale whiff of aspen and musk in his sheets. His eyes snapped open, his hands fumbling for the warmth he'd cuddled up with last night. Greg had been real. The sex had been real.

He looked down at himself. His skin was pale, normal, his belly flat.

The baby.

Dale sat upright, his heart stumbling. "I'm pregnant?" he murmured. "I can't be."

But he remembered the five tests yesterday, the double blue lines, and Greg standing beside him, counting down the minutes with his phone. They'd met for dinner to discuss the baby. Except they'd gotten distracted, and Dale had a meeting with Bernard Hastings this afternoon.

He groaned, grabbing his phone. 7:14 AM. A minute before his alarm went. Dale killed the alarm, rolling out of bed. Vaguely, he thought about pulling shorts on. But there wasn't any point anyway, when he and Greg hadn't just fucked once.

They'd slept together twice, Greg had watched him pee, and it was ironic how he didn't need contraceptives now—not because he was infertile, but because he was pregnant. *I still can't believe it.*

He pressed his hand to his belly, wandering to the kitchen.

Greg stood at the electric stove, shirtless, his jeans hanging from his hips. When Dale stepped in, he turned, his dark eyes wandering over Dale—from his face to his hips to his feet, and back up. "Morning," Greg said, his voice rasping.

Dale swallowed. Gods, could this alpha get any sexier? "Hello," he croaked, clearing his throat. "Sorry. I didn't expect you to be up this early."

"I'm making breakfast," Greg said, nodding at the pan.

Dale crossed the kitchen, rubbing his arms. Maybe he should've pulled a shirt on—it was March, and still a little chilly. "You found my favorite food."

"Bacon?" Greg laughed. "I looked in the cabinets. Should I be sorry?"

"Not if you're making me breakfast," Dale said, his chest filling with warmth. This, he hadn't expected either. "Sex and bacon—are you trying to get into my good books?"

"Maybe your science journals." A grin played on Greg's lips as he opened the cabinets. He pulled out a mug, filling it half-full with coffee. "Cream? Sugar?"

"It should go to three-quarters full," Dale said, his lips twitching. "But yes. Three tablespoons of sugar, and cream."

"You're pregnant, so no. Half a cup. That's all for today."

Dale sighed. "So I'm really pregnant."

Greg slanted a look at him, opening the fridge for milk. "We could visit the doctor in a month's time if you want to be sure."

"'We'?"

"Yeah. I'm not leaving," Greg said.

"Oh. I thought... you might drop me and run."

Greg snorted, stirring sugar into the coffee—he'd only added one tablespoon of it, Dale noticed. "I'll grab some clothes from home before I come back," Greg said. "Any plans this week?"

"No." Dale accepted the mug of coffee, breathing in its bittersweet fragrance. "You're... really staying the week."

"Yeah." Greg drank from a mug he'd poured himself. His coffee was black, like Dale had suspected. "So you'll get used to me."

"Why?"

"Because I'm the kid's dad. You're going to be seeing a lot of me."

Dale's pulse skipped. "You're handling the news a lot better than I expected," he said. "Most unbonded alphas your age would flee."

"I'm not most alphas."

"I guess not, if you're sleeping with me." Dale ducked his chin, staring into his mug. His coffee was paler than usual, and less sweet. Probably a healthier dose than he usually poured

140

himself. "You left out two tablespoons of sugar."

"Three tablespoons would be too much for half a cup." Greg raised an eyebrow. "Or do you want me to indulge you with unhealthy food?"

Dale smiled to himself, hiding his face behind his mug. Greg's concern was endearing."One tablespoon, I guess. I'll have to get used to less caffeine. My usual is three cups in the morning."

"Three?" Greg stared incredulously at him. "No wonder you smell like coffee in class."

"You've been smelling me?"

"Yeah." Greg's nostrils flared. "But you smell like me today."

The heat on Dale's cheeks intensified. Greg had marked him last night, after he brought in a damp towel to wipe Dale down. Then they'd kissed and cuddled, and Dale had savored the tangle of their limbs, the whisper of Greg's skin on his own. And now, he smelled like Greg.

A ribbon of horror shot down his spine. "I have a meeting with your dad this afternoon."

Greg tensed. "Crap."

"He'll smell you on me. I'll have to look for a scent suppressant."

"The school pharmacy should have one." Greg winced. "Sorry."

"I don't know if you should be. Last night was... nice. I enjoyed it. Thank you."

"You don't have to thank me," Greg said, but he smiled, his cheeks darkening. He turned to flip the bacon in the pan.

Dale watched him, melting a little. Greg had helped him through the pregnancy tests in the college bathroom yesterday, and he had seemed too good to be true. Except he was still here, and he was now making Dale breakfast. "You really don't have to do all this."

"You deserve a good time," Greg said.

"Then you're spoiling me. Who's going to give me a good time after you leave?"

"I'll come back. I meant what I said about this week, you know." Greg turned fully to look at Dale, his expression honest. "Let me stay until Sunday. Give me a chance."

Dale rolled the mug in his hands. If it weren't for his heat last week, he wouldn't even have agreed to meet Greg. But after two months of Greg asking him out, Dale's resistance had eroded from rock to sand. "Fine."

Greg smiled, laying bacon strips out on a wad of paper towels. "Do you want eggs, too?"

"Yes, please."

Dale watched in silence as Greg cracked eggs into the pan. They sizzled, their yolks a sunny yellow, their whites turning opaque.

Even though it was a school day, it didn't feel like one. Breakfast was cooking on the stove, and Dale's body was relaxed, aching a little after last night.

"My first class is at 9 AM," he said, sipping from his mug.

"Yeah, that's my class."

"Gods, I hope no one notices. I smell like you. I mean, I smell like we had a thorough fucking."

Greg smirked. "Want more tonight?"

Dale shivered, his nerves lighting up at the memory of Greg's touch. "If I make it through today alive, sure."

"You'll make it through."

"Because you believe in me?"

"Because you want to be back in that bed." Greg laughed, and Dale tried to scowl, failing miserably. Instead, he stepped closer to the stove, elbowing Greg.

"Hey! That's not what a prof's supposed to do."

"Don't sully my reputation, Greg Hastings."

"You sully it enough yourself," Greg said.

"Do I?" Dale hesitated, trying to remember if any of the students had looked suspiciously at him. Then he glanced down at his naked body, and at the blinds.

"No, I don't mean that. Damn it." Greg winced, nudging Dale's foot with his own. "I was kidding."

"Oh."

Greg turned the heat down on the stove, took Dale's mug out of his hands, and set it on the counter. Then he gathered Dale in his arms, pulling him against his bare chest. Dale leaned in. Greg felt good. Safe. His arms curved solidly around Dale's back, like a protective cage, and Dale didn't want him to leave.

"You're carrying my baby," Greg murmured into Dale's hair, his breath warm. "I won't let anything happen to you."

It was nice of him to try. Dale sighed. "You can't do everything, Greg. You're not old enough. As much as I hate to say it, you don't have the rank or power your father has."

Greg stiffened. Dale rubbed his back, trying to console him.

"I'm gonna do better," Greg said. "Once this semester's over, I'll look into a full-time job."

"Promise me you'll return to school when the semester starts," Dale said, a streak of anxiety winding through his chest. "Please don't jeopardize your career because of a baby. I make enough to support it."

"Still not what I want. I've told you, fifty-fifty. I'm not letting you do all the work."

Greg glared down at him, and Dale's heart skipped. *This is insane. You're twenty years younger than I am. You shouldn't give up your future because of a mistake.*

"We'll talk about it when the time comes," Dale said, reluctant to argue about this right now. Not when the eggs were sizzling, and they could be doing better things. Like snuggling closer, Greg's mouth brushing over his. "Breakfast first."

He pressed a kiss to Greg's shoulder, savoring the heat of his skin. Then he trailed kisses up along Greg's throat, licking at his pulse point.

Greg swallowed, slipping his hands down to squeeze Dale's ass. "Breakfast? You mean, you?"

Dale laughed, and Greg shut off the stove, pushing Dale up against the wall. This close, Dale was only aware of Greg, and the hint of musk that coiled from his skin. So he pressed his hand against Greg's abs, sliding it past his waistband. No underwear. Just hot skin, and a growing cock.

"Very nice," Dale murmured.

Greg smirked, kissing him, and breakfast slipped entirely from his mind.

12
Dale

"YOU SMELL like alpha," June said the moment Dale stepped into the lab. "And you're late."

Dale winced, sniffing at his arms. It was 8:30 AM. He'd scrubbed at his skin earlier, but no matter how vigorously he'd showered, Greg's aspen scent still lingered in the creases of his body.

Desperate, he'd gone to the school bookstore, grabbing a couple different brands of scent suppressants. The cashier had joked with him; Sam Brentwood had been working there part-time for the past five years, and he was familiar with most of the campus staff. Of course, Sam had to ask who the new alpha was. Dale had brushed the question away, his cheeks burning as he left.

In his car, he'd spritzed the suppressant all over his clothes, coughing when the spray stung his nose.

"I've muted the scents somewhat," Dale muttered, glancing around his lab. This early, only the grad students and post-docs were around, working on their own experiments. Glass rods clinked in test tubes, and the machines whirred quietly in the background.

"Relax," June said, leaving her desk. "It's not

strong."

But her eyebrows quirked knowingly, and Dale couldn't meet her gaze. "I'm not sure what I can say," he muttered. "I'm aware of the consequences."

She sighed, spreading her arms. Dale stepped into them. He liked hugs. And he liked June in a purely platonic way, but her birch scent still comforted him. "So am I still your pretend alpha?" she whispered. "Or are you transitioning away?"

Dale bit his lip. "I don't know. I told him I'd try this for a week."

"Oh, gods, Dale." June's shoulders sagged. "I'm happy that you're happy about the baby, but this... it's risky."

"Don't you think I know that?" But Dale remembered the warmth in Greg's eyes, the heat of his embrace, and his stomach swooped. He hadn't needed anyone this badly in years. "I just... It's nice."

"I'm sure you'd be able to find other alphas out there if you looked."

"I guess. I might be in a little deep."

"You think?" She rolled her eyes, but hugged him tighter. The birch helped mask the aspen scent, too, so Dale wasn't complaining. "I know Meadowfall isn't exactly a tiny town, but it's still risky."

"I'll do my best," he said. "He's staying over at my place."

"Merciful gods. His dad—"

"—Is having a meeting with me later," Dale said. "You might want to have 9-1-1 on speed dial."

"I should come along with you," June said,

146

peering worriedly at him. "Geez, Dale. I've known you for four years. You've been scandal-free this whole time!"

"With any luck, I'll have my tenure in the next two years, and Greg will graduate and leave for good." Dale bit his lip, glancing down. Right now, his chances of tenure were growing slimmer. Probably in inverse proportions with his belly.

"I hate that omegas are held to a different standard," June muttered. "With ten years, you'd have gotten tenure as an alpha."

Dale sighed. "Not much I can do about that. But the suppressants don't work especially well."

The lab door creaked open. Dale and June both looked up, and Greg stepped in. Dale's stomach flipped.

Greg had changed his clothes—T-shirt, new jeans, basketball shoes. He paused at the door, his gaze flicking between Dale and June, his nostrils flaring. Then he narrowed his eyes, and Dale gulped, unable to look away.

So Greg didn't like June's scent on him. That was too bad, because June was a friend. Except part of Dale also wanted Greg to smile, wanted Greg to sniff at him and smirk. This morning, in the kitchen, Greg had whispered, *Who am I?*

My alpha, Dale had said. And he was. Dale's body hummed, acknowledging Greg as his bedmate. Dale *didn't* want Greg to be his alpha.

Greg brushed by them, his eyes anchored on Dale the entire time, and Dale's pulse rushed in his ears.

When Greg had parked himself at the other side of the lab, facing them, Dale turned back to

June.

"He smells like you," June whispered.

Dale hid his face behind his hands. "I'm seeing his father in five hours."

The aspen scent wouldn't dissipate by then, but maybe the suppressants would work if he applied more.

"I'm still here if you need an alpha for show," June said, her expression sympathetic. "And I'll pretend to be the proud mother if you need me to."

Dale gave her hand a squeeze. "Thank you."

June was about to say something else when one of the grad students made her way over—Penny Fleming, the brightest unbonded omega in Dale's lab. He'd submitted her name to Bernard Hastings, and he was sure the meeting today would be about her.

Penny beamed at them, her glasses winking in the fluorescent light. She'd be a nice fit for Greg, too—all soft curves, her red curls bouncing as she walked. She was pleasant, cheerful and friendly. "Professor Kinney! If you have a moment, I have a few questions on the carbon tubes."

"Sure," he said, stepping away from June.

"Oh, congrats," Penny said.

Dale's stomach tightened. *Did she smell the pregnancy?* "What?"

Penny waved at June. "I hadn't noticed the ring before. Is it a tradition if only the alpha wears a ring?"

Dale glanced at the silver band on June's finger, swearing inwardly. He'd forgotten about that.

June looked pointedly at him. *It's up to you*

how you spin this lie.

On Dale's other side, Penny waited for his answer, bright-eyed and smiling. Greg's stare prickled his skin; Penny's voice had carried across the lab.

In that moment, it felt as though everything hung in a delicate balance—the fake relationship, the pregnancy, his mess with Greg.

"I leave mine at home just in case," Dale blurted, regretting the lie the moment it left his lips. He looked up at Penny, then chanced a glance at Greg over her shoulder.

Greg's eyes had narrowed, and Dale's stomach plummeted.

It wasn't as though they were bonded. But he'd agreed to spend this week with Greg, sort of like a date, and this... Well. Maybe Greg would fume and leave now, and Dale would have seen it coming from a mile away. Maybe this was what it took to shift Greg's focus onto omegas who were younger and a better fit for him.

"We're still deciding on a wedding date," Dale said. June sighed.

Penny beamed. Dale followed her through the lab, to where she'd left her experimental setup.

Greg's stare burned into his back the entire time.

AT 3 PM, Dale knocked on Bernard Hastings' office door.

"Come in," the voice inside boomed.

Dale heaved open the wooden door, hiding

his grimace.

Bernard Hastings' office was a place Dale liked to visit as rarely as possible. It was wide, oval, a row of windows stretching from one wall to another. Rows of textbooks filled the ceiling-high bookcases. On two sides of the office, gold-framed plaques hung in columns, and leather couches sat in one corner of the room, surrounding an elegant glass table.

Dale avoided the expensive furniture, smiling politely at the alpha behind the gleaming steel desk. Bernard Hastings was as tall as his son, broad-shouldered, his countenance shrewd. Strands of silver streaked through his chestnut hair; his eucalyptus scent wafted around him.

"Mr. Hastings."

"Dr. Kinney."

Bernard rose to his feet and extended his hand. On the other side of the desk, Dale accepted the handshake, quailing at the stranglehold the president locked his hand in. It was nice of Bernard to treat omegas as his equals. Not as nice to crush their delicate knuckles.

When Bernard released his hand, Dale waited for him to sit, before settling into his own chair. "I hope you received the list well," Dale said. "Just in case you haven't, I've printed it."

He slid his sheath of papers across the desk, Penny's photo on the front. Bernard raised his eyebrows. "I appreciate the pictures," he said. "There were none with the email."

After the lab this morning, Dale had redoubled his efforts to please the college president. Regardless of what Dale wanted, and regardless of which alpha fathered his child, Greg needed a decent shot at life. He had his entire future ahead of him, and Dale wanted him to be happy. Not be stuck with an aging omega, an unwanted baby curbing his dreams.

"If I read your email right, you're searching for the perfect omega for your son," Dale said, smiling confidently.

"Yes. This is a good list," Bernard said, his eyes gleaming. "I appreciate the descriptions of your students — brilliant minds, engaging personalities."

"They are a fascinating bunch to work with," Dale said, relaxing a little. Bernard didn't seem to remember the fucked-up presentation, or the lab fire. Maybe Dale could still salvage his chances at tenure. "I might be exaggerating, but I believe my students have been the driving force behind the lab's success."

Bernard Hastings studied him, those austere black eyes boring through Dale. "They may very well be."

He hadn't forgotten Dale's mistakes at all, had he?

Dale's stomach twisted. He should leave the list with Bernard, get out of here. "I have coached them to the best of my abilities," he said, wishing he was better at sucking up to people. "If you come across an omega you'd like to meet, do arrange a meeting with them."

"Definitely," Bernard said, flipping through the papers. Dale held his breath, watching as the president paged through photo after photo. There were none of Dale in that stack. "The reason I asked you here—I believe my son may be in your classes. Which omega do you think is best suited to Greg?"

And even though an arranged marriage had burned him once, Dale put on a smile. "I believe that Penny Fleming may be his best match."

Bernard scrutinized her photo. "She seems familiar. Is she the police chief's daughter? Stan Fleming?"

Dale hid his wince behind a smile. Was she? Penny had never mentioned it. "It's very possible. She is the friendliest omega I've ever come across—capable, inquisitive, adaptable. Slightly older than Greg is, if you don't mind a three-year difference?"

Bernard's forehead furrowed. "Three years?"

"Yes," Dale said, hesitating. "Their ages aren't shown, but you'll be able to judge by their birth years."

Bernard flipped past Penny's profile to the next omega. Dale watched him with a morbid fascination. *Three years, and you're dropping her like a hot beaker. What about a twenty-year difference?*

The college president paged through the stack again, his lips thinning with distaste. "Very well. This is a valuable list. I'll look through it again and reach out if I find another suitable candidate."

Dale exhaled, relief crawling through his bones. *Time to go.* "Feel free to contact me anytime, sir. My lab is very accommodating with requests."

They stood to shake hands, and Bernard eyed him, his gaze critical. Then his nostrils flared, and Dale's heart stopped beating.

"You smell like aspen," Bernard said, meeting his eyes.

Dale froze. Three full-body coats of suppressant hadn't been enough. Heart thudding, he tilted his head, hoping it conveyed confusion. "Yes. I've been around a few alphas with that scent lately."

"Oddly enough, Greg's scent is the same," Bernard said, eyeing him.

"Oh? I had no idea. It's been a while since I've talked to the undergrads—my post-docs are the ones guiding them."

"Very well," Bernard said. But doubt lingered in his gaze, and Dale needed to get out of his office. Before Bernard somehow identified the scents Greg had left on his skin.

"If you have nothing else for me, I'll take my leave," Dale said.

"I'll see you again. Thank you for coming down."

Dale couldn't escape the suffocating silence quickly enough. But even after the door closed behind him, he still felt Bernard's stare, analyzing and suspicious.

Bernard had smelled his son on Dale.

They weren't even a week into this dating thing, and Dale had to stop seeing Greg.

13
Greg

GREG SPUN on his feet, took aim, and shot.

The basketball arced through the air toward the backboard, dropping neatly through the hoop. The netting hugged the ball for a split second, and the ball hurtled toward the floor, bouncing back up.

Greg jogged across the court for it, his soles squeaking across the tan floors. In the other courts, people played casual games — there was no practice today. His court happened to be unused right now.

He caught the basketball, barely focusing on his moves. He'd come here after class so he could work out some of that pent-up unease in his chest, and it was working. Slowly.

Without the press of opposing teams around him, Greg thought about Dale again. This morning in the lab, when Penny had gone up to the professor, asking questions so loud the entire lab heard. He'd wanted to stride up and step in front of Dale, and snarl at Penny, *Mine.*

He knew he shouldn't blame Dale for his lies. But damn, if Greg could get over *We're still deciding on a wedding date.*

Dale had known he was listening. He'd

known Greg would return to his apartment this evening. And it had felt like a slap, Dale pretending to be engaged to June. June wasn't his alpha. He was carrying Greg's baby.

This morning, in Dale's kitchen, Greg had sunken to his knees, sucking Dale off. Dale had grasped his hair and writhed, moaning Greg's name.

To have him ignore that an hour later, well. It hurt.

Greg took a running leap, dunking the basketball through the hoop. It felt empty when the ball fell through the net, bouncing away. Unlike in a game, this goal meant nothing.

From every angle, the situation couldn't last. If Greg stuck with Dale and married him, his dad would find out. He'd probably fire Dale. If Greg left Dale, he wouldn't be able to live with himself. Dale's ex had let him down, broken him, and Greg wasn't going to pull that same shit on his omega.

I don't love you, Dale had said yesterday, his eyes solemn. Except he'd huddled up in Greg's arms, clinging to him like he had nothing else to hold onto. He hadn't wanted to step away today, either.

So maybe Greg could understand why Dale had lied. Regardless of what Dale wanted, his job was at stake. Greg shouldn't be a jerk, demanding Dale acknowledge the baby's alpha father.

But Dale wasn't the only one with doubts. Greg was still trying to process the baby. It spoke too much about a future, about making promises he wasn't sure he could keep.

Aside from his parents, he'd never told

anyone about Tony. About that camping trip four years ago, when they'd spent hours on the inland sea. Greg had shared so much with his best friend. The time they'd skipped school together, the time they'd ridden through town cosplaying as Super Alpha and Vilso. The time Greg had fooled around with Tony, and the condom had torn.

They weren't going to be mates—they had dated, and then broken up, returning to being best friends. But Greg had still loved Tony as a friend. In a moment of Greg's idiocy, Tony had lost his life, and their dreams had shattered in a night.

All it had taken was a candle flame leaping onto a curtain, and a cabin made of dry wood.

If Tony were still around, what would he have said about Dale? About Greg becoming a dad? Would he have clapped Greg on the back? Greg could almost hear Tony's voice, as though Tony was trying to talk to him though rush of water. Throat tight with guilt, he pushed Tony's voice out of his mind. Tony wouldn't forgive him. Not when Greg was alive, and Tony wasn't.

Greg's footsteps slowed. The basketball thudded dully by his feet. He wasn't looking at the court anymore, only the flickering embers, the red lights of a fire truck. His throat closed.

It had taken him years to forgive himself after Tony's death. How could he promise Dale anything, when he wasn't even certain about his own future? Anyone could die, or make a stupid mistake. Tony was gone. Greg hadn't trusted in his future for a long time.

The basketball hit his foot, bouncing off. Greg stared as it skipped across the court, losing momentum.

He needed to talk to Dale. He knew he needed to be there for Dale, for the baby. But beyond what he could foresee, how much could he really promise Dale?

Greg didn't know. He didn't think Dale had answers, either.

14
Dale

THE RED sports car was parked at his apartment when Dale pulled in that evening. His stomach flipped as he remembered — June, Bernard Hastings, Penny's awkward questions.

Dale lying about his relationship with June.

Between Bernard's office and his own lab, Dale had decided on one thing: he needed to stop this pseudo-relationship with Greg. As soon as possible.

Except Dale pulled in to the empty parking spot in front of his apartment, and Greg was there by his front door. Greg's eyes were solemn as he leaned away from the brickwork, his arms folded across his chest. Dale parked the car, his heart sinking.

Greg was still here — that meant something. Even if he looked like he brought bad news.

Dale stepped out of his car, locking it. Greg waited for him to reach the door.

"I didn't think you'd still be here," Dale said, fishing his keys from his pocket. "I haven't... been fair to you."

Greg looked away. "We should probably

talk."

Dale's mouth twitched. Yes, they should have been doing that from the start. Not fuck first, and trip over everything else while they tried to make amends. "Inside," he said.

When the front door was locked, Dale set his satchel down, pulling his shoes off. "I'm sorry about this morning. I'm aware that it upset you."

Greg shrugged. He smelled like soap, like he'd gone home for a shower first. "It's fine. I understand."

"Do you really?"

"Yeah, your job's at risk," Greg said. "You did the right thing, faking that thing with June. Took me a while to work it out of my system."

"But something's still bothering you."

"The baby. Essentially, all of this." Greg followed Dale to the tartan couch, meeting Dale's eyes. His own glimmered with uncertainty, and Dale's chest tightened. He wanted to set Greg at ease. Greg didn't need to go through this mess; it had been Dale's fault.

"This isn't the way a relationship should go," Greg said.

"No, it isn't."

"I shouldn't have pushed so hard with this staying-together thing," Greg said, sitting on the couch adjacent to Dale's. "I kinda got ahead of myself."

Well, this was easier than Dale had thought. They would part ways from here, and that would be that. "What's got you changing your mind?"

"The baby," Greg said. "But not exactly. I still want to do a fifty-fifty thing. It's not so much the baby as the future."

"I don't blame you," Dale said, even as a pang hit his chest. Greg was leaving. And maybe Dale had been looking forward to the week with him more than he'd thought.

"No, I just... How do you even have a kid when you don't know how your future's turning out?"

Dale frowned. "What do you mean?"

"See, this." Greg pulled his phone out. He tapped on the screen, and that same picture came up again, the one of Greg with that other boy, with a sparkling sea behind them. "That's Tony. My best friend. He died four years ago."

Dale's breath froze in his lungs. This wasn't what he'd been expecting. He'd thought maybe Greg was pining for that boy, or maybe Greg was somehow seeing him on the side. He hadn't thought the boy was a dead best friend.

For a long moment, Dale looked between Greg and the boy, their smiles in that photo. The boy with the blond hair was Tony, and four years ago, he'd been alive.

"You... couldn't have been more than eighteen," Dale said, chest aching. Whatever Dale had been through... Greg had had it worse.

"We were about eighteen, yeah." Greg flipped the phone over, setting it on the coffee table. "We were on a camping trip. I had a lit candle by the window. The curtains caught fire and it spread. I—I tried to get him out. There was fire everywhere. I had to carry him over the burning floors. He died of smoke inhalation."

And Dale suddenly understood the shadows

160

in his eyes, the jadedness Greg harbored when he looked at the other students. The crimson fire-shaped scars on his calves, the way he glanced at the windows when he stepped into the apartment.

Greg wasn't like any of the other students. Of course he wasn't—and it shouldn't have taken Dale this long to realize it.

Four years ago, that other boy had been alive. With his death, he'd taken part of Greg, and Dale couldn't imagine the grief Greg had suffered. The guilt. No wonder he'd protested when Dale talked about his future.

Dale's skin felt two sizes too tight. "I'm sorry about that. I—I don't know what else to say."

Greg watched him carefully. "My dad said I should move on. Tony and I were never bonded. We'd dated, but then we'd decided we were better matched with other people."

Dale wanted to comfort him somehow, but Greg's eyes held uncertainty, not grief. "I want to make you feel better," Dale said. "How do I... how do you want me to help?"

And Greg cracked a smile, his shoulders relaxing. "You don't have to do anything. You care. That's enough."

"That isn't what we came here to talk about, though."

Greg sighed. "Yeah. See, the thing is, life is transient. Why would anyone have a baby if—if they could die at any moment?"

Dale opened his mouth, but realized he had no answer to that. "I don't know. I hadn't thought about it."

He looked down at his flat belly, imagining

the life growing inside. Greg looked, too, but he didn't move closer. "I just... I don't know how much of the future I can promise you, is all."

Dale read honesty in his eyes. "I guess this is why people buy life insurance."

But from the way Greg looked at him, this went deeper than that. Greg was still hurt, Dale realized. Dale could understand not trusting a future, and it was brave of Greg to admit to it. Brave of him to tell Dale, especially as an alpha who wanted to provide.

"Are you scared?" Dale asked, holding his hand out.

Greg curled his fingers around Dale's. "I don't... No. I don't think so. But I just... I don't want to make promises I can't keep."

"Then make the ones you can," Dale said, squeezing his hand. "That's enough for me."

Greg stared at him for a long moment. Then, something fell away from his face, leaving him raw and open. Vulnerable. "Really?"

"Yes. I don't want you to make promises you'll regret," Dale said, his heart squeezing. He liked Greg. Didn't want to see him hurt. And right now, Greg had exposed a part of himself that he'd held close, like a dog with an injured paw. "Sit with me."

Dale patted the couch next to him. Greg stared at it. Then he edged around the coffee table, settling cautiously beside Dale. He smelled like aspen and soap, and in his eyes, Dale glimpsed the jagged edges of his soul.

Slowly, Dale eased his fingers into Greg's hand, holding him. "I can't promise that everything will be fine," he said. "But we have resources. I have some savings, and you have status. That'll help."

As the college president's son, Greg had access to important contacts, had a reputation that would benefit him. He could get far on those.

"Yeah," Greg said, squeezing Dale's hand. "That'll help."

"Are you feeling better about this?"

Greg sucked in a deep breath, looking at Dale's belly again. "Somewhat. I... I could be gone in a day. Just like that. We should get married, or be bonded. Then at least you'd have access to my savings."

Dale stared at him, at this alpha who was just twenty-two, trying to promise Dale all his possessions. His heart thudded. "You're adorable," he breathed, leaning close. "I can't believe you'd do so much for me."

"Well, yeah." Greg frowned. "I want to. I don't want to leave you to raise a baby alone."

"Let's not think about death for a while," Dale said. "You might be hanging too much on what-ifs. What if you survive until you're eighty? I'd love to see you still healthy at that point."

Greg hesitated. "There's that."

"Do you have dreams? Hopes? Travel plans?"

Greg rolled his shoulders, eyeing the mug stains on the coffee table. "Kind of. They disappeared when Tony died."

Dale squeezed his hand, leaning into his arm. "Do you want to return to them, or make new ones?"

"New ones, probably. I tried to go back to them after—after the death. Couldn't concentrate on any. So I took up basketball instead."

"Then let's make some new plans," Dale said, wanting to help. Wanting to see Greg trusting in his future again. "Just some small goals. Like next week."

"What about next week?" Greg raised an eyebrow.

"I'll watch your game next week," Dale said. "You have one, don't you?"

"I have one this week, too."

"That's too soon. I'll be at your next game," Dale said. "So it's something to look forward to."

"You could be at both games. I'd still look forward to them."

Dale paused. "Will that help?"

"One step at a time," Greg said, a smile curving his lips. "Small steps, you know?"

"Fine, small steps," Dale said. "I'll be there."

"Thanks." Greg's smile widened then, hopeful and boyish, and Dale leaned in, brushing his fingers through Greg's hair.

"You act like you've never had anyone else go to your games," Dale said.

"My mom goes to some. My dad doesn't have time."

"Ah." Dale winced. "Your dad. I had a meeting with him today."

Greg tensed. "Shit, yeah. I forgot. How did it go?"

"I'm crap at lying," Dale said, squirming on the couch. "He smelled aspen on me."

"Lots of people smell like aspen."

"I know. But like I said, I can't suck up to people. He looked at me, Greg. Really looked at me. He even asked if you're in my lab. I told him I didn't know."

Greg snorted. "'Didn't know.' Like this counts as not knowing you."

He leaned in, dropping a kiss on Dale's nose. Dale's pulse pattered. "That's not knowing me, huh?"

Greg kissed his lips. "Yeah. I don't know you at all."

He caught Dale's lower lip in his mouth, sucking on it, and Dale smiled. "I wonder how far your not-knowing stretches."

Greg chuckled, his hands slipping around Dale's waist. "This? Or this?"

He shuffled around on the couch, scooping Dale up into his arms. Then he deposited Dale on the couch, stretching him out. Dale's heart fluttered. Inches away, Greg's eyes were dark, his lips damp.

"I thought we were going to end this," Dale whispered. But this intimacy was nice. Good. It distracted him from feeling like a pile of crap, and he wanted to see Greg smile. Wanted to forget about everything except Greg.

Greg swallowed, meeting his gaze. "Do you want to?"

Carefully, Dale touched his fingers to Greg's chest, following the planes of his pectorals. He brushed his fingers up, tracing Greg's clavicles, then his throat. Whatever was between them—it felt too new, too fragile, like a bolt of lightning trapped in glass. "I agreed to a week," Dale said.

Greg breathed in, closing his eyes. When he opened them, he had calmed a little, his lips twitching up in a smile. "I don't want to forfeit this."

"Then don't."

Greg surged in, kissing Dale's lips, his chin, his neck. Then he dropped kisses down Dale's chest, his heart, trailing all the way to his belly. Dale's throat grew tight. Greg wanted him, and Dale hadn't the strength to push him away. At his waistband, Greg looked up. "There's really a baby in here, huh?"

"You tell me." Dale held his breath, watching as Greg crouched over him, his hands on either side of Dale's hips, his mouth a hairsbreadth from Dale's belly.

Greg tugged Dale's shirt out of his pants, exposing his abdomen. He studied it for a while, before pressing his nose to Dale's skin. "You don't smell as strong today."

"I used the suppressants."

Greg sucked in a deep breath, air rushing cool against Dale's skin. "I smell you faintly. It's still sweet."

"So the tests are probably right."

"Very likely." Greg kissed his belly, right over where the baby was, and Dale's cheeks burned. *He cares.*

"You're my student," he croaked.

Greg glared. "Not here, I'm not. You know what you're supposed to say."

Dale swallowed. Yes, he knew. And it felt right when he murmured, "You're my alpha."

Greg kissed further down Dale's abdomen,

then back up, over Dale's heart. At his lips, Greg whispered, "You're my omega," and Dale's pulse thumped so loud he thought Greg might hear it.

"Really?" he asked.

"Yeah." Greg kissed him again, soft and languid. For a while, Dale lost himself in Greg, just holding him, savoring the strength of his body. Greg had fathered his child. He was *here*, promising his care, and Dale felt safe with him. Felt as though Greg would never abandon him, not like Charles had.

It was a relief, knowing that Greg would stay.

The phone buzzed on the table. Greg paused, glancing at it.

"Over here," Dale whispered, tugging on his shirt. "I'm your omega."

Greg hesitated. Then he looked back at Dale, and his next kiss scorched through Dale's nerves, all the way down to his toes.

MUCH LATER, when they were peeling themselves apart on the couch, their clothes strewn around them, Greg glanced at his phone again.

"Were you expecting a message?" Dale croaked, his voice hoarse. Hopefully, he hadn't been too loud. Greg had worked him into a frenzy, and he'd forgotten himself. And that was probably the third time they'd fucked in twenty-four hours.

"No." Greg grabbed the phone from the coffee table. The lock screen flashed, then the app notifications. Dale pushed himself up, peering over his shoulder.

In a text message from *Dad*, Dale read, *I met with your professor today. Dale Kinney. I thought that hibiscus scent smelled familiar.*

"Shit," Greg said.

Dale's breath hitched. "What?"

"He smelled you on me the other day. After your heat. I told him I'm dating some imaginary guy on the basketball team."

Dale swallowed, his heart thumping. Not only had Bernard recognized Greg's scent, but he'd recognized Dale's, too. "I screwed up big time, huh?"

Greg shrugged, tapping on the Reply button. *I've told you, Ivan smells like hibiscus too.*

"I hope he doesn't start looking into the basketball team," Dale said, pressing a hand to his damp chest. His heart thudded against his palm. "He certainly has the means to."

"It's not like hibiscus is a rare scent, either," Greg said. "There are a few others on campus who smell like you."

Dale gulped anyway, squirming, his stomach a heavy lump.

"I'll distract him with this Ivan," Greg said, waving his phone. "Just that Ivan is busy and doesn't have time to meet with him. That'll take his mind off you."

"But what if he finds out you're lying?"

"He'll cut my tuition and board." Greg leaned back into the couch, glancing up at the ceiling. "I'm fine with that."

"You are?"

"Yeah. Actually, I was going to talk to you about my career yesterday. Before the pregnancy tests." Greg smiled, looking at Dale's bare chest. "But I guess we can talk now. It's probably easier, since you know what I think about my future."

Greg set his phone back on the table, rubbing down his calves. Up close, the pink burn scars covered most of his shins. Their edges were uneven, like watercolor soaked through paper, and Dale couldn't imagine how much pain Greg had been in. Or how long he had taken to heal.

"Does it still hurt?" he murmured, reaching down to stroke smooth skin. Greg's calf twitched against his touch.

"Sometimes," Greg said. "I had to have physical therapy for a bit after the fire. I don't remember much of it."

And from there, Greg had pushed himself all the way to become an MVP.

"You're amazing," Dale breathed, dragging his hands up Greg's legs, admiring the strength in his body. "You've come a long ways in four years."

Greg snorted. "More like it was something else to focus on. Some days, I couldn't think of Tony without puking."

Dale winced. That, too, had to have been difficult. "But you've changed for the better. You've climbed out of all that to become someone stronger." Dale swallowed, looking at Greg's calves, then at his own hands. "I'm still... well. Still not much to speak of."

"You're a professor, aren't you?" Greg angled a glance at him, leaning in, his shoulder warm against Dale. "You've been doing well yourself. You've got your own lab and everything."

"It took nineteen years. I had to go back to

school. Get my PhD. I was bussing tables on the side." Dale chuckled, looking up at the ceiling. And all that time had somehow passed in the blink of an eye. "It didn't only take four years."

"Then you're stronger than I am," Greg murmured, leaning in to kiss his cheek.

Dale blushed. "It just means I'm slow. I don't even have tenure yet."

"How much longer will it take?"

"Two years." He sighed.

"You can do it," Greg whispered, sliding his arms around Dale, tugging Dale against his damp chest. "I'll believe in you."

Dale's heart squeezed. Greg was incredibly sweet. He talked to Dale like there weren't twenty years between them. Like they were both equals. Like he was genuinely interested in Dale for who he was. Few others had done this for Dale, and Dale... didn't want to let him go.

"Come on," he said. "We'll talk about your career through a shower. I'm sticky."

Unwillingly, Dale pulled away from Greg, glancing down at the smear of cum on his belly. He wriggled his fingers; Greg caught them with a tiny smile, standing up.

The bathroom was one of Dale's favorite parts of his apartment. Rich blue mosaic stretched up from the bathtub like a tapestry of jewels, lighter blue tiles swirling around the small window like waves cradling a treasure chest. The mirror was mounted amidst smooth river rock, and little conch shells decorated the corners of the bathroom counter.

"You've spent a lot of time on this place,"

Greg said, lifting a wooden sailboat from a shelf.

Dale ran the shower, waiting for the water to warm. "Well, I could afford it after some teaching stints. With no family, I thought I might as well make this a pretty place."

"You've never considered adoption?" Greg asked, setting the boat down.

Dale shrugged. "I don't know if I'll be a good dad."

"'Course you will."

He smiled wryly. "I'm a bad omega, Greg. Surely you know that."

"No, you aren't." Greg narrowed his eyes. "Do you think that because of your ex's shitty parents?"

Dale opened his mouth, remembering *If his body is rotten, then so is his mind,* and *If he can't bear a child, how can you be sure he'll raise one right?*

"Damn it," Greg said. "No. Stop thinking about them. They're crap. You're every bit worthy, Dale Kinney."

Dale looked up at him, his heart sore. When he'd failed to conceive several times over, he'd begun to believe Charles' parents, and their insidious words. "I tried so hard to meet their expectations, Greg. For the three years I was married, I was never good enough."

"You're plenty good," Greg growled, his eyes flashing. He cupped Dale's cheeks in his hands, glaring down at him. "I don't care if you're fertile or not, okay? I care about you because you're humble and kind and so damn strong. That's enough for me."

Dale forgot to breathe, his heart thudding in

his ears, drowning out the hiss of the shower's spray. It was difficult to believe that Greg would think that. That a good omega... didn't necessarily have to be fertile.

But maybe Greg was wrong. He was still young, and maybe his priorities might change in the future. Dale's pregnancy was risky. Just how risky, he hadn't dared find out. But it might fail, and Greg might want someone who could give him a family one day. Someone who wasn't broken like Dale.

Dale swallowed, shrugging. "Maybe."

"You don't have to believe it now," Greg said, rubbing his shoulders, his expression sincere. "Just think about it."

"Okay."

When the water was the right temperature, Dale stepped to the tub. Greg followed, his broad shoulders crowding out most of the space. Greg turned them around, placing Dale under the shower first. Dale couldn't help a smile.

"You've barely been here a day, Greg Hastings, and you're already pushing me around."

Greg rolled his eyes. "This is your home. I'm just letting you have the water first."

"That's incredibly nice of you."

"That's *polite* of me." Greg frowned. "Just because I'm alpha, it doesn't mean I have to be an asshole."

"Only too true." Dale leaned his forehead into Greg's chest, savoring the patter of warm water on his back. "I grew up in Drakestown, you know. Back in Arizona, the alphas aren't... so nice."

"Gods, you really need all the nice things,"

Greg said grabbing the soap. He rubbed it down Dale's back, soaping him up. "You deserve to be treated well, okay?"

Dale snuggled closer to him, purring when their skin slid damply together. "Are you promising to do that?"

"Yeah."

"I don't know what I did to deserve this," Dale said, wrapping his arms around Greg's back. "This is... nice. You're nice."

"I need you to step back so I can soap the rest of you," Greg said, but his eyes danced with humor.

Dale laughed. He drew away, and Greg washed Dale's neck, his back, his arms. Unlike this morning, when they'd kept to themselves, Greg scrubbed down Dale's chest, his strong hands slipping up under Dale's jaw, his calluses catching on Dale's skin.

"You look like you're having a good time," Greg murmured.

"I have you."

When Dale cracked his eyes open, he found Greg smiling to himself, looking at the bar of soap in his hands. Dale's heart fluttered. They shouldn't be doing this. But he was far too comfortable with Greg, and maybe this could work. He liked this alpha. Cared about him.

Then Greg met his eyes, and a jolt shot down Dale's spine. Maybe he was in this a little too deep. They'd only been doing this two days.

Dale fumbled for a change in subject. "You wanted to discuss your career?"

"Yeah. Like what I can do with a chemistry

173

degree."

"That would depend on your interests—there are lots of positions in the research sector, or you could work for the government."

"The government?" Greg squeezed shampoo into his palm, lathered it, and worked his fingers slowly through Dale's hair, firm points of pressure on his scalp.

Dale moaned. "Yes. Lots of positions in quality control, public health, environmental protection. I believe Meadowfall is always looking for people to fill these positions—a lot of students graduate with a degree, and move out trying to find better-paying jobs in Highton."

"You'd be staying here for the next ten years?"

Dale glanced at him. "What happened to not trusting the future?"

Greg shrugged, but he was smiling a little. "I don't know. Just looking at my options. The kid's gonna be nine years old by then. I want to stay close."

A slow heat crept up Dale's chest, up his throat, to his ears. "You're not going to pursue basketball?"

"I'm sticking with chemistry," Greg murmured, leaning in. He kissed Dale's forehead, and Dale's heart stuttered. "I'm gonna look out for you, too."

The shower pattered warm on his back. Dale swallowed, stepping closer. Through the whole of tonight, Greg had been nothing but kind. Warm. He'd cuddled with Dale, touching him, getting angry on his behalf. It was such a change from his marriage with Charles, and Dale... wanted more. Wanted Greg closer.

"You shouldn't keep saying things like that," he whispered, his chest tight.

Greg's hands stilled in his hair, his thumb tracing Dale's ear. "Why not?"

"Because I might...." Dale gulped, looking down. "If you keep it up, I might actually, well..."

I might actually fall in love.

He didn't speak, and Greg continued to massage his scalp. But Greg wore a smile, never asking for the rest of his sentence.

And maybe, just maybe... he'd heard what Dale had been too afraid to say.

15
Greg

IN THE following days, Greg watched as the unease in Dale's shoulders fell away.

The first morning, Dale tried to wake early to make them breakfast. Greg beat him to the kitchen, grabbing the coffee grinder when Dale turned to put the coffee beans away. Dale tried to wrestle the grinder back. Greg hung on with brute strength, and Dale pouted.

The next morning, Dale set his alarm for half an hour earlier. Greg didn't realize Dale had disappeared from the bed until he woke up. He pulled on his rumpled boxers and wandered to the kitchen, where he found Dale puttering between the fridge and the stove, a sheepish smile on his face.

"Go back to bed," Greg rasped. "It's too fucking early."

"I'm making you breakfast," Dale told him.

"Make me dinner."

Greg stepped over to the stove, shut it off, and wrapped his arms around Dale. Dale protested the entire way back to bed, but Greg didn't miss the way he wriggled his hips, rubbing their bare skin together.

After that morning, Dale stopped climbing out of bed early.

Sometimes, Greg would crack his eyes open when the alarm rang, to find Dale's face in his chest, his eyes closed, his nose pressed against Greg's skin. Other times, Greg would wake with a gasp, his body taut and needing, Dale's hand between his legs. He'd growl and pin Dale down against the mattress, teaching him a lesson for waking him early.

Except Dale didn't learn anything from it, but to wake him more frequently instead.

Sometimes, Greg would wake first, and Dale would be asleep, his mouth hanging open, the worry lines absent from his face. He looked younger this way; Greg realized Dale probably didn't know this. Didn't realize that maybe twenty years wasn't that big a difference in the grand scheme of things.

When their schedules roughly matched, Dale drove them both to the college—his white Volkswagen blended in with the rest of traffic, and they arrived far too early for students to glimpse Greg stepping out of his car.

They each went about their days. Greg watched the students around Dale; some of them glanced curiously at the professor, but with Greg on the other side of the lab, tending to his own experiments, their stares lingered on him, then drifted away. No one questioned the increasingly-prominent aspen scent that Dale wore, except Penny.

At noon, Greg would bring lunch to Dale's

office. In the evenings, Greg would return, and they'd drive home for dinner. Dale would cook, while Greg would set up his laptop in the living room, going through his homework.

At night, after dinner, Dale would read the latest science journals on the couch. Greg would sit at the coffee table, typing out reports. Dale's feet would skim across his shoulders, and every so often, Dale would lean in, pressing a kiss to Greg's nape.

And even though Greg hadn't foreseen it, they settled into an easy routine, one they both looked forward to.

A WEEK passed.

In the second week, Dale attended Greg's basketball game. He sat in the front-row seats, and during the half-time break, Greg jogged by him, just to see Dale light up, his cheeks rosy.

In the third week, Dale taught Greg to fold the paper cranes. He had had a new delivery of paper squares waiting for him at the mailbox, and when Greg asked, Dale pulled out two squares of polka-dotted paper, showing Greg the creases to make.

Greg had folded them decently, or as decently as he could, with the corners slipping when he tried to match them. His first crane took half an hour, and tore when he tried to unfurl its wings. The second turned out better. Dale said, "It'll get easier as you practice."

"How many have you made?" Greg asked

when Dale folded his fourth crane that night.

"I've lost count," Dale said, the tips of his thumbs whitening as he made a crease, "but I've made five hundred this year. A Japanese myth says that if you fold a thousand in a year, your wish will come true."

"What do you wish for?"

"If I tell you, then it won't happen, will it?" But Dale glanced at his belly, and Greg pulled another sheet, determined to help.

The next day, Greg presented him with ten cranes, and Dale's mouth fell open.

Two days later, while Greg did his homework, Dale set a plain white envelope next to him.

Greg glanced at it. He solved the equations on Dale's second assignment. Dale's toes skimmed over his shoulder, and Greg had to make himself focus, get through the rest of the homework before he picked the envelope open. Then his heart skipped.

"The NY Rockets game?" Greg blurted, staring at the glossy tickets in his hands. He'd been thinking about attending the match this weekend, but had decided not to, so he could save up for the baby.

"I dropped by your Facebook page," Dale said, smiling wryly. "You said Phil O'Riley is your favorite star. I did a bit of sleuthing."

Greg couldn't help his grin. "Two tickets? Are you watching it with me?"

"Do you want me to?"

"Yes!"

Dale's eyes sparkled. "I thought you'd, you

know, watch it with a friend. From your basketball team or something. You have lots of friends on Facebook."

"But you're my omega," Greg said, climbing onto the couch next to Dale, tackling him in a hug. Dale yelped. "You're coming with me."

"I thought it might give you something to look forward to," Dale said, pressed against Greg's chest, his hands stroking down Greg's sides. "Granted, it's not very far into the future."

Greg nuzzled his throat, breathing in hibiscus and honey. "It'll be like a date," he said. "But at least people won't recognize us in Highton."

Dale cracked a smile, and when Greg kissed him, Dale melted in his arms, sweet and omega and so very needy.

THAT WEEKEND, Greg drove them to Highton in his Porsche, and no one gave them a second glance at all.

They had dinner at a French restaurant. At the basketball arena, before the game started, Dale leaned into Greg's shoulder. No one booed, or even looked their way. Dale's darting glances finally stopped, and as the game kicked off, Dale squeezed Greg's hand, leaning forward, excitement on his face.

Somehow, Greg knew this was what Dale looked like back home, when he was watching the Meadowfall Lions' games. How he looked as he watched Greg, cheering him on.

Despite the fact that they were there to watch

Phil O'Riley, Greg found himself watching Dale half the time, admiring his omega, the way his shoulders tensed when the other team had the ball.

Dale had stopped worrying about himself, or their relationship, and he looked so much younger, so much more alive than he did back home.

As Greg watched him, he realized that Dale was important. That despite his reluctance to think about his future, a future with Dale sounded... good. Comforting. He could see them living together, raising a baby. They would take turns changing its diaper, or feeding it, or coaxing it to sleep.

Greg couldn't bear to think of a future for himself, but a future with Dale made him *want.*

And that was when he realized... he'd fallen in love with Dale Kinney.

16

Greg

IT WASN'T until the end of the fourth week, as they were heading out of Dale's apartment, that Greg grew tired of not knowing.

"Hey," he said when Dale locked the door. "About this."

Dale's eyes flickered up to his, mint-green and questioning. "This?"

Greg wetted his lips, his heart thudding. "Yeah. Me and you."

Dale's cheeks turned a faint pink. He glanced down at his belly, which was still flat as ever. But the honey of his scent was heavier now, and Greg knew without a doubt that Dale carried his child.

"What about us?" Dale asked.

"You haven't asked me to leave."

Dale opened his mouth. Closed it. His eyes darted around them, but at 8 AM, the few neighbors around were getting into their cars and heading away to work. "Should I be?"

"Do you want me to?"

Dale tucked his keys into his pocket, looking down. For a long moment, he didn't answer. "This really shouldn't be happening."

Greg knew that. "But what do you want? Should I leave?"

Dale swallowed, shaking his head.

Greg's heart leaped. After the two months of pursuing him, after the past month staying with Dale... Dale wanted him, and this felt like a dream.

Over the past few weeks, he'd learned more about Dale. Little things, like Dale's stash of sweet wine, that he eyed but didn't touch. Like Dale's favorite craft channel on TV, and the curtains of miniature cranes he sold, made with cranes from previous years. More than once, Greg had helped him string the birds, sending it off to new homes around the world.

Dale cared about him. He understood the situation with Tony, and never cast judgment on Greg.

And all this felt like a legitimate relationship. They'd curl up in bed, and Dale would tell him that three research projects were close publishing papers. That the cats next door were having kittens. That the sausage casserole Greg made was the best he'd ever had.

If they weren't teacher and student, theirs would have been just another alpha-omega relationship.

"So," Greg said, unsure how to proceed. "Does this mean...?"

Dale bit his lip. "We can't go public with this."

"We can't."

Dale rubbed the scent gland at his wrist, where the old scar was—left by an alpha who no longer wanted him. Looking at it made Greg's chest heat. "I still want to mark you," Greg murmured. "Want you as my bondmate."

Dale's cheeks darkened. "I know."

"You believe me now?"

"Yes." Dale lifted his hand, hesitating. They were outside the apartment, and anyone could see them. But Dale slipped his hand into Greg's for a second, and squeezed his fingers.

Something in Greg's chest roared. *He wants me.*

Dale pulled his hand away, flushing right to his hairline. He was adorable, and Greg wanted to pull him close, drop kisses all over his face.

He followed Dale to the Volkswagen instead, slipping inside. It was only when the doors shut, when Dale locked them inside, that Greg leaned in, pressing a kiss to his cheek.

"I love you," Greg whispered, his heart thudding in his ears.

Dale froze. He blinked rapidly, his gaze darting to Greg's, like he couldn't believe what he'd just heard. "I... I..."

"You don't have to say it back," Greg muttered, looking away, his cheeks burning. He couldn't believe he'd said it, either. But he knew he felt it, knew what his instincts told him. "I just wanted you to know."

Dale stared at the steering wheel, his cheeks pink. "I... Well, thank you."

Greg shrugged. "You don't have to thank me."

"I know. I just... It's special. Nice."

"I thought you had a better vocabulary than that," Greg said. "You're a professor."

Dale laughed, his eyes sparkling. He opened his mouth to say something else. Then he blanched, glancing desperately around the car, one hand flying up to cover his mouth.

"What do you need?" Greg asked, preemptively looking at the backseat.

Dale shook his head, scrambling against the car door. When it opened, he dashed out, reaching for his house keys. Before he could get them into the door, he doubled over, puking behind the bush by the front steps.

Oh.

Greg was out of the car, bottled water and a wad of napkins in hand. Dale's face was pale, his chest heaving.

Greg rubbed his back. "I've got water and napkins. Which do you want?"

"Water first," Dale croaked, wincing. He spat, washing his mouth out. Then he wiped his mouth with the napkins, and Greg brushed away the sweat that had beaded across Dale's forehead.

"Still feeling bad?"

"Kind of. I'm still nauseous, but it's... not as bad now." Dale leaned against the front door, breathing deeply.

"Sorry," Greg said. At Dale's raised eyebrows, he said, "I knocked you up."

Dale chuckled. Then he laughed harder, doubling over until he gasped for breath. Through Greg's stay, the only time he'd seen Dale laugh this hard was when Greg had made a dirty science joke. Greg watched him now, mystified.

When Dale calmed, Greg offered him more water. Dale gulped a mouthful, then another. "I'm really fine, you know," Dale said between gasps. "I guess the pregnancy feels real now."

Greg shrugged; he still felt bad. "You didn't ask to be pregnant."

"But I'm glad that I am." Dale's smile softened. He cradled his belly with his hand, reaching out to trail his fingertip along Greg's forearm. "I've wanted a child forever."

He looked so joyful about the pregnancy that Greg relaxed. He'd thought the morning sickness might make Dale a grump, but Dale took this in stride. When Dale leaned away from the front door, Greg supported his by the arm, leading him to the passenger side of the car.

Dale paused. "I'm driving."

"No, I'm driving," Greg said. "You're pregnant."

"Greg Hastings." Dale tried to look stern. He turned to the driver's side, and Greg held on firmly, pulling the car door open with one hand. "I'm just pregnant, not—"

On impulse, Greg kissed him hard, on the lips.

Dale froze, and Greg pulled away, looking around. He'd known there weren't witnesses.

"I'm not having you drive when you're feeling sick," Greg said. "Get in."

Dale pouted. But he slid into the car, and Greg rounded the hood, settling into the hibiscus-scented driver's seat.

When the car door slammed shut, Dale muttered, "That was risky."

"It got you to shut up." Greg smiled, sagging when Dale continued to frown. Well, Dale had a point. "I understand. Not gonna do that again."

Dale sighed. He reached over, though, squeezing Greg's thigh. "You're forgiven."

The little coil of tension released Greg's lungs, and he could breathe again. This, he hadn't expected either, not for himself to need Dale's approval this much. He drove them out of the parking lot, pulling onto the main road. "There might be something for morning sickness at the bookstore. Want to go look?"

"I probably should. I've got two lectures and a short class today." Dale shuddered. "I can't imagine emptying my guts during a lecture."

"Gods, yeah, that would suck."

The bookstore parking lot was mostly empty when they pulled in. At 8:30 AM, most students were making their way to class, not buying emergency supplies for a pregnancy.

"Morning," Sam Brentwood chirped when Greg opened the door for Dale. "Two customers at the same time—it's getting crowded in here!"

Greg blinked. With his concern for Dale, he'd forgotten that they shouldn't be seen together. *Crap.* He stood back, allowing Dale to move through the store first.

The college bookstore was a place Greg had visited time and again. At eighteen, he'd gotten into law school, going to the bookstore for the textbooks his lecturers had listed. At nineteen and unable to focus, he'd dropped law, entered med school, and bought a whole new set of first-year books.

Then he'd dropped out of med school and gone into chemistry at twenty, and Sam Brentwood had raised his eyebrows, looking dubiously at Greg's textbooks. *I had no idea law school made you study med and chem,* he'd said.

I switched majors, Greg had told him.

Then he'd taken his second year of Chemistry, and Sam had finally shut up about Greg not staying in his majors past a year.

Today, there was a couple at the cashier stand—an alpha and an omega, from their pine and lavender scents. The omega cradled a smiling baby girl to his chest. Greg watched as Dale sucked in a breath, his hand coming up to touch his belly.

They hadn't been out shopping together before. Dale had been the one doing the groceries, in case someone spotted them together. And the basketball game in Highton had been an exception.

But the way Dale looked at the baby now... there was a deep yearning in his eyes, joy mixed with anticipation and longing, and Greg could've kicked himself for not noticing sooner. How long had Dale watched infants, wishing for his own? It had to be decades.

Greg wanted to reach out for Dale, pull him close.

"Morning, Sam," Dale said, glancing at the register. "Busy today?"

"No, no, this is family," Sam said, grinning. He was tall for an omega, his dark hair falling over his eyes. He waved at the couple with him. "Kade's my brother, and Felix is his omega. They're just visiting before they head on a road trip."

Kade nodded at Greg and Dale. He seemed to be in his thirties—not the typical college student, if he were even a student here. His omega seemed the same age, blond with green eyes, leaning into his side as he cuddled their baby girl.

"Hello," Dale said, before turning to Sam. "I need help with nausea pills. Do you know a good brand?"

Sam winced, glancing at Felix. "Do you think you could help, Felix? I'm not very familiar with those pills at all."

Felix brightened. "Sure!" He grinned at Dale, hefting his daughter in his arms. She gurgled and patted his chest. "I'm not sure what the bookstore carries, but let's see what they have."

Greg watched as Dale and Felix headed past the shelves, murmuring quietly between themselves. He was tempted to follow—Dale was his omega—but both Kade and Sam were watching him now. His cheeks prickled with heat. *Shouldn't have stared at Dale so long.* "I need ballpoint pens. They still in the same place?"

"Yeah. Over in the corner with the notebooks. See the sign?" Sam pointed.

"Thanks." Greg ducked down an aisle.

"We're headed for Red Rock Canyon," Kade rumbled at the register. "Felix wants an adventure. I told him it's way too ambitious. Bethy's one—she won't remember the Grand Canyon, anyway."

"We'll take photos, Kade," Felix called from the other end of the store. "Tell Sam about the mule ride! We're going to be taking that down to the bottom of the canyon. It'll be fun! There's even a ranch there, you know."

"Sam will see the photos on Facebook," Kade said. "Not like you won't be posting pics every hour."

"I've seen the three hundred photos of Bethy, yes," Sam said dryly.

"Can't wait for your own?" Kade asked.

"I'll wait," Sam replied. "I'm not ready yet."

At the stationery section, Greg picked a couple of pens, drawing loops on messy scraps of paper to test them.

The conversation about Facebook nagged at him. He'd been thinking about it lately — this thing he had going on with Dale. No one could know about it. His friends on the basketball team had been posting pictures of their bondmates, pictures of couples flying kites, or eating out, or going to the movies.

Greg had never felt the need to post about his personal life. But looking at Dale, he almost wanted to share pictures of them. Pictures that said, *This is my omega.*

Greg was proud of Dale. He wanted, at least, for his friends to stop nagging at him. *When are you settling?* the alphas on the basketball team had asked. *You've been smelling like the one omega for weeks. Are you dating him?*

It was stupid, but he wanted to show off his omega. Wanted to mark Dale, wanted people to know Dale was his.

Except he couldn't.

Greg brought the pens to the register, tugging out his wallet. Dale stepped out from the shelves then, his eyes bright as he turned to speak with Felix. He was wearing his button-down shirt, his black pants, his steel-rimmed glasses. But back home, Dale had worn Greg's jersey, its neckline gaping down his chest, and he'd looked just as gorgeous. Maybe even more so.

And Greg couldn't stop staring at him.

"Greg? I'll need to scan those pens if you want them," Sam said, following his gaze. "Is there something wrong? Looks like Felix got Professor Kinney—"

Sam's nostrils flared, and his eyes widened. He looked between Greg and Dale. "*Ohhh.*"

Shit. Greg slapped the pens down on the counter, trying to fight the blush crawling up his neck. "I'm buying these," he said, his heart thumping.

Dale had turned, his gaze flickering between Greg, Kade, and Sam. And Kade's eyes must've darted between Greg and Dale, because Dale tensed.

"I won't say a word," Sam breathed, but his eyes gleamed. "Cross my heart. I promise."

"You promise," Greg blurted, his insides coiling up. This was bad. He shouldn't have been looking at Dale.

"Nothing happened. I swear." Sam rang up the pens and read the total to Greg. But he glanced back at Dale, and Dale had frozen like a statue at the other end of the counter.

It wasn't like any of them could avoid the giant elephant in the bookstore. And because Greg knew Sam well enough, after visiting the bookstore for four years, he could afford them a bit of truth.

"Dale's my omega," Greg said, calm as he could. His heart pounded. "I'm marrying him."

Dale's eyes snapped up to his. His throat worked, except no words came out.

"Congrats," Felix said, looking meaningfully

at Dale. He squeezed Dale's hand. "I'm sure Greg will be good to you."

Dale huffed a weak laugh. "That… is actually the least of my concerns, but thank you."

Greg paid for the pens. Dale came to stand by him, setting on the counter a bag of ginger drops, a set of origami paper, and a wrapped sandwich.

"I'll pay for those too," Greg said.

"Will you invite me to the wedding?" Sam asked when it became clear that neither of them would speak. He smiled uncertainly. "I mean, I'm happy for you guys. I really am. I've known you for so long."

Greg glanced at Dale. This, he wasn't sure about. They hadn't even discussed marriage.

Dale stared hard at Sam. "Only if you promise not to leak. I know where you live, Sam Brentwood."

Sam looked between them, gulping. Then he glanced at his brother, and Kade shrugged. "Not my business," Kade said. "You stepped into this yourself."

Sam made a face. "You're my big brother—you're supposed to protect me!"

"Not if you're getting into someone else's mess." Kade smiled at Greg and Dale. "Congrats."

Greg nodded stiffly at them. Then he headed out of the bookstore with Dale, his back prickling under three different sets of eyes.

"Bye-bye," Bethy said, waving when Greg glanced back at her. He waved back.

It wasn't until they were back inside the car that he sighed, rubbing his temples. "That was not good."

"You really want to marry me?" Dale asked, an odd inflection to his voice. Greg glanced up. Dale looked a little distraught, like he wanted to say no.

Greg swallowed. "You don't want to?"

"You're young," Dale said.

He sighed. "I thought we've been over this."

"Yes, but not marriage. That's... a little much."

"You're my omega," Greg said. This was the one truth he'd been hanging onto, when Dale eyed him in class next to omegas his age, doubt in his gaze. When Greg thought Dale might tell him to leave.

Dale looked down at his ginger drops. "You have so much ahead of you. I don't want to trap you into something that'll clip your wings."

"You aren't clipping my wings," Greg said. "I'm making my decision, and it's staying with you."

Dale rubbed his face, sighing. "I'll think about it."

Greg wasn't sure what else he could say—he'd tried convincing Dale every way he could. And unlike when he and Tony had decided they wouldn't be mates, this was... different. It hurt.

With Tony, there had been subtle differences, like Tony had said Greg gave him no space to breathe, that Greg clung too much to him as a lover. With Dale... Dale liked Greg this close. He liked Greg nudging him around, crowding into his space.

In his gut, Greg knew he and Dale were a good match. Everyone had their good sides and bad, and some of those things wouldn't change. In love, there was no perfect mate, only the mate that fitted best with you, who could compensate for where you were weak.

Greg wanted to be needed, and Dale needed him around.

To have Dale reject the idea of marriage, well. Greg wasn't sure what to think of it, other than it was the wrong decision. Even if he himself could not promise a future.

He stayed silent through the trip to the science faculty, dropping Dale off at the lab building. Dale had one foot out of the car when he turned back, his eyes searching out Greg's.

"I'll park the car here and walk," Greg said. "Text me if you want me to drive you anywhere."

"Okay." Dale hesitated, glancing around them. The entrance to the building was empty. There were no cars pulling into the parking lot, and no students walking around them.

Dale leaned in, pressing a brief kiss to his mouth. Greg's heart missed a beat.

"See you later," Dale whispered, his eyes heavy with guilt.

"I love you," Greg said when he pulled away.

Dale bit his lip, looking at the dashboard. "I know. See you in class."

The car door slammed shut, and Greg watched as Dale made his way to the lab building, disappearing past its doors.

So maybe they weren't going to marry. But Dale liked him enough to risk kissing him in public, and that... had never happened before.

Greg took comfort in it.

17
Dale

DALE POPPED a ginger drop into his mouth, trying to quell the nervous patter of his pulse. His thoughts whirled—Greg proposing, the morning sickness. Someone on campus *knew*.

He breathed in deeply, then released his breath. Breathed in, breathed out.

No matter how hard he tried to shove it from his mind, Dale remembered Greg's fierce eyes in the bookstore. Greg had been serious when he'd said, *Dale is my omega. I'm marrying him.*

In the store, Dale's heart had given an excited little thud. Then the rest of reality had sunken in, and Dale had realized that they had had an audience. That Sam Brentwood knew.

Sam's relatives weren't part of the college— Dale had learned that much. But Sam was still a college employee. He dealt with hundreds of people in the bookstore every day. Just the thought of him *knowing* sent goosebumps marching down Dale's skin.

He slipped into his office and shut the door behind him. Locked it. Hands still shaking, Dale sank into his chair, setting down his things.

He could trust Sam. He'd chatted with Sam ever since Sam began working in the bookstore six years back. Sam was a cheery omega who pointed out all the things Dale looked for, even the simplest pencils and plastic files. Never once had he gossiped, or shared someone else's secrets with Dale.

Their secret was safe with Sam.

He powered on his laptop, picking at the plastic wrap around his sandwich. Then he nibbled on it. The tuna-and-mayo filling was light on his tongue, moist, flavorful chunks of fish.

In the bookstore, Felix Brentwood had sniffed at Dale, his eyes lighting up at the scent of pregnancy. Dale had been quietly glad when Felix waited until they were hidden by shelves of snacks, before he asked, *Is it a wanted child?*

Very much so, Dale had answered.

That alpha with you?

Dale had nodded, and Felix had beamed, squeezing Dale's hand. If Felix had known that Dale and Greg were teacher and student, Dale was sure his reaction would be different. But Felix didn't know, and in those minutes, he'd let himself soak up Felix's excitement.

When is it due? Felix had asked, hugging his daughter close. *Is your alpha taking care of you? Is this your first child?*

Dale had answered his questions, bubbles of joy rising in his chest. In those moments, he'd thought of himself and Greg as alpha and omega, and nothing else. And that thought had lifted a weight off his shoulders.

He liked Greg as his alpha. Greg brought him

lunch, joked with him, promised to listen if Dale had problems.

I love you, Greg had said this morning.

Dale's throat tightened. He didn't know if the ache in his chest was love. But he did know that they couldn't get married, not when Greg was so young. Hell, Greg might not even know what he wanted — Dale hadn't. Dale had been married at twenty, and he'd followed Charles' desires, staring at pregnancy tests, hoping to see two blue lines.

Greg was twenty-two. To bind him into a marriage... It was unthinkable.

Dale opened his email, nibbling on his sandwich. He needed coffee to wake up properly — Greg had banned him from drinking more than half a cup a day. His coffee machine sat neglected in the corner of his office, untouched for weeks.

Months ago, before Greg, Dale had had breakfast at his desk every morning, the coffee machine gurgling as it kept him company. Ever since Greg moved into Dale's apartment, they had had breakfast together every day. Dale hadn't realized how much less lonely he was, until now.

He focused on the screen. At the top of his unread emails, there was a quick note from June.

Dale — Read this first.

He winced, clicking on it. June rarely had urgent news; she was training to become an assistant professor, and Dale relied most heavily on her to run the lab.

Just received word - a group in Texas State U is also working on nano Au-enzyme synthesis. Same materials as ours. They're projecting research completion to be the end of this month. Our estimate was completion next month. Penny and I are working on the project now. Gonna be lots of OT, but we can get an article submitted in 3 wks if we hurry. -June

Dale held his breath. If the Texas State U group published the same synthesis method before Dale's group did, they'd have a higher chance of catching someone's eye. Especially if that someone was a large biosensor company. And the company could well offer the Texan group a research grant, instead of Dale's group.

Dale rubbed his temples, sighing. If he lost a grant... his chances of tenure would slip further. Bernard Hastings would look down his nose at Dale, asking what Dale did wrong this time.

He was tempted to drop everything to help June with the research. But June had banned him from experiments, and Dale had his own lectures to deal with.

The semester ended in four weeks. He had assignments to grade, exam papers to write. With his post-docs and grad students stepping up their research, they wouldn't be able to help with his workload.

And the pregnancy would only make him more fatigued as the month drew on.

I'll be there in five, Dale typed.

He made notes on the stacks of ungraded assignments, closed the laptop, then headed for the lab.

A WEEK later, the nausea had only added to Dale's growing fatigue. He was tired when he woke.

Classes drained him faster than he expected. By midday, he was out of energy. When Greg visited for lunch at noon, Dale hardly wanted to move at all, and Greg would drag his chair over to Dale's, feeding him bites of sandwich.

Dale's fatigue was compounded by the nagging task he'd been putting off: doing research on his pregnancy.

He'd done the basics, of course. Finding out which foods he needed. Doing exercises. Looking up his symptoms and how to remedy them.

What he'd been avoiding was the one thing he couldn't change: the risks of pregnancy at his age.

He was forty-two. The pregnancy had been too new, too surreal at first. And last week, when Dale had glimpsed Felix's daughter at the bookstore, he'd remembered the burgeoning life in his own belly, and a slow, secret happiness had built in his throat. He hadn't wanted to lose hope by doing research this soon.

But now... with the lights dimmed around them, and with Greg sleeping peacefully beside him in bed, Dale thought about Greg's proposal again. *Dale is my omega. I'm marrying him.*

If Dale didn't have a baby, Greg wouldn't feel the need to propose. Without the responsibility of child-raising, Greg would be free to leave, and seek out his own future.

And Dale had been selfish all this time, wanting to keep him close. He really shouldn't.

He held his breath and opened the email from Bernard Hastings, sent four days ago.

I have decided to arrange a dinner with my son

and Penny Fleming. Penny mentioned that her parents will be out of town for the duration. Would you be interested in joining us as Penny's reference instead?

Dale stared at the message, his breath caught in his throat. In the bluish glow of the screen, he admired the curl of Greg's lashes, the point of his nose, the bow of his lips. Greg was beautiful. Clever. Full of potential. And he deserved so much more than what Dale could give him.

Dale switched out of the email app, typing, *Pregnancy risk forty years old.*

The search engine returned with an answer: *In omegas older than 40, the incidence of miscarriage has been found to be 50%, but the risk may be greater, depending on the individual's medical history.*

Dale stopped breathing. *Fifty percent?*

His fingers shook as he tapped on the first website. Then the next website. And the website after that.

All of them gave the same answer: he had a one-in-two chance of losing the baby he carried.

Dale stared at the too-bright screen, his heart stumbling. He'd spent a month thinking about the baby he'd cradle in his arms. He could just as easily lose his child.

His throat closed, and his vision blurred. He couldn't breathe.

He couldn't lose his baby.

Dale sobbed, clapping his hand over his mouth. Behind him, Greg's breathing remained steady; he was still asleep.

If Dale lost this baby... Greg would be free to go.

A soft, keening whine slipped from his

throat. Dale bit hard into his palm, trying to stay silent. His chest ached. This was a precious child; Greg had given it to him, and he couldn't possibly lose it.

Dale cradled his belly, burying his face in his pillow. *I'll keep you safe,* he thought to his unborn child. *You are loved.*

But if the baby miscarried, Greg would be free to leave. He could bond with Penny, or some other omega younger and more fertile than Dale. Someone who had a brighter future. Dale bit his lip and breathed, turning the possibilities over in his head.

It was hours before he fell asleep.

HOURS LATER, Dale woke to Greg gently shaking him. "Hey, it's almost eight," Greg murmured, frowning. "We gotta get up."

Dale groaned, burying his face in the pillow. His eyes felt as though bits of sand had crusted in them, and he couldn't pry them open at all. The sun stung when he squinted. "It's too early."

"What do you want for breakfast? I'll make it for you," Greg said, pressing a kiss to his forehead. "I've been trying to wake you for the past hour."

Dale peered at him, his limbs heavy as lead. Greg was already dressed, his hair brushed, his face shaved. "You look good," Dale croaked. "Gods, my voice is terrible."

"Thanks. Breakfast?" Greg scooped an arm behind Dale's back, helping him sit up.

"Anything I won't puke."

201

"Bread and cheese?"

"Sounds good." But his eyes ached with lack of sleep, and Dale flopped down onto his stomach, burying his head under the pillow. "Who invented mornings?"

"You tell me. You're older."

He was. Dale whined, pulling the pillow firmly over his head. "Don't remind me."

But his thoughts connected — he was older, he was tired because he was old, because he was pregnant, and there was a fifty percent chance that he'd lose his baby because of his age.

Dale froze, icy dread sliding into his stomach. Then he groaned, choking, and Greg's hand settled on his back.

"What's wrong?" Greg asked, concern in his voice.

Greg couldn't know. Dale was already older than he was — he didn't need Greg thinking less of him, all because he couldn't carry his child to term. He couldn't bear to tell Greg that his dream held such a huge chance of shattering.

"I'm fine," Dale said, breathing through his mouth. He was just five weeks pregnant. Not eight months. "Make me breakfast, please."

Greg rubbed his back, peeking under Dale's pillow. Dale hid his face in the sheets. "You're not okay," Greg said, his gaze prickling Dale's skin. "Tell me what's wrong."

"It's too early. It's just my hormones," Dale said. "Go away."

Greg hesitated. Dale hated lying to him, but he didn't want his alpha knowing right now. Didn't want Greg to face just how useless an omega

Dale was. Charles had annulled the marriage. With Greg... there wasn't even a bond for him to break. He could just leave.

Dale bit his lip, hot tears welling up in his eyes.

A sturdy warmth settled down beside him, nestling against his back, his thighs, his calves. Greg circled Dale's waist with his arms, burying his face in Dale's neck.

"I'll wait in the kitchen," Greg murmured. "If you think of something, tell me what I can do."

He held Dale for a long moment, until Dale stopped shaking. Then he dragged his wrist down Dale's arm, pressed a kiss to Dale's nape, and pulled away, padding out of the bedroom.

Dale clung to his pillow, the information from last night trickling back into his mind. Some omegas would lose their babies closer to term. Some would birth stillborns. Some would miscarry earlier on, even when the ultrasound went fine.

And there was little he could do about it, because he was old. Because his body was no longer what it was at twenty.

Dale sucked in a deep breath, pushing those thoughts away. He had work to do. A lab to lead. He couldn't let his own worries drag him down.

He peeled himself off the bed, heading to the bathroom.

MORE HOURS later, the same sick dread hadn't dissipated. Greg had visited his office during lunch, and Dale had pasted on a smile, pretending everything was fine.

Except Greg hadn't believed him then, either. He'd sat close to Dale, rubbing his neck, shrewd eyes studying him. Just like Bernard Hastings watched Dale before he decided Dale wasn't up to par.

Dale had all but pushed Greg out of his office, locking him out after lunch.

The next classes were hell to get through. Dale couldn't forget the betrayal in Greg's eyes, the confusion and worry. And he'd caused it all, keeping his secret from Greg. Knowing he should tell Greg about the risks, so Greg could leave.

Greg had texted him, asking when he wanted to leave for home that evening. Dale had stared at the text message, turning his phone face-down. He didn't know. And he had no energy left to deal with this.

By the time 7 PM rolled around, Dale still hadn't replied to Greg's message. Greg had come to Dale's office twice, knocking at the door, but Dale had locked it, pretending he wasn't around.

His belly was still flat. He shouldn't be this worried about a pregnancy he couldn't even see.

Weary, Dale pulled on his lab coat, dragging himself to the lab. He had to go home at some point. He had to tell Greg about the baby. He didn't want to.

In the lab, he found June with a bench full of vials—some on the magnetic stirrer, some neatly in a grid, some clustered to a side. When the door clicked shut, the rest of the lab occupants looked over. Penny waved from another bench, and Greg's eyes flickered up from his pipette, his lips growing thin.

Dale's stomach squeezed. *Are you angry?*

June peeled off her gloves, hurrying over. He met her at her desk.

"Something's bothering you," June muttered, scanning him. "Your eye bags are worse than usual. Like, they're bad on a whole different magnitude."

Dale winced. "I didn't sleep well."

There were a few other grad students in the lab, and Dale knew both Greg and Penny were listening in. Penny had been eyeing him ever since he started wearing Greg's aspen scent, but she hadn't said a thing about it. He was thankful for that.

"It's not just the sleep, though," June said.

Dale swallowed, trying not to think about the statistics he'd found. "I'm fine. How is the project going?"

"We're on schedule. I've got experiments for the last three enzymes, and Greg volunteered to verify the procedure for me. Penny's testing some silver-gold nanoparticle combinations."

"Right," Dale said. He followed June to the bench, avoiding the other two sets of eyes on him. Greg hadn't moved an inch. Penny glanced at him, then at Dale.

"You don't look so good, Professor," Penny said, her forehead furrowed. "June's bringing you home, isn't she?"

Dale froze, needing to look at Greg, to see how he reacted. "I'd need to know the project status first," he said. "How have you been doing?"

Penny briefed him on her procedures, and

Dale half-listened to her. He sneaked glances at Greg instead, catching his narrowed eyes, his clenched jaw.

Funny how he could read Greg so easily now, when he hadn't been able to two months ago. Funny, too, how Greg's disappointment made his own heart ache.

"Very good," Dale said when Penny stopped talking. "Please keep it up."

"I do have some questions about the experimental variations, though," she said with a tiny frown. "Is it okay if I ask you about them later?"

"Sure," Dale said. "Or you could ask June — she knows just as well what the project needs."

Penny opened her mouth, glancing at June. Dale hadn't noticed before, but Penny seemed wary of his first-in-command. Had June said something to her?

Shelving the thought away, Dale stopped briefly next to Greg, breathing in his comforting aspen scent. He wanted to step closer, wanted to lean into his alpha's chest. Greg's eyes locked with his. Dale fought down the anxious little whispers of *You'd leave if you found out about the baby,* and smiled. "Everything okay?"

"Maybe," Greg said. "You look like you need to go lie down."

"I..." Dale sagged. He thought about the couch in his office, the soft pillows and wide cushions, and every cell in his body yearned for it. Greg's chest looked comfortable, too, all flat planes, and Dale remembered the musk of it, the safety of his arms.

"Can you get to the office yourself?" Greg asked.

Penny was looking at them again; he couldn't acknowledge Greg's question; it seemed too intimate. Dale's heart pattered. "How are your experiments going? Are your results comparable to June's?"

"Yeah." Greg glanced sideways, as though trying to see if Penny was still listening. "But the current set will only be done in two hours. Maybe check with me then."

Between his words, Dale understood *Rest for two hours. I'll see you after that.*

He turned away, leaning his shoulder into Greg's arm so it looked like an accidental bump. The brief touch was comforting, and Dale wished he could have had more. "I'll speak with you again later."

"Get some rest," his alpha said.

Dale's heart swelled. When he glanced back, he found Greg's gaze soft and warm, tinted with concern. "I'll be fine," Dale said. "June will accompany me to the office. There are some things I'll need to discuss with her, anyway."

"Fine," Greg said.

Dale stopped by June's bench, where she was working on her current procedure. While he waited, Dale looked at his phone again, scrolling to Bernard Hastings' email. Greg couldn't possibly want to spend his life with Dale. Not when Dale could miscarry anytime, and Greg would be free to go. He could fall in love with someone else, like Penny.

I'll attend the dinner, Dale typed. Then he hit

Send, and slid the phone back in his pocket.

When June accompanied him out five minutes later, she steadied him by the arm, frowning.

"What did you say to Penny?" Dale asked, massaging his stiff shoulders. "She seems terrified of you."

June sighed, glancing down the empty hallways. "She was getting nosy about my relationship with you. I said it wasn't her place to question your choices, but maybe with a few harsher words."

She smiled sheepishly. Dale groaned. "I hope it doesn't get worse. That was awkward."

"You did land yourself some trouble," she said, shaking her head. "How are you doing? I haven't talked to you properly in weeks."

Dale looked over his shoulder. This late at night, the only people staying in the labs were the grad students and post-docs, rushing projects and working on journal articles. There was no one in the corridor right now. "I'm doing fine. Greg's been... really patient with me. I don't even understand why he's still putting up with my crap."

"Oh, Dale." June squeezed his arm. She smelled like birch, with faint petunia undertones. Her fiancée's scent. "I can see why he likes you. You're so serious all the time—you need someone to drag you out of your shell."

"I don't need to be dragged anywhere."

"You do seem happier, though."

Dale glanced down at his belly, oily unease unfurling through his stomach. "Maybe."

"Something happened. Is it the baby?"

"Yes." He caught his lip between his teeth. "The... the risks. I only looked them up last night."

June winced, turning them round a corner. "Bad? I've never researched it myself."

"Bad enough that I don't want to think about it," Dale mumbled, wringing his fingers.

"Oh, Dale." June held his hand, giving him a squeeze. Dale squeezed back.

"If I lose the baby, he might — might leave."

"I don't think he will," June said. "Have you seen the way he watches me when I hug you?"

Dale smiled, his heart thudding. He hadn't thought Greg cared that much. "I'm just worried."

"You don't have to worry about Greg. That much, I'm sure of."

But there was everything else to think about — the baby, the tenure, Greg's father. Greg finding out about the risks, and leaving. No matter how much he said he loved Dale, surely there was a part of him that wanted a family at some point. If the pregnancy failed, Dale wouldn't be able to provide that.

As they walked, Dale's limbs weighed him down, his head heavy with fatigue. He didn't speak until he reached his office. There, he unlocked the door, pushing it open.

The sight of the couch had him swaying on his feet. It called out to him, promising peaceful rest.

"Sleep," June said firmly, guiding him over to the couch. "You look like you desperately need it."

"I should be working harder," Dale said. But

he kicked his shoes off, curling up on the couch. It smelled like himself, and he snuggled into the cushions, taking comfort in its familiarity.

"You can't work if you don't have rest," June said. She checked the room, then waved at the key in the door. "Do you want this?"

"Hand it to Greg. Please, and thank you." Dale set his glasses on the side table.

June nodded, worry in her eyes when she looked back at him. "Call if you need anything. You have a couple of alphas who will do anything for you."

Dale smiled. "You should spend more time with Cher—I'm sure she misses you while you're cooped up in the lab."

June cracked a smile. "Will do, once we get this project over with. Or, if we call off this fake engagement, maybe she can step into the lab or something."

"We really should do that," Dale mumbled. Before he could linger on that thought, his eyelids drooped shut, and fatigue pulled him under.

18
Greg

TIME PASSED a lot slower without Dale around. Greg looked up when the lab door opened again, but June was the only one in the doorway.

She'd delivered Dale safely to his office, then. That was far better than the alternative: Dale staggering to the office himself, prone to collapsing along the way. He hadn't looked okay the entire day.

June walked up to Greg, nodding at him. "Everything good?"

"Yeah," he said. "I'm waiting for the oxidase powder to dissolve."

"Great." June glanced at Penny, who was frowning at her own experiment. Without missing a beat, June set a key on the bench inches from Greg—Dale's office key. "Someday, I want to have a couch in my own office," she said.

So Dale was sleeping on the couch. That was a relief to hear.

She smiled at him, then turned back to her own bench, where glass vials sat on the magnetic stirrer, little magnets spinning inside them.

Greg slipped the key into his pocket,

imagining Dale curled up on the red couch. All week, he'd snuggled up to Greg in bed, his lips pulled up in a smile.

I'm trying to decide on the baby's name, Dale had said. *What do you think?*

I don't know, Greg had told him. *Why don't you come up with a list?*

There are superstitions that given names will influence personalities, Dale had answered. *That makes it such a heavy decision.*

Names are what you make of them, Greg had said, tapping him on the nose. *What matters more is how we raise the baby.*

Through the times they lay in bed, Dale would shift Greg's hand from his hip to his belly, his eyes warm. At five weeks, he wasn't showing yet. But Greg liked cradling his omega's belly, liked touching where their baby grew. It pleased Dale greatly. Several times, they'd spooned in bed, Greg holding Dale's abdomen as they slept. Dale had purred in his arms, snuggling closer.

So it hadn't made sense when Dale flinched from him this morning, his eyes glittering like fragile glass. It couldn't have been the proposal, or Sam Brentwood finding out about them last week. It couldn't have been Bernard Hastings—Greg's father didn't email anyone at 10 PM. Bernard adhered rigidly to office hours, as he did with everything else in his life.

Greg had gone to sleep with Dale at nine, and Dale had smiled when Greg showed him a picture of a bunny onesie, asking if he liked it.

If Dale was distraught... maybe it was something else he'd seen. Or maybe it was the baby.

Uncertainty slithered up Greg's spine. Why hadn't Dale told him if there was something wrong? Was the baby in danger?

He glanced at June, wondering what Dale had confided in her. But she didn't seem overly worried. Instead, Penny was the one looking distraught, and Greg almost felt sorry for her. She glanced at June, then her own notes, tapping into her phone. Not something Greg could solve, probably.

The minutes crawled by, until Greg tested his nanoparticles for fluorescence. Then he keyed in his results on a spreadsheet, forwarding it to June.

"I'm done with this," Greg said, washing up his apparatus. "Results okay?"

June scanned through the document he'd sent. "Yeah, this looks fine. Thanks for helping."

Greg shrugged. He'd come to the lab because it was the only place Dale couldn't avoid him. For an excuse to stay, he'd volunteered to help June with her project.

Then Dale had shown up, looking worse than he'd done all day, and Greg had hated that he was stuck on the damn experiment, instead of bringing Dale home to rest.

And now he was finally free to leave.

"Are you including my name on the paper?" Greg asked, grabbing his backpack.

"Yours might be the last name." June grinned. "Dale's name will be first, of course."

He waved, pulling open the lab door. As it closed behind him, he heard Penny say, "Maybe I should talk to Professor Kinney about this."

June would stop her—Greg trusted June now, when she'd backed off on Dale, not marking him. Over the last few weeks, Greg had been the one to mark Dale, leaving his scent on his omega. June respected that. And Greg had slowly let go of his resentment, chatting casually with her when he showed up for lab class.

He strode to Dale's office, his unease settling when the lock clicked open. Dale was asleep, and even though the college seemed safe, Greg liked that his omega was secure. That Dale trusted Greg with his office key.

Greg switched the lights on, stepping into the office. Dale had curled up on the couch, his arms wrapped around a pillow, his glasses folded on the side table. The shadows under his eyes had faded slightly, and Greg was glad that he was getting some rest.

He eased onto the couch, sitting in the half-circle of space between Dale's knees and his face.

Asleep, Dale looked so much more relaxed than he'd done all day. Greg was hesitant to wake him—Dale needed all the rest he could get, with his body still adjusting to the pregnancy. So Greg leaned in, pressing a kiss to Dale's cheek. Dale stirred lightly, then settled.

Carefully, Greg slid his arms beneath Dale's back and knees, to turn him into a manageable position. If he could get Dale to the car without waking him somehow...

Dale sucked in a sharp breath, his eyelids fluttering open. "Greg?" he mumbled, his gaze forest-green and unfocused. "What're you doing here?"

"Getting you home," Greg said.

Dale nestled against him, slipping his arms around Greg's waist. "Missed you."

Greg's heart fluttered. After a whole day of Dale avoiding him, he was relieved that Dale still wanted him on a subconscious level. "Feel better?"

"A little." Dale squirmed closer, settling his cheek in Greg's lap. "I'm still tired."

"C'mon, let's get you home," Greg said, stroking his hand down Dale's side. "Get you a shower. Then you can sleep in bed."

"I should be doing more," Dale mumbled, burying his face in Greg's abs. His breath puffed through Greg's shirt, and Greg ran his fingers through Dale's hair, just touching him. "The lab..."

"You're pregnant. Gotta get more rest."

"I'm..." Dale breathed in deeply, his fingers curling into Greg's shirt. "The baby."

Something shifted in his body then. Dale tensed, his breaths growing short and sharp. "The—the baby," he said, and his voice grew strained. "I—I can't..."

A sliver of ice shot down Greg's spine. "What about the baby?"

"I... looked up the risks last night." Dale blinked himself awake, the corners of his lips pulling down. And that same dismay slipped into his eyes again. "The risks are awful. Fifty percent."

Greg froze. He must've heard wrong. "Fifty?"

Dale nodded, huddling into himself. "Anytime during the pregnancy, the risks of losing the child are one-in-two. I don't—don't expect you to stay if I lose it. I can't—I don't know—"

His face crumpled, and Greg's heart squeezed. This couldn't happen to Dale. Not when he'd waited so long to carry a child. Greg gathered Dale up in his arms. "C'mon, don't... don't think about that right now. Things are fine."

"But I could lose it tomorrow," Dale said, his voice tapering into a whine. His lip trembled, and when he looked up at Greg, his eyes were wide and scared, vulnerable. "I-I can't lose the child. It's yours. I don't—don't want—"

"Shh," Greg said, pulling Dale tight against his chest. "It's gonna be fine."

"I don't even know if it'll turn out fine. I can't control it." Dale's voice broke, and he shivered in Greg's arms, tears rolling down his cheeks. "You gave me the child and I—I—I can't lose it, Greg. I d-don't know if I can h-have another one."

Dale sobbed, his hands fisting in Greg's shirt, his entire body wracked with shudders. Greg's eyes burned.

It wasn't fair. Dale had wanted a child for decades. And now that he was pregnant, the risks of losing the child were so high. The mere thought of a miscarriage filled Greg with horror.

For a month now, he'd been coming to terms with the child. Of him and Dale getting married, caring for a baby together. They'd raise their baby, bring him or her to the park. Dale would teach their baby about bugs and plants, and together, they could all play ball when they were older.

To be faced with the possibility of losing this child... Greg's chest ached like someone had gouged a hole in it. He hadn't known he'd wanted the baby this much. Hadn't known he was looking forward to a family with Dale.

We could adopt sounded consoling enough, except it would imply losing this baby. Greg's stomach shriveled.

"We won't lose the baby," he said, his own voice tight. "We'll go to the doctor. See what they say. I'll watch out for you, okay? We're gonna be fine."

Dale trembled against him, his body thin and fragile, and Greg wanted to hide his omega at home, protect him from everything he could. He stroked Dale's back, aching at the tears that soaked through his shirt. He wanted to solve this, but he didn't know what options he had.

"C'mon, let's get you home first," Greg murmured, stroking Dale's back. "Get you a hot shower. It won't be so bad once you're comfy in bed."

Dale huddled against him. "You'll leave, won't you? I-If there's no baby."

Really? Greg's chest squeezed. "That's what you think? That's why you've been avoiding me all day?"

Dale nodded, his hair mussing against Greg's midriff. He couldn't look at Greg, and in that moment, Greg understood how humiliated Dale felt, back when he'd been with Charles and that bastard's parents. *What else did they say to you? How dare they hurt you like that?*

"I'm not Charles," Greg muttered, holding him tight. "I'm not going to leave because of a baby. I want this child, but if anything happens, I'm not going to abandon you, okay? I'd still marry you."

Dale whimpered. He pressed himself closer to Greg, his thin arms slipping around Greg's waist, his shoulders shaking as he cried.

Greg held Dale snug against himself, stroking down Dale's shoulder, his arm, his flank. "I'm not leaving," Greg said, rubbing down his back. "I want the baby too. I want it just as much as I want you."

He lost track of how much time passed, instead rubbing Dale's neck, massaging his scalp, careful not to displace Dale from his lap. And as Dale's sobs quieted, Greg brushed his hair away from his face, gathering Dale up into his arms.

The fabric of Greg's shirt was soaked through with tears and snot, and Greg didn't care. It would be worse with a baby, anyway.

Dale looked up at him, his face blotchy, his nose red. Greg felt just as helpless as he did, uneasy and upset, his heart sore. He didn't want to think about losing their baby. He hadn't felt this raw since Tony died, and it scared him, a little. Scared him that he was vulnerable again. That he could get hurt again.

He hadn't expected that since the fire, and maybe... he was in a little too deep.

But Dale seemed more fragile than Greg was right now. Greg took his glasses from the side table, unfolded them, and slid them onto Dale's nose. "Better?"

"I can see you now," Dale said thickly, breaking into a wan smile. "Before, you were just a blob of color."

Who even told their lover that? Dale was different. Funny.

"Gods, I love you," Greg murmured. Dale blinked at him. Greg cupped his cheeks, wiping his tears off. "I'm not leaving you, Dale Kinney, whatever happens with the baby. I promise."

Dale stared at him, his mouth falling open, tears welling in his eyes again.

Greg winced. "C'mon, I didn't mean to make you cry."

"I..." Dale gulped, his cheeks darkening. "Oh gods, I think I love you."

Greg's pulse missed a beat. "Really?"

Dale lowered his gaze. "I think so, yes."

Greg's heart swelled by three sizes. He hadn't expected Dale to. Not when Dale had been skittish about love, had been worried about getting too close.

Greg pressed their foreheads together, staring through Dale's glasses into his eyes. They'd been living together a month, and Greg had learned so much about this omega—the way Dale wrinkled his nose at pickles, the way he loved crosswords, the way he wanted to snuggle under the sheets all day.

If there were something in his future that could be guaranteed, Greg would want it to be Dale. He wanted Dale by his side for all the years to come.

With Dale's face cradled in his hands, Greg kissed him on the lips, on the nose, on the cheeks. He kissed Dale's forehead, his chin, and when he returned to Dale's mouth, Dale whimpered and pulled him close, opening for him, his lips so familiar that Greg could recognize him with his own nose stopped and his eyes blindfolded.

"Wanna marry you," Greg murmured against Dale's lips, kissing him fervently. "Make you mine."

Dale moaned, kissing him back, his lips sliding silky against Greg's. His musk coiled through the air between them. "Greg, please—"

Greg kissed his words away, scooping Dale onto his lap, thinking about reaching into Dale's pants, stroking him right here on the couch. They hadn't fucked here before, and maybe they could. The couch was comfortable. Dale would writhe beneath him, spreading his legs wide, and Greg would reach down—

The door squeaked open.

Penny tumbled into the office just as Dale jerked away from Greg, but there was no mistaking how close they had been, Dale's lips kiss-swollen, their scents mingled.

"Professor, I hoped you might be around..." Penny frowned at the empty desk and turned, her eyes growing wide when Dale eased toward the other end of the couch. A flush crept up his neck.

Greg frowned. *The hell?*

Before he could speak, June skidded into the office, lab coat fluttering around her legs, her forehead creased. "I've told you, Penny, he's left for home—"

June's eyes snagged on Greg, then Dale, who had curled up in the corner of his couch. Dale looked beseechingly at her, his fingers curled into his pants. June sighed and rubbed her face.

"You knew this was going on?" Penny asked, looking accusingly at June.

What a nosy bitch, Greg thought.

"I've told you, Penny. This is none of your business," June said, her voice edged with impatience. "Office hours are over. Dale's not working right now."

"But you told me he's your bondmate!" Penny said, her voice rising. She looked between Greg and Dale again, scandalized. "How could you let him and Greg—"

"Dale's not actually my bondmate," June said, at the same time Greg snarled, "He's mine."

Greg stood, shielding Dale from Penny, anger thrumming through his veins. Penny had no right to barge in here. No right to walk in on him and Dale, even if Greg had left the door unlocked. All he'd wanted to do was get Dale home, damn it.

Penny's mouth fell open. She tucked her curls behind her ear, looking between Greg and June. "You've been hiding this all along?" she asked June, uncertainty flashing through her eyes.

"Get out," Greg started to growl, except Dale slipped his fingers into Greg's, squeezing them. Greg shut up.

Dale climbed to his feet, looking sternly at Penny. "I should have told you to leave your questions for tomorrow, Penny. This concerns June, Greg, and I. Your attention would be better spent on our research project."

Penny frowned at him, a flush rising on her face. "You told me you were engaged to June."

"And that is what you shall continue to believe." Dale exhaled. "If you consider yourself a part of my lab, please understand that my personal relationships aren't something you should worry about. What you saw here—I'd really appreciate it if you could keep it to yourself."

Dale's fingers squeezed tight around Greg's, as though he was trying to put up a brave front. Greg held on to him.

"I'm not feeling well right now—Greg will be sending me home. June has her own fiancée to return to tonight." Dale smiled at Penny, reaching out for a handshake.

Penny's mouth fell open. She glanced at June, who shrugged.

Privately, Greg would've cornered Penny and growled at her until she promised to keep silent about him and Dale. But Penny reached out, taking Dale's hand, and maybe Dale's was the better solution instead.

"You're an important part of my lab," Dale said, looking at Penny. "I appreciate that you're sharp and willing to experiment with new ideas. You borrow concepts from other fields and give us new directions to take our projects. I'm glad to have you as part of my team, Penny, and I'd hate to have to send you away. Is that clear?"

Penny glanced at all of them, flushing scarlet. She shook Dale's hand. "I understand. I'll mind my own business. Sorry."

"If you have questions, please do ask June. Or if you'd rather me answer them, drop me an email—I'll get to it in the morning."

Penny grimaced. "I really am sorry, Professor."

"And you're forgiven." Dale smiled, kind and beautiful. Greg wanted to pull him close. Hold him. He was precious, and Greg had never told him that before.

Penny glanced at Greg and Dale, then at June, discomfort in her eyes. Then she nodded and ducked out of the office, leaving behind a trace of lily.

For a moment, Greg glanced between Dale and June, wondering how safe it was to talk. Whether their secret could still remain one. Sam Brentwood was an exception, and so was June. But Greg didn't know Penny Fleming well at all. For all they knew, she'd return to the lab and spread the news.

"Can we trust her?" he asked.

Dale sighed, leaning into Greg's arm, fatigue slipping back into his face. "I don't know, to be honest."

"You did great with her," June said, closing the office door and locking it. "Sorry. I really did try to stop her, but she got out of the lab while I was in the middle of pipetting. Merciful gods—I'll have to redo that again—it'll be 1 AM before that's done."

Greg winced. June's experiments needed hours of prep, and having to redo all of that? He felt sorry for her.

"Work on it tomorrow," Dale said. "Take a break. Go home early, June, spend some time with Cher. You and Penny have been staying late this entire week. I'd rather you not push yourselves so hard."

"But the paper—"

"The research will still be here. Take some time off." Dale smiled tiredly, lacing his fingers with Greg's. "Go home and cuddle. Cuddling is nice."

June snorted. "You're a lot happier now than you were before, Dale. More relaxed."

"I was?" Dale nuzzled Greg's shoulder. Greg pressed a kiss to his temple.

"Yes. Remember me taking two weeks off for the vacation? You were so reluctant to let me go."

"Because I needed you to mark me." Dale glanced at Greg, a bright flush creeping up his neck.

"Why?" Greg asked, narrowing his eyes. He remembered Dale smelling like June, but Dale *needing* to smell like her? That was new. And it made him want to growl.

"So I had a reason to decline coffee with you." Dale blushed to the tops of his ears, looking away. "It was difficult to say no to you, Greg. Just so you know."

Greg blinked. Dale had smelled like birch the entire semester, since the second day of school. "You... wanted me from the start?"

Dale's throat worked. June rolled her eyes. "Gods, yes, he did," she said. "He had the basketball email open most mornings, Greg. You don't want to know what he was doing with them."

Dale's entire face was red. He looked away from Greg, picking at his shirt. "June, don't tell him more than he needs to know."

A thrill shot down Greg's spine. *What were you doing with them?* He tucked the question away for later, nuzzling Dale's hair. "So, about Penny."

Dale groaned. "We'll play it by ear. For now, the lab group still thinks I'm engaged to June. We'll keep it that way. See what Penny does."

"Fine," Greg said. He didn't know how he'd speak to Penny tomorrow, but it would probably be twice as difficult for Dale. Especially when she knew her professor was sleeping with a student. "C'mon, let's go home. You look beat."

"Yeah, you might want to take tomorrow off," June said, eyeing Dale. "I can cover for you."

"No! You do still have to work on the project." Dale frowned.

"I'll help," Greg said.

Dale sighed. Then he leaned in, pressing his nose to Greg's shoulder. "You're incredible. I think I'm really in love."

Dale hadn't said that in front of anyone else before, and from the way June's eyebrows inched up, it was something special. Greg's heart pounded, his chest too small for everything he felt for this omega.

"Then marry me," he said.

Dale looked up at him, his gaze soft, his cheeks rosy. Before Greg could kiss him, June broke the silence.

"I'm getting out before you drown me in your sap," she said, pinching her nose. But she grinned, her eyes sparkling. "You really need a break, Dale. I'm serious."

"And I'm coming back to work tomorrow," Dale said, smiling wryly. "But I may end my office hours early."

"Good," Greg said. "Maybe watch my game or something. Relax a bit."

"Yeah, do that. I'll see you guys tomorrow." June waved.

"Thanks, June," Dale said. "Say hi to Cher for

me."

It was only when the door had shut behind June, that Greg looked at Dale again, studying him. "You sure things will be fine with Penny?" he asked. He'd only known Penny for two months, since he joined Dale's lab.

Dale sagged further; he'd been pretending to be less fatigued in front of June, too. "I can only hope," he said. "But I don't want to think about it right now. Please?"

"Fine." Greg checked him over, then began gathering Dale's paperwork. Dale had a little stack that he'd always bring home with him, set on one corner of his desk.

"You really don't have to," Dale said, but he didn't move to stop Greg.

"I do because I care," Greg said. When he clipped Dale's satchel shut, he found Dale watching him, a tiny, warm smile playing on his lips.

"I meant it when I said I love you," Dale murmured. Greg's pulse quickened. He still wasn't used to hearing that.

"Love you too," he said, brushing a kiss over Dale's mouth.

In the office, with the windows dark and the streetlamps shining gold, nothing mattered quite as much as Dale in his arms, and the world at peace around them.

19
Dale

IT WASN'T until they'd returned home that the situation with Penny began to sink into Dale's thoughts. She'd walked in on them. This was the second acquaintance who knew about him and Greg, and another person who could expose their secret. Possibly bring the information closer to Bernard Hastings' ears.

With that came the risk of Dale's tenure, and maybe even his job. His stomach turned.

"Worried?" Greg asked in the bedroom doorway, a glass of water in each hand. He crossed the hardwood floors, setting the glasses on their bedside tables. Then he crawled into bed next to Dale, the scent of olive soap clinging to his skin. "How much can we trust Penny?"

"I don't know." Dale sighed, thinking over the students in his research group. Of the grad students and post-docs, his favorite had to be June, then Penny. The two didn't always agree, but they had their good points. And Dale had liked Penny enough to recommend her to Bernard Hastings.

That had been before he'd found out about the pregnancy. Now, with the child in him, he wasn't so sure he could give up Greg anymore. Wasn't sure he could bear the thought of Greg marrying someone else, even if Dale wasn't good for him.

Because as horrifying as the thought was, Dale loved this alpha. Wanted to be with him. He'd only realized it when Greg had held him in his office, promising to stay no matter what. And it felt a little like a manacle, and a little like a hot air balloon lifting him up.

At the end of the day, Greg was still his student. Dale shouldn't be sleeping with him, or carrying his child.

And now Penny knew.

"Penny has been in my lab for a couple of years. I suggested her to your father, you know."

Greg frowned, wrapping his arms around Dale. "My dad?"

"Remember the omega list?"

Greg winced. "Is he still on that?"

"Yeah," Dale said, thinking about his reply to Bernard. That had been before Dale realized he was in love. And he couldn't possibly back out of the dinner now.

"So you had Penny on that list," Greg said flatly, slanting a glance at Dale. "You know I'm not into girls."

Dale cracked a smile. "No, I did not know that. Does this mean if you find a male omega younger than me—"

"Stop that."

Sheets rustling around him, Greg leaned in, pressing a kiss to Dale's lips. His stubble scraped along Dale's jaw, and Dale curled his fingers into

Greg's boxers, pulling him closer. It was seven weeks after Greg had moved in, and Dale still hadn't had enough of him. Would possibly never have enough of this man.

"What did my dad say about her?" Greg asked.

Dale kissed him, savoring Greg's warmth. "He passed on her profile when I said she's three years older than you."

That thought sobered him up. How could Bernard Hastings even accept Dale as a son-in-law, when Dale was old enough to be Greg's father? Dale was Bernard's employee; for all Bernard knew, Dale had manipulated his son.

What would Penny think of him now, and what would she say to the rest of the lab? Would his students leave him? Would they eye him and secretly think he was perverse, for sleeping with someone their age?

"I'm twenty years older than you," Dale mumbled, glancing down at himself. Greg had never mentioned it, but Dale saw the stray blemish here, the gray hair there. His body had lost some of its definition from his youth, and if he squinted hard enough, crow's feet clustered at his eyes.

What did it mean that Dale was in love with an alpha half his age? He'd tried so hard not to get to this point. Except Greg had stayed, and Dale... had allowed him to fit their lives together. He'd allowed himself to fall in love with Greg.

Bernard Hastings would scoff at him, his lips turning down in distaste.

Dale swallowed. "I think we might've made a mistake."

Greg's lips thinned. "You mean, us?"

"Yes."

"You're not a mistake," Greg growled, pushing himself up to hover over Dale. "The baby isn't a mistake, either. I want both of you."

"You said you weren't certain about a future," Dale whispered, looking into his eyes. They'd been working on this for the past few weeks—Greg's basketball games, that game in Highton with the NY Rockets. "Are you any more certain about your future now?"

Greg paused, his mouth open, half-formed around an answer. He ran his tongue along his lip, and Dale was glad that he was giving it some thought.

Greg closed his mouth, looking at the sheets. Dale saw the hesitation in his eyes—they could not proceed.

Just as Dale couldn't set aside their age difference, Greg couldn't envision a future for them, either.

"Are you sure you want to marry me?" Dale whispered, trailing his fingers over Greg's heart. "I don't want you to regret it."

Greg breathed out, pressing his lips to Dale's forehead, his breath puffing through Dale's hair. "I can't promise you my future," he said quietly. "I don't even know what's in it. Not for more than a week at a time."

Dale slipped his fingers into Greg's hands, holding on to him. "You'll have a future if you believe in it."

Greg's throat worked; pain flashed through his eyes. Could they really have a future together?

They were both still broken.

"Let's think about something else," Dale murmured, caressing Greg's jaw. "Let's take things one day at a time. I'm here. And I'm all yours."

Greg cracked a smile, warmth glimmering in his gaze. When he leaned in to kiss Dale, heat sparked between them, and Dale's body arched into his alpha's touch.

Someday, maybe Greg would believe in a future. Then he would leave Dale, to find an omega who was worthy of his love.

IN THE days following, they trod carefully at school. Dale texted June before he arrived at the lab—she reported no leaks. In the afternoons, Dale stepped into his lectures with bated breath, scanning the crowd. No one said anything, and hardly anyone glanced between him and Greg.

The first time he met Penny at the lab again, Penny watched him with trepidation in her eyes. She glanced warily at June, too. No one else gave Dale a second glance. They didn't know about the scandal in his private life, then, and Dale was happy to keep it that way.

"I'm sorry about the other day," Penny said, her gaze lowered. The cheery light in her expression had vanished, and dark splotches lingered under her eyes.

Dale winced. He hadn't expected his relationship with Greg to give her sleepless nights. "Don't worry about it. I value you as a part of my team, Penny, and I hope you understand that."

She glanced dubiously up at him. "Really?"

"I believe in second chances," Dale said. He believed in second chances for everyone but himself — the baby was a miracle, and anything that happened with Greg was a dream. "Have you spoken to June?"

"Briefly." Penny bit her lip. "June's been cool about it. I'm really sorry for intruding."

She seemed genuine. In that moment, Dale knew he could trust her, more than he trusted the risks of his pregnancy, or Greg staying for its duration. So he patted Penny on the shoulder, giving her a smile. "As far as I'm concerned, you didn't see anything, okay?"

"Okay." She smiled weakly at him, hesitating. "For what it's worth, I've thought things over. I hope it goes well. Things between, you know, you and your bondmate."

Dale stared at her, his skin flushing hot. He'd fantasized about being Greg's bondmate before. Several times, in fact. But to have someone else think they were bonded, and send them goodwill... It gave him hope that this relationship could work. That not everyone would glance askance at them, thinking Dale perverse for mating with his student.

And if Greg truly wanted to bond with him... Dale's heart thumped, the old scar on his wrist itching.

"Thank you," he said, his throat tight. "If you encounter any problems with June, please feel free to tell me about them."

Penny beamed, light returning to her eyes. Something lifted from Dale's chest. "Thank you," she said. "For having me in your lab."

Dale spread his arms, offering a hug. Penny stepped into them, relief rolling off her in waves.

BY THE next week, their schedules were crammed full.

Greg's classes became more intense as his professors scrambled to finish their lectures, piling homework and assignments on top of large group projects.

Dale graded his assignments feverishly — he'd tried to lessen the students' workload toward the end of the semester. Somehow, that had never worked through the years. There were always more things he wanted to cover in his classes, more things he thought his students should know.

Greg stopped visiting Dale's office. He'd taken to delivering Dale's lunches between classes, and when noon rolled around, Dale would find him tucked away on a bench, his laptop open, textbooks and papers spread across the table.

Dale didn't have the heart to interrupt him. When he found Greg's study spot by the lecture halls, he took time off his own break, walking by the open atrium to peek on his alpha. Greg would frown, his eyes scanning his laptop screen, and on occasion, he'd remember to take a bite of his sandwich.

Sometimes, Dale would tuck himself into the space between a potted plant and a wall, and send Greg a message. *Eat your lunch.*

The first time it happened, Greg smiled, took a bite of his sandwich, and forgot about it for the next five minutes. So Dale sent another text. *Finish your sandwich. 10min to class.*

When Greg finally dragged his eyes from the

screen, he blinked at the text. Then he looked around, his lips curving into a grin when he found Dale watching him. Dale's heart skipped.

You could share the bench, Greg texted.

That would be too obvious, Dale answered.

But his presence kept Greg from working, so he left the atrium, heading back to his office with a smile.

As the days edged closer to the finals, Greg stayed up later at nights, his project deadlines looming. Dale accompanied him when he could, lounging on the couch after dinner. He'd fall asleep to Greg's typing, and when he woke, he'd be in their bed, or cradled in Greg's arms as Greg carried him to the bedroom.

It was sweet of Greg. Adorable. It was frightening, how much Greg meant to him. And maybe there was something intrinsically wrong with Dale, with him loving an alpha so young.

But there was no going back now. Dale was in love, and he couldn't retract his feelings even if he wanted to.

20
Greg

GREG SLAMMED the Porsche door shut, jogging up the short path to his old apartment. In the four weeks since he was last here, nothing had changed. The grass was still lush and trimmed, the trees were perfectly manicured, and the apartment buildings were freshly painted.

Not so different from Dale's place, except his parents had paid for his lodging here, whereas Dale's apartment was something Dale owned. Not something Bernard Hastings could hold over his son's head.

Greg scanned the closed windows of his apartment, but didn't enter. The last time he'd visited, it had been to grab the rest of his textbooks, and a shirt or two he'd missed. The rest of his things weren't important—this place wasn't home anymore, not since he'd begun living with Dale.

And Dale was the reason why he'd come back at 7 AM on a Saturday... not that Dale knew Greg had slipped out of bed.

Greg had gotten a gift delivered to his own apartment, so it wouldn't somehow arrive early to Dale's mailbox and ruin the surprise.

Dale was still asleep back home, the sheets tucked around him. Greg had turned off the alarms and sneaked out of the apartment, careful to close the doors quietly behind himself.

At the mailboxes, Greg searched out his own. Inside, a stack of cards and magazines and flyers had been crammed into the tiny space. For a moment, he held his breath—the package hadn't arrived.

But the email had said *Product delivered*, so Greg pried the wads of paper out, his heart skipping when he found the plastic envelope squashed at the very top.

It was wrinkled, folded at the corners, and slipped around the product inside. Greg tore it open.

With the receipt came a bundle of printed white fabric—cartoon rabbits on a bunny-shaped onesie, the one with the fluffy tail that Dale had laughed at. It was tiny, maybe twelve inches long, and in another seven months, a baby would wear this. Their baby.

Dale would love this. And Greg wanted to surprise him with it.

Grinning, Greg slung the onesie over his shoulder, sorting through the mail. Mostly junk. A card from his mom. Some wedding invites from his friends from school. He emptied the mailbox, kept the onesie and cards, and headed back to his car, wondering how he'd wake Dale up in bed. With a kiss? With the onesie stretched across his chest? Over his belly?

As he made his way back down the sidewalk, Greg opened the envelope from his mom. It wasn't until he looked up that he found his father standing by his car, a disapproving frown on his face.

Greg froze. *Crap.*

Bernard Hastings stepped forward, a deep frown creasing his forehead. "You haven't been here in a while. I've dropped by a few times to see if you were home."

No, he hadn't. And he'd been ignoring his dad's prying texts for the past few weeks. "Hey, Dad."

Bernard's gaze slid to Greg's shoulder, where he'd left the bunny onesie, its fuzzy tail sticking up. Greg cleared his throat. Not his dad's business. Especially not right now, when the pregnancy was just over a month in.

"What's that?" Bernard asked, nodding at the onesie.

"It's a gift."

"Have you chosen an omega?" Greg's father sniffed at him, his gaze appraising. "Or are you still with Ivan? You're still wearing that same hibiscus scent."

Who's Ivan? Greg blinked, his mind racing. *Oh.*

When he'd first moved in with Dale, Greg had mentioned the imaginary omega to his dad a few times, to throw him off Dale's scent. Then he'd forgotten the name in the midst of ignoring his father's texts.

As Bernard Hastings stared him down, Greg breathed in, his thoughts filling with a sleepy-eyed professor. *Yes,* he wanted to say. *I've chosen my omega and it's Dale Kinney.* But his father was the college president, and Dale would lose his job in a day. "I haven't decided yet."

"Good," Bernard said, checking his watch. "I've picked out a few better choices for you. Dale Kinney suggested Penny Fleming from his lab. I've been trying to find someone more suitable, but she's still the most prominent omega I've come across. Her father is the police chief. She comes from a good family. A marriage to her will boost your status."

Greg's stomach had flipped at Dale's name. Then it had begun to sink in slow-motion. He remembered Dale's office, and Penny's wide eyes last week. The way she'd looked at him and Dale, scandalized. "Penny? I know her. She's okay."

"So you'll be agreeable to dinner with her, then. I've reached out to her for an introductory meeting next week."

Sounds like a mess. "Finals are next week. Everyone's gonna be busy."

"Penny has agreed." Bernard checked his phone. "And so has your professor. You owe it to them to be there."

"Da—Kinney will be there?"

"Yes. He replied to me two weeks ago."

"Two *weeks* ago?" Dale never said anything about the dinner. *What the fuck?* Two weeks was before the mishap with Penny, but surely Dale wouldn't agree to this train wreck of a dinner. Why hadn't he told Greg about it?

"Is something the matter?" Bernard raised an eyebrow.

"No," Greg said. "Just seems redundant that you'll ask my—my professor along."

"He seemed interested in matching the two

of you," Bernard said. "So I'll see you at The Apex this Wednesday, at 7:30 PM. Yes?"

For a heartbeat, Greg wanted to say no. He wanted to tell his father he already had an omega. He wanted to say, *Screw that crap about my status,* because he didn't need his father paying anything for him. He didn't need favors from his dad.

Except it would also involve telling his dad who his omega was, and Dale had been talking about tenure, had been bouncing on his feet when he said his lab had published eighty journal articles. Dale had talked about the newest students in his lab group, had beamed when a piece of equipment came in two weeks ago.

Greg couldn't possibly take that away from his omega.

"Fine," Greg said, his heart thumping loud in his chest. "I'll go."

Bernard Hastings nodded, satisfied. Then he turned and paused. "I hope you'll make full use of your lodgings here. It's a waste spending your time with an omega you won't marry."

Greg opened his mouth. He wanted to marry Dale, mark him. He wanted to tell his dad that. Instead, he watched as Bernard drove off, the rumble of the silver Rolls Royce fading into the background.

Greg stepped up to his own car, dropping the cards into the passenger's bucket seat. The few times he'd asked Dale to marry him, Dale hadn't given him an answer. He'd smiled and looked down, but there was always a shadow in his eyes.

And maybe Greg could understand why Dale had agreed to the dinner. Dale didn't think he was good enough for Greg. And Greg couldn't give him a positive answer on his future.

Greg shut the Porsche's door, looking down at its sleek console. Everything else about his life — the luxury, the apartment, the paid tuition — he could do without. But he had a fondness for his car, and he hated that he liked it this much. Especially when his father had given it to him for his twenty-first birthday, and it screamed *money*.

He set the onesie down on his lap, pulling out of the parking lot. Did Dale think Greg was a spoiled rich kid who couldn't support himself? That Greg had gone from one paid apartment to another, so he could leech off his professor?

Because Greg could damn well support himself, plus Dale and their baby. He didn't need his father's help doing it. And maybe that was the solution — moving to somewhere they wouldn't be judged. Except Dale's job was in Meadowfall.

I'll find a job for when semester ends. Save up some money. Buy Dale a ring. See if he says yes.

He needed to believe in his future. But he remembered the fire, remembered Tony's pale face as he gasped for air, and his stomach shriveled.

How could he promise Dale anything, when life was so easily snatched away from them? When Greg had done everything he could to save his best friend, and he'd still failed? What if they moved out of Meadowfall, and Greg couldn't support them somehow?

He still didn't have an answer.

Fifteen minutes later, he pulled up in front of Dale's apartment. Greg breathed in, then out, counting to five.

Dale was still asleep. As far as he was concerned, Greg had just left the bed. And Greg wanted to present the rabbit outfit to his omega, watch his reaction to it.

Heart skipping, Greg headed through the apartment, stopping at their bedroom doorway. For a moment, he watched as Dale stirred, the sheets rustling off his back. This seemed so... normal. Peaceful.

Dale rubbed his eyes, peering at Greg's half of the bed. Then he looked up. "Where'd you go?" he mumbled, his voice rough with sleep. "You weren't here."

"I was getting you something." Heart thudding, Greg stepped over to the bed, holding out the onesie.

Dale squinted at it, then slipped his glasses on. His mouth fell open.

"Like it?" Greg murmured, crawling onto the bed. He lay the onesie on Dale's chest. "It looks big on you."

"I—" Dale blinked rapidly, pressing his hand over the outfit. "You bought this. It's so soft. It even has the bunny tail."

"Yeah, you laughed when I showed it to you."

"I can't believe you bought it for the baby. Our baby." When Dale looked up, his eyes were damp with a sheen of tears. Greg swore.

"C'mon, I didn't do that to make you cry." He gathered Dale up in his arms, pulling him close, breathing in his hibiscus scent. "Thought you'd like it."

"I love it. I—I wasn't expecting this so soon.

It's just been seven weeks."

"Long enough to me."

Greg kissed him, and Dale wrapped his arms around Greg's waist, lips parting for him. "I'm looking forward to our baby," Greg said.

"Oh, gods, Greg. I love you." Dale's fingers pressed into his skin, and Greg straddled his omega, kissing his mouth, his nose, his cheeks. When he pulled away, he found Dale with his throat flushed, his eyes sparkling. "The onesie is perfect. I don't even—I wasn't expecting you to buy it when you showed it to me."

The onesie had pooled on his belly. Greg leaned back, watching as Dale inspected the tiny sleeves on the garment, the snap-on buttons and the fluffy tail.

In the sunlight streaming through the room, Dale's hair was lit a vivid coppery brown, his eyes bright green. Before this relationship with Dale, when Greg had been watching his professor step in and out of class, Dale hadn't grinned much at all. He'd go over his lessons, a smile occasionally on his lips.

But that was nothing compared to the awe on his face right now, the spark of excitement in his eyes.

Greg's chest was way too small for the affection he felt. He wanted to preserve this moment forever, this image of Dale happy.

He slid his phone out, snapping a photo of Dale, capturing his lit eyes, his slender fingers, the onesie stretched out along his body.

"Hey!" Dale yelped, yanking the onesie further down. "I'm naked!"

Greg blinked. "Oh."

"'Oh'?" Dale narrowed his eyes. "Surely that doesn't mean you never look at me, Greg Hastings."

He canted his hips up, spreading them, and Greg smirked. "'Course I look at you. I just wanted a picture of you and the onesie."

Dale raised a skeptical eyebrow, so Greg opened his phone gallery, showing him the picture. In it, Dale's delight had been real, and he'd been preoccupied with the outfit, his face radiant in the sunlight.

"I look old," Dale said, frowning.

Greg stared. "What? You look fine."

Dale took the phone from him, zooming in on his hair, where there were a few streaks of gray. Then he showed Greg his abdomen, and his face. "See?"

"I don't see it. You look good." Greg tapped out of the gallery, pressing a kiss to his lips. "You look like someone I want to marry."

Dale's breath hitched. "I'm too—"

"You're perfect," Greg said, settling on the bed next to him. He started up the phone camera again. This time, he switched the view to the secondary camera, and angled it so they were both in the image—Dale with his glasses on, Greg with his hair mussed. "C'mon, smile."

Dale leaned out of the image. "You're not posting this on Facebook, are you?"

"'Course not. But I want pictures of us. I want pictures of our family."

"Our..." Dale looked down, stroking his still-flat abdomen.

"Want a photo of me kissing it?" Greg smiled, handing Dale the phone. Then he kissed around Dale's navel, down the line of his belly, to the bare skin right before his groin. "Or I'll blow a raspberry here."

Greg puffed his cheeks and pressed his lips to Dale's skin, and Dale pushed his face away, laughing. "No!"

"Okay, fine. What about a picture?" Greg kissed his belly, right over where the baby was. And Dale blushed, his smile mellowing.

"All right." When Dale took the picture, the look in his eyes had softened. Greg wished Dale could see himself the way Greg did—the way he shone with his kindness, his humor, his affection.

Greg kissed all the way up Dale's chest, to his lips. Then he looked at the picture Dale had taken, of him and their unborn baby. And a low, hot possessiveness growled in his chest.

"Mine," Greg whispered, kissing him on the mouth. He traced his wrist along Dale's jaw, down his throat, to his chest and belly and cock, marking Dale as his.

Dale flushed scarlet, but he watched Greg, a tiny smile on his lips. "Yours," he murmured.

"Gonna marry me?"

"I'll think about it."

Greg kissed him again. Then he settled down beside Dale, angling the camera back at them. "Are you smiling for this one?"

"I will." Dale nestled close. Greg snapped a picture of them together, Dale more at ease with the camera than before.

"You look good," Greg whispered.

"I do not."

Greg slipped his arms around his omega, hugging him anyway. Next week, Greg would have his finals. Then he'd start working, buy his omega a ring with his own money. Start working full-time. Make enough to support his family, instead of relying on his father and his conditional gifts. But first, he had to get through that damn dinner with his father and Penny.

"You agreed to dinner with my dad," he said, frowning. "Why didn't you tell me?"

Dale blinked. Then his eyes widened. "Oh. Shit. I forgot—I thought... Well, I really do think Penny would be a better omega for you. Except that was before you told me about the not-being-into-girls thing."

Greg stared at him, incredulous. "I'm not marrying anyone else but you."

Dale squirmed. "You say that, but you aren't looking at yourself, Greg. You're so young. So full of potential. You have bounds of energy and confidence and strength, and some days I can't keep up with you."

He looked down at his stomach, his expression faltering. "I'm still not sure about myself," Dale said. "How can I be a good father? I've never had practice. I couldn't even bear a child until now. I don't know if I'm fit to raise a child—"

"You're perfect," Greg said, kissing his lips. "Stop thinking about Charles. You're not even married to him anymore. You don't need to believe what his parents say. And your body and mind are two different things. Just because you couldn't conceive doesn't make you a bad parent."

Greg thought about his own father, who sneered and said *Tony wasn't your bondmate. Move on. You'll do better spending your life with someone worthwhile,* and his gut simmered with old rage.

Dale had never once put down his relationship with Tony. He'd listened to Greg talk about Tony's death, and he'd never judged Greg for any of it, not even when Greg knew the fault was his. And that would make Dale a better father than Bernard Hastings ever would be.

"You're patient, and kind, and I've never met anyone as humble as you," Greg said, kissing the tip of Dale's nose. "I want you to be my baby's father."

Dale met his eyes, a little skeptical, but also trusting and warm. "I'll try to believe it," he said, linking their fingers together. "I don't think I can back out of the dinner, though. I'm not sure your dad will like that."

"It would be so much easier with anyone but Penny." Greg sighed, pressing his forehead to Dale's. "Maybe suggest another omega to him next time."

Dale chuckled, brushing his lips over Greg's cheek. "Okay. But let's not talk about that."

"What do you want to talk about?"

"The onesie. We're going to have a nursery, aren't we? And a photo album. And we'll need to do all the research about raising a child."

"Yeah, we do."

"And that's seven months away," Dale said, his eyes soft. "Can you believe we'll be fine until then?"

Greg opened his mouth, hesitating. He

remembered Tony again, and the flames razing up the dry curtain. Remembered Tony's last gasping breaths. Remembered his own carelessness and stupidity, hating himself for it. "I'll try."

"Good," Dale whispered, kissing him. "We'll take things a month at a time."

21
Dale

DESPITE DALE'S fervent pleas for Wednesday to vanish, it didn't.

On Monday, he distributed the final exam through the exam hall, watching as his students scribbled on their answer sheets, tapping frantically on their calculators. Amongst them, Greg worked steadfastly through his questions, glancing up when Dale passed his desk, recognizing him by scent alone. He smiled, and Dale smiled back.

On Tuesday, Dale made pulled pork, the recipe he'd told Greg about when they'd first had dinner at El Asado. Greg kissed him when dinner was over, tasting like wine.

On Wednesday, Dale paced in his office, his attention anchored to the ticking wall clock. June had banned him from the lab, and Dale needed to take his mind off the dinner. It was three hours away.

Bernard Hastings was shrewd. He would smell his son on Dale, see the way they exchanged glances, and maybe he'd be able to deduce their relationship from that. Or maybe Penny would blurt a detail, and the truth would be laid bare. It would be a disaster.

His knees weak, Dale flopped into his chair, opening his email. The pictures of Greg in the basketball newsletters calmed him a little, allowed him to remember the games he'd attended.

Greg's games had slowed in frequency lately; Dale had watched every one of them, though. He remembered Greg searching him out during the halftime breaks, remembered them driving to the Highton stadium to watch the NY Rockets. They'd covered their knees with a rumpled blanket and held hands beneath it, and no one had given them a second glance.

Those weeks had been a dream, and maybe with this dinner, it would all be over.

Dale wished he hadn't accepted Bernard's invite. It had been a stupid decision. But if he didn't show up... Bernard Hastings would scorn him either way, wouldn't he?

At 5 PM, the office door opened. Dale jumped. Greg stepped in, backpack slung over his shoulder, his shirt clinging to his pecs. Dale sucked in a deep breath, smiling. "How did your paper go?"

"Good. Couple of questions I wasn't sure about." Greg studied him, his eyes locking on Dale's face. "You look like you're scared to death."

"I am." Dale wrung his hands. "June banned me from the lab, so I've been stuck in here all afternoon."

"That's a long time."

"I think I shouldn't attend the dinner."

"You probably should." Greg winced. "My dad wouldn't have minded if you declined, but if you accept and drop out, he'll throw a fit."

Dale groaned, covering his face. Bernard Hastings would fire him, wouldn't he? "I'm still convinced he'll find out about us."

"He won't." Greg set his backpack on the couch. "You still have the scent suppressants?"

"Yes, but I don't know if they'll be enough." Dale pulled the two bottles out from his drawer, setting them by his laptop. Then he rounded the desk, burrowing into Greg's chest. "Help."

"Help with what?" Greg locked the door with a resounding click. He wrapped his arm around Dale's waist, pressing his palm to Dale's chest. "Shit, your heart's pounding."

"You think?"

Greg pulled Dale against his own chest, one arm on his back, the other around his waist. In the tight grip of his embrace, Dale finally felt secure, felt like he wouldn't shake out of his skin.

"Gods, you feel good," he whispered, breathing in, then out. Greg's scent surrounded him, all sharp aspen and musk, and it was a scent that he had come to associate with safety. Belonging. Home.

Greg's breath puffed through his hair, warm. He pressed kisses to the top of Dale's head, and Dale tried to sink further into his chest, mold himself to his alpha so they couldn't be pulled apart.

"Whatever happens today, remember that I love you," Greg murmured, running his hands up Dale's back, then down. He worked his thumbs into the knots in Dale's neck, easing the tension there, one spot at a time. Dale moaned.

"I need... I need more." Dale curled into his alpha, slipping his hands under Greg's shirt, just to feel Greg's warm skin against his palms. Nothing mattered outside Greg's arms. Not his job, not his tenure, not Bernard Hastings. In the heat of Greg's body, all Dale wanted was a shred of refuge, and he found it in Greg's lips on his ear, Greg's fingers massaging his shoulders. "I need to relax. Or forget. Or something. Please."

"Yeah, you do." Greg slipped his arms around Dale's back, scooping him off his feet. Then he stepped around the room, releasing Dale into his chair.

Before he could lean back, Dale cupped Greg's face, pulling him close for a kiss. He wanted Greg closer. Wanted Greg to not leave him.

Greg's lips slid soft against his. His tongue tangled with Dale's, silky and damp, and electricity jolted down Dale's spine. He spread his legs, inviting Greg closer. But Greg only pulled away, his gaze raking over Dale's body.

Then he glanced sideways, at Dale's laptop screen. Greg raised his eyebrows. "You were looking at me?"

Dale squirmed. He'd left the basketball newsletter open on the screen—it had been an attempt at distracting himself. It was his favorite email, too, the one with Greg's picture at the top, the email subject in bold: *Greg Hastings named this season's MVP!*

"I like looking at you," Dale mumbled.

"That was an old email." Greg smirked, nudging Dale's further knees apart. "June said you do things with those emails. Were you really that obvious about them?"

A surge of heat washed through Dale's face. Two months ago, June had caught him in his office, rubbing himself through his pants. She never let him forget that. "I didn't even have my cock out," Dale mumbled. "She only smelled the musk."

Greg's eyes gleamed. He knelt between Dale's legs, rubbing his hands over Dale's thighs, the heat of his palms soaking through thin fabric. "Remember what you were thinking about?"

Dale gulped, pushing his hips forward, trying to tempt Greg into touching higher. "You're always in your jersey in the newsletters. Take a guess."

"Too many possibilities." Greg pressed a kiss to Dale's inner thigh, then another, trailing his lips up to his hip. Then he kissed the spot just next to Dale's cock, blowing through cloth. Humid air flooded around Dale's skin, hot like Greg's mouth. "Tell me."

Dale's throat went dry. He wanted to push past Greg's lips, wanted Greg to strip him and suck him. Greg dragged his mouth lightly over the tip of Dale's cock, his lip catching on the cloth of his pants. Dale groaned. "Oh gods, you have no idea how many times I've thought about you. I wanted you all sweaty, pinning me. I wanted you keeping me open with your knees. I wanted you just watching me come."

A smirk crept over Greg's lips. "How many times did you come, thinking about me?"

Dale's cheeks scorched. He'd looked at Greg's photos with his hand down his pants, knowing no other professor did that. He was terrible. And he had come so hard every time, spread open on his bed, pretending Greg was behind him, holding him down, pounding into his ass. "I—I don't remember. Maybe twenty. Forty. Fifty."

Greg's smirk widened. He slipped his fingers into Dale's belt, tugging it open, the length of it pressing around Dale's waist. A reminder that Greg could touch any part of him, and it would feel exquisite. "And you wanted my knot?"

"Fuck, yes." Dale held his breath when the belt loosened. Greg undid Dale's too-tight pants, sliding the zipper down against his cock. His bulge pushed out past the V of his fly, and Greg eyed it, rubbing his thumb down the underside of Dale's cock, his touch muffled through the cotton. "I wanted you breeding me. Every time."

A growl rumbled through Greg's chest. Musk slipped through the air between them, and Greg leaned in, licking over the damp spot on Dale's briefs, tasting him. "Wet for me?"

"Yes." Dale groaned, pushing his hips up. Greg held him down against the chair, took Dale's tip into his mouth, underwear and all. He ground his tongue against the sensitive spot on Dale's head, sending pleasure through Dale's body. Dale panted, his fingers digging into the leather of his chair. "Greg, please."

Greg ran his lips over the crown of Dale's head, licking it. The wetter it became, the more keenly Dale felt his touch, until the fabric of his briefs was soaked around his tip, stretched thin, his ruddy skin visible through its weave.

"You're so goddamn hard," Greg murmured,

kissing down Dale's cock, then back up, his tongue catching on damp cotton. Then he took Dale's cock into his mouth, sucking it, and Dale felt the pressure all the way in his balls. He arched, rocking up. Greg paused, leaving Dale's tip between his lips. "You said you had condoms in your office. What were you using those for?"

Dale blushed. This had been a secret; even June didn't know about them. "Plugs. I have a couple here."

Greg's gaze sharpened. He glanced at the desk drawers. "You've mentioned that once. Back when you were in heat."

"I might've used them. Thinking about you." He'd fucked himself with them, too, late at night, pretending they were Greg's knot inside him. Pretending Greg was filling him with cum over and over.

And a slow smile spread across Greg's lips. "Where are they?"

"Bottom drawer. Inside the box."

He held his breath, waiting as Greg leaned away, sliding the drawer open. Behind stacks of notebooks was a cardboard box, completely white. Discreet. Greg pulled it out, picking it open. Then he smiled, examining first the smaller red plug, then the larger glass one, that Dale now knew was a little narrower than Greg's knot. He hadn't needed the plugs in a while.

Greg met his eyes, setting the glass plug on Dale's desk. He closed the box, returned it to the drawer, and leaned in. "You'll wear that through dinner."

"What?" Dale squeaked. On his desk, the

glass plug was teardrop-shaped, with a flared base on its wide end. He thought about it inside him, spreading him open, and quailed.

"Whatever happens during the dinner, you'll remember that it's my knot in you," Greg said, his eyes gleaming. "If I pretend to like Penny, or if you even think about getting jealous... give it a squeeze. Remember who put it there. When dinner's over tonight, you'll take my knot."

Dale thought about Greg bending him over, sliding into him, swelling inside him, and his cock ached. "You're not giving me your knot now?"

"Later," Greg said, rubbing his knuckles over Dale's cock, a dark promise in his eyes.

Dale whined, squirming. He wanted his alpha inside him. Wanted Greg filling him with seed. Wanted Greg stretching his body open, pleasuring him, until all he knew was his alpha and nothing else.

Greg pressed a light kiss to Dale's cock, then curled his fingers into Dale's pants and briefs. "Up."

Dale kicked his shoes off, lifted his hips, then his legs, so Greg could slide his clothes off. His pants and briefs landed on the floor with a rustle. Dale fitted his knees around Greg's shoulders, shivering when Greg's gaze raked over his bare thighs, his balls, his cock.

"Very nice," Greg murmured, pushing himself up on his knees, his fingers whispering over Dale's shirt. With each button that popped, cool air brushed over Dale's skin, tightening his nipples. "Gonna take that plug for me?"

"Yes." Dale swallowed. Maybe it wasn't a

good idea. But he needed the distraction, needed to know he belonged to Greg, and he couldn't wear Greg's scent tonight.

Greg smiled, kissing Dale's nipples. He stood and pressed kisses up Dale's chest, up his collarbones to his throat. When he met Dale's mouth, his tongue slid in, hot and possessive. Dale moaned. He needed Greg. Needed to feel him inside, needed to feel as though Greg wanted him.

"Fuck me, please," he gasped, finding Greg's hand, pushing it down on his cock. Greg ran his fingers over Dale's balls, squeezing them, stroking around them, until Dale squirmed, his hole damp. Then Greg wrapped his hand around Dale, pumped him, and the pleasure in his cock intensified.

"Fuck my hand," Greg whispered against his lips. Dale whined, bracing his feet against the floor, thrusting up. His flushed tip pushed out of his alpha's fist, his foreskin pulling back, and it was lewd, slick. And he couldn't stop.

With each thrust, Greg's fist tightened, forcing pleasure through Dale's body. Dale whimpered, his hips jerking unevenly as he tried to keep his momentum, fucking up, his alpha witness to how desperate Dale was. Except Dale grew so close to the edge that he couldn't stop trembling, his precum dripping down Greg's fingers.

Greg planted his hand on Dale's thigh, pushing him back down against the seat.

"Very good," he whispered, sliding his hand down to Dale's base, just holding him. Dale's cock jutted up, exposed and hungry, aching for release. Dale gasped, squirming, and Greg kissed his parted lips. "Ready?"

"Yes," Dale hissed.

Greg pulled his hand away, leaving Dale's cock neglected. He wiped down the plug with his shirt, rubbing it over Dale's tip, catching streaks of precum. "Spread for me."

Dale's cheeks burned. They were in his office. And here he was, curling his legs up, pulling his cheeks open to show his student his hole.

Greg's nostrils flared. He breathed in Dale's musk, a hard line in his own jeans. Then he reached behind, pulling his phone out. "Fuck, you look good."

Dale's entire face scorched. "You're going to take a picture?"

Greg lowered his phone, meeting his eyes. "You don't want me to?"

"I—" Secretly, the thought gave Dale a dark thrill. Holding himself open, spreading for his alpha, letting his slick opening be captured on photo. It was humiliating. And it made his cock throb harder. "I want you to."

Greg's lips curved in a smile. He held his phone up, and Dale dug his fingers into his cheeks, pulling them apart. Greg growled, snapped the picture, and shoved the phone in his pocket. "Gods. I want to be inside."

Greg rubbed his own cock through his pants, his gaze dragging down Dale's body, from his chest to his belly to his hips. Dale leaked. "Then get inside."

"You're so damn needy." Greg took the plug, rubbing its cool, hard surface along Dale's cock. Then he touched the point of the plug to Dale's tip, gathering his precum, slicking it over rounded glass. When all of it was covered, he slid it down Dale's cock, over his balls, to his hole.

But he didn't push it inside. Instead, Greg circled his hole with the plug, a light, steady touch, until Dale quivered, his hole clenching. "Greg, you can't just tease!"

Greg met his eyes, pressed the plug against his entrance, and pushed. Dale's body stretched open around it, a cool solid weight making its way inside.

"You're so tight," Greg murmured. "Fuck."

"Maybe I need your cock first," Dale panted, his hole squeezing around the cool glass plug.

"You're gonna take my knot just like that." Greg slid the plug out, until it almost left Dale's body.

Then he pushed it back in, stretching Dale wider and wider, until half of the teardrop had disappeared into his body, a thick solid weight. Unlike Greg's knot, which swelled inside him, the plug required Dale's hole to stretch wider than usual. And it snared every bit of his attention, feeling himself open up, feeling Greg slide the plug in and out of him.

Greg stopped pushing when the plug was halfway in, and held it there.

"Greg," Dale whined, his legs shaking, his hole spread open. And Greg could see every bit of it. "I need more."

"Really?"

"Yes!"

"What about this?" Greg whispered, then slid the widest part of the plug in. Dale arched, his body opening around it, opening for his alpha.

"F-fuck," Dale gasped, his cock jerking. "I-I can't—F-feels so good."

"It'll feel better later," Greg said, pressing on the plug, until the widest part of the teardrop pushed past his hole, and Dale's body closed around the thinner neck between bulb and flared base. The plug sat inside him like a knot, cool and heavy, and Dale's body hummed with pleasure.

"I'm gonna breed you when we get home," Greg said. The base of the plug pressed against Dale's cheeks.

Dale whined, thinking about Greg's cum inside him, about Greg knotting inside. Greg tugged lightly on the plug; it moved in Dale, a smooth, intimate touch.

Greg kissed up his thigh, biting lightly on his skin, his teeth gentle, sharp points. Then he kissed Dale's balls, up his cock, and licked slowly over his head, at the same time the plug shifted inside Dale.

"Come for me," Greg whispered, sucking Dale's cock into his mouth. The pressure in his cock spiked; Greg pushed the plug deeper, grinding it against Dale's prostate, and pleasure crashed through his body, his spine arching, his cock releasing spurt after spurt of cum onto Greg's tongue.

When he could think again, Dale found Greg standing over him, wiping Dale's sweat off with his own shirt. The plug was still inside. Dale stared up at his alpha, his limbs weak as jelly, his mind fuzzed over.

"I can't think," he panted.

Greg smirked. "That's what you wanted,

wasn't it?"

"Oh, gods, I don't know if this is worse." Dale rubbed his face, looking down at himself. His chest was pink, his thighs splayed around Greg's knees, his cock damp. He wasn't in any shape for a dinner. "I need all my wits about me."

"So you wanna remove the plug?" Greg dropped a kiss on his forehead. "You can—I won't mind."

Dale opened his mouth, about to say yes. It would interfere with his ability to think. But he was also going to a dinner where Greg would be looking at another omega. Where Greg would be considering other omegas as his mate, and... Dale couldn't stand the thought of that. He didn't want Greg thinking about any omegas but himself.

But maybe this had been the last fuck they'd ever have, before Bernard Hastings convinced Greg that he wanted someone younger, someone better than Dale. With the pregnancy as risky as it was, Greg didn't need to stay. He could find someone better suited to be his mate.

Dale's heart squeezed. "No, I'll keep it. I'll pretend it's your knot."

"Yeah?" Greg nuzzled Dale's temple, kissing him on the lips. He was still hard. Dale reached down, thinking about returning the favor. But Greg caught his hand, lifting it up to press kisses to his palms.

Dale's throat grew tight. Even after all this time, he still didn't believe that Greg would stay. Not when there was so much at stake, not when Dale couldn't see much about himself worth loving. "I need the plug as a reminder."

"Okay." Greg gathered Dale into his arms, kissing down his neck to his scent gland. He dragged his lips over it, then his tongue, and his teeth, and Dale's breath shuddered out of him. Was Greg going to bite?

"I still want to bond with you," Greg murmured against his skin. "You know that."

Not after tonight. But Dale nodded, his heart aching. "I know."

"We'll be fine. You'll see." Greg squeezed him. "We've been okay for almost two months. The next two years will go quick. Then you'll have tenure, and I'd have graduated."

If it were that easy! Dale sagged into Greg's chest, breathing him in. If things went south tonight... he wanted to remember Greg's scent, wanted to remember the heat of his body, the gentleness of his touch. "I can only hope."

"I love you," Greg whispered, kissing him again.

"Love you too," Dale said, closing his eyes. It was an hour until dinner. He didn't want to leave Greg's arms before then.

22
Greg

AT 7:20 PM, Greg stepped into the carpeted foyer of The Apex.

Inside the restaurant, a chandelier hung from the ceiling; two fountains ran down the sides of the lobby, lit blue, each with orange-and-white carp swimming around their miniature waterfalls. In the middle of the foyer, a host smiled—omega, from his oleander scent. "Reservations for you, sir?"

"Hi. Bernard Hastings. 7:30."

"Right this way."

Half an hour ago, he and Dale had gone home to shower. Greg had let Dale pick an outfit for him—a button-down shirt and black jeans. They'd sprayed on the scent suppressants, ten coats on each of their clothes, and Dale had climbed into the Porsche with Greg.

Three minutes ago, Greg had dropped Dale off amidst the boutiques and antique stores along Prime Road, where the rest of Meadowfall's more-expensive stores were. It should take him five minutes to walk to The Apex.

Greg followed the host past the general dining area, into an elevator with silvery walls. The doors slid shut, and the numbers blinked. On the third floor, the host showed the way out into a corridor of private rooms—some enclosed within mirrored walls, some with wide glass windows overlooking the restaurant's garden dining area.

The Apex was one of the taller buildings in Meadowfall, built five years ago when an influx of wealthy folk moved into town. Greg remembered his father grinning with the news. *This will increase the College's attendance,* Bernard Hastings had said. *We'll hire more professors, increase its prestige over the next few years.*

Greg had shrugged at that point, too distracted by the camping trip with Tony to care.

At the end of the hallway, the host stood by an open door. Two picture windows met at the far side of the room, the sunset sky beyond filled with deep pinks and golds. His father sat at a wide square table, Penny Fleming to his left. The air carried a trace of poplar and lily; they hadn't been here long.

Greg breathed past the thudding of his heart, nodding at them. "Dad. Penny."

"You're early," his father said, scrutinizing him. Dressed in a coat and tie, he looked older than usual, his long face stern, his eyes disapproving.

Nothing new there. Greg shrugged, taking a seat across from him. "Traffic was light."

Penny gave him an apologetic smile. She'd dressed up, too, leaving behind her lab outfit for a demure dress. "Hello," she said, glancing past his shoulder, as though expecting Dale to show up. "Sorry for the inconvenience."

"It's not an inconvenience to Gregory,"

Bernard said, cracking a smile at her. "He's been looking for an omega for a while."

Penny glanced at Greg. Then her nostrils flared, and Greg knew she couldn't smell Dale on him. Her eyebrows lifted with surprise.

Maybe he should've contacted her in advance. With Dale nervous before the dinner, he'd forgotten about texting Penny, asking her to play along. "I'm not sure I need you to pick out an omega for me, Dad."

Without looking at him, Penny nodded slightly to show that she'd gotten his message: *I'm still with Dale.* And Greg was suddenly glad that Dale had been polite with her the night she walked in on them—she was playing along with the secret now, and maybe she wasn't the nosy bitch he'd thought her to be.

Bernard chuckled. "Gregory always says he isn't looking, but he is. You two have met in Dale Kinney's lab, haven't you?"

"Yes, we have." Penny smiled, her gaze flickering to the doorway. Greg wanted to follow her glance, catch Dale's entrance, but it would be far too obvious. "I've been working in Dale's lab for three years, ever since I was an undergrad."

"How old are you, again?" Bernard asked, a crinkle on his brow.

"Twenty-five, but age is just a number, isn't it?" She glanced at Greg. Greg froze, wondering if she was talking about Dale.

"Yeah. Age doesn't mean anything to me."

"It should," Bernard said, frowning at him. "You'll share more interests if you're closer in age. You'd also be more biologically compatible, but I guess a three-year difference isn't quite so terrible."

Penny's smile faded, and Greg stopped looking at her. He didn't want her pity. He'd known what he was heading into, pursuing Dale.

A waiter breezed in then, setting a glass of water down for Greg. Greg gave him his drink order, and the waiter left.

"You seem a bright young omega, Penny. Why don't you share your interests with us?" Bernard asked. "I'm sure Greg would love to know more about you."

Greg sighed. His father's watch read 7:25. Dale was taking his time, wasn't he?

Penny listed crafts and sewing, talking about each in detail. Bernard nodded along; Greg smiled at her, thinking if he showed some interest, his father would stop inviting more omegas to dinner. And maybe he would eventually accept that Greg wanted to live his own life, prestige be damned.

"I figured I would try mountain-climbing this year," Penny said, sipping from her glass. "I have a couple of friends who—"

The host moved across the doorway, and Dale stepped in with an easy smile, running his hand through his hair. "I hope I'm not late—it's not even 7:30, and you're all already here!"

Greg had intended to glance at his omega, then look away. But Dale strode into the room, his damp hair gleaming softly, his dress shirt clinging to his arms, his pants hugging his thighs. He was wearing his favorite leather shoes, all polished for the occasion, and even though Greg had already admired him back home, his omega looked radiant now, his posture at ease, his smile charming.

He was putting on an act, and he could've fooled everyone, Greg included.

"Oh," Penny said softly.

Greg glanced at her—she had been staring at him, not Dale, and Greg's stomach tightened. He'd been obvious about Dale, hadn't he?

But Bernard Hastings was still looking at Dale, that same appraising look in his eyes. He stood, reaching out to shake Dale's hand, his nostrils flaring. "Dr. Kinney," Bernard Hastings said. "Thanks for joining us."

"It's my pleasure to meet all of you," Dale said, still smiling. He nodded at Penny, never once looking at Greg. When Bernard released his hand, Dale sat in the last seat between Greg and his father, his scent a faint hibiscus. Greg's aspen scent was no longer on his skin.

"I could have remembered wrong from the last time we met," Bernard said, his nostrils flaring. "But it seems your scent has changed."

Greg tensed, and so did Dale.

"When are you expecting?" Bernard asked, the sternness melting away from his face. "Forgive me. I got ahead of myself. Congratulations to you and...?"

The breath in Greg's lungs turned into ice. After weeks of smelling the faint honey notes of Dale's pregnancy, Greg had missed it while spraying down Dale's clothes with suppressant.

Dale's smile slipped for a second. Then he grinned brighter than before—ten thousand megawatts of a fake smile. "Charles," Dale said. "Charles and I are expecting in December."

Greg's heart pounded loud and angry, a

visceral reaction he barely controlled. *Mine,* he wanted to say.

But why had Dale mentioned Charles, instead of a make-believe alpha? Had Charles been so deeply burned into his mind that it was the only other name he could think of?

Greg wanted to pummel this Charles person into mulch, and pull Dale close and hug him. Both of which he couldn't do right now.

Dale still hadn't looked at Greg. Bernard Hastings nodded approvingly. Next to Greg, Penny's mouth had fallen open. Her eyes darted between Greg and Dale, and Greg wanted to say, *That's my baby.*

"Congrats, Professor," Penny said, glancing at Greg.

Greg dipped his chin, and Penny smiled. It cooled the heat in his chest somewhat; Penny, at least, acknowledged him and Dale without judgment.

"Gregory," Bernard said, forehead creasing. "Your manners. Your professor is expecting."

He stared at his father, a million thoughts flooding through his mind. *Of course he's expecting.* But when Greg glanced at Dale, he found his omega watching him hesitantly. As though Dale was afraid Greg would snap at his father, maybe ruin this dinner.

Greg swallowed. That wasn't his intention. He held his hand out over the table, waiting for Dale. "Congrats."

Dale blinked, surprised. Then he slipped his sweaty hand into Greg's, like they hadn't held hands a hundred times before. Except they were touching in front of Bernard Hastings now. And Greg hadn't actually said congratulations, had he?

"I mean it," Greg said, smiling when he squeezed Dale's hand. Dale had thought himself infertile for so long. Charles' parents had shamed him for it. That he was carrying Greg's child now... It was a miracle. And Greg hadn't told him that enough.

Dale's shoulders relaxed by a fraction. He squeezed Greg's hand, and Greg held on a second longer, before releasing him.

"Thanks," Dale croaked.

The table was too wide. They were seated too far away for their knees to touch. But Greg stretched his leg out, hooked his foot around Dale's ankle, and Dale looked down at his cutlery, a blush rising up his neck. He was beautiful like that, beautiful every time Greg looked at him, and Greg wanted to present him with a ring. Before Dale decided he wasn't good enough.

"Greg," Penny said.

He glanced up to find his father looking between him and Dale. He'd been staring at Dale too long. *Fuck.*

"Your interests," Greg said to Penny. "You were talking about mountain-climbing."

"Oh, yes. My friends and I are planning a hiking trip this year," she said, smiling at Bernard. Bernard refocused on her. "We were planning to explore some dormant volcanoes. Did you know that there are some in California? The Panum Crater is a volcanic cone east of the Sierra Nevada—the scenery along the 395 is *beautiful*. Especially if you visit the little towns along the way, like Big Pine and Lone Tree."

"Oh yeah?" Greg leaned forward. Dale's gaze flickered toward him, but Greg didn't dare look at his omega again. So he dragged his foot up Dale's calf, then down. Dale relaxed slightly into his seat. "Found anything special when you visited?"

"Yes, actually. We found a rusted chunk of metal that looked like a spaceship." Penny grinned. "It had a pointed nose and all! I wanted to bring samples back for Professor Kinney, but he said the lab doesn't deal with metal identification."

"We should expand into that, shouldn't we?" Dale said, some of his false brightness seeping back into his voice. "A trip up north sounds great."

"Really depends on the company," Greg said. "You don't want to be stuck in a car with someone you can't stand."

"Are there people you can't stand, Greg?" Dale asked, glancing at him. He was still wary, his eyes drawn, but Greg knew Penny and his father couldn't tell.

"It's easier to count the people I like," Greg said. *And you're at the top of that list.* "I guess Penny and I could go on a trip."

"It would be fun, wouldn't it?" Penny said. "I could show you the mountains and the trails—but especially the junipers. Those are my favorite trees. What do you think, Professor? A field trip for the lab students would be great!"

Dale glanced at Bernard, then back at Penny, as though trying to gauge where he stood with his employer. "We really should! Especially if the whole lab does some prior research. I think we could all benefit from such a trip. Broaden our

269

experiences, refresh our creativity. We've been having some really successful experiments in the lab recently. I'd like to see that continue."

"How would you afford a trip like that?" Bernard asked, his eyebrows drawing down. "Surely not with your current lab funds?"

Dale quailed in his seat, his smile flattening. "I'm sure our students won't mind paying for the trip themselves."

"I wouldn't mind," Penny said.

"I wouldn't either," Greg added. Penny smiled at him.

The waiter delivered Greg's drink—a Sprite, and took Dale's order. Raspberry iced tea, like before. And Greg realized they hadn't eaten out since that very first week, back when they'd just found out Dale was pregnant. Dale's leg twitched nervously against his. Greg eased his foot out of his shoe, then slipped his toes up Dale's pants to try and calm him.

Dale jumped. "I—I'm sorry, I lost my train of thought. The field trip?"

Bernard frowned. Greg swore inwardly. He needed to stop focusing on Dale. Stop worrying about him. Except Dale still wasn't okay with this dinner. He wasn't himself at all, and every time Greg glanced at his omega, he wanted to comfort him, hold him. So Dale wouldn't feel so alone.

"Now that I'm thinking about it, I realize that lab groups hardly go anywhere," Penny said. "Mostly, there are conferences, but not everyone gets to go. A trip for all of us would be nice."

"I'd go," Greg said, swearing at himself. He needed to suck up to his dad. Take Bernard's attention off Dale. "Probably a good chance to meet more people."

Bernard smiled. Dale stiffened, his hand shaking a little when he picked up his water glass. He was nervous, and Greg hated seeing him uneasy. He needed to end this dinner, maybe convince his dad that this was the last time they all needed to meet.

Greg met Penny's eyes, putting on a smile. It felt like a wince. "Do you have siblings?"

Penny hesitated, sighing. "The short answer is yes. I have two siblings."

"So fertility runs in your family," Bernard said, his eyes glinting.

"It's a bit complex. My oldest brother, Wyatt—he's an omega. But he's actually my stepbrother. Raph and I have the same mom, but we're unmarried. So since Wyatt's already got a child, the pressure's on me to get married and all that."

"You do want children," Bernard said.

Penny nodded. "I'd like to have a couple, maybe more. Maybe I'll even have twins! Dad said my biological mom came from a large family."

Dale gulped, his eyes locking on his empty plate. Greg's heart ached. He shouldn't have talked about siblings.

Bernard nodded. "So you are likely to be exceedingly fertile as well."

Penny blushed, nodding.

Dale glanced at the door, his shoulders tense. Greg watched as he carefully set his glass down. "If you'll excuse me—I'll be in the washroom for a minute."

Bernard frowned when Dale rose from his seat. Dale all but ran out of the room, and Greg resisted the urge to follow him. Not this soon.

"I'm vaguely concerned," Bernard said, his eyes still on the doorway. "Kinney doesn't seem to be feeling well."

Penny opened her mouth, but Greg beat her to it. "I'll go check on him."

He slipped his shoe back on and left the room, his father's eyes burning into his back. But Greg didn't care about that. He cared about his omega, and maybe they shouldn't have come to this dinner at all.

23
Dale

DALE SUCKED in a shaky breath, barreling past the black-and-white photos in the blue-lit hallway. The waiters of The Apex had been friendly, pointing him down the corridor to the washrooms. He pushed through the first door he saw, stepping into pine-scented air.

Before the dinner, he'd thought himself prepared for conversations about babies. It would have happened during the introductory dinner, and Dale would have smiled and ignored the things Bernard said about fertility and families. Dale would have said Greg was better suited to a younger omega, one who could easily bear children when both of them were ready.

He hadn't expected to talk to Penny, who would face no problems with getting pregnant. He hadn't expected Greg to look at her with interest, even when Greg had said this was all pretend.

In a day, Dale would be exactly two months pregnant. His belly was still flat as ever, and it had been a surprise when Bernard caught his scent. Dale hadn't expected to fumble for a name that wasn't *Greg*.

So he'd blurted Charles' name, and Greg had glared at him, ferocity glimmering in his eyes.

Dale bit his lip, his heart wrenching.

He stepped up to the tall mirrors over the sinks. In the silvery surfaces, he saw the mess that was himself: droopy mouth, bonding scar on his neck, streaks of gray through his hair. Next to Penny and Greg, he'd felt immensely old.

Bernard Hastings was ten years older than Dale. There was no way he'd accept Dale marrying Greg, not when Dale had seen the mix of disapproval and pride in Bernard's eyes. The college president loved his son. But he also had high hopes for Greg, and Dale... would only weigh Greg down.

By the time their baby was ten, Greg would be thirty-two, and Dale would be fifty-two.

Dale cringed. Would their child be embarrassed by Dale at school? Would Dale still be healthy at that age?

He held his hands under the automatic faucet, watching as cool water drizzled onto his skin. In the shower an hour ago, Greg had hugged him, cleaning around the plug in his body. It sat inside him now, warm and heavy like an egg, a reminder of when Greg had slid it in, his eyes dark with promise.

If they went through more introductory dinners with other younger, better omegas, then Greg would surely leave Dale. Bernard would somehow convince Greg of other better omegas, and he would leave Dale tonight; Dale had seen the way Greg looked at Penny, and that interest could be genuine with someone else.

Dale hugged himself, the damp from his fingers soaking through his sleeves. *Your body is rotten,* Charles' parents had told him. *We're embarrassed to be seen with you.*

At some point, Dale would grow older. And Greg would really look at Dale, and realize the sort of relationship he'd gotten himself stuck in.

When that truth finally sank in, Greg would leave him like Charles had all those years ago.

His heart hurting, Dale wiped away the fresh tears in his eyes.

The washroom door opened. Dale tensed, turning to the urinals. No one cried at the most expensive restaurant in town. People did their business, and left.

"Hey," Greg said behind him.

Dale turned, his heart missing a beat. The sight of his alpha eased the tension in his shoulders. Black eyes glimmering with concern, Greg stepped forward as the door closed, pulling Dale into his arms.

"Wanna go home?" he murmured. "You're not looking so good."

Is that because I'm old, or because I'm crying? Dale sagged against his chest, running his hands down Greg's spine. Greg smelled like aspen, like comfort. "I'll be fine," Dale said.

The creases on Greg's forehead deepened. "You're not fine. I've never seen you step into the alpha washroom before."

"Oh. I did?" In his rush to get away, Dale hadn't thought the pine scent meant anything. He should've been more aware than this.

"I checked in the omegas', but you weren't

275

there."

"Did anyone squeak?" Dale chuckled weakly.

"No, but I didn't smell you in there." Greg rubbed down Dale's back, pressing a kiss to his forehead. "I can't hold you for long. Someone might come in. Just wanted you to know I lo—"

"I know. You don't have to say it," Dale mumbled, looking down. Maybe he shouldn't hear it, if Greg would be leaving him anyway.

Greg cupped his cheeks, the calluses of his hands catching on Dale's skin. Then he tipped Dale's face up, forcing Dale to meet his eyes. "You still feel the plug?"

Dale nodded.

"Give it a squeeze."

"I am." It sat wide inside him, keeping him open for Greg. He'd felt it every time he squirmed at the table.

"That's my knot inside you," Greg whispered. "I'm your alpha."

Dale nodded, his chest squeezing. If he closed his eyes, he could pretend that the solid, smooth weight inside him was his alpha's. Was Greg touching him intimately, even here. Heat prickled on his cheeks. "I want today to be over," Dale said.

"I know." Greg dipped his head, brushing his lips over Dale's, a quick, light touch. "Love you."

Dale gulped. "I know."

With his thumbs, Greg wiped the tears off his cheeks. Then he turned Dale toward the sinks, standing next to him, close enough their arms touched. Dale leaned into his bicep, breathing in, admiring Greg's face in the mirror.

"I'm sorry about earlier," Dale said. "About

Charles."

Greg narrowed his eyes. "Baby's mine. Not that bastard's."

A thrill shot down Dale's spine. He opened his mouth, about to say *It's yours,* when the restroom door opened. Dale jerked his gaze toward the faucet.

"Dad," Greg said. "Is the first course there yet?"

Dale's heart sank. *Why does it have to be my boss?* He looked up just as Bernard's eyes flickered between him and Greg. "It's there," Bernard said. "Didn't expect to see you here, Dr. Kinney."

"I brought him here," Greg said, shifting to put himself between Dale and his father. It was a protective gesture, and Dale wasn't sure Bernard read it that way. "I couldn't go into the omega's restroom."

"Ah." Bernard stepped around him, studying Dale. His gaze lingered on the damp splotches on Dale's sleeves. "Are you all right, Dr. Kinney? You seem a little pale."

"I'm fine," Dale said, forcing a brighter smile. "Thank you, sir. I'd best be heading back."

As he strode out of the washroom, Bernard said, "Drying your hands on your clothes, son? I didn't raise you to do that."

Dale's cheeks burned. He checked his hands halfway down the corridor, grimacing at damp creases of his fingers. The hug had been impulsive, and he'd forgotten about leaving behind handprints. *I hope Bernard doesn't figure it out.*

He only remembered to breathe back in the dining room. Penny picked at her salad, looking up

277

when Dale returned. "Are you okay, Professor?"

Dale laughed weakly. "Probably. It's not so bad." He sat gingerly in his seat, swallowing when the plug—Greg's knot—moved inside him. "How are you finding the dinner?"

"It's very nice." Penny glanced at the doorway. In a muted tone, she said, "I'm really sorry about this. If I'd known earlier, I'd have turned the invite down."

"No, I don't blame you for that. No worries."

But Penny squirmed, her gaze darting down to his abdomen. "The baby..."

"As far as you're concerned, it's my alpha's," Dale said, his heart skipping. He hadn't said that to anyone other than Greg. *My alpha.* A tiny part of his chest swelled—he belonged to someone, he belonged to Greg—but he also knew that this relationship couldn't last.

Dale rubbed the scar on his wrist, wondering what it'd be like if Greg bit him there. If Greg marked him permanently. The knot sat inside him, soothing as a promise.

"I understand," Penny said, glancing up at the doorway. Dale felt the moment when someone stopped behind him, a warm palm settling on his shoulder. Greg.

Dale almost leaned into his touch. Greg squeezed him lightly, as though he meant *I'm here,* and Dale could have cried with relief.

Greg's hand lingered for a second. Then he pulled away, settling back into his chair.

"I really do mean it," Penny said, smiling at them both. "Congrats on the baby. I'm sorry I didn't realize it before."

Dale touched his belly, cradling the life that nestled in him. "Thanks. We're looking forward to it."

When he looked up, he found Greg staring at him, his eyes solemn, intent. Dale's throat tightened.

"I feel like a third wheel," Penny whispered. "This is really weird."

Dale almost laughed. He dragged his gaze away from Greg, looking down at his salad. It was an artful display of lettuce leaves, with sliced olives and cherry tomatoes dotting the plate, and prosciutto petals tucked between the greens. "This is beautiful."

"You've never eaten here?" Greg asked.

Dale shook his head. "I've never even thought about it—it's all the way across town. But it's a stunning place."

"It's a first for me as well," Penny said, glancing at the doorway again. "What's your favorite dish here, Greg?"

Bernard Hastings rounded the table, glancing between Greg and Dale. Dale forced a smile, the plug a distinct weight inside him. *If you knew about your son's knot in me right now, you wouldn't still be sitting down to dinner.*

Pregnant or otherwise, Dale had no doubt that the college president remembered his past mistakes—the botched presentation months ago, the one time Dale had drunken too much at a staff party, the nanoparticle fire during Bernard's lab visit.

Greg chatted with Penny about politics, education, and travel. Before long, Bernard's attention had returned to Penny and his son. Dale was content to fade into the background, quietly eating courses of braised lamb with mint, pasta splashed with truffle oil, and duck confit on a bed of mashed potatoes.

It wasn't until the dessert course, during a conversation on post-grad studies, that Bernard said, "I'm pleased to see you aren't associating with many older omegas, Greg. Of course, Penny is a delight to have around."

The peppermint ice cream in Dale's mouth turned tasteless. His heart thudded slow and loud. From the corner of his eye, Dale watched as Greg stiffened. For a moment, Dale almost wanted Greg to stand up to his father, to say *Dale's my omega.* Except Greg also knew the risks involved. Greg's lips thinned, and Dale couldn't breathe.

"I really like older omegas," Penny said. "And older alphas, too. I've dated an alpha ten years my senior in the past—it was really nice. She provided a whole new perspective on things."

Greg breathed out. Dale scooped another spoonful of ice cream, his hand trembling as he brought it to his mouth. *Don't look up. Don't catch Bernard's eye. Let's get through the next ten minutes.*

"Age doesn't make a person," Greg said, his voice low, tempered with anger. "I want someone I'm comfortable with. That's all."

"And I'm sure you'll find one," Bernard said. "Don't you agree, Dr. Kinney?"

Dale forced a smile, but it felt like a porcelain mask on his face. "Yes, of course."

Greg narrowed his eyes.

"When you go on that lab tour, Gregory, start

with omegas in your class first." Bernard wiped his mouth on a napkin, signaling to the waiter for the bill.

Dale remained frozen in his seat, Bernard's words echoing in his ears. *I'm pleased that you aren't associating with many older omegas.*

The waiter brought the bill. Dale scooped the rest of his ice cream into his mouth, just so he had something to do with his hands. He needed to get out of here. Maybe leave Greg for a while, let him clear his head. They'd been living together for weeks, and maybe that had tainted Greg's perspective on what he really wanted.

Dale climbed to his feet when the rest of them stood. Greg and Penny talked as they took the elevator back down to the first floor, with Bernard occasionally joining in.

At the foyer, Bernard turned to Dale, extending his hand. "Thanks for joining us, Dr. Kinney. Do pass my congratulations along to Charles."

Hearing Charles' name felt like a slap. Dale couldn't look at Greg, but he could feel the waves of possessiveness roll off his alpha. When Bernard glanced at his son, Dale said, "I will pass it along to Charles. Thank you, Mr. Hastings."

Bernard's nostrils flared. Could he smell Greg on Dale? But Bernard nodded and turned, stepping out of the establishment, the omega host pulling the glass door open for him.

When the door closed, Greg growled, "I can't believe you went through that."

"I'm really sorry as well," Penny said, her eyes downcast. "The food was delicious. I just wish... it had been under better circumstances."

Dale pulled her into a hug. "Don't worry about it. I'll see you in the lab tomorrow?"

She gave him an uneasy smile, hugging him back. "I will. Goodnight, Professor, Greg."

Penny disappeared past The Apex's glass doors. It was only after she'd gone that Dale sucked in a breath—the first deep one he'd managed all evening. "That was an awkward dinner."

"No shit." Greg studied him, his shoulders still taut. "How do you want to get home?"

"I should walk for a distance. Or maybe all the way home."

"Ten miles? You have to be kidding." Greg narrowed his eyes. "I'm driving, and I want you at home with me."

Dale breathed in again, the murmur of conversation washing through his ears. The plug sat heavy in his body, and he wanted Greg closer, wanted Greg to help banish the dinner from his mind. Dale couldn't forget Bernard's scrutiny, couldn't forget the sick dread that had never left his chest the entire night.

"Is your dad gone yet?" he asked, looking at his feet. "I'm just... I'd rather not walk alone out there. It's dark."

Greg walked to the glass doors, peering out through them. Then he returned to Dale, his shoulders relaxing slightly. "I don't see my dad's car. C'mon, let's go."

Dale followed him out of the restaurant, glancing around. Bernard Hastings drove a silver Rolls Royce, but it was nowhere in The Apex's parking lot. Dale fell into step next to Greg, cracking a smile when Greg pulled open the Porsche's passenger door for him. "You really don't have to."

"Get in."

"Fine." But Dale's smile grew a little wider. They'd survived the dinner.

Greg slid into the driver's seat, shutting the door. In the dim ceiling light that came on, he was handsome, with his strong jaw, his dark eyes, his full lips. He watched Dale, his gaze raking over Dale's face, down his chest to his thighs. "Gods, I've missed you," Greg murmured. "Dinner took forever."

"It did," Dale sighed, reaching over to squeeze his thigh. Greg's warmth soaked into his palm, steady and comforting.

The ceiling light shut off, plunging them into darkness.

For a beat, nothing happened. Then Greg slid his hand around the back of Dale's head, pulled him close.

They met in a desperate kiss, Greg's lips on Dale's in a brief, chaste touch, before he pushed his tongue into Dale's mouth, tangling them together. Heat spiraled through Dale's gut. He opened for his alpha, curling his fingers into Greg's shirt to drag him closer. Greg tasted like peppermint, like dessert and alpha, and Dale hadn't had enough.

Greg's palm slid down his chest, heavy and hot. Then he dipped it lower, past Dale's belly, cupping him between the legs. Dale gasped. Greg massaged his cock, and Dale moaned into his mouth, his hips rocking up, his pants tight. The entire car smelled like musk.

"Want something?" Greg breathed against his lips, grinding the heel of his palm down on Dale's cock. Pleasure jolted up his spine. Dale whined, his fingers digging into Greg's thigh, nails scraping on denim. They shouldn't be doing this, not out here.

Dale shoved himself away, panting, his nipples hard. "Home. Get home. I want your knot."

A groan rumbled in Greg's throat. He pushed his key into the ignition, started the car. In the faint orange glow of the dashboard, he looked fierce, predatory, and Dale wanted his alpha closer. Wanted Greg pushing him down into their bed, his teeth on Dale's scent glands, marking him.

He slid his hand between Greg's legs, caressing the hard line in his pants. Greg hadn't come this afternoon, and Dale wanted to return the favor, pleasure his alpha. Greg bared his teeth, pressing Dale's palm flush against his cock. It strained in his pants, and Dale's throat went dry. Greg wanted him.

"We're heading back," Greg said, his voice hoarse.

They pulled out of the parking lot and onto the road, the streetlamps glowing orange around them, casting moving shadows through the car. Dale held his breath, breathed out. He shouldn't distract Greg right now, not while he was driving.

"I know dinner was a shitshow," Greg said. "But did you have any favorite parts?"

"Possibly the duck confit. Mm, dark meat." Dale sank back into his seat, willing his distracted mind to focus on food. "Possibly the ice cream. It wasn't too minty, you know? Just smooth vanilla with a hint of peppermint. And the chocolate chips. Mmm. Which was your favorite dish?"

"The lamb wasn't bad." Greg flicked on a turn signal, glancing over. "But I like your cooking more."

Dale grinned. "You're just sucking up to me."

"Have you known me to suck up to you?" Greg snorted. "Maybe suck *on* you, but that's it."

"Ha! You were sucking up to your dad, though."

Greg blew out a breath. "Yeah, well."

He sobered, and Dale looked at the textured surfaces on the inside of his door, thinking about his own childhood. His parents were gone. They'd been insistent that he marry a good alpha, and bear his alpha children. It wasn't the best way to grow up, or the best life motto to adopt. But some of it had stuck, and he couldn't help the yearning for children of his own.

"I don't suppose your childhood was all that pleasant," Dale said.

"Could've been worse." Greg rolled his shoulders. "I loved comics, though. Had bookcases of them."

"Really?" Dale perked up, groaning when the plug shifted inside him. "I've never seen you read for pleasure."

"Not these days. But I still have a wall of them in my apartment. Used to act them out—in fact, that was what I did with Tony. We found our favorite parts of Super Alpha and my mom made costumes. He played the villain, Vilso, and I was Super Alpha. It was goddamn cheesy." Greg met his eyes at a stoplight. "You wanna see? We took some photos—there's a whole album or two."

Dale's smile had been growing at Greg's recount. He'd wondered what Greg looked like as a boy, wondered about his childhood. And the vision of Greg in superhero costumes was too adorable to refuse. "Sure."

Greg smiled, making a U-turn. Dale squirmed with excitement. It was different from the desire a few minutes ago, but just as potent.

They drove through winding roads into a different part of town. Dale hadn't realized before, but Greg lived close to him—perhaps an hour's walk away. The apartments looked nicer than his own, their landscaping more exquisite, and he was reminded of Greg's status, of his potential as an alpha.

If Dale had been twenty years younger, he would've wanted Greg for his status, wanted him for all that wealth. That had been what Dale saw in Charles.

He was no longer that boy, though, and he was glad for it.

They pulled into an apartment complex minutes later, similar to Dale's own. At the door, Dale peered past Greg at the hardwood floors, the ebony trimmings along the walls, the recessed lights that threw a soft glow on the black leather couches.

"Nice apartment," Dale said.

"My dad pays for it. I'd rather live in a hole than keep this place."

"You love the car, though."

Greg sighed. "I do."

He shut the door, leading Dale past a steel-

and-metal kitchen to the study. There, he flicked on the lights, nodding at the wall by his desk. Dale stared.

Four bookcases stood side by side, stained auburn. Each shelf was crammed full of tall, thin volumes, several wrapped in plastic jackets. There had to be at least fifty comics on each row, and at least a thousand books in these bookcases, staring back at him.

"Wow," Dale breathed. "That's like collecting science journals, only more exciting."

Greg laughed, trailing his hand across their spines. "The Super Alpha comics are in these three bookcases. The rest are the Mad Scientist comics— have you read them? He did weird experiments. Mostly with bubbling liquids instead of nanoparticles, but with way more explosions."

Dale shook his head. His own childhood had been full of origami books, and stacks of colorful paper. "I had no idea you were a science nerd."

Greg shrugged. "The Mad Scientist comics were from way back, when I was a kid. I told you, I... lost interest in my hobbies when Tony died. So I never returned to reading these things."

He glanced away, breathing in deep. Dale winced. He shouldn't bring up Greg's past, when it had caused him such pain. "So you're majoring in chemistry."

"There's a reason why I stuck with chemistry, you know." Greg met his gaze. "And it's not just because of you."

Dale's heart thumped. *I thought you were kidding about that.* "I'm glad it's not just because of me. That wouldn't be wise."

Greg rolled his eyes. "The thing was, I'd been switching courses since I was nineteen. I took a year of law. Then I dropped out and did med school. Then I decided I'd try chemistry because I loved it in high school. At the end of last semester, I was thinking about dropping out again when I saw you."

Dale froze, his pulse thudding in his ears. Greg had never mentioned this. "Me?"

Greg crouched by the bottommost shelf of a bookcase, sliding out a couple of four-by-six albums. He flipped through them, then handed them over. "Yeah, you. I didn't realize you were a prof. at first. Saw you hurrying between classes, but you looked so damn worried."

Dale bit his lip. There never was reason to hurry between classes. "The only time I ever ran last semester... was when some solid iron nanoparticles caught fire in the lab. I was getting out of class. June called. And your dad saw the mess. Gods, that was embarrassing. I'd asked June to prep the sample so I could do a demo."

Greg grimaced. "Oh. But yeah, I saw you running that day, oxfords and all. Your lab coat was flying off your shoulders. I thought you looked good, so I asked around."

Dale flipped through the photo albums, his cheeks hot. He'd thought Greg's fascination with him had started on the first day of classes this semester, not way before that. "That was in November. It's been six months since then. I can't believe you'd pursue me for that long."

Greg shrugged, a red tint crawling up his neck. He was adorable. "Are you looking at the pictures, or not?"

"I am!"

Tucked into the album were several faded photographs. In them, Greg looked a decade younger, with the same brown hair, the same dark eyes. His shoulders hadn't bulked up yet, and he was thinner, lankier, his smile brighter.

Through the pictures, the boy from his phone accompanied him. They were always dressed the same way: Greg in a scarlet spandex suit, a black cape trailing down his back, Tony in a midnight-blue suit, with white V lettering on his chest.

In one photo, they'd both struck the same pose: one arm outstretched, the other pulled back, as though they were drawing imaginary bows. In another, Greg exchanged punches with Tony, scowls on their faces. A third photo had them both lying stomach-down on a table, fists thrust forward, their legs stretched straight behind them.

"You're so cute," Dale said.

"We were flying in that one," Greg said dryly. But he glanced away, blinking hard, his gaze focused on the comics on the shelves.

Dale's chest ached. He knew grief; his parents had passed away fifteen years ago in a car accident, and he had had time to adjust. Tony's death was still recent; Dale hardly dared bring up the subject at all. "Does it still hurt?"

"Sometimes." Greg blew out a breath, his gaze pausing briefly on the pictures. "I—I try not to think about it."

Dale swallowed. He shouldn't be upsetting Greg, reminding him of his late best friend. In his excitement to see these pictures, he'd forgotten to consider Greg's feelings. Greg had probably yielded because he loved Dale, regardless of how the pictures would affect himself.

What kind of partner was Dale?

I hate myself. His chest tight, Dale closed the photo album, holding them against himself. Greg and Tony had looked like childhood sweethearts in the photos. And Greg was still young. He still had so many opportunities waiting for him out there. All he had to do was find the right omega.

"I'm sorry," Dale said, setting the albums on a shelf. "I shouldn't have asked to see the pictures. I didn't mean to hurt you. And you deserve better. You deserve to have someone else you can act out comics with, another second chance. There are so many omegas—"

"I don't care about that anymore. I told you." Greg met his gaze, his eyes dark with pain. "I lost interest in that when Tony died."

"But surely someone else—"

"You're my second chance," Greg said. "Stop saying you're gonna leave."

Dale stared, his breath snagging in his throat. "I'm just an old professor," he said. "I can't see this working out."

Greg stepped closer to him, his shoulders tense. "But what if it can?"

Dale froze. There had been instances, on and off, when Greg had cooked with him, when Greg had cuddled up with him in bed, that he'd thought this relationship could last. But it couldn't. Not if Dale wanted to keep his job, not when the pregnancy still carried such a huge risk.

"We should stop this," Dale said, his throat

tight. "I don't—don't think this relationship is doing either of us good."

Greg's breathing hitched. "It is," he growled, his eyes glittering. "Don't you dare say that."

Then he leaned in and kissed Dale, firm and warm, and wetness smeared between their cheeks.

It was only a second later, when Greg's breath soughed on his skin, that Dale realized those were Greg's tears.

24

Greg

DALE PULLED away from him, his soft hands cupping Greg's cheek, his eyes flying open. "Greg—"

"I don't want to talk about it," Greg said, pulling him closer, claiming Dale's mouth again. His heart ached. With that dinner tonight, he hadn't expected to bring Dale back to his apartment, hadn't expected to show Dale those pictures of Tony. The ones where he'd been happiest with his best friend, when he and Tony had talked about how they'd buy neighboring houses, and cosplay with the silliest poses ever.

Greg missed him. He remembered the blaze, remembered blowing air into Tony's mouth, pumping his chest, trying to get him to breathe. During that camping trip four years ago, he'd shared that cabin bedroom with Tony, but Tony had gone to sleep first. Greg had been in the bathroom. When he'd stepped out, he'd found smoke seeping from under the bedroom door.

He'd opened the door to find the curtain in flames, his candle and the bedside table swallowed in fire. Smoke had filled the room, and Tony had been coughing, frozen in fear. It had been too late when Greg carried him out of the fire.

"Greg," Dale said. His eyes glimmered with concern; they'd stopped kissing somewhere in between, and Greg hadn't realized it.

He leaned into Dale, his heart fragile.

"I lost him," Greg croaked, pressing his forehead against Dale's. "And it was my own damn fault." He blinked his tears away, breathing in deep, filling his lungs with his omega's scent. "I don't want to lose you."

Dale cupped his cheeks, pulled him close, and Greg lost himself in the heat of Dale's mouth, sliding in, their tongues tangling. Dale opened beneath him, soft and damp. He was familiar—so familiar—by now, that Greg knew the press of his body before Dale's chest even sank against his.

He slid his palm down Dale's back, following the dip of his spine. Past his tailbone, Greg found the smooth disk of the plug through Dale's pants, the one he'd slid in this afternoon.

Dale had held his knot through all of dinner, held it through smiling at Greg's father. Greg growled, heat surging through his chest.

"Mine," he murmured, kissing Dale, scooping Dale up against him. He pushed the plug deeper, wedging it firm into his omega. Dale gasped, his fingers curling painfully tight into Greg's hair.

"Greg," he moaned, his cock pressing hard through his clothes. "Your—Your knot."

"Like it?" Greg leaned away, staring down at Dale, at his glistening lips, his blown pupils, the way his chest heaved. In that moment, Dale wanted

293

him, needed him, and a slow, sweet ache unfurled in Greg's chest.

I love you, Greg wanted to say. But he didn't want Dale to refuse it again, didn't want Dale to tell him why this was wrong. So he lifted Dale up into his arms, stepping out of the study into the living room. The plush couches reminded Greg of the one in Dale's office, the one he'd imagined Dale sleeping on, time and again.

Gently, Greg dropped him onto the couch, admiring the slender lines of his body, the way Dale's clothes hugged his chest, his thighs. He leaned in to kiss Dale on the lips, and Dale moaned, squirming, his hands sliding down Greg's abs, yanking his shirt from his pants.

Against the black leather of the couch, Dale's skin was pale, his hair a bright reddish-brown. He spread his legs, tugging at his own belt. Greg almost laughed, catching his hands. "In a hurry?" he growled, pinning Dale's wrists up above his head.

"Maybe," Dale whispered, smiling up at him.

With his knee anchored by Dale's hip, Greg leaned in, kissing Dale until Dale gasped for breath, his eyes half-lidded, his breath stuttering from his lips. He was beautiful like that, beautiful every time Greg saw him. And Greg pressed kisses down his jaw, following the arch of his neck, flicking his tongue over the flutter of Dale's pulse.

"You're tormenting me again?" Dale whined, lifting his hips, trying to entice Greg's touch. But Greg left his cock neglected, kissing down to the crook of Dale's neck, where his scent gland was. His hibiscus scent rolled off his skin, heavy with musk. Beneath that, notes of honey lingered.

Dale was carrying his child. And Greg pushed away his nagging doubts, dragging his lips over the sensitive spot, where Dale's ex had marked him. Something angry and primal roiled in his belly. He wanted his mark on Dale's skin, wanted Dale to know Greg would be there for him.

"I want to bond with you," Greg murmured against his scent gland, licking it, kissing it, until Dale's scent had smeared over his lips. "Want to make you mine."

Dale groaned. Greg closed his lips around his scent gland and sucked, and Dale's hips bucked up, his cock straining against his fly. "Greg, please."

"Please what?" He ran his teeth over Dale's skin, thinking about biting through it, writing over that damn scar.

But it also involved an oath, and looking at those photos had reminded Greg why he couldn't do this. He didn't want to make empty promises. Didn't want to mark Dale like his ex had, and then disappoint him.

Just to be sure, Greg whispered, "Do you want my mark?"

Dale shivered, his breath puffing through his mouth. "No."

And that was fine. It was. Greg's chest squeezed.

He looked down to hide his dismay. It surprised him, how easily he'd thought of Dale as his. There had never been a clear line drawn, when they had ceased being teacher and student, and when they'd started being alpha and omega.

He sucked on Dale's scent gland, slow and

firm. Dale jerked beneath him, panting, his hand pushing into Greg's jeans, past his boxers. Then his fingers wrapped around Greg's cock, an insistent pressure. Greg growled, growing hard in his hand. Dale knew he liked his tip played with, knew he liked being massaged slow and firm.

Dale teased him, his fingers sliding slow, a teasing touch that gripped all of Greg's attention, sent pleasure shooting up his spine. Greg almost bit down on Dale's scent gland. He sucked a last time on it; Dale shuddered, his hips rocking up, his neck arched, offering himself to Greg by instinct alone.

"I'm not gonna bite," Greg murmured, kissing down his clavicles, down his chest, along the buttons of his shirt. At Dale's nipples, Greg paused, licking them through thin fabric. They tightened, their pink tips barely visible through the thin weave.

With impatient hands, Dale tugged on Greg's belt, undid his fly. The pressure at his hips eased; Greg's cock slipped out, tenting his boxers, hungry for touch. Dale's eyes raked appreciatively over it, his tongue darting over his lips.

"Want it?" Greg asked, pushing the waistband of his boxers down, showing Dale his thick, flushed cock. Dale groaned, leaning forward, his eyes fixed on it.

Greg planted his hand on Dale's chest, pushed him back down on the couch. Dale whined. "Let me suck it!"

"Later," Greg murmured, kissing down his belly. At Dale's waistband, he tugged the dress shirt up, exposing his pale abdomen, and the tiny mole by Dale's navel. He licked the mole. Kissed it.

Dale squirmed, bucking up at him.

Then he kissed down the line of hair on Dale's belly, right over where their baby was. Dale trembled. Greg tugged on Dale's belt, slid off his pants and underwear, and Dale's musk washed over him like a wave, going straight down to his cock.

He growled, stroking himself, nudging Dale's thighs open. Between Dale's cheeks, the base of the plug glistened, his hole dark through the flat glass base. Dale had been stretched open for him the past five hours, had thought of the plug as Greg's knot the entire time.

Greg traced the base of the plug with his finger, his own cock aching. Then he pulled on it, just a little, so Dale would feel his touch all the way inside. "What's this?"

Dale gasped, his body clenching, his cock dripping. "Y-your knot."

A slow, possessive heat crept through Greg's chest. He rubbed his cock over Dale's tight balls, smearing precum along his taint. "Ready for my real knot?"

"Yes," Dale hissed. Greg worked his fingers beneath the base of the plug, pulling it out slightly for a better grip. Dale swore, his chest heaving, his cock jerking against his body.

"Feel good?"

Dale nodded, breathing hard. When Greg could fit his thumb between the plug's base and Dale's skin, he massaged Dale's hole, kneading his slick muscles. Then he eased the plug out, a little at a time, and Dale's voice dipped into a moan.

"Relax for me," Greg whispered, taking

Dale's cock into his mouth.

Dale writhed beneath him, dripping salty precum onto Greg's tongue, his nails scratching down the leather. "F-fuck."

Greg pulled slowly on the plug, watching as Dale's hole stretched around it. He left Dale's cock, kissed his inner thighs, and Dale squirmed, cock straining, his tip pushing out past his foreskin.

"Almost there," Greg murmured, pushing the plug back in. A visceral sound slipped from Dale's throat. Greg paused, sliding the plug out a little ways. Then he pushed it back in.

Dale whined, his breaths coming short and fast, his legs trembling.

"Does it hurt?" Greg asked.

Dale shook his head, his eyes dark, his chest flushed. "More."

So Greg eased the plug out of him, the widest part of it cresting his hole, before the rest of it slid out, glistening with slick. Dale panted, his cock flushed a dark red, a sheen of sweat on his body.

"Okay?" Greg asked.

"Yeah. Gods." Dale reached down, rubbing his fingers over his stretched hole, his pupils blown wide. "I'm so ready for you."

Greg groaned, setting the plug down on the floor. Dale had trusted him with the plug, had trusted him to ease it out, and his body was vulnerable like that, open for his alpha. Greg's cock ached. "Want me inside?"

"Yes!"

"C'mon, suck on me first," Greg whispered, sliding his arm around Dale's back, rolling him forward.

Dale's gaze dragged over his cock, his lips curving in a smile. "You liked seeing that."

"I'm that obvious?"

"You can't hide anything from me," Dale said, meeting his eyes.

In that moment, Greg wondered how much his omega knew. Dale knew Greg's reluctance to swear an oath. He knew about Tony, about the relationship Greg used to have with his best friend. Dale knew about Greg's parents, too, and there was little he *didn't* know.

Greg had nothing to hide from this man. Dale had seen all of him, and Greg was afraid he'd run. Dale didn't want to hear his *I love you*s. Didn't want to be bonded. Greg couldn't promise him a future.

All he could do was show Dale how much he cared, and hope Dale would feel safe in his arms.

Greg angled his cock down toward Dale's lips. Dale took him inside with a soft moan, his mouth wet and snug, his tongue flicking over Greg's tip. He stroked himself, sucking Greg deeper until he hit the back of his mouth.

Then Dale took him down his throat, and Greg's breath punched out of him.

He trembled, winding his fingers through Dale's hair just to hold him, stroke his face. And Dale moved, his tongue sliding against Greg's cock, his throat tight. He lifted his gaze, meeting Greg's, and Greg read the trust Dale had in him, the fondness and love and...

Greg could read every bit of Dale, too, and he was afraid of losing him.

He slid out of Dale's mouth, his cock throbbing. "Gonna fill you," he whispered, easing

Dale back onto the couch, kissing him softly on the lips.

"I'm not fragile, you know," Dale said hoarsely.

"I know." Greg hovered above him, unwilling to stop kissing him.

Dale curled his fingers around Greg's cock, angling him downward, rubbing Greg's tip against his open hole, fitting his tip inside. He was hot, slippery. Greg groaned, sliding in, pushing into the tight, unstretched parts of Dale's body. Dale moaned, his spine arching, his nails biting into Greg's sides. "Need—need you."

Greg slid all the way into him, as deep as he could get, watching as Dale's eyelids fluttered shut. Then he began to move, pacing his thrusts, the pressure in his cock building as Dale took him inside, his hole stretched around Greg's cock.

With every thrust, Dale made a little breathless gasp, biting his lip, his cock taut, smearing precum over Greg's abs. Greg curled his fist around Dale's length, stroking, and Dale jolted, his cock jerking against Greg's palm. He was completely open beneath Greg, his face a study of pleasure and need.

Greg stroked him, flicking his thumb just under his head where he liked, and Dale cried out, spilling onto his belly, his body clenching hard around Greg. The tight pressure hauled Greg over the edge, sent pleasure sluicing through his body, and Greg roared, fucking in deep, emptying himself into Dale.

He pressed his face into Dale's shoulder, panting, his body damp with sweat. Dale pulled him closer, damp clothes and all, and kissed him softly on the neck.

"Thank you," Dale murmured, nuzzling him. "That was—that was so good."

"Gods, you always feel incredible." Greg kissed him on the lips, gathering Dale up in his arms. Dale's skin brushed sticky against his, warm and soft, and Greg thought about hauling him into the shower, washing him down. Dale purred against him, and Greg kissed him slow and deep.

"I've never been here before," Dale said when they broke apart, his gaze flickering around the living room. Greg didn't care for the LED lamps, or the wide-screen TV, or the brushed-steel coffee table, but Dale was studying them all, admiration in his eyes.

Greg kissed down his throat, his knot swelling in his omega's body. Dale stretched around him, moaning, languidly hooking his leg around Greg's waist. "My parents have the key to this place," Greg said. "We probably shouldn't be here right now."

"Damn it. You should've mentioned it earlier," Dale said, glancing at the door. Worry flashed through his eyes.

"Yeah, but we just had dinner. I'm pretty sure he's gone home. He's already seen me today." Greg rolled his hips, pushing his knot deeper into Dale. Dale gasped. "Think I should grab a change of clothes first. These are soaked."

"Soaking through your clothes?" Dale smiled. "Like an omega?"

Greg smirked, kissing him. Midway through, his phone buzzed in his back pocket, the insistent vibration of an incoming call. He frowned, tugging it out.

Dad, the caller ID read.

His heart thudded. Greg rejected the call, sliding his phone onto the coffee table. He wasn't answering that right now, not with his knot inside Dale.

"Who was that?"

"My dad."

Dale squeezed around him, worry flashing through his eyes. "We should leave soon," he said, glancing at the door. "It's not safe here."

Greg sighed, hugging Dale closer. He knew Dale's pulse was skipping, knew Dale would squirm away if they weren't locked together right now. "C'mon, relax," Greg whispered, running his fingers through Dale's hair. "We'll be fine."

"Why didn't you tell me they have the key?" Dale groaned, throwing his head back into the couch. "This is the most—"

Greg kissed him, slow and coaxing. "Shh. Stop worrying. We'll leave the second I'm out, okay? We'll be fine."

But Dale squirmed, clenching tight around him. "I really don't know. He was looking at me over dinner. He might be suspicious."

Greg sighed, kissing his chin. "I'll pull out. Then we'll get going. Okay?"

"Yeah. Please do."

Greg leaned back, his knot catching behind Dale's hole. "C'mon, you're gonna have to relax."

"I'm trying," Dale said, whining when Greg pulled gently on his knot. "At least I had the plug in before."

"It's still not as big as me," Greg said. "I don't wanna hurt you."

Dale sucked in a deep breath, reaching between them, his fingers sliding around the snug fit of Greg's body against his. Slowly, Greg rolled his hips back, watching as Dale stretched around his knot, his own flushed skin a stark contrast against Dale's.

Little by little, Dale opened around him, a low moan falling from his lips. Greg kept the pace slow, waiting for Dale to stretch, massaging his hole to help him relax. "Easy does it."

"I'm not a horse," Dale said.

"I didn't say you were."

Dale snorted, a smile creeping up his lips. "Back when I was a boy, there used to be a cartoon about a horse. Its rider would say, 'Easy, easy. I won't hurt you,' and the horse would eventually listen. I began associating 'easy' with horses."

Greg smiled, rolling his hips, the tightness of Dale's muscles squeezing pleasure through his knot. They were almost at the thickest part of it, and after that, Greg would slip free, separating them. "You ever had a horse?"

"No, but I wanted one." Dale groaned as he stretched. "My parents wouldn't allow it—it was dry in Drakestown. Horses are expensive to keep there. When I was nine, we passed a store selling books—they had one opened to a page on origami horses. That's where I learned to fold them."

"And then you switched to folding cranes," Greg said, slowing when they reached the widest part of his knot. Dale's mouth fell open; he dug his fingers into the couch. "C'mon, just a little more.

How many cranes do you have now?"

"I think we might've folded four hundred since the start of this year —"

The door opened just as Greg's knot slipped out of Dale.

Past the doorway, Bernard Hastings stood in the shadowy night, a deep frown creasing his face.

25
Bernard

Five minutes ago

BERNARD HASTINGS frowned at his phone, leaning back into the seat of his loaner car. Today had not gone well.

He'd been busy with board meetings all afternoon, arguing with the college shareholders on the declining student intake. Then he'd tried to convince them that Meadowfall College still held rank, only to meet with resistance on his proposed logistical changes.

The meeting had dragged on, and Bernard had forgotten about his service appointment at the Rolls Royce dealership until 5 PM. The staff there had been very pleasant about it, of course, offering him a complimentary loaner car for his use. Even so, Bernard still wasn't pleased with the BMW, even when it had all the controls he could possibly want. It didn't have the prestige the Rolls Royce gave him.

The dinner, at least, had gone well. Until he'd noticed that Greg's attention drifted, time and again, to Dale Kinney.

Bernard had studied his son, watched as he ran after the professor. And in the bathroom, Greg had stepped between Bernard and Kinney, the way an alpha shielded his omega. There had been water marks on his back, at angles that Greg couldn't possibly reach with his own hands.

A dreadful suspicion roiling in his gut, Bernard had left The Apex first, sat in his loaner car, and watched as Greg peered out of The Apex's glass doors. Minutes later, Greg and Kinney both stepped into the Porsche. Not incriminating, in itself. Greg could've been offering Kinney a ride.

Except Greg's car didn't start for a good five minutes. Maybe they'd been typing an address on the GPS. But Bernard wasn't sold, and Greg had made a U-turn, heading all the way back to his own apartment.

Weeks ago, Greg had smelled like hibiscus, claiming it belonged to an omega on his basketball team. That exact same scent belonged to Dale Kinney. Greg hadn't been wearing it today, but Bernard could've punched himself for not making the connection earlier.

He wanted to think they were headed to Greg's apartment for a discussion on schoolwork. But it had been a while since Greg had been there— Bernard had checked the apartment a few times— the fridge was empty, most of Greg's clothes were gone. He'd all but moved out, and never moved back in.

Just as Bernard had been about to head over to the apartment, his broker called. Then they'd spent half an hour arguing about the foreign stock market, and Bernard had watched the minutes tick away on his watch.

Half an hour later, Greg and Kinney still hadn't stepped out. If they were doing something upstanding, Greg would answer his phone.

Bernard called. Greg rejected it.

He gave them five minutes, his pulse rushing in his ears.

When he opened the front door, Bernard expected to smell dust, or maybe Greg's aspen scent. Instead, a wall of musk rolled over him, overpowering, prickling through his nerves. *What in the gods' names,* Bernard thought.

On the couch, Greg eased away from Dale Kinney, pulling the glistening length of his cock out of Kinney's hole, his knot flushed and swollen.

They froze, all three of them.

"What the fuck," Bernard said, disgust crawling up his throat. He'd forgiven Kinney for his blunders, time and again, even going so far as to invite him to tonight's dinner. And *this* was how Kinney repaid him? By seducing his son?

Fury roaring through his veins, Bernard stepped into the apartment, slamming the door behind him.

This atrocity would cease tonight.

26
Dale

THE DOOR slammed shut. Bernard Hastings prowled forward in the living room, his stare flickering between Greg and Dale.

Dale's stomach squeezed into a hard lump. The moment Greg released him, he closed his legs, trying to hide himself.

They shouldn't have come to Greg's apartment. Dale shouldn't have encouraged him, shouldn't have coaxed him into sex out here on the couch.

For the past two months, he'd sometimes woken with nightmares of this happening, Bernard pronouncing the words *You're fired,* and expelling Dale from the college. He'd dreamed of packing up his belongings, his students sneering at his disgrace. He'd woken in Greg's arms with a gasp, his heart crashing into his chest.

Now that Bernard Hastings was here, Dale's mind had gone blank. He couldn't think. Didn't know how to save himself, not when he was half-naked beneath Greg, damp and open from sex.

Greg moved. He pulled himself off from Dale, crouching to snatch up Dale's pants. Then he dropped them on Dale's hips with a cool rustle, and stood in front of him, his shoulders tense. "You could've knocked," Greg snarled. "About damn time you learned that."

Bernard's mouth curled with distaste. "No, I really didn't need to see this," he said. "I expected more from you. Kinney, too."

Dale flinched. Was there any chance that Bernard would forget who Dale was? *All the gods of the world, please kill me now.*

"This isn't just a one-off event, is it?" Bernard glared at Greg. "You've been lying to me for months."

Then he looked at Dale, and Dale's cheeks burned. *I need to move.* He pulled his pants tighter around his hips, trying to cover his exposed skin.

"This is none of your business," Greg said, glaring.

Dale wanted to tell him to stop. Wanted to get out of this place, before everything burned down around them.

Bernard scoffed. "None of my business?" He looked at Dale, his eyes mocking. "I thought I'd be benevolent for once, Kinney. Give you a chance tonight. And what do I find but you seducing him? Have you no shame?"

Have you no shame? Charles' parents had said nineteen years ago. *How dare you marry our son, and not give him a child? How dare you even call yourself omega?*

"He didn't seduce me," Greg snapped.

"Bribed you, then?"

What had Dale bribed Greg with? He didn't know. Sex? The baby? He'd never understood what

309

Greg had seen in him.

"He's my omega," Greg snarled. "I don't need anyone bribing me."

"*Your* omega? Kinney said it himself—his alpha is Charles." Bernard's mustache quivered. He cut a broad, domineering figure across the living room, and Dale felt like cowering. Bernard looked down his nose. "What of the baby, Kinney? Whose is it? Or don't you know?"

Dale's cheeks scorched; his skin might've peeled. He wanted to hide his face. Burrow into a hole and pretend this never happened. He wanted to be somewhere far away, so he wouldn't have to hear his boss putting him down in front of Greg.

"Don't you fucking say that about Dale. The baby is mine," Greg growled, low and dangerous, his fists clenched. "Charles is his ex."

"So that was a lie? And how do you know he hasn't been lying to you as well?" Bernard spared Dale a glance. Then he raised a challenging eyebrow. "You see just as clearly as I do—there are bonding marks on his skin."

"I'm divorced," Dale said quietly, closing his eyes. He needed someone to shoot him, or kill him, take him away from here. "The baby is Greg's."

Greg stepped closer to Dale, the heat of his body radiating through the space between them. "You heard him. The baby's mine. You're not touching him."

Bernard stepped closer, his mustache bristling. He looked at Dale like Dale was scum on the bottom of his shoe, and Dale wanted to shrivel up and wither away. "If the fetus is yours, then it'll have to go. You will not be seeing Kinney again.

He's fired."

Dale swayed.

The words rang in his head, loud and clanging like a death knell. He was fired. Just like that, he'd lost his job, and he didn't know which was more embarrassing—telling his students, or packing his things from his office. Or meeting Bernard's gaze, scorn blazing in the college president's eyes.

"What the hell? You can't do that," Greg snapped, baring his teeth. "You can't fire him."

"He breached the most important rule," Bernard said, meeting Dale's eyes. Dale wanted to look away, but he couldn't. "You don't engage the students in sexual activity. Anyone found guilty will be terminated immediately."

"I forced it on him," Greg said, his voice low with fury. "I bribed him. Leave him out of this."

"Then he should have reported it to the Dean." Bernard's nostrils flared, his features twisting into a scowl. "You are a disgrace, Gregory. And Kinney—I have no words for you, except to say I wish you had never been hired."

Dale held onto the couch, trying to stay upright. He couldn't collapse right now. Couldn't let Bernard Hastings see how weak he was.

"Gregory, you're moving back in with me. Your education will be terminated otherwise—"

"Fuck my education," Greg said, stepping forward. "I'm not obeying your backward rules."

Dale's nails dug into the couch, sweat coating his palms. He couldn't let this play out, not when Greg's future was at stake. It was bad enough that Greg and his father were tearing each other apart because of him. He couldn't stay and continue to ruin Greg's life, couldn't drag him down with a baby.

"I'm leaving," Dale blurted. "Greg, you're not my alpha."

Greg stared incredulously at him. "No."

"Yes," Dale said, fumbling with his clothes. "Don't follow me, please. Move your things out of my apartment by tomorrow."

Greg's jaw went slack. Then, as though he thought this was a ploy to deceive his father, he relaxed. "Okay."

Dale shook his head. "No, I mean it. Return my key."

Greg blinked. Dale met his eyes, holding his hand out. For a moment, Greg stared at him, his gaze raking over Dale's face. Dale left himself open, let Greg read the despair he felt. And horror flickered through Greg's eyes. "You can't—"

"Yes. This is over. Listen to your father."

To the side, Bernard Hastings watched them, his eyes narrowed, his arms folded across his chest.

Dale found the opening of his pants, stepping into them. He didn't want to know what Bernard Hastings thought about his pasty thighs, his half-naked body. He tugged his shirt down, the material too thin to hide him away. "The key, please."

"You promised—"

"I promised nothing," Dale said. His chest ached. "*The key.*"

Greg searched his gaze, but Dale looked away, his eyes burning. This had to stop. He was fired, and he needed to quit ruining Greg's life. Needed to find his footing again, find a job somewhere that didn't involve this scandal. Would the Dean even give him a decent reference?

"You can't go anywhere," Greg said, slowly slipping his hand into his pocket. "It's not—not easy for you to find another job."

Dale closed his eyes, wanting to cry. He knew he was old. They couldn't be having this conversation in front of Bernard Hastings, not like this. "I'll manage."

"The baby is mine! I promised I'd care for it."

"No. Please." Dale breathed in. He couldn't break down. He still had shreds of his pride left.

Greg turned to his father, his eyes beseeching. "Dad. You can't fire him. He's been adding to the reputation of your college, damn it! Haven't you seen his lab? His students?"

Bernard Hastings studied him, then Dale, and Dale needed to get out of this suffocating place right now.

"I may consider it if the fetus is aborted," Bernard said, glancing at Dale's belly. "I will have no scandal connected to Meadowfall College, Gregory. I've spent twenty damn years building it up, and I will not see it fall."

"We're not aborting it," Greg said, pulling his hand from his pocket. "Dale—"

Dale pressed his hand to his abdomen, to protect his child from them. He wasn't losing his baby. Not now, when he'd wanted it for two decades. "I'll send in my resignation letter first thing tomorrow," he said. "I'm deeply sorry about this."

When neither Greg nor his father moved, Dale stepped over to Greg, slipping his hand into

313

Greg's right pocket, where the key was. Greg's jeans were tight like a hug, warm, and Greg caught his wrist. "You can't walk home like that."

Dale couldn't help looking up. *Don't go,* Greg's eyes said.

"Sorry. I'll catch a cab," Dale mumbled, curling his fingers around his key. He pulled it out of Greg's pocket, and Greg yanked him close, leaning in for a kiss.

Every cell in his body wanted that kiss. And that meant he had to leave, before everything fell further apart.

He twisted out of Greg's touch. Stepped into his shoes, striding across the hardwood floors, his footsteps clicking loud in the silence.

Then he pulled the door open, walking out into the cool night air.

The door shut behind him with a note of finality. Dale sucked in a shuddering breath, and crossed the parking lot, hugging himself to ward off the cold.

Back at the apartment, Greg's silhouette darkened a window. Dale yanked his gaze away, turning down the sidewalk. His heart ached.

Greg never saw his damp cheeks.

27
Greg

GREG SPUN away from the window, heat bubbling through his chest.

Dale had left. Dale had taken the key, and after all these months of watching his omega, Greg knew he hadn't just left the apartment. Dale had left *him*.

And it hurt.

He rounded on his father, glaring. "Damn you. Dale's my omega!"

Bernard Hastings glanced at the door, unimpressed. "Kinney said it himself—he isn't. And he's gone, isn't he? A good thing, too. I won't have you bonding with an omega that old."

"I was gonna marry him. Damn you, and fuck you."

His father narrowed his eyes. "Watch your tongue, son."

After all those months of his father ignoring his protests, Greg had had enough of it. "No. I told you when Tony died, and I've told you a million times. Fuck my future."

Bernard clenched his jaw. "Tony is gone. You'll have to keep facing forward. I did not raise you to destroy your future with such an unworthy omega. I expected you to be above that."

Why the hell don't you understand? Greg's heart pounded. "He's worthier than you'll ever be. Dale didn't bribe me, or seduce me, or any of that shit. And we're not aborting that child."

The frown on his father's forehead deepened. "If you get with him again, I'll make sure he'll find no employment in the whole of Meadowfall. That seems to be the only way you'll end this."

Greg's stomach turned into ice. "You can't do that. That's illegal."

"He breached his contract. You should be glad I'm not suing him for two million." Bernard looked down at him. Greg stood taller, trying to intimidate his father. It didn't work. "He's been taking risks with the college's reputation. I will not have some harebrained omega tarnish my hard work."

He had a point, and Greg hated it. Hated that it had been a losing battle right from the start. "Dale's not hare-brained. But I'm not staying in this apartment. I'm not feeding off your money. I don't need it."

"And then what? You'll find a job? With no degree? You don't even have a mate to boost your status."

Greg looked down at his wrist, his scent gland free of bonding marks. He'd wanted to exchange marks with Dale, wanted to make him promises, even when he couldn't.

"I'll talk to Dale about it," he said.

Bernard snorted. "I'll make sure you won't. But even if you did, he has no job to support the both of you. Without your degree, you'll get nowhere."

That wasn't true. But Greg couldn't focus on it, not when he'd lost Dale his job. And maybe that was why Dale had gone. Dale loved his lab, his students, and Greg had no power to reinstate it. He'd fucked up.

"I will talk with the apartment manager," Bernard said. "The apartment's lease will end this month. You have a choice: move back in with your mother and me, or find your own lodgings."

"I'm not moving back," Greg said, his throat tight.

"We'll see."

Bernard turned and left. Woodenly, Greg stepped over to the window. He couldn't have missed the Rolls Royce in The Apex's parking lot. Gods knew he'd scanned the place for it.

But what he saw was a shiny black vehicle pulling out of the parking lot, instead of the silver car he'd looked for.

Greg dragged his hand over his face, his heart squeezing. He'd told Dale his father had left, when he hadn't. His dad had probably followed them home.

They'd been caught off-guard, and in the span of an hour, Dale had lost his job. His second home at the college. He'd taken his apartment key and left.

Greg didn't know how he could fix any of this.

28
Dale

WHEN THE alarm clock rang, Dale groaned, cracking open his sleep-sticky eyes. He wanted to burrow into Greg's warm chest, cuddle up against him. But when he reached across the bed, he found the sheets empty. The bedroom was still dim; the sun hadn't risen yet.

At first, he'd thought Greg was in the bathroom, or he'd woken up early to make breakfast. But his spot on the mattress was cool, and there was no aroma of coffee, or bacon. Was this another onesie surprise?

Dale trawled through his memories of last night, of Bernard Hastings and the dinner, and Bernard walking in on them.

His stomach twisted.

He'd been fired. And he'd walked out of Greg's life, knowing Greg could do so much better than him.

Dale wiped the dried tear tracks off his cheeks, dragging himself out of bed. He had to pack the rest of Greg's things, leave them out on his doorstep. He couldn't risk bumping into Greg, couldn't let Greg convince Dale to take him back into his life.

He stumbled to the bathroom, drooping at the sight of Greg's toothbrush, his razor, his red-and-black can of shaving cream. Any moment now, Dale expected Greg to show up at his door, demanding to be let in. And Dale couldn't let him destroy his own future. Because Greg had a future, despite him thinking he hadn't.

Dale fumbled through his morning routine, drank a cup of milk, and began tucking the rest of Greg's clothes into his empty moving boxes. Greg would collect them. He'd take some time to settle into being omega-less, and then he'd move on to the next person. And he'd be happier than he'd ever been with Dale.

When all of Greg's things had been tucked into boxes, Dale sank into his couch, worn out, his head rolling against the backrest. For a moment, he focused on catching his breath.

Then he slid onto the floor, pulling a paper square from the stack on the coffee table. It was printed with bamboo patterns, gray brushstrokes on a white surface.

The movements came to him from memory. Dale folded the sheet into triangles, then unfolded it. He folded it into rectangles next, scratching creases into paper to form the crane's base structure. He tucked the sides in, folded the corners up, so it became a condensed diamond shape, with neat folds toward its middle.

When the crane was done, he pulled out a smaller sheet from the stack above: white diamonds on a background of wine-red.

The third sheet was a colorful amalgam of

leaves, and the fourth, black lightning on a scarlet backdrop.

That one's my favorite, Greg had said.

Because it's red and black? Dale had asked.

Greg had taken the sheet from him, folding his own crane. *I just like the colors. They're vibrant.*

Dale swallowed hard, tempted to place the sheet back in the pile. Instead, he made himself work through it. He needed to get over their relationship, needed to forget about Greg. And that would have to start now.

Twenty minutes later, he had four cranes. Dale scooped them up, dropping them into the glass bowl in his study. But the red-and-black crane stared up at him, and he paused, looking at the pile of cranes he had folded together with Greg. They had laughed and joked around, folding those. Greg had tried perching cranes on Dale's hair, and Dale had tried to keep still, balancing those cranes on his head.

Dale picked up the crane, tucking it into his pocket. At the door, when he was moving the rest of the boxes out onto the front step, Dale opened a cardboard box, dropping the crane inside.

Maybe it was a farewell gift, or maybe he was returning a fraction of the luck and hope Greg had given him. Dale piled more boxes onto the cardboard box, then locked the door, climbing into his car.

HALF AN hour later, he arrived at the chemistry lab building, looking around. Everything seemed so familiar—the trees planted through the parking lot, the steel doors leading into the building. The empty corridors that led the way to his lab.

June looked up from her computer when he pushed the lab door open, her gaze falling to the flattened cardboard boxes under his arm. "You look terrible," she said. "What happened?"

Dale met her eyes. He didn't know what to say, not really. June had warned him about the relationship. She knew the risks, too. And she had been one of his best friends through all this time.

"I've been fired," he said.

She paled. "What?" Then she leaped up from her chair, horror darting through her face. "The dinner?"

He rubbed his face. "It was after. I don't know how Bernard knew where to find us. We... we went to Greg's apartment. Bernard had keys to it. I just..."

June squeezed past the cardboard boxes and wrapped her arms around him, her birch scent comforting. It wasn't anything like Greg's, though. "Oh, gods, no. Really?"

"I left him," Dale mumbled, pressing his face into her shoulder. He had no more tears. But he needed a hug, and there wasn't much time before school started, or before the rest of the lab students came by. "If he asks, tell him I don't want to see him."

Her arms tightened around his shoulders. "I can't believe that bastard would fire you. I'll start a petition—"

"No, don't." He breathed out. "I've thought about it. It's best that Greg doesn't see me again.

I'm... just going to let it go. He'll do better without me."

"But—"

"No."

"He made you really happy, Dale."

Did he? Dale hadn't thought about it, but maybe he had indeed been happier. He cradled his belly. *Maybe you'll meet your other dad someday. He's a great guy.* "I'm too old for him, June. I'm just here to pack and submit my resignation letter. That's all."

"What about the baby?" Concern glimmered in her eyes. "Greg will have visitation rights."

Dale sighed, rubbing his face. He hadn't thought that far yet. "If the pregnancy is successful."

"Gods, this is just not fair. You're the nicest person I know."

He chuckled weakly. "I guess that's a good thing."

"It is, and I doubt Greg Hastings will drop you just because you left him."

June was right; Greg wouldn't leave that easily, not when Dale had allowed him so close. "He needs to."

"And you need him."

The thought of waking up alone every morning made him cringe. And that was telling, wasn't it? He'd become too dependent on Greg, even without meaning to. And it had gotten him fired.

"Can we stop talking about this?" Dale groaned, looking at his watch. He needed to leave. Needed to get away from the college, before his students somehow saw him. He couldn't stand the thought of them looking at him right now, when they'd soon discover that he'd been fired.

"I can't believe you're leaving." June pulled him close, squeezing the breath out of him. "I'm going to miss you so much."

"You'll find a better professor, I'm sure."

"No, I won't. And I think Greg will say the same. You know how he feels about you, right?" She leaned away to stare hard at him. Dale shook his head, his throat tight. "He loves you."

Greg had said *I love you* countless times, and Dale wished he'd recorded it, so he could play it on his phone when he was lonely in the coming nights. "I don't—don't want to think about it," he said. "I just... I need help packing. Please?"

"Fine." June pulled away. Then she hesitated. "Hey, what's your address? I've got a couple of things I want to mail to you."

He frowned. "What are they? You could hand them over now, if you have them. I'll be back over the next few days to grade the finals."

She winced. "You don't want it now, trust me."

"You can't do that. You're going to drive me insane wondering about it."

"I..." June sighed, picking up a pastel-pink envelope. "It's my wedding invite. Four months from now. I was going to ask if you wanted to be our best omega."

June was getting married. Dale had forgotten, caught up as he was with Greg. And now that he no longer had an alpha, the thought made his chest squeeze. Especially when Greg had asked Dale, time and again, to marry him. "Oh."

"Yeah, I told you. I figured it'd be better if I just mailed it."

Dale took the envelope in his hands, picking it open. The invite was scented lightly with birch and petunia, and Dale's chest ached, looking at the names printed in swirling gold letters. He could've been handing cards like this out, too. Inviting the few friends he had to a private wedding. With Greg, marriage had almost seemed plausible. Good. Wonderful.

"I'll... just not think about it," Dale said, swallowing hard. "But I'll be there."

"As my best omega?"

"Yes. I'd—I'd love to. Thank you for asking me. I'm very honored."

She peered at him in concern. "Tell me if you can't make it, okay? You have my number. Call me if you need help."

"I will." Dale tucked the invite into his cardboard boxes. "What's the other thing you wanted to send?"

June smiled wryly, handing over a flat, wrapped gift. It was square, covered in polka-dotted paper, and tied up in twine—probably more origami paper. "It's your birthday," June said. "I thought paper would be a good gift."

"I didn't... realize it was my birthday."

June winced. "Happy birthday?"

"Some birthday it is." He sighed.

She wrapped her arm around his shoulder, steering him toward the door. "Come on, let's get you away before the rest of these guys come in."

29
Greg

FOR THE past three weeks, they'd been leaving Dale's apartment at 7:30 AM, heading for school in Dale's Volkswagen. They'd pull into the campus parking lot at 7:45. Greg would drop Dale off, and park the car.

The morning after The Apex, Greg pulled into Dale's parking lot at 7:15, his heart sinking at the boxes stacked by Dale's front door.

You'd meant it when you said you were leaving.

He hadn't slept at all last night. Several times, Greg had considered driving over to Dale's apartment, just to see if he'd gotten home safe. But he knew Dale wouldn't have answered the door. Dale never replied to his texts, and Greg had slept with his phone nestled in his hand, waiting for a call. Dale never rang.

The Volkswagen wasn't in the parking lot. When Greg stepped up to the front door, he found his basketball jerseys folded in the topmost box, laid on top of T-shirts and jeans. They smelled like aspen and hibiscus and laundry detergent — Dale had picked them from the laundry hamper and washed them last night. Laundry day wasn't supposed to be until tomorrow.

In the second box, Greg found his toothbrush, toiletries, his boxers and socks. In the third box, Dale had stashed his mug, his stationery and backpack, and some textbooks. There were more boxes beneath these, but he hadn't the heart to see what else Dale had thrown out.

For a heartbeat, he considered leaving the boxes here, so he wouldn't have to move them when Dale welcomed him back.

He tried the doorknob. It was locked.

The curtains had been drawn, and the apartment looked spotless. There was no sign of movement. No textbooks or stray clothes on the couch.

He pulled his phone out, dialed Dale's number again.

"The number you're calling is currently unavailable. At the tone, please leave your message."

He hit the End Call button, shoving his phone back into his pocket. Dale hadn't answered any of his calls, either.

Dale didn't want to see him. Greg hadn't wanted to believe it last night, but it was slowly sinking in. And he'd failed as an alpha, hadn't he?

Slowly, Greg moved the boxes into his car. It was a tight fit in the Porsche—with no backseat and a tiny trunk, he had to squeeze boxes into the passenger's leg compartment, cramming them all the way to the ceiling.

Then he drove to the college, faster than he should, and breathed a sigh when he found Dale's car in the chemistry lab parking lot. The car was empty. But Dale had been well enough to drive, and that meant something.

The lab was locked when he reached it. Greg turned, heading down the hallways to Dale's office. Midway there, he bumped into June.

She wasn't surprised to see him. "Didn't take you long, did it?"

"Where's he?"

"Around." June glanced over her shoulder. "He said your name will still be on the nano-gold research paper."

Greg frowned. What paper? The one he'd helped with, when Dale had gone to nap in his office? "I don't care about the paper."

"Dale thought you might." June shrugged, nodding at the hallway where he'd just come from. "Walk with me?"

"I'm looking for Dale. Is he in his office?"

"He should've left by now."

But I just saw his car! Greg spun around, and June grabbed his arm. She was surprisingly strong—he jerked to a stop, frowning back at her. Then he sniffed. There was a faint hibiscus scent on her, mixed with birch and petunia. *Dale hugged you?* His heart kicked.

"Look, let him be for a while," June said.

"He's my omega." Greg looked down the empty hallway. If Dale was still around, if he could catch Dale, tell him he was sorry.

"It's his birthday today. Don't make this harder on him than it has to be."

His stomach dropped. "It's Dale's *birthday?*"

"He never told you?"

"It never came up." Greg winced, thinking about Dale hurt and jobless, fired the day before his birthday. If he'd known... He'd been such a bastard alpha. "Oh, hell."

"Give him some time to recover. You've hurt him enough."

Knowing was one thing. Having another alpha tell him that... Greg flinched, ashamed of himself. "I don't need you to tell me."

June shrugged, sympathy in her eyes. "Dale's been a professor for ten years," she said. "If he were an alpha, he would've gotten his tenure by now."

Greg's heart sank. Omegas in Meadowfall were treated well—better than in some other parts of the United States. But Dale had never mentioned the double standards in his employment here. Greg rubbed his face, wishing he could've done more to help. Wishing he wasn't twenty-two, and with hardly any influence on anything. "I hate this."

"Thing is, he's been saving up," June said. "He can afford to be alone for a while. You don't have to think you need to provide for him."

She meant *Dale doesn't need you,* and for a moment, Greg's breath caught. "I—"

"Sort out what you want in life," June said. "That's what he wants for you."

"He won't even answer my calls."

June studied him, as though she was deciding how much she wanted to share. "Look, I'm getting married in four months. He's agreed to be my best omega."

Greg opened his mouth, his heart thudding. Before he could answer, June continued, "I can invite you to the wedding, if you'd like. But you won't be allowed to talk with him until after the ceremony. I won't have you scaring him off."

She met his eyes, honesty in her expression. And Greg felt guilty for all the times he'd glowered at her, thinking she was Dale's alpha. "Thanks. That's really generous of you. I mean, I was a bastard to you at the start of the semester."

June cracked a smile. "Anything for Dale, really."

Greg nodded, looking down the corridor again. Was Dale still around? Could he salvage this?

"I wouldn't speak to him again this soon," June said, releasing his arm. "You know why he became a professor, don't you?"

He stared at her, about to speak when he realized he didn't know. Dale had never mentioned it. "No. Why did he start teaching?"

"Because it was his second chance at proving that he could do something right. You know how upset he was by his infertility." June stared hard at him. "Tenure was his stretch goal."

Greg froze, horror creeping through his veins. Even if Dale had a baby now, it didn't mean he should be robbed of his other dream. Especially when the pregnancy wasn't guaranteed to be a success. "I..."

"Think about it," June said, patting his shoulder. "I warned him at the start, but I think you knew the risk you were both taking."

He nodded, his heart heavy with regret. Did Dale hate him now? Greg had shattered his dreams, and he didn't have the power to restore Dale's job. He looked down the corridor, wondering if Dale was still around. If Dale would even want to speak to him again.

"I'll be in the lab," June said. "Drop by if you need questions answered."

Greg trudged to Dale's office, his heart aching at how his omega must be feeling. He'd known that Dale had been upset about his infertility, but to have the professorial job be this important...

The office door was locked when he reached it. There were no sounds from within, and Greg waited outside, hoping to hear movement inside the room.

Five minutes passed. He heard nothing, and only smelled a faint hibiscus scent leading away from the office door. Had Dale already left? Greg swore, jogging down to the parking lot. June had delayed him on purpose.

Dale's car was no longer parked next to his. On the asphalt next to the Porsche, something glimmered.

When Greg reached his car, he realized that the shine came from shards of glass—a sugar jar had smashed on the ground, a tiny metal spoon left among the scattered white granules. It was one of Dale's favorite spoons, too, one with a cross-hatched pattern on its handle.

He'd been in a hurry to leave.

Greg crouched to pick up the spoon. Scratches marred the back of it. He wiped it off on his jeans, before rounding his own car.

Dale didn't want to see him again. He hadn't stopped to talk, even when he'd probably recognized Greg's car next to his.

And that told Greg everything he needed to

know. June had tried to give him hope. But Dale himself was no longer interested in this relationship—Greg had fucked up way too badly.

Maybe Dale was right. Maybe Greg was too young for someone like him.

Greg slid the metal spoon into his pocket, furious with himself.

HOURS LATER in his own apartment, Greg stared blankly at his textbook. His last exam was tomorrow, and he couldn't concentrate.

Weeks ago, he'd been looking forward to the end of finals. He'd planned on building a pillow nest, lining up a menu, charging up their phones so they wouldn't need to leave the bed. They'd spend all day snuggled together, and Greg would devote hours to touching every inch of Dale's skin.

He was back in his own apartment now, the luxurious decor alien after weeks of comfort and warmth.

This was not his home. None of this was— not the shelves of comic books, not the lavender-scented bed, not the polished shine of his kitchen.

Home was back with Dale, with the paper cranes hanging in the bedroom, the mosaic walls in the bathroom, the memory of his omega curled up in their bed, cotton sheets slipping off his shoulder.

He fought down the pang in his stomach, sick with longing. *You're not my alpha,* Dale had said. Except when Greg thought *omega* and *bondmate*, all he remembered was Dale's smile, the warm glow of his eyes. The way Dale's belly was soft under his touch, the way he leaned so easily into Greg's chest, his limbs loose and relaxed.

Nothing in this apartment smelled like home. Greg climbed to his feet, padding to the boxes he'd stashed by the door. He opened the box with his clothes, breathing in the whiff of hibiscus and aspen.

Gods, he missed Dale, and it hadn't even been a day.

One by one, he opened the boxes. Breathed in lungfuls of hibiscus. Then he opened his textbooks, pressing his nose to smooth paper.

If he thought hard enough, he could imagine Dale's cheek pressed against his back, the soft ends of his hair tickling Greg's skin. Greg opened the last box, wishing he had the self-restraint to leave one box sealed, to try and trap the air from Dale's apartment.

In the box, he found things he'd forgotten about: a free mug from the campus bookstore, a cluster of used pens, a stuffed goat plushie Dale had bought on a whim, and tucked down the back of Greg's shirt.

There was a paper crane behind the goat. Frowning, Greg pulled it out. Lightning print covered its surfaces—his favorite in Dale's stack of origami paper. The crane perched in his palm, its wings elegant and pointed, not a fold out of place. One Dale had made, then.

Through his stay at Dale's apartment, Greg had folded twenty, maybe thirty cranes. It was nowhere near the thousand Dale wanted, and Greg couldn't fathom why Dale would return just one crane, and not all those Greg had made. Had this crane fallen in by mistake? Or had Dale given this to him?

We're at four hundred now, Dale had said last night.

Greg flipped through the rest of his textbooks, looking for the origami squares he'd used as bookmarks. He found ten sheets.

At his desk, he made creases through the paper. *You can't fold them like a production line,* Dale had said. *That's cheating. For cranes to count toward the thousand, you have to fold them with your heart. One at a time. And when you've got a thousand cranes, your wish will come true.*

So Greg folded the first crane, running his nail along the folds like Dale did. He brought the corners together, tucked the sides in, flipped the paper around. Fifteen minutes later, he had one crane.

For the rest of the night, he folded the cranes, remembering Dale's hands on his, Dale's breath on his cheek, the way Dale had watched his handiwork intently.

Then Greg thought about next week, next month, and what it would be like if Dale wasn't there. He shoved the thought away, bowing his head, working on the ninth crane. *Please let the baby be okay. Please let Dale be okay.*

It was well past midnight when the tenth crane was done. Greg leaned back into his seat, his eyes tired, his mind unable to rest. He picked his phone up, opening his speed dial list. Dale's number was at the top.

He tapped on Dale's name, pressed the phone to his ear, and closed his eyes.

The dial tone rang twice. Then it clicked like someone answered it, and Greg's heart skipped, just like it had all the other times.

An automated voice said, "*The number you're calling is currently unavailable. At the tone, please leave your message.*"

He sighed. The phone beeped.

"Hey," Greg said, his voice rough with fatigue. "I don't know if you've listened to my other voice messages. Just wanted to say I miss you. I'm sorry for everything, okay? I didn't mean for my dad to show up. He switched cars, I had no idea. I just... I wish I'd been better with all this. I'm sorry. I know it's better that I don't see you anymore, but I just—just wanted to say I love you. That's all."

He wanted to say so much more—wanted to tell Dale he missed his laugh, wanted to say he missed having Dale in his bed, having Dale's lips on his skin, but maybe that would be too much. Dale had left. He wouldn't want to hear why Greg wanted him back, what Greg missed about him. Greg couldn't return Dale his job.

So he shut up, hitting the End Call button.

From the living room, Greg fetched one of the boxes his things had been packed in. He tucked the cranes carefully into them, then set the box beside his desk.

Tomorrow, he'll buy some paper, and fold more cranes for Dale. For their baby.

30
Dale

IN THE first days after The Apex, Dale adjusted to not having an alpha again. It wasn't easy. He was afraid to step outside his apartment, for fear of his neighbors recognizing him. Of someone spilling the news, or a nosy alpha coming along, smirking when he said, *So I heard you were sleeping with your student.*

Worse, maybe the cashier at the grocery store would know, or maybe rumors had spread about him at school. Maybe Greg had found someone new, and he'd tell his omega, *I knocked Professor Kinney up.*

Greg wouldn't do that. But he *could,* and Dale remembered Bernard Hastings' eyes burning into him, revulsion and scorn dripping off his lips.

He wasn't fit to be a professor. Like Bernard said, Dale had breached the first rule of teaching. But Dale still needed income, so he sent in applications to the childcare centers in Meadowfall, hoping someone would think him employable. Maybe he should move to Highton instead, where no one would recognize him. Maybe he should move before his belly grew too big.

But he'd also promised June he'd stay here for now, and he didn't want to break his word.

Secretly, Dale wished he'd glimpse Greg in town somewhere. In the grocery store, or in a sporting goods place, or maybe on the road.

The days passed, and the hole in his chest lingered.

Three weeks after The Apex, Dale landed an interview.

The childcare center was looking to fill a permanent position. It was on the other side of town, far away from Bernard Hastings' home. In the daytime, children ran through the center playground, watched over by two omega teachers. Dale eyed the children's smiling faces, his chest aching.

He couldn't help touching his own belly. At eleven weeks, the baby bump was starting to become noticeable. He'd been talking to it, cradling it, and sometimes, he read to it at night, wishing he'd taken one of the comic books from Greg's bookshelves. Their baby would love to listen to things from Greg's childhood, he was sure.

Dale stepped through the colorful doorway of the childcare center, glancing at its jangling bells. Cheerful rainbows and clouds had been painted across the walls. A smiling lady looked up from behind a shelf of schoolbags—omega, from her apple blossom scent. "Hello! Can I help you?"

"I'm here for an interview," he said, dreading the questions. *Why did you leave your previous job? How can we trust that you'll keep your oaths as a teacher?*

"You must be Dale," she said, brightening.

She rounded the shelves, extending a hand. "I'm Lisa, the principal. Did Cindy mention that I'll be doing the interview?"

"Yes, she did," Dale said, his stomach twisting into knots. He wanted some pickles, suddenly. Wanted them smothered in ketchup and tuna and cheese, when he'd cringe at the combination before. But first, the interview.

Lisa led the way to her office, where more rainbows adorned the walls. In a corner, acrylic handprints were scattered around a calendar, and pictures of children hung between some clouds. "Congratulations, by the way," she said, glancing down at his belly. "We especially love expecting omegas here."

Dale cradled his abdomen, relaxing a little. That was why he'd applied for a job here — so he'd be prepared for children. It had been too long since he'd read those books on pregnancy and childcare, and this would give him some firsthand experience with toddlers. And if the pregnancy failed... maybe he'd still get to be around the little ones. "It's my first. I hope you don't mind...?"

"That's great!" Lisa beamed, her curls bobbing around her face. "We've got all kinds of omega teachers here — some of us have adult children, and some of us have given birth not too long ago. If you're worried about training, we'll provide that."

The interview proceeded like he expected: Lisa asked about his previous jobs, about his experiences and achievements and interests, and Dale leaned into his seat, his nerves starting to calm. He was getting through the interview fine.

Lisa seemed to like him, with her smiles and nods, and all his interview preparation was paying off.

She flipped through his printed resume, meeting his eyes. "So it says here that you were a professor for ten years in Meadowfall College. Why did you leave that job?"

His stomach hardened into a piece of rock. Dale stared at her, then at the resume, wishing he could erase those words. But he hadn't anything else to fall back on—before he became a professor, he'd spent his days on his PhD, and before that, he'd been working part-time as a waiter, struggling to pay off his tuition.

All it had taken was one alpha, and Dale's painstakingly-repaired life had shattered into pieces again.

"I... It was no longer suitable for me to stay on," he said, all his carefully prepared-answers fleeing his mind. He needed a smart reply. Needed Lisa to trust him with clever words and confident smiles. Instead, he remembered Greg, his warm embrace, his cocky smile. Greg's forehead pressed against his, his clumsily-folded cranes sitting in a row on Dale's study shelf. Dale's throat tightened.

It had been three weeks, and Dale couldn't forget about him.

Lisa nodded for him to go on. Dale sucked in a deep breath, then blew it out, his eyes burning. He couldn't cry in front of a potential employer.

"You don't have to mention it if you don't want to," she said, concern creasing her forehead. "I'll understand."

"I met my alpha there," Dale blurted, his fingers pressing into his abdomen.

The moment he said it, he knew it was the truth. That Greg was his alpha. That Greg would *always* be his alpha, and it would never change.

And Dale had left him behind.

"That's a good thing, right?" Lisa asked, leaning forward. "Or should I call Omega Support Services?"

"No! No, it isn't that," Dale said, horrified. "Greg isn't abusive. He's just... someone I shouldn't have gotten involved with. It's complicated."

Lisa settled back into her seat, doubt lingering on her face. "If you're sure," she said. "But do remember that there are help lines you can call."

Dale nodded. He'd dug himself into a hole, and the only way out was to explain himself. "My alpha was my student," he said, looking at his hands. "I was fired for that."

His cheeks burned so hot they felt like peeling. Lisa was in her fifties, and Dale was prepared for her judgment. *Guess I botched this interview.*

Instead, she peered at him, her eyes filled with worry. "Is Greg supporting you now?"

"I left him," Dale said. "I'm starting over."

She nodded gravely. "Then I'll wish you the very best on your new journey. Thank you for your honesty, Dale."

He wasn't sure what she had to thank him for. It was a job interview. But Lisa stood, extending her hand.

"Well, this has been a trying time for you," she said, shaking his hand when he scrambled to his feet. "Go home and get some rest. You'll start work next Monday."

He stared at her, mouth hanging open. "What?"

Lisa smiled, her eyes crinkling. "You care for your students, Dale. Your work history has proven that. And you've been holding onto your child this entire time."

Dale wanted to say, *This is insane. I've breached my previous contract. How can you trust me?*

It must've shown on his face, because Lisa added, "We aren't defined by single mistakes, Dale, but by who we are as people. Does that make sense?"

He wanted to argue. A mistake lasting two months was enough for almost everyone to judge him by. But Dale was *hired,* and he wasn't going to mess this up again. "It does. Thank you, Headmistress."

"Just Lisa," she said, walking him to the exit. "I look forward to working with you."

When he first joined the college, Bernard Hastings' welcome hadn't been so kind. Dale swallowed, ducking out of the childcare center. But Lisa had seen past his mistakes, and he was determined not to disappoint her.

He strode to his car, glancing at the bits of papers strewn in the backseat. He should clean his car. Return Greg's sunglasses, his pen, the one NY Rockets shirt Dale never returned. Greg hadn't called him about the missing things; he probably didn't know they were still with Dale.

And Dale was still holding on to them, damn it all to hell.

In silence, Dale drove home, his thoughts

whirling. Bernard Hastings had promised to make life difficult for him, but Dale now had a job. He didn't know the sort of reach Bernard had. If Dale saw Greg again... would Bernard pull strings? Get Lisa to fire him? Or would he get the entire childcare center shut down?

Dale shuddered. He shouldn't even think about meeting Greg again. He was letting Greg go, giving Greg a chance to spread his wings. See the world. Find a better omega, not someone who had lost his job sleeping with a student.

At the apartment, Dale slipped through the front door, setting his interview folder on a side table. Then he pulled his phone out, tapped on the voicemail app, and played the first message.

"*Hey, it's me again,*" Greg's voice said, tinny in his ear. But it was close, filled with warmth. Dale closed his eyes, sinking into his couch.

"*I don't know if you're listening to any of these messages. Or if you're even getting them at all. I'm calling anyway. I got a second job two weeks ago at the community center. They were looking for part-time coaches, so I went and filled in.*

"*We've been doing all sorts of sports — football, soccer, hockey, and all that. The kids are fun. Mostly from elementary school. I've been thinking... I hope you and the baby are doing fine. When he or she gets older, I was thinking I could show our baby how to play sports. Basketball. Just thought it would be fun.*"

Dale bit his lip, his eyes growing wet. Greg couldn't still be thinking about their baby.

"*I've been doing well. Moved in with my mom and dad. It's a pain. I'm moving out as soon as I get my paychecks, but it's still two weeks away. Been thinking about you. Miss you.*" Greg stopped for breath, and Dale breathed along with him, his heart sore. "*I love you, okay? Don't forget that.*"

The voicemail ended, leaving silence in his ear. Dale replayed the message, curling into a ball on the couch. Then he played the previous message, where Greg had told him about his other job—an internship at Meadowfall's environmental regulations department.

The doorbell rang. Dale's heart leaped. *Greg?* A moment later, a truck rumbled off outside. Not Greg. He sagged. *But it can't be a delivery, either. I haven't bought anything.*

Phone in hand, Dale rolled off the couch, padding over to the front door. He peeked through the viewfinder. No visitors. So he opened the door, staring at the parcel on his doorstep.

There was no sender information, just Dale's name and address. But he recognized that bold handwriting anyway, the sharp curves of the D and Y. *Greg.*

Heart pattering, he picked up the box. It was surprisingly light, as though Greg had sent air. With the next voicemail playing on the phone's loudspeaker, Dale picked open the box, wondering if Greg had sent him legal paperwork, or something for school.

The first thing he saw, when he opened the box, was a mess of pastel colors. Blues, purples, pinks. They were paper cranes, Dale realized, his breath catching. And there had to be a hundred of them crammed into the box—big ones, little ones, ones that perched nicely in his palm.

The last time Greg had made these, he'd

taken half an hour for each crane. Dale didn't know how long Greg had to have spent, folding all of these.

Slowly, he lined the cranes around him: large ones on the floor, small ones on the coffee table. They sat in rows by his feet, watching him. Greg had to know he'd love them, didn't he? Dale swallowed past the lump in his throat, wishing he could see his alpha.

There was an envelope taped to the bottom of the box, lumpy, as though it contained some kind of fabric. *There's more?* Dale pulled it out of the box, tearing the flap open.

It was another onesie—this time with paper cranes printed all over it. Dale stared, his heart thudding loud in his chest. Next to him, the voicemail played on.

"*I love you,*" Greg said. "*The baby, too.*"

"You need to stop doing that," Dale groaned, covering his face with the onesie. It smelled like aspen, and he couldn't stop breathing it in.

He needed to forget that Greg Hastings ever existed.

Except he couldn't. Not in the past, and certainly not now.

31
Dale

THE ULTRASOUND was due at twenty weeks, right when semester began.

Dale stepped into the prenatal clinic, his hands shaking. The baby hadn't begun to move. Fetuses were supposed to do so anywhere between sixteen to twenty-two weeks, and four weeks had passed in that window. In the days leading up to the appointment, Dale had convinced himself that the baby would miscarry, that it had stopped developing, that it would die.

He'd cried himself to sleep the past two weeks, and he hadn't any more tears right now.

"Hello," the receptionist said when he stepped up, giving him a friendly smile. "Here for an appointment?"

"Yes," he said. "My name is Dale Kinney."

She handed him a clipboard with a form. Dale sat in a corner of the reception area, trying not to stand out.

Couples filled the rest of the waiting room—mostly pairs of two women, and a couple of men. Dale's nape prickled under their stares. It seemed unusual for an omega to show up alone, but it would probably be worse if Greg had accompanied him to this visit.

Around them, pictures of babies and baby animals covered the walls. Pastel colors filled the room. A tinkling lullaby played in the background, and baby magazines were strewn across the chairs and tables, with adorable little faces smiling up at the reader. A young girl smiled up at her mother, swinging her legs.

Dale pressed his hand to his belly, filling in the form. At the line for his alpha's name, he paused, thinking about Greg. He wouldn't implicate Greg in this; Greg was far too young. So Dale left the space blank, wincing when he filled in his age.

At the counter, the receptionist's eyes widened when she scanned his form for blanks. Dale swallowed. *She probably knows it's a risky pregnancy.* She smiled at him, though. "Thank you, Mr. Kinney. Please have a seat."

He flushed, retreating to his corner.

To kill the minutes, Dale pulled his phone out. Looked up Greg's Facebook profile. Greg's name was at the top of his search history; Dale had been following his page for the past weeks, secretly saving selfies that Greg had posted. In those photos, Greg sometimes smiled, but it was a tiny one, like his heart wasn't in it.

Greg didn't use to share pictures of himself. But he did now, and Dale had no idea why. Was he advertising himself? Looking for a new omega?

There wa a new photo, posted two hours ago. It was faded out with some photo filters, cropped to show Greg's lips on someone's abdomen. Dale's stomach twisted. *You found someone.*

Except he recognized the tiny mole right next to the omega's navel. It was *Dale's* belly, and that picture was of them, taken two months ago, when Greg had given him the rabbit onesie. Dale's heart raced.

Beneath the photo, there were a few comments. *Who's the lucky omega? That a baby? Who did you hook up with?*

Greg hadn't replied to any of them. He didn't know Dale had been stalking his Facebook—at least, he shouldn't. Dale had been talking to June, giving her updates on the pregnancy. In return, June told him when Greg dropped by the lab, offering to help with more research.

Dale swallowed. He missed being in the lab. Missed his experiments, his humming machines, the glint of fluorescent light on glass vials. Did he regret meeting Greg? If he hadn't met his alpha, he'd still have his job now.

In the clinic, a nurse opened a door, calling out a name. Dale jumped, glancing up.

He almost didn't want to see the doctor. Didn't want to do the tests, in case bad news came up.

He breathed in, then out. No, he needed to do the tests—there were things he would need to know now, and he needed to be brave.

Dale looked back at the photo. It had been taken so long ago. He still knew the touch of Greg's lips, knew the warmth of Greg's smile. What would Greg do if there was bad news?

Suddenly aching for his alpha's voice, Dale

looked at the contacts on his phone, his thumb hovering over Greg's Call button. He'd spent weeks listening to the same voice recordings, playing them on loudspeaker so their baby could hear its other dad. But Dale had memorized all of those messages now, and he wanted to hear Greg say something different. Have Greg next to him, just lending a shoulder for him to lean on.

Dale held his breath. *If he doesn't answer, I'll take that as a sign. I'll hang up and forget I ever called.*

Heart thudding, he hit the Call button, and pressed the phone to his ear.

Greg answered after three rings. "Dale?"

His voice rumbled into Dale's ear, sharp and concerned. Dale sank bonelessly into the chair, his heart squeezing. Greg's voice was so familiar, and he hadn't thought he'd hear it again. The tightness in his chest eased.

"Dale?" Greg said, his voice tinny across the line.

In the background, children shouted, and whistles beeped. Greg had to be at his coaching job, then, standing in a sunny field, dressed in coaching slacks and a T-shirt. The image burned into the backs of Dale's eyelids, vivid and precious.

"C'mon, I know you're there," Greg said.

Dale didn't answer. He hadn't meant to start a conversation. Hadn't even thought of what he'd say to Greg, if Greg answered the call. And now that Greg was speaking in his ear, Dale felt like he'd cry if he started talking. He hadn't realized he'd missed his alpha this much.

The nurse opened the door again, announcing another name. Dale jumped.

Greg heard it, too. "Where are you?"

The clinic, Dale wanted to say. *I've missed you so much and I don't want you to stop talking.* Instead, he kept silent, breathing in, listening to yells and laughter and the sough of Greg's breath.

"Tell me," Greg said.

Dale squeezed his eyes shut. They weren't supposed to be doing this. Bernard Hastings could find out. And Greg was supposed to be looking for a new omega. Dale shouldn't be dragging him back into the past.

"Look, if you aren't talking, I'll hang up," Greg said.

Dale's stomach dropped. "No," he blurted, then regretted it immediately. He should've just shut up. He shouldn't have called Greg at all.

Greg breathed out, and Dale imagined him closing his eyes, phone cradled to his ear. "How's the baby? Is that where you are? The clinic? Are you sick?"

And *now* Dale wanted to laugh and cry at the same time. Greg wanted to know everything. It was just like him, and Dale loved him, and he should be ending this call before he begged for Greg to return.

"C'mon, don't stop talking," Greg said. "I haven't heard from you in two goddamn months."

If Dale had any self-restraint, they wouldn't have talked for the rest of their lives. "I'm waiting for the ultrasound."

Greg sucked in a breath. "How's everything else?"

"I don't know."

"Gods, I should be there," Greg said. He

paused, as though he were looking around. "Where are you? I'll come."

"You're working," Dale said, his pulse fluttering. "You can't just leave."

"It's my baby. I don't care."

"Well, I care. Stay where you are," Dale said. He swallowed, wishing Greg would come anyway, wishing Greg would take Dale into his arms, hold him close. Gods, what wouldn't he give for a hug?

There was a pause. "How are you?"

Dale swallowed. He didn't know. "Fine, I guess." *I miss you.* "How are you?"

"Fine."

"Really?"

Greg snorted. "What do you want me to say? Good? 'Cause I'm not happy, Dale. I need to see you."

Dale bit his lip hard, his eyes prickling. He was in a clinic with other people, and he couldn't cry here. "No, you don't."

"Look, I'm sorry," Greg said. "I need to make things up to you. I—"

The door opened, and the nurse looked around. "Dale Kinney!"

Dale swore. "I have to go."

"I have a match next week," Greg said. "School's starting. You gonna be there?"

Dale's stomach squeezed. He wanted to attend the game. Wanted to see Greg on the court again, all sinewy muscle and hard body. He'd missed that, too, missed seeing Greg all fierce on the court, his focus razor-sharp.

"Dale—"

"Mr. Kinney," the nurse called.

Dale winced. "No. I'm not going. Bye."

He hit the End Call button before he could change his mind, shoving his phone into his pocket. Then he stood up with a smile, waving at the nurse. "I'm here! Sorry!"

But the conversation lingered in his mind. As the nurse took his weight and blood pressure, Dale imagined the disappointment on Greg's face when he said he wasn't attending the game.

When Dale knocked on the doctor's office door, he remembered the edge of desperation in Greg's voice. *I need to see you.*

The doctor was a beta, from the faint scent of grass in the room. Dale barely noticed. She explained the visits he'd need for the pregnancy, the extra tests he'd have to do because of his age. Dr. Smith spoke to him with smooth neutrality, never once asking where his alpha was. Dale relaxed into his cushioned seat, his anxiety easing.

"As long as you continue to eat healthily and exercise every week, the pregnancy should proceed as normal," she said.

After she answered his questions, Dr. Smith took him through the ultrasound. She showed him the beat of his baby's heart, and Dale sagged into the exam bed, relief soaking through his bones. The baby was fine. Still alive. It would be a boy.

"I want two pictures of him," he said. One for himself, and one for Greg. Because Greg deserved a picture of their baby, too.

She nodded, tapping the print order into the computer.

Unlike the frown he'd been expecting, Dr. Smith looked him in the eye, smiled, and never once gave him bad news.

"You may experience the first flutter soon," she said. "Maybe over the next day or two. Sometimes, it just takes a while. Come back in two weeks if you haven't felt it yet."

He held his belly as he dressed, leaving her office a lot calmer than before. Maybe he didn't need Greg, after all. Maybe he could do this by himself.

The thought both scared him, and gave him strength. He was omega, but he could get through this. He didn't need an alpha for everything.

But as Dale settled into the next room to do his blood tests, he couldn't help remembering Greg again, knowing he'd have felt so much better with his alpha by his side.

32
Dale

DALE KEPT his head down, weaving through the spectators' seats in the college arena.

He'd told himself he wouldn't return. He'd spent the whole of yesterday saying *No, I don't need to see him. He's moving on.*

Except he'd opened his email this morning, and *First playoff of the season!* had screamed bold across his screen.

They'd included a photo of Greg on the team. Dale's stomach had swooped, and all his resolve had crashed and shattered.

Five minutes before the game started, Dale picked a seat close to the walls of the arena, so Greg wouldn't be able to see him. No one gave him a second glance—not when the baby bump was hidden under a loose T-shirt and flowing pants.

The crowd murmured around him. The basketball teams clustered on opposite ends of the court. Dale kept his head down, picking out Greg from the mess of scarlet jerseys.

Greg looked the same—spiky hair, focused eyes, full lips. His skin had tanned from coaching, and Dale couldn't look away, not when he'd spent hours on Greg's Facebook, just looking at his photos.

The teams scattered, falling into position on either half of the court. Greg stood on one side of the referee, staring down his opponent, the basketball between them. Dale held his breath.

The whistle screeched. The ball soared into the air, and Greg snatched it, twisting, passing it to his teammate. Then he tore across the court, his eyes on the players and the ball, and caught a pass. Thighs pumping, he slipped out of his opponents' defenses, dodging arms all the way to the hoop. Then he leaped, dunked the ball in, and the crowd roared around Dale.

Dale clapped along with them, a deep yearning whispering through his veins. He'd missed this. Missed the adrenaline of Greg's games, the sweat and ticking clock and fast-paced passes.

Through the previous semester, Dale had sat in the front row seats, cheering on Greg's team. Greg had been doubtful about making promises, and Dale had shown up week after week, trying to prove that they were still unhurt and alive.

They were both still safe, and Dale wondered if Greg still thought about Tony, afraid of making promises. He shouldn't be. He was young, healthy. He had his whole life ahead of him.

When the halftime whistle blew, the players split into their own sides of the court. Greg wandered to the edge, scanning the crowd.

Dale's stomach flipped. *He's looking for me.* Greg didn't believe his lie, then. He knew Dale would come. And Dale had, hadn't he? If he had had a shred of self-restraint, he wouldn't be in this mess. Wouldn't have gotten pregnant with Greg's baby at all.

He ducked down when Greg's gaze swept closer, pressing his face into his knees. Sixty seconds later, Dale peeked up over the beta seated in front of him, breathing a sigh when he found Greg jogging back to his team. The red jersey clung to his back, damp with sweat. Dale dragged his gaze away. He'd probably dream about Greg tonight, like he had last night, and the night before last.

When the halftime whistle blew, Dale straightened in his seat. Greg had called again yesterday, two hours after Dale left the clinic. Dale had rejected the call, and Greg had left another voicemail. Dale had listened to it three times, damned creature that he was. But at least Greg didn't know.

The game passed far more quickly in the second half. The score was 53-27 in favor of the Meadowfall Lions, but the other team was now on the offense. Dale gulped, watching as Greg flew through the court, his muscles flexing, his skin gleaming with sweat.

He couldn't deny that he still wanted Greg. Wanted Greg in his jersey, his strong, toned body pressed against Dale, his callused hands dragging over Dale's skin.

Dale swallowed, his nails biting into his palm. The pregnancy hormones had only made him want Greg more.

Greg sprinted through the court, accepting passes, shooting the ball at his teammates, dunking them into the hoop. He was a joy to watch, his expression sharp, his movements smooth like a prowling beast.

Dale could understand why he'd escaped into basketball after Tony's death.

The game ended far too soon. The Lions won 91-54, and the team gathered around, clapping each other on the back. Dale twitched. He had to leave now, before the team broke for the day. Before Greg spotted him somehow, found him secretly watching.

Pulse thrumming in his ears, Dale stood, keeping his face away from the court. He jogged up the stairs to the furthest exit, hesitating when he approached the door. When would he see Greg in person again? Maybe never.

He gulped, turning back.

Greg stood stock-still by his teammates, scanning the crowd again. Dale's breath caught. He couldn't see Greg's expression from this far away, didn't know if Greg had spotted him against the white backdrop of the arena wall. But Greg stepped toward him, and Dale's instincts said, *Run.*

He turned for the door, not daring to look over his shoulder. Greg would leave for the debrief. He'd joke with his teammates, forgetting about Dale. That was the way it should happen.

Dale barreled down the stairs. At ground level, he pushed through the stairwell door, blinking to adjust from bright fluorescent lights to the dim sodium lamps that lit the parking lot, trying to remember where he'd parked his car. This soon after the game, no one had left the arena yet.

He didn't see me. He couldn't have.

Dale stepped toward the half-full parking lot,

gravitating toward an alcove, where decorative trees cast dark shadows on the arena walls.

A hidden door flew open in front of him. Dale yelped, stumbling backward, his heart crashing into his chest.

Greg charged out, glancing around. Then his eyes locked onto Dale, and Dale couldn't move. Couldn't stop staring at Greg's face, at the dark gleam of sweat along his jaw, at the glisten of damp on his neck, his shoulders. He smelled like aspen, like fresh sweat, and Dale had dreamed of seeing him too many times to even run.

Greg crossed the space between them in three strides, snagging his hand. His palm was hot, callused. He parted his lips, but no words came out.

He was trying to figure what to say. Dale wasn't judging. He had no words, either.

Greg reached up with his other hand, tracing the backs of his fingers over Dale's cheek, the heat of his body whispering into Dale's skin. For two months, Dale had missed his touch. And Greg was being far too tender.

"No," Dale whispered.

Greg leaned in and kissed him.

His lips were soft, careful. Familiar. In the shadows of the parking lot, Dale needed more. Needed to feel the press of Greg's body before he left him. So he parted for Greg, licking at Greg's lips, and Greg groaned, sliding into his mouth, his tongue tangling with Dale's. He tasted like the electrolyte drinks he loved, and the possessive stroke of his tongue weakened Dale's knees, had him sinking against his alpha.

Greg pressed him against the cool arena wall, his large hands smoothing down Dale's chest, following the curve of his belly. Dale arched into his caress. He almost thought Greg would touch lower, but Greg's hands slowed, rounding his sides, then back again to hold their baby. His fingers were right above Dale's cock, and Dale whined, his blood rushing south.

"Greg," he whispered, his hips rocking. Greg growled, stroking him through his pants, a firm, hard pressure. They'd done this before a few times, pressed up at home, or in school, when Dale had needed to jerk off quickly, and Greg had helped.

In the shadows of the parking lot, Greg tugged open Dale's pants and reached inside, his palm hot through Dale's briefs.

Dale hissed, jerking, and Greg kissed him harder, swallowing his moans. His fingers slid down the bare skin of Dale's cock, dragging down his foreskin, touching his sensitive tip.

In a few minutes, there would be people flooding out of the arena. All Dale could think about was his alpha, his alpha's touch on him, his cock throbbing for Greg.

He ran his hands down Greg's damp chest, sliding his fingers under Greg's jersey. Greg's abs were solid, his pecs flat and smooth, and this wasn't the after-match sex Dale had envisioned for them ages ago.

"Missed you," Greg growled against his lips, his breath hot on Dale's cheek, his callused fingers squeezing Dale's tip, slipping under his foreskin, circling his head. Pleasure jolted down his nerves.

Dale shuddered, panting, his cock so hard he

357

couldn't think. Greg traced two fingers down his balls, stroking them, rubbing his slick hole, and Dale's breath rushed from his lungs.

They shouldn't be doing this here. But Greg shielded him from view, his fist working slow and knowing around Dale's cock, and Dale's legs trembled. He'd been dreaming about Greg's touch for two months. And when Greg slowed his fist, leaving it snug around Dale's cock, Dale thrust up, fucking into his hand just like he'd done tens of times, back when they'd still been seeing each other.

"Want another baby?" Greg murmured against his lips. "I'd give you a second one."

Dale whimpered, remembering Greg inside him, Greg filling him with seed. Greg putting a baby inside him. The tension between his legs spiked. Pleasure crashed through him, and he was coming, spilling, moaning into Greg's mouth as he shuddered, clinging to his alpha.

Greg pressed him against the wall. Dale panted against his lips, trying to think.

He felt safe against Greg like this. No one was shouting. There were no camera flashes, no speculative murmuring. Just his breathing, and Greg's chest snug against his, his sweat smearing on Dale's skin.

Dale groaned, pressing his face into Greg's shoulder. Greg smelled like pure alpha — aspen and musk. He didn't have another omega's scent on him, and Dale wanted to drag his own wrists over Greg, mark Greg as his own.

"How did the ultrasound go?" Greg whispered, curving his arm around Dale's back.

His other hand stroked Dale's cock slow and smooth, milking him for the rest of his cum.

"The baby's fine," Dale mumbled. "I had some blood work done. The results of the abnormality tests aren't in yet."

Greg exhaled, his breath riffling through Dale's hair. "Okay. Keep me updated."

"It's a boy."

"Thought of names yet?"

Dale huffed, almost laughing. "I don't... I haven't even processed it all. I'm just..."

And his mind cleared. He was in the campus parking lot, his pants open, Greg tracing his thumb languidly over Dale's cock. It was wrong. And yet he felt the safest he had had in the past two months, curled up against Greg's chest. Greg felt like home.

"I missed you," Greg murmured, kissing his cheek. "I'm sorry. I want you back. I don't know how to fix this. I—"

"We shouldn't be doing this here," Dale muttered. He needed to pull away. Leave Greg. But Greg's touch drifted up to his belly, and he slipped his hand under Dale's shirt, running the backs of his fingers over his baby bump. Dale's throat tightened. "You shouldn't be seen with me."

Greg didn't answer. Dale didn't know what Greg's circumstances were like with his parents, but he knew he couldn't risk his new job, couldn't risk Bernard Hastings shutting down the childcare center. This didn't only involve him now; he would not repay Lisa's kindness with destruction.

"You should go," Dale said, closing his eyes.

"Am I still your alpha?"

Yes. Yes, you are, Dale wanted to say. Except he couldn't have Greg pining for him, posting pictures of them on his Facebook. Greg needed to set his sights higher, find someone who wasn't forty-two and on his probation period at his new job.

"No. I'm leaving," Dale choked. He hadn't had enough of Greg. He wanted Greg's teeth marks on his skin, wanted Greg's scent all over him.

Greg brought his wrist up, rubbing his scent gland along Dale's throat, over his shoulder. Then he dragged it down Dale's chest, over his belly, and Dale heard *Mine,* in his touch. His entire body ached to be pressed against his alpha's.

Dale forced himself to step away, his heart thumping. "No."

"You wanted me." Greg drew his hand back, hurt in his eyes. Streaks of white glistened on his forearm.

Dale did up his pants, swallowing hard. Greg was still wearing his team jersey. He wasn't even out of college yet. "Date someone else. Three other omegas. Ten. I don't care. Find someone better," Dale gasped. "I don't believe you can't."

"But the baby—"

"The baby will be fine," he snapped. "Don't pull that on me again. *Find someone else.* I won't have your father ruin everything else I care about."

Greg flinched. Dale took another step back. In a smaller voice, Greg said, "I lov—"

"No." Dale turned away, his chest tight. "I don't need it."

Greg looked at the sidewalk. In that moment, he looked fragile, like he was going to break.

"I don't want any more of your voice messages," Dale said, his voice wavering. He spoke louder, to pretend this didn't feel like a knife wound. "I don't want any of your boxes, or your cranes. I don't want to see you ever again."

Dale stepped off the sidewalk, crossing the road before he could change his mind. He needed Greg to stop thinking about him. To at least find someone who could stay with him the rest of his life. Who wouldn't drag him down with a child at the wrong time.

He strode down the rows of cars, closing his eyes when he found his own by chance. Dale slipped inside, then locked the doors.

When Greg didn't approach, Dale sank his forehead against the steering wheel, and cried.

33
Greg

GREG SLAMMED the front door, his teeth grinding. He was leaving. After two months of staying in this damn mansion, saving money and putting up with his father's rules, he'd run out of patience.

He needed to get away. Needed to fix Dale's life. Needed to set everything straight again, except he didn't know how.

They should have spoken the night his father walked in on them. Sorted things out. But none of that had happened, and they'd hung in limbo, Dale throwing Greg out of his apartment.

And in the weeks since, Greg had had alternating nightmares of fire, of losing Dale, of Tony dying over and over in front of his eyes.

He couldn't think about his own future, even now. But he could think about Dale's, and he wanted to help Dale with the baby, help him any way he could.

Back at the basketball arena, Dale had watched the game. He'd lied about attending; Greg had thought he might.

In the weeks before this, June had asked

discreet questions about Greg's Facebook pictures. It was only then that he'd realized she'd been talking to Dale. That Dale was looking at his page. So he'd posted more pictures, earning a tiny smile from June when he'd posted that old photo of him kissing Dale's belly.

An hour ago, he'd glimpsed Dale leaving the basketball arena. He'd caught up to Dale, kissed him, and Dale had melted in his arms the moment their lips met. And he'd been so *hungry*.

Dale had squirmed and bucked and gasped, and all Greg had been thinking of was touching his belly. In the two months they'd been apart, Dale's baby bump had become far more pronounced. Greg had kissed him, knowing Dale was caring for their baby, protecting it, making sure it was loved.

It's a boy, Dale had whispered, after he'd squirmed and come all over Greg's forearm. Greg had held him, breathing in his honey-and-hibiscus scent, filling his lungs and memorizing the musky notes of it.

Then Dale had told him to leave, told Greg he didn't need him anymore. With a sting of guilt, Greg had remembered losing Dale his job. Dale couldn't forgive him for it, and Greg's father would continue to hurt Dale for as long as they were together.

Angry heat swirled in his gut. Greg stalked through the mansion, barely glancing at the vast paintings of Meadowfall College, the bronze bust that his father had commissioned of himself. Two months ago, Greg had moved back into his family home, thinking he could convince his father of his relationship with Dale.

Countless arguments and slammed doors later, Bernard Hastings still scoffed when Greg mentioned age differences.

Greg couldn't subject Dale to that treatment. And Dale no longer acknowledged Greg as his alpha.

His heart hurt.

He was halfway up the grand staircase when his mother stepped out of her bedroom. She was in a nightgown, her graying hair in curlers. When she saw him, she hurried forward, a smile splitting her face. "Greg!"

"Hey, Mom," he said, barely keeping his voice even.

She was the only bright point in his move back here. Greg had spent most of the past five years away from his family, when his father refused to acknowledge what Tony's death meant to him. He'd called her on and off, but it wasn't the same as seeing her in person.

"I'm moving back out," Greg said. "I'm not living with Dad. He's a bastard."

Henrietta slowed down as she reached the landing, giving him a doleful look. "Do you really have to? I missed you when you were living on your own."

"Yeah." He grimaced when she reached for a hug. He was still in his basketball jersey—his sweat had dried on it, and he'd wiped the remnants of Dale's cum on the jersey, after he'd licked the rest off his arm. Not the best time for a hug. "Mom, no. I need a shower."

She paused with her arms outstretched, almost touching him. "Well, go shower, then. I demand my hug."

He cracked a smile. She followed him to his bedroom. Inside, the furniture hadn't been updated since he'd left at eighteen. The shelves were empty — he'd left his comics in the moving boxes — and the bedspread still had Super Alpha printed on it. He'd turned it face-down to hide the graphics.

"What happened?" Mom asked when he shut the door.

"Dale was at my game. The ultrasound went okay. We don't know about the other tests yet."

"Ah." She sighed, settling on the side of his bed while he grabbed his shower things.

"He didn't manipulate me, you know."

"So you've said."

Through the arguments with his dad, his mom had stayed silent, listening to Greg when he had to vent. But she'd never stepped in to defend him, either.

"I don't get why you married Dad. He's... backward. He doesn't understand."

Mom pressed her lips together, the wrinkles on her forehead deepening. "He's still a good man, Greg. He just has different priorities from you."

"He fired Dale!"

"But you understand why he did."

Greg closed his eyes. This, too, was always difficult. "Yes."

He'd known, back when he'd first pursued Dale, that Dale could lose his job. And Greg had been reckless then, had gotten careless later on. His father wanted the college's reputation to grow, so he could continue to see his life's work prosper. By firing Dale, his father was preserving his own goals, the way Dale had clung to his dreams of tenure.

"Sometimes I wish I wasn't so young," Greg said, rubbing his face. "I'm an idiot."

"There's still time for you to grow," his mom said kindly.

He grabbed his towel, glancing at her. "You've never said what you really think about Dale and me." And maybe he'd been afraid to ask, when he was closer to his mom than his dad. He was afraid that she'd think poorly of Dale, or of their relationship. "Or the baby."

"When all's said and done, you're still my child." She smiled tiredly at him. "My heart hurts for you. I don't want to see my baby in pain. And that's why your father is so opposed to this—what will happen when you grow old? Chances are, you'll outlive Dale. Your relationship will raise eyebrows. We think you'll be hurt somehow or other, by continuing with him."

He swallowed, fingers clenching around his towel. "Dad has hurt us most. Everyone else accepts us, damn it. Three different people know about me and Dale, and they've all been really nice about it."

"But what about everyone else? They don't know yet."

"It's none of their business. Dale is—he wanted to be my omega."

Henrietta sighed. "You're Bernard's son. You know the importance of making good impressions. Your relationship with Dale will have others judging you before you even try to influence them."

Greg knew that, too. "I've thought about it. There's no point living my life based on what everyone else thinks. They don't know the other side of the story. They don't know what I feel for Dale, and they don't need to."

She didn't answer, so Greg headed into the bathroom. By the time he finished showering, she was still outside, waiting for him.

"I just want you to be happy, Greg," Mom said, smiling sadly at him. "That's all."

"I'll be happy when I fix all this," he said. "Thoughts on the baby?"

"I'll care for it as my own grandchild," she said. "Try that with your dad. He may be swayed."

Greg closed his eyes, imagining his dad scoffing at his newborn. Dale and the baby didn't deserve that. "Some other time. I'm not ready to talk to him again right now."

His mom rose from the bed. Greg stepped into her arms, hugging her tight. She smelled like morning glory, like *Mom*, and he'd miss her when he moved out again.

"You're not encouraging me to get back together with Dale," he said.

"You aren't trying very hard either, are you?"

Greg swallowed, looking at the worn covers of his bed. On the other side of the duvet, Super Alpha haunted him, reminding him of old costumes and broken dreams.

He'd tried placing hope in his future, a week at a time. Those had gone well. In two months, June would hold her wedding, and Greg would see Dale again.

Maybe... if he and Dale were still unhurt, if

no accidents had befallen them when the wedding rolled around... Maybe Greg could start trusting in the future.

34
Dale

"ARE YOU ready to be married?" Dale asked with a grin.

June rolled her eyes, sitting still while the makeup artist did her eyebrows. "I was ready about six months ago, Dale."

He laughed, nudging her foot as he waited for his turn. In the mirror, June looked beautiful, with her coiffed short hair, her bright hazel eyes, her suit with its lapel and tie. In another room. Cher and her best alpha were dressed and ready— they were all in a mansion by the sea, rented for Cher and June's dream wedding.

"Why Cambria?" Dale asked. "There are lots of towns along the coast. We had to drive two whole hours to get to this place."

June chuckled. "Cher said vampires are rumored to live here. I told her she's been reading too many vampire books."

"They'll prowl the streets at night?"

"No, they'll walk amongst us in the day." She pretended to shudder. "I may be alpha, but I'm not sure I can win against an undead."

Dale smiled. "I guess I'll be at a greater

disadvantage, then, being omega and all."

"Who knows? Maybe you'll have some special vampire-defeating powers." June grinned, her gaze slipping down to his belly. "You know, that looks really uncomfortable."

He followed her gaze, touching the large bump of his abdomen. The baby kicked.

It had been four months since the breakup. Two months since he'd met Greg outside the basketball arena. Since then, little had changed— Dale was still following the basketball emails, peeking at Greg's Facebook when he dared.

The only difference was, Greg had stopped leaving the voicemails. There had been no more cranes and baby clothes. Every so often, the doorbell would ring, and Dale would hurry to the door, expecting his alpha.

Greg never showed up.

He didn't know what he'd do if he saw Greg again. Dale had made it plenty clear that he'd wanted Greg gone. And Greg had listened. The pictures he posted now were of him and his basketball team, and Dale couldn't bring himself to ask if he'd found another omega. June never mentioned it, either.

He was starting to dread going to the store, for fear of somehow bumping into Greg, and whichever new omega he'd found.

"How are things at the childcare?" June asked.

"They're going fine. I'm now officially out of probation." Dale smiled wanly. He liked his new job well enough. He got to spend time with children every day, and his coworkers liked him.

Not quite like his research lab, but it wasn't bad, either. Something to distract him from Greg.

"That's great," June said. "Congrats!" The makeup artist frowned; she gave a sheepish grin.

Dale cracked a smile. "Well, at least no one at the childcare recognizes me."

June sobered. "Has anyone else found out?"

"Other than you? Sam Brentwood and his relatives. Then there's Penny, and Bernard Hastings." Dale winced. That particular memory still set his cheeks burning. Bernard had seen Greg's knot slipping out of him, and that, well. That was the nightmare of the century.

"That's more people than I expected," June said. "How did the rest react?"

Dale opened his mouth, pausing. He'd shoved those memories away, repressing them so he wouldn't feel terrible each time he remembered. "They've been fine, I guess. Sam wanted to attend our wedding, but that's not going to happen."

June raised her eyebrows at 'wedding'. "So aside from that damn bastard who fired you, everyone else accepts you and Greg."

He stared. "I... guess?"

Dale had never thought of it that way. Not when his first priority had always been making sure that word never got out, because he didn't want Bernard Hastings to discover the relationship.

"I'm guessing that you won't find it as stigmatized in some circles," June said, closing her eyes when the makeup artist moved to brush powder on her nose. "Think about it. How many people have actively rejected you and Greg?"

He paused. "One. But he has power over

everything."

"But you still love Greg."

Dale's heart fluttered. "Does it matter?"

She cracked a smile. "Are you ever going to talk to him again?"

"Probably not."

June snorted, but her smile lingered. Dale watched her, wondering how this was funny at all. "Why are you smiling?"

"Because you're an idiot, Dale. The worst things have happened, and you're still refusing to get together with him."

He fixed his gaze on the large picture windows looking over the ocean. Outside, the skies were a clear azure. Golden sunlight slanted through the windowpanes, lighting the oaken floorboards and tiny dust motes in the air. It was all so beautiful here, and it scarcely matched the loneliness that nagged at him inside.

"Bernard could still threaten the childcare center," he said. "Or he could make Greg's life miserable. Or something. I don't even know if Greg has another omega. Maybe he's already bonded with them."

June snorted again, louder and ruder, and the makeup artist sent her an offended look. "Sorry. But seriously, Dale. You're getting nowhere with your life like this. Your baby deserves to meet his other dad."

He knew that. He figured he'd make that decision when things got to that point. Or maybe never, with his current streak of avoiding Greg at all costs. "I'll think about it."

June sighed, still smiling. "I guess we'll see."

THE WEDDING took place on the front lawns of the mansion, early September sunlight glinting off a delicate white gazebo.

To the right, gentle waves rumbled along the private beach, seagulls soaring above the glittering sea. To the left, a fountain tinkled in a garden of rose bushes, water spilling off three tiers of carved marble.

The guests were gathered in the seats facing the gazebo. They murmured and waited, turning to look when the flower girls walked down the aisle. Someone played on a piano to the side.

At the start of the carpet, Dale squirmed. There had to be two hundred people here, and he wasn't used to that kind of attention, not anymore. Not when he was six months pregnant, and anyone could tell just by looking at his belly. There were probably some of his ex-students in the audience; June had mentioned inviting Penny.

Dale tugged on the white cotton blouse, wishing it were long enough to be tucked into his pants. It was a beautiful shirt, with lace collars and sleeves, and pearl buttons dotting down his chest, over his belly. It barely veiled his abdomen, allowing cool air to brush his skin from beneath.

"Are you ready?" the best alpha asked, offering Dale his elbow. Cam Brown was one of Cher's best friends, all blue eyes and blond hair, his smile stunning. He was older, too, maybe in his fifties. Probably the sort of person who had his life together, complete with sailboat and private beach house.

If Dale wasn't already in love with someone else, he'd have given Cam a second glance. Cam was the sort of alpha he *should* be seeing. But all he felt was weariness, and the ache of missing someone.

Dale smiled wanly. "Yes, I'm ready."

He slipped his hand into the crook of Cam's elbow. Behind, June whispered loudly, "You can do it!"

Dale wasn't sure if she was talking to him, or Cher, but her words cheered him up. It was better than thinking about how he'd never have his own wedding, or his own alpha, or...

Cam led him down the aisle when the flower girls reached the end, their violet petals dotting the red carpet. Around, the guests murmured. Dale held his free hand by his side, fighting the urge to hold his belly, shield it from all the stares. He was old. He didn't want to be reminded about how risky the pregnancy was.

Instead, he pretended that this was what his own wedding would look like: family and friends around him, people who cared that he'd be spending his life with someone he loved. Greg would be by his side, smiling at him, and everything would be okay.

In those moments, Dale allowed himself to think that maybe June was right, that there were people who would accept him and Greg despite their differences. Their friends would clap when he walked down the aisle with his alpha, and it wouldn't matter that Greg was twenty-two, and Dale was in his forties.

They would exchange rings, and maybe their son would watch from the front row, his eyes alight with joy.

Dale breathed out as he stepped along the carpet, scanning the crowd for faces he recognized. He glimpsed Penny, who beamed and waved. He saw a couple of other post-doc students from two labs over, whom he'd seen around once in a while.

He saw Greg, his dark eyes fixed on Dale's face, his lips pressed into a thin line.

Dale froze, his heart stumbling. *Greg?*

Greg still looked the same—tanned, his chestnut hair short, his inky eyes boring through Dale. He was wearing a crisp suit, a black jacket with a white shirt beneath, and black pants to match. For four months, Dale had thought about him every day, thought about his lips and his skin and his smile, and listened to his fifty-nine voice messages on repeat.

Looking at Greg now, Dale *wanted* like he'd never wanted before.

"Dale?" Cam murmured, squeezing his arm.

Dale blinked, suddenly too aware that there were people around them, that they were supposed to be walking down the aisle. His face burned. This was June's wedding, not his. "Oh. I'm sorry."

He looked at the carpet, matching his footsteps to Cam's. His mind whispered, *Greg's here. Greg's watching you.*

When they turned at the end of the aisle, standing to one side of the gazebo, Dale chanced a look at the crowd again. Greg scowled from two rows away, glancing at Cam, then Dale. *Does he think I'm with Cam?*

Then Greg's gaze dropped to Dale's belly, and Dale slipped his hand over his abdomen, needing to touch his baby. He couldn't deny that his baby was Greg's, couldn't deny the flush of warmth that unfurled through his chest. *Greg's looking at me.*

The mellow notes of the piano grew louder, a cheerful wedding melody. The crowd turned to watch as June stepped down the aisle. Dale glanced at her — she looked fantastic, confident, but her eyes searched him out briefly. He frowned at her; she smiled, and Dale knew she'd set him up with Greg. He didn't have the heart to swear.

And Greg was still watching him.

For the past two months, Dale had buried himself in work at the childcare center, reading up on how to care for babies and toddlers. He'd kept himself focused on fixing meals, eating healthy food, cleaning up his home to prepare for his baby.

But he'd ached for Greg the entire time, only allowing himself one voicemail a day. He'd followed Greg's Facebook. Flipped through the pictures he'd secretly saved. Several times, he'd shoved his hand down his pants, thinking about his alpha, and he'd always felt a surge of guilt after those thoughts.

Greg had to have found an omega. But he was seated next to an older woman at the wedding, and Dale had forgotten to breathe when he'd passed Greg. Was he wearing another omega's scent?

June came to stand beside him. The crowd turned to look at Cher, who wore the most elaborate dress Dale had ever seen, with sequins and ribbons and layers of lace, and a sparkling train that followed her down the aisle. During the times Dale had met her, she'd dressed casually, in

T-shirts and jeans. Today, she looked radiant, with her tumbling red hair all done up, and joy rippling off her in waves.

Dale wanted to look radiant, too. He wanted to be married to his alpha, wanted his alpha to tell him he was beautiful.

"How are you?" June asked under her breath.

"Oh, gods, June. I can't believe you invited Greg." He wanted to cover his face. But there was a touch of makeup on his skin, and he didn't want to ruin it. "He's still looking at me!"

She rolled her eyes. "I wouldn't have invited him if he wasn't going to look at you."

"I almost had a heart attack. Don't pull that on me!"

"You said it yourself. You weren't going to see him again."

Dale looked at his hands. She was right. "Does he have an omega?" he whispered, half-afraid of the answer.

June only smiled. "Ask him yourself."

Dale groaned. Cher stepped down the aisle, and June grinned at her bride, her attention slipping away from Dale. Dale admired Cher again, with her red-orange curls and the cute pair of glasses perched on her nose. He really was happy for them.

But right now, all he could think about was the alpha two rows away. Dale both wanted to touch him, and run as far as he could. He shouldn't distract Greg from a younger omega. He needed to leave, so he could stop aching for Greg.

When this was over, he'd catch a cab or bus home, get as far as he could from Cambria.

The rest of the ceremony passed in a whirl. Dale tried not to think about Greg. Greg hardly looked away from him, and Dale wanted to step closer, check if Greg still looked the same. If he still smelled the same. Dale wanted a hug, and *gods,* it was difficult, watching June get married when he wanted his own wedding. He shouldn't be jealous.

The moment June began thanking the guests for their attendance, Dale turned. He slipped into the rose garden, heading for the quiet road.

He felt a little bad, leaving June while her wedding wasn't over yet. But he needed to get out of here before Greg cornered him. Before Dale fell into his arms and made a mistake in front of so many people.

He needed to get away.

35
Greg

GREG SWORE, darting between the wedding guests. Damn all the tiny clauses June had made him agree to—no leaving before the other guests did. No attracting attention to himself. No hunting down Dale on the mansion grounds.

He loosened his tie, jogging toward the mansion's exit. He'd seen Dale head that direction, leaving behind a trace of hibiscus. The scent was barely there, faint in a blend of other scents, and when Greg reached the mansion driveway, he was almost afraid that he'd lost Dale.

Auburn hair flashed at the end of the street, right down from where he'd parked his car. It would be faster to drive.

The wedding had been painful to watch. Especially when Dale had held on to the other alpha, looking up at him. Dale had looked beautiful in that loose shirt and pants, his eyes bright in the sunlight. Greg had wanted to pull him close, hug him, and the entire time he'd watched Dale and that alpha, Greg had thought, *Mine.*

At six months pregnant, Dale's belly was swollen with their child, and Greg wished he could touch Dale, talk to their baby. Gods, he'd wanted nothing more than to hold his omega close.

He slipped into his car, slamming the door shut. The Porsche rumbled to life around him. Greg checked the street, waiting for three slow cars to drive by. The streets of Cambria were narrow, grassy stretches to either side.

When he pulled out onto the road, Dale had gone. Greg swore, urging the Porsche forward, scanning the roads leading into the other housing estates. After the initial burst of traffic, the streets had returned to being sparse. He stepped down on the gas pedal, appreciating the smooth hum of the Porsche's engine, the way it obeyed his steering at the slightest touch.

And now, when Greg needed a car most, he was glad he had the Porsche with him, despite everything else he hated about his father's money.

He wound through the lanes of homes, searching for red-brown hair.

It was only when he pulled away from the narrower roads, when he turned in the direction of the highway, that he found Dale. On the roadside a hundred yards away, Dale held his belly, his strides lagging. Greg's chest squeezed. *Don't strain yourself!*

Further down the road, some cars drove by. There wasn't any divider, just a lane for traffic in each direction, and grass bordering them. It seemed safe enough. Not somewhere he'd want his omega, though, not when he was just a lane away from traffic.

Greg was about to accelerate when a truck drove into view two hundred yards down, weaving along the road. It careened into Greg's lane, then swerved back into its own. Then it veered out again, its side squealing against the guard rail. Greg tensed. Dale was right between them, with only a grassy drop-off and a steel railing to his side.

Greg glanced in the rear-view mirror. There were a couple of cars slowing down behind him, and some cars to his left, getting the hell away. Dale had seen the truck, too, wrapping his arms around his belly. He had nowhere to run. Not with empty land to his side, and no buildings or lampposts to shelter behind.

Fifty yards from Dale, the truck rumbled ever closer, weaving between the two lanes. Between the guard rail and the other cars, there was no space for Greg to make a U-turn. They were trapped.

Unbidden, Tony's face flashed through his thoughts. Tony had frozen like Dale, paralyzed by fear. And Greg had taken too long to rescue him.

In that moment, Greg knew the choices he had. He swallowed the bile in his throat, stepping down on the gas pedal. Dale was his omega.

And the only sure way to protect him was to stop the truck.

Greg urged the Porsche forward, ten yards, then twenty, passing Dale. He didn't pull his eyes away to glance at Dale's face, but gods, he wanted to. Instead, Greg gripped his steering wheel, slowing down when he neared the truck. The truck careened into his lane again.

He held his breath as the truck loomed up before him, shifting the gears to neutral.

The truck headed for him, ten yards away, then five, then one.

Then it crashed into the Porsche and Greg hit the brakes, and all he could think about was his omega, that he'd protected his omega this time.

36
Dale

One minute ago

THERE WAS nowhere to run.

On Dale's left, there was the road with its oncoming cars. On the right, the grass dropped off past the guard rail, closed off by another road. Dale wasn't sure he could climb the guard rail in time, if it would offer enough protection from the truck.

For moments, he stood, holding his belly, wishing he'd never hurried down this road. The truck rumbled ever closer. It could stay in its lane and completely miss him, or it could veer into the guard rail, and flatten him.

Except a red Porsche sped by, heading for the weaving truck. Dale stared, struck by the familiarity of it.

It couldn't be Greg's car. It couldn't.

But he recognized the license plate, with *Meadowfall Lions* in bold print on the plate frame, and his breath froze in his lungs.

"Greg," Dale cried, horror crawling up his throat. But maybe Greg couldn't hear him, because he was speeding away, hitting his brakes as he headed straight for the truck. The truck's brakes shrieked.

With a sickening crunch, the Porsche crashed into the truck's chrome bumper, and Dale's heart stopped.

The hood of the car crumpled, and the truck shoved it backward, slowing to a halt. Dale staggered, dizzy, unable to breathe.

Please don't die. Please don't die, Greg.

In the steps it took to bring him closer, Dale regretted all the months he'd spent away from Greg. He regretted pushing Greg away, regretted thinking that their differences mattered.

Because right now, none of that did. All he cared about was whether Greg was alive. If Greg died, if he was gone... Then what did it matter if Dale was twenty years older? That he'd lost his tenure? That Bernard Hastings shut the childcare center down?

He loved Greg, and Dale wished he'd gotten the chance to say it to Greg one last time, to tell Greg he'd always be Dale's alpha.

He stumbled toward the wreckage, tears dripping down his cheeks. Behind him, cars honked, and someone yelled.

The Porsche's door opened. Dale sucked in air, his heart pounding. *Greg?*

He checked the road, then staggered forward, rounding the Porsche to the driver's door. Black shoes met the asphalt. Greg pulled himself out of the car, swaying a little. He met Dale's eyes, his gaze darting over Dale to see if he was hurt.

Greg's fine. Dale cried out with relief, stepping forward.

He couldn't continue to push Greg away, not anymore. Not when Greg had been so close to death, and Dale had been so close to losing his most important person.

Greg Hastings was his alpha. Dale could no longer deny him their bond.

37
Greg

IN THE seconds after the crash, Greg panted, his hands shaking. The leg compartment had compressed. The airbags had deployed.

He wasn't dead. He'd expected to die, or at least be in a great deal of pain. He could've been crushed by the truck. But he moved his legs now, finding them unharmed. He turned his hands over, then stared down at himself.

He wasn't hurt. His car was totaled, but he was alive. *Dale* was alive. Greg had saved him, had saved his omega. It felt like a boulder had rolled off his chest, so he could breathe again.

He exhaled, tipping his head back. The truck's chrome grill loomed over his windshield.

Unlike the cabin fire five years ago, they'd escaped from this accident unharmed. Tony would've said, *Look, get up and move on! We don't have time to waste!*

It was a voice that was familiar and strange all at once. Greg had kept it suppressed all these years, because he couldn't stand the thought of having failed his best friend.

"I'm alive," he muttered. "I'm still alive. And

you're not."

I forgive you, Tony whispered in his mind. *You did your best. It's time to move on.*

Greg breathed out his guilt from Tony's death, his thoughts whirling.

There was no future he could rely on, not really. But in avoiding the future, Greg had also forgotten about the present.

All this time, he had been afraid of committing to Dale—and for what reason? He'd been afraid of getting hurt again. Of disappointing his omega. Of failing somehow. Maybe he couldn't be around forever for Dale, but he could be around *now,* and that was most important.

He needed to spend time with his omega, so if anything happened to either of them, they could tell their son what their other dad was like. He should have held Dale close, tell him how important he was. He should have stayed, and fought for their relationship, and be the alpha Dale needed.

He shouldn't have left Dale at all.

Greg swore at himself, feeling like an even bigger idiot. *I've wasted so much time.*

He pushed the door open, stepping out. Dale hurried across the road to him, tears streaking down his face, his arms wrapped around his belly.

If Greg hadn't stopped the truck, Dale could have died. And that single thought sent his stomach plunging, set his hair on end.

"Greg," Dale said, his voice stretched thin. He looked up at Greg, his eyes wide, and tumbled into Greg's chest, thin and familiar and precious.

"Gods, I'm sorry," Greg murmured, slipping

his arms around Dale. "I shouldn't have left you. I shouldn't have put you in danger. I—"

"I love you," Dale said, his voice muffled in Greg's shoulder, his tears soaking through Greg's shirt. "I love you, and you're my alpha, and I shouldn't have pushed you away for so long. I'm sorry."

"You want me back?" Greg whispered, his heart squeezing.

"Yes. Yes!" Dale's fingers pressed into Greg's back, his belly pushing against Greg's hips. "Gods, I've missed you so much." Then he stiffened and pulled away, his eyes glittering with tears. "Are you hurt? Did you have a concussion? Oh, gods, I should've checked before I hugged you, I—"

"I'm fine," Greg said. "But I'll call 9-1-1 just in case."

"I'm not even thinking straight right now," Dale said. "I was so worried. I thought you'd died. I saw your car and you were headed straight for the truck and I just—"

His voice tapered off in a high whine. Greg pulled him close, guiding him to the side of the road. Behind the Porsche, other cars had stopped, and people were on their phones. Greg wrapped his arms around Dale, running his hands down Dale's back, then his belly.

"I thought *you* were going to die," Greg murmured into his hair, breathing in lungfuls of hibiscus and honey. After months of separation, Dale's scent was so very welcome, and Greg wanted it all over his skin. "The bastard was gonna hit you. Gods."

The thought alone made him shudder. It had

388

been instinct, driving headlong into the truck. Greg knew he'd do it again in a heartbeat.

"I'm not leaving you," he said. "I don't care about my dad. I'm not fucking losing you, you hear?"

Dale sobbed into his chest. Greg held on to him, closing his eyes. Of all the times he'd thought about them making up, never once had he imagined it would be by the side of the road, their lives a hairsbreadth from ending.

"I don't care where we have to go," Dale said into his chest, his hands curling into Greg's shirt. "I'm not leaving you again."

"Good," Greg murmured, dropping kisses on his head. He dragged his wrists over Dale's back, down his arms, masking the other alpha's willow scent. Dale finally wanted to be his. Sweet relief soaked through his chest. "I'm glad."

He lost track of how long he held Dale, just standing by the roadside with his omega in his arms. Greg pressed a kiss to Dale's temple, then his hair, his ear, holding him tight. When Dale looked up, hiccupping, Greg kissed his lips.

Dale melted against him, his mouth pliant and hungry against Greg's, his breath unsteady on Greg's skin.

Greg had lost track of how long they kissed, too, when a little whimper slipped from Dale's lips. Greg kissed him quiet, his fingers slipping through Dale's soft hair.

"How's the baby?" Greg murmured against his lips.

"Oh," Dale breathed, catching Greg's hand, pressing it to his belly. "He kicked right after the ultrasound. I was so relieved."

Greg waited. Then he slid his hand over the warm firmness of Dale's abdomen. "I don't feel anything."

Dale chuckled, patting his hand. "Be patient, young alpha."

Greg pulled away to look him in the eye. Dale's eyes were red, his face was blotchy, but his lips curved with mirth. "You can laugh about that now?"

"I've decided that I don't care about our ages anymore," Dale murmured, sliding his hand up Greg's forearm, his wrist dragging against Greg's skin. He was marking Greg, leaning against him in public. Greg stared, stunned silent with disbelief and wonder. "Except when I tell age jokes," Dale said. "Then it becomes relevant."

Greg rolled his eyes, but an overwhelming relief surged over him. "Good."

In the distance, an ambulance turned on its sirens, police cars trailing behind it. When they pulled up around the wreckage, paramedics leaped out of the ambulance. Greg released his omega reluctantly.

"I'm glad you're fine," Dale said. "But you really should be checked out by the EMTs first."

"Yeah." Greg kissed his forehead, looking over as the truck driver climbed unsteadily out of the cabin. "Sit somewhere safe. I'll get back to you soon."

"I'm not an invalid, Greg Hastings."

"You're pregnant," he said. "And I'm your alpha."

Dale's face lit up, even as he looked down at

the ground, suddenly shy. "You are?"

"Yes," Greg said, rubbing their wrists together. "Wait for me."

Still smiling, Dale stepped over to the guard rail, cradling his belly. He looked good in the white shirt and pants; Greg hadn't told him that yet. But they had time now—he'd lost his car, and they were probably stuck in Cambria for the near future.

Greg had new plans for tonight, plans that involved learning his omega, all over again.

38
Greg

HOURS LATER, Greg shut the door to their hotel room. "Gods, that was a pain in the ass."

"They didn't lube you up enough?"

Greg snorted. "Seriously?"

Dale grinned. Then he snagged Greg's collar in his hands and hauled him down, capturing his lips in an open-mouthed kiss.

With that kind of welcome, the low snarl of anger in Greg's chest seeped away.

Earlier, the paramedics had sent him to the Cambria Hospital for observation, citing possible concussion. Greg would've been fine with that, except the police wanted statements from both of them. Then reporters from the Cambria Weekly had swooped in, and there had been question after prying question, people brandishing cameras, and Greg had wanted them gone so he could kiss his omega in peace.

Dale moaned against him, and Greg slipped his arms around his omega, following the curve of Dale's spine to his hips. He dipped his fingers lower, between Dale's cheeks, and Dale gasped against his mouth, pushing back against his touch.

Greg smirked; this was still the same. "How are you guys?" he murmured, nipping on Dale's lower lip.

"You guys?" Dale paused, blinking.

"There's two of you." Greg kissed him again, slipping his hand around Dale's side, caressing his belly. Dale's ears turned pink, and Greg kissed his cheeks, then his lips. "Remember?"

"Oh, gods, I love you," Dale breathed, pulling him closer. "But I really am sorry about the car. You were so fond of it."

Greg shrugged, scooping Dale into his arms. Dale curled his legs around Greg's waist; he was heavy with child, and Greg wanted to look closer at him, see how much his body had changed in the last few months. "I'll get something else. Something that can fit a car seat."

A huge grin spread across Dale's face. "Why haven't you proposed already?"

Greg laughed, another weight rolling off his chest. "I don't have a ring! I didn't—didn't expect you'd say yes today. Give me some time."

Dale smiled, his eyes glowing with warmth. Greg's heart swelled. Gods, he loved Dale, and now that he had Dale in his arms, he didn't want to let his omega go.

Gently, he deposited Dale on the king-sized bed. The sheets were silky beneath them, ivory in the lamplight, and Dale stretched his arms up, squirming on the mattress like a languid cat. "Mm, this is nice."

It was a nice room, too—a brick-facade fireplace faced the bed, life-like logs behind the grate. Polished bedside tables stood on either side of the headboard, their legs curved elegantly, the knobs on their drawers gilded. They'd found the hotel after searching futilely on the internet—June had recommended it, looking on in horror when Dale told her about the crash.

"Anything's nicer than those reporters," Greg said.

"I was surprised you told them who you were." Dale sobered, his forehead crinkling. "It may be county news, but your dad may still catch wind of it."

"Yeah, but you heard what I said. 'My dad's always told me that my omega is the most important.' That isn't gonna bring the college's rep down. You're not even working there anymore."

Dale chuckled wryly. When Greg had first mentioned it to the Cambria Weekly's journalist, Dale had stared, his eyes almost falling out of his head. "And now the entire county knows we're alpha and omega."

Greg leaned in, kissing his omega again, his abdomen bumping into Dale's belly. "Yeah. He can't threaten the childcare center now, or it'll make even bigger news."

"I guess."

By stretching, Dale had pulled his shirt up, thin cotton hiking up to reveal pale skin. A line of fine hair dusted his abdomen, leading down past his waistband. Greg sat back, sliding his shirt up past his belly, dragging his fingertips over supple skin.

"Gods, I haven't touched you in so long," he murmured, pulling Dale closer, wedging Dale's hips against his own. "You look so fantastic."

Dale chuckled, squirming, pushing his hips up, his legs spread wide around Greg's waist. "Are you only going to look?"

"Maybe." Greg met his eyes, hungry, and Dale shivered.

Slowly, Greg tugged off Dale's shoes, then his socks. Then he undid Dale's belt and pants, pulling those off, too, leaving him in his briefs, and the white lace shirt.

"I really like the shirt," Dale murmured, half-hard behind his briefs. "June and I searched online for a bit, but most of the pregnancy wear is boring. Then it turned out that Cher knew someone who could sew. We did measurements—aah!"

Greg slipped his fingers out of Dale's briefs, grinning. "You were saying?"

"I, uh. What was I saying?" Dale's pupils had dilated. He rocked his hips up, his hard cock straining against thin cotton. Greg had slipped his finger beneath Dale's foreskin, circled his tip, and just like that, Dale had gotten distracted.

"The shirt." Greg slid his hands up Dale's thighs, squeezing his muscles. Then he eased his thumbs under the elastic of Dale's briefs, pressing them against Dale's cheeks. The movement spread Dale open, exposing his hole, and musk rolled through the air between them, sharp and heady.

Greg's pants grew tight. Dale wanted him. After so long apart, his omega desired him, and it sent relief and desire flooding through his veins.

"The... the shirt." Dale's nipples had peaked, little points on white fabric. Greg leaned in, kissing them through the weave. Then he licked over them, biting them lightly, and Dale gasped, his spine arching, his hand curling around Greg's, nudging him toward his cock. Greg drew his fingers away.

Dale whined. "Touch me."

"Tell me about the shirt, and I'll touch you." To encourage him, Greg rubbed the tip of Dale's cock through his briefs, squeezing its blunt head, following the rest of his hard shaft down to his balls. "Or do you want me to fuck you, too?"

Dale sucked in a sharp breath, his hands reaching down, slipping between Greg's thighs and his own. Then he spread his ass again, leaving himself open. It was an invite, one Greg could barely resist. Greg growled.

"You know you want to be inside," Dale whispered. "You haven't knotted in me for so long."

Greg moaned, grinding his own cock against Dale's ass, letting him feel the thickness of it.

He remembered the tight heat of Dale's body, the way Dale had stretched around him. "I haven't even seen all of you."

"You can see me later," Dale said. "Fuck me first."

"No," Greg whispered, reaching for Dale's shirt. He popped the lowest button, following the trail up Dale's chest, rubbing Dale's sternum with his knuckles. Dale squirmed beneath him, and Greg caressed his nipples, tweaking them.

Dale's breath rushed out. He thrust his hips up, and Greg slid his briefs off halfway, exposing the damp of his hole. Then he grabbed Dale's pants, crumpled part of it into a ball, and wedged it up his ass, right against his sensitive hole.

Dale gasped, trembling. The pants held him

open, and Greg knew Dale would feel the cloth spreading his cheeks. His cock slipped out of his briefs, its tip dusky red, slippery with precum. He was so hungry, and Greg could hardly stop caressing his hipbones, his sides, the soft skin of his belly.

In the past four months, Dale's body hadn't changed much—his limbs were still slender, his skin pale. But his belly had grown fuller, and Greg regretted not having been there, watching as his omega's body grew along with their child.

Greg rubbed his dry thumb over Dale's tip. Dale jolted against him, his breath rushing out, his eyelids fluttering shut. The touch left a smear on Greg's finger; he brought it to his lips, licking Dale's precum off. It was salty, tasting like *him.*

This, too, hadn't changed. A slow heat built between his legs; he was hard, but he wanted to savor his omega, pleasure him. Greg wanted to hold Dale close, make him feel good like he hadn't been able to the whole time they'd been apart.

He'd wanted Dale ever since he'd glimpsed his professor back in November, but Greg had only wanted Dale more since the pregnancy. He needed to show his omega he'd missed him, needed to get his fill of Dale's warmth.

Except he would never have enough of Dale; Greg knew that.

He undid the rest of the buttons on Dale's shirt, spreading it open to reveal his chest. The shirt was intricate. But Dale looked better without, his skin creamy, his nipples taut, his cock jutting up at Greg, begging for touch.

Greg scooped Dale up, pulling the shirt off

his arms. And now his omega was bare, save for the scrap of cotton around his hips. The moment he looked down, Dale wriggled his hips, yanking his briefs along his thighs, showing Greg his cock and balls, and his ass. The crumpled pants fell damply away from his ass, and his hole was small and tight, open for Greg.

"You're so damn ready for me," Greg murmured, reaching down, rubbing over Dale's slippery hole. Dale gasped, his slippery entrance fluttering against Greg's fingers, inviting him inside. Greg teased his hole, pressing down just enough for Dale to feel his touch, but not enough to slip inside. Dale groaned.

"That means you should be filling me up, shouldn't you?" Dale breathed.

In the orange light of the room, his cheeks glistened, wet with slick.

Greg throbbed in his pants, needing to slip inside, spread Dale open with his cock. Instead, he leaned in, kissing Dale full on the lips. Dale moaned into his mouth; Greg ground their cocks together, sharing his pleasure with his omega. Dale squirmed against him, panting, his tongue tangling hungry and wet with Greg's.

So Greg caught his knees, pushing Dale's thighs to either side of him, spreading him open. Dale whined, his hips rocking, four months of pent-up desire dark in his eyes.

He watched Greg trustingly, his body held open, his belly heavy with their child. And Greg knew he'd never love anyone else this much, not like he loved Dale Kinney.

He kissed down Dale's chest, down his belly

and up his thighs, and back to his leaking tip. Dale's cock jumped against his lips. Greg took it into his mouth, licking over his velvety skin. Dale groaned. Greg took his whole cock into his mouth, down his throat, so Dale choked and shuddered, his body shaking beneath Greg.

"That—that feels—f-feels good." Dale held his legs open, his toes curling, his chest heaving. Greg rubbed his tight balls, down the curve of his ass, spreading his cheeks. Then he released Dale's cock, leaving it wet with spit, and sucked on Dale's balls, one at a time, until Dale wound his fingers into Greg's hair, pulling him up, pushing him down, as though he couldn't decide where he wanted Greg.

Greg made the decision for him. He slid his fingers into Dale's hole, pushing into its tight warmth. Dale gasped, clenching around him. So he swirled his fingers around inside, finding Dale's prostate, pushing down hard on it.

Dale jerked off the bed, his cock jumping, his legs trembling. "Greg, please don't tease," he cried. "I need—-need you inside."

"Want me to breed you again?" Greg murmured, pushing his fingers in to their knuckles. The thought went straight to his balls, made them heavy. "Want me to fill you full of cum? Until it's oozing out of you when you walk?"

"Gods, yes," Dale gasped, squeezing around him, his chest flushed pink.

Greg paused, his gaze snagging on Dale's belly. "What about the baby? Will I hurt him?"

"He'll be okay," Dale said, his face turning a beautiful shade of scarlet. "I checked with the doctor."

So Dale had wanted him enough to ask, and Greg needed to be inside. Needed to claim his omega. "Gonna take my knot?"

"Yes! And all your cum."

"And another baby?"

"Fuck yes," Dale said, his lips quirking in a smile. "Especially another baby."

Greg's throat went dry. He rubbed himself through his pants, pulling his fly open, breathing a sigh of relief when the pressure on his cock eased. He unbuttoned his shirt, shrugged out of it, and Dale purred as he watched Greg strip, languidly stroking his own cock, pointing it at Greg.

With a grin, Greg stepped out of his boxers, climbing onto the bed to hover over his omega, taking both their cocks into his hand. Then he stroked them, and Dale pushed his hips up, rocking into his palm, his hands sliding down Greg's chest, over his back, his nails biting into Greg's skin. "Fuck me now."

"You're so pushy," Greg said, but he rutted against Dale's cock, squeezing him, gathering the drop of precum that oozed from his tip. Dale bucked beneath him, spreading his ass again, and this time, Greg slid his cock up between his damp cheeks, grinding against his tight hole. For four months, he'd thought about this, wanting to be this close to his omega again.

Dale's gasp tore out of him. And Greg slicked himself up with Dale's wetness, his hand smearing Dale's precum onto his cock. Then he slid into Dale, burying his cock completely, and Dale's spine arched, his ass stretching hot around Greg's cock like the very first time Greg had fucked him, back in his office.

Greg groaned, pumping in, his cock throbbing, dripping precum into Dale. He needed more of his omega, needed his omega to belong to him. As Dale reached up to touch his face, Greg linked their fingers together, kissing down Dale's wrist, right over the scar on his scent gland.

"Gonna be mine?" Greg whispered, licking over his pulse point. Dale's pulse beat beneath his tongue. Then Greg dragged his teeth over the bonding scar from Dale's ex, possessiveness roaring through his gut.

He needed to mark Dale. Make Dale his.

"Yes," Dale said, rocking back against him, his fingers squeezing tight around Greg's. "Mark me everywhere. I'm yours."

Greg bit down hard over the bonding mark, sinking his teeth into soft skin. Dale arched off the sheets, clenching around Greg, his cock jerking.

"M-more," he panted, his chest heaving.

So Greg brought Dale's other wrist to his lips, thrusting deep, licking over where the hibiscus scent was strongest. "Yeah?"

"Yes!"

He bit into Dale's unmarked scent gland, and Dale jerked again, whimpering, his cock a dark red, his body gleaming with sweat. When he could speak again, Dale's eyes were glazed, his limbs trembling, his balls drawn up tight. The bites on his wrists welled with crimson blood, along the curve of Greg's teeth marks, and Greg's heart swelled.

"Last one?"

"Yes," Dale whimpered, slipping his hand

against Greg's nape, pulling him close, until Greg's lips pressed against his throat. Greg sucked along his skin, his tongue swirling against Dale's pulse. Dale writhed.

Greg found his scent gland easily. They'd been in this exact position back in his apartment, when his dad had found them. Except Greg would not let his father get in the way again, would not let his fears cripple him. He wanted Dale to be his.

Dale grasped Greg's forearm, bringing it up to his panting lips. Greg pulled back to watch him. Dale's tongue dragged against Greg's wrist, soft and wet, right over his scent gland, and Greg knew this was no mistake. Not when Dale's teeth scraped over his skin, his eyes dark with desire and resolve.

"Mark me," Greg whispered, thrusting deep into Dale, his balls heavy with cum. "I'm gonna fill you up. Make you mine."

Dale groaned, biting down hard. Pain and pleasure jolted through Greg's nerves, down his spine, all the way to his cock. Dale was marking him as his own. Greg fucked in deep, sinking home. And Dale took his other wrist, his teeth dragging over Greg's scent gland.

Dale finally wanted him, and that thought was heady in itself, sending so much blood to Greg's cock he couldn't think.

"Gods, I'm gonna come," Greg panted, reeling with the bite, with the pleasure, with his belonging to Dale.

"Come inside me," Dale rasped, biting down hard on Greg's other wrist. Pleasure sluiced through his body, down to his cock, and Greg snarled, so hard it hurt. He leaned in, finding

Dale's scent gland, licking over it. His cock pulsed. Dale found Greg's scent gland, his lips hot on Greg's neck, his teeth pressing sharp indents into Greg's skin.

Greg bit down hard, burying his cock inside his omega. Dale shuddered beneath him, crying out, his teeth sinking sharp into Greg's scent gland. And pleasure seared through Greg's nerves, ripped his release so hard through him that he was coming, his vision blanking out, waves and waves and *waves* of pleasure bursting through his body.

Faintly, he felt the damp warmth of Dale's cum on his abdomen. It took Greg a while to process that, then another moment to realize that they'd marked each other, that Dale wasn't going away, wasn't going to leave him anymore.

"You're really staying?" Greg mumbled, his voice weak, his body trembling around Dale's.

"Yes," Dale whispered, his arms slipping around Greg's waist. "I'm all yours."

Greg sighed, relief washing through him. He leaned to the side to avoid crushing their baby, turning Dale to face him. As his knot grew inside Dale, Greg slid his thigh between Dale's, holding him close.

He hadn't done this in months, just watching his omega from inches away.

When Dale had left, Greg had realized that he'd taken their two months together for granted, until Dale was suddenly no longer by his side. Then he'd regretted it, wishing he could've had his omega back. Just touching Dale's skin was special, and Greg didn't know how much he'd missed it until he slid his arm around Dale's waist, pulling him close.

Dale smelled like hibiscus and honey, like Greg's, and holding him was like coming home.

"I'm just glad to have you back," Greg murmured, tracing the new mark on Dale's neck, where his own bite had written over Charles'. Dale was his. Dale had agreed to be his, he had marked Greg, and this had gone beyond Greg's wildest dreams. "Gods, I missed you so much."

Dale tucked his head beneath Greg's chin, his fingers tracing faint lines along Greg's side. "Same here. I shouldn't have left you in the first place."

"There's no point regretting that now." Greg scooped him close, running his fingers through Dale's sweat-dampened hair. "But I'm really sorry about your tenure. I tried everything I could to get you your job back."

Dale chuckled against him, pressing a kiss to his chest. "Thank you. I've made peace with it."

"Really?"

"Yes. I realized there was no point in me pursuing tenure, not anymore. It was a way for me to find value in myself. A goal to work toward, you know? But I have different goals now. I have our baby. I have you. And I have a job—I don't need to be a professor anymore."

Greg mulled over his words, the guilt in his chest easing a little. "Okay. I'll remember that."

They held each other, Greg lulled into a doze, his omega safe in his arms.

He was woken by a faint buzzing noise—his phone?

When he pulled away, Dale made a soft sound of protest. This, too, was something precious, when Greg had missed Dale, missed every bit of their relationship. "I'll be back," he said, slipping out of Dale's body. Sometime while they'd napped, his knot had receded. "I'll just see who's calling."

He grabbed his pants, fumbled in its pockets, and slid the phone out.

Dad, the caller ID read. Greg breathed in, glancing at the door. It was locked; they were safe here. He hit the Answer button.

"Dad?" he asked, watching as Dale tensed. Greg crawled back, rubbing Dale's back. *We'll be fine,* he mouthed. But Dale remained frowning.

"I saw the news," Bernard said across the line, his tone severe.

Greg swallowed, his stomach flipping. "I'm sorry about the car. It was a pity."

"Your picture is on the front page of the county news, and the first thing you mention is the car?"

"I saved my omega with it. I think that's all you need to know."

Dale winced.

"I didn't bring you up to throw your status and abilities away, Gregory," Bernard said, disapproval thick in his tone. "Dale Kinney is an embarrassment—"

"I was saving my baby, too," Greg said, glad that his phone wasn't on loudspeaker. Some things, Dale didn't need to hear. "Your grandson."

"My..." Bernard paused.

Greg let the information sink in. "We're calling him Phil," he said, then winced. He'd made that up on the spot. Dale raised his eyebrows. "Phil

Hastings."

It occurred to him that his dad had forgotten the importance of family.

Gone were the days when Bernard Hastings brought Greg to the park to play ball. Gone were the days when Bernard clapped Greg on the back, telling him jokes. That had been close to a decade ago, and Greg hadn't realized his dad had been so absent from his life, until now. Greg had gotten too distracted with Tony, and then with Tony's death, to notice.

"You don't have a say over my family, dad," Greg said. "This is my choice. I've chosen Dale."

"You almost died in that crash," his father said.

"Yes. Because Dale is worth saving to me."

Dale was staring at him now, his mouth hanging open. Greg shrugged. It was the truth.

"I'm still not paying your tuition," Bernard said.

"That's fine. I'll take a loan out." He had savings, had monetary gifts from his parents over the years. There was maybe twenty grand in his bank account that he'd refused to touch on principle—he could fall back on that if necessary. "I'll finish my course in Meadowfall College. If you have a problem with that, we'll move out of town."

"You're allowed to continue your studies," Bernard said. "At least succeed in that."

Greg heaved a sigh.

When his dad said nothing else, Greg said, "I'll have to go now. Take care. Say hi to Mom for me."

He ended the call, setting his phone on the

side table.

"I'm worth saving?" Dale blurted, his eyes wide, his voice strangled.

Greg settled back into bed with him, pulling him close. "Yes."

"Oh."

"Why do you think I hit the gas back there?" Greg said, sliding his hand down to Dale's belly, holding their baby. "You're important to me, Dale. You're my bondmate."

Dale blinked rapidly, glancing down at his wrists, where Greg had marked him. Greg showed Dale his own wrists, where Dale had bitten him, and Dale's mouth quirked in a tiny, disbelieving smile. "I... I guess I am. That was a little impulsive."

"It needed to be done," Greg murmured, kissing his nose. "I wasn't gonna wait any longer."

Dale laughed softly. "Sometimes, I can't decide if you're patient or impatient."

"Maybe both," Greg said, slipping his arms around Dale. The phone conversation with his dad had gone better than he'd expected. He didn't know if it would last, but they were out of Bernard's influence in Cambria.

And maybe, if things went right, maybe Bernard would see the futility in trying to break them up. Maybe, with this accident, Greg had won a second chance for them both.

And maybe, unlike the last time, things will turn out all right.

39
Dale

Two months later

DALE WOKE to an empty mattress. For a second, his stomach clenched. *Greg?*

It took him another second to remember that Greg had moved back into his apartment two months ago, that Greg was probably in the bathroom, or the kitchen. The sheets were still warm, aspen-scented, and Dale relaxed. "Your dad's still here," he murmured, cradling his belly. "He's just busy right now."

The baby kicked against his hand. Dale smiled, nestling into Greg's side of the bed, Greg's scent surrounding him. It was a habit left over from the months they'd been separated, when Dale would huddle on the other side of the mattress, wishing for Greg to return.

These days, burrowing into Greg's spot earned Dale a smile, and Greg climbing into bed behind him, snuggling up close.

Dale slipped his hand under Greg's pillow, frowning when paper crinkled against his fingers. He pulled the sheet out, holding it to his nose to read it.

In Greg's handwriting: *When you're ready to wake up, head to the kitchen.*

Dale frowned, looking at the blurred doorjamb. The hallway beyond was dim, and there were vague shapes hovering in the air. He rolled himself upright, grabbed his glasses, and slipped them on.

"Oh. Wow."

Paper cranes hung from the ceiling. But these weren't the ones that Dale had strung up. The closest crane hung close to eye-level from his spot on the bed, the next crane a little higher, a little further away. Words had been scrawled across their wings.

His heart skipping, Dale climbed out of bed, pulling on Greg's T-shirt for warmth. On the first crane, Greg had written, *In the mornings, your eyes are green like a pine forest.*

Dale smiled, releasing the jade-green crane. It twirled in midair. The second crane was sky-blue, with the words *Your nose is damn cute.*

He laughed then. "My nose, cute?"

The third crane was violet, hanging at chest-level. *Actually, so is your mouth.*

"Greg Hastings," Dale said, a smile tugging on his lips. Past the doorway, there were more cranes hanging from the ceiling, and Dale had no idea when Greg had done all of this. Or how long it had taken to put this together. Or what on earth he was trying to do. Or maybe Dale *did* have an idea.

The fourth crane was sand-brown. *I'm running out of compliments, okay. I'm not good at this.*

Dale bit down a smile.

The fifth crane was pale pink, and Greg had written *I think you'll make a really great dad* on it. Dale's heart squeezed. After all that he'd worried about being good enough... Greg had known, somehow, that Dale needed to hear that. His eyes prickled. Dale blinked his tears away, calling out, "You just made me cry, Greg. I hope you know that!"

Somewhere in the apartment, Greg laughed. "Need me to come get you?"

Something eased in Dale's chest. Greg really was at home. And he'd meant for Dale to follow the cranes alone, if he'd left the note under his pillow. "No," Dale called back. "I'll tell you if I need dire assistance."

"What do you mean, 'dire assistance'?"

Dale laughed. He followed the cranes out of their bedroom, sniffing at the burnt, lush aroma of coffee. He'd been having hot chocolate lately, and the scent of coffee made his heart leap. This was a special occasion, then. Enough for a hundred paper cranes to twirl in their apartment, and an exception to the no-coffee rule.

Dale followed the paper cranes into the kitchen. The birds were colorful, ranging from emeralds to cream to ocean-blue, one crane landing on the coffee machine.

Coffee first, Greg had written on its wings. *But no more than half a cup!*

Greg had brewed the Colombian beans, too. He'd laid out Dale's mug, a tiny pitcher of cream, and a jar of sugar. Next to it all, Dale found the sugar spoon that he'd left behind, back when he'd packed his things from his office and dropped his sugar jar.

He picked up the spoon, marveling at the glint of light on its crosshatched handle. It was one of the first things he'd bought himself, back when Charles had annulled their marriage. He'd bought it to remind himself that he was worthy, that he had the freedom to decide things for himself.

To think Greg had salvaged it... Dale swallowed. There were a couple of scratches on the back of the spoon, but the spoon was intact, in his hands, and Dale would tell Greg its story later.

For now, he fixed himself sweet, milky coffee, cradled the mug, and sought out the next crane.

I love waking up with you, Greg had written on a parchment-brown bird. Then, on bright orange wings, *When you smile at me, it's like standing close to a warm fire.*

I want to grow old with you, another crane said.

Maybe we'll take dancing lessons, and we'll dance until our son's thirty.

Then he'll be embarrassed by his dads, but I kind of like that thought.

But you'll never be old to me.

Dale laughed, following the winding trail into the living room, where the cranes dipped toward the coffee table. There was a large photo album on the middle of the table. The first picture was of them the day after June's wedding, when Dale had texted her, and she'd invited them back to the mansion for more photos.

The second picture was the oldest, from when Dale had laid the rabbit onesie on his chest, and Greg had snapped that picture of him. A flattened crane next to that picture read, *This is still my favorite pic of you.*

The photos after that came from the various selfies they'd taken together, when Greg had snapped pictures of Dale, or when Dale had taken pictures of him. Dale had returned to the lab once, and June had set a camera on a tripod, taking a timed picture of the entire lab group. That photo was in the album, too, and Dale lingered on the white lab walls, the memories from when he'd shied away from Greg in school.

Three of the album's pages were filled. The rest had been left blank. Another crane said, *For the future,* and Dale's throat tightened. Greg believed, then. And that meant so much more than the pictures did.

He followed the cranes through the apartment, smiling when they landed on a pile of baby clothes — cat-shaped mittens and booties — and a crane that read, *I don't really care if our baby is alpha or beta or omega. I want him to be happy.*

The next crane said, *Or if he's really a she, or a they. Fine with me.*

Dale grinned. The cranes led down the hallway to the bathroom, where the door was ajar. No cranes led away from there.

He pushed the door open, unsure what to expect.

Inside, Greg leaned against the counter, dressed in boxers. His eyes flickered over Dale's chest, brightening when he recognized the shirt.

But instead of Greg's shirt, Dale's attention had snagged on the crane in Greg's hands. It was the largest crane of all, its wings spanning Greg's palms, watercolor leaves speckling its wings. This crane had no words, only two silver rings slung around its neck. Dale's breath punched out of his chest.

Then he smiled so wide it felt as though his face was going to split. "The bathroom, Greg? Really?"

Greg laughed. "To be honest, this is my second favorite room in the apartment. Bedroom's my favorite." He nodded at the mosaic tiles around the bathtub, the stone pebbles on a shelf. "It's like being in a totally different place when I step in here."

Dale followed his gaze, looking at the wooden sailboat on a shelf, the indigo oyster shells by their toothbrush holder. Next to the mirror, there was a watercolor painting of a ship at sea, signed *Felix Henry* in one corner. That was new.

"I haven't looked closely at the bathroom in years," Dale said. It felt like he'd taken this for granted, all the decorations he'd once painstakingly collected for this room. "The painting and the oyster shells are new. I love them. But I'm also confused—is there a reason you added to the bathroom before you proposed?"

Greg laughed. "I just wanted to surprise you. But if you wanted a... more romantic reason, I guess you could say it's for a new beginning. I didn't have time to redecorate the entire house. 'Sides, you'd probably want it all done to your tastes."

Dale fell silent. Greg was right, though. Up until now, they hadn't changed the apartment any. Greg had moved in twice, but each time, he had only moved his things in, fitting them around

413

Dale's. He hadn't made any decisions on how he wanted the place to look, and all the other decorations had been from Dale's old life.

"We'll redecorate together," Dale said, his chest squeezing. "Are you going to propose, or not?"

Greg laughed.

They were already bondmates, of course. The bite marks on Dale's scent glands had healed; Greg's marks silvery, Dale's own bites bright on Greg's skin. But this was another part of the glue that bound them together, and Dale wanted to be tied in every way to Greg Hastings.

Greg sank onto one knee, his confident grin falling from his mouth. He slid the rings off the crane's neck, holding them out in his own hands. Then he met Dale's eyes uncertainly, as though he was afraid Dale would return to his old ways, and reject him all over again.

"Are you gonna—" Greg cleared his throat, a hint of red creeping up his neck. "I mean, Dale Kinney, will you marry me?"

Dale's heart swelled. For the past few months, since this all began, he'd never once thought that marriage was possible between them. But Greg had bonded with him. Greg had rejected his father's opinions to stay with Dale. Greg believed in their future, and they were both looking forward to raising their child.

Dale loved this alpha, this man who had taught him to see past his age. Greg had offered Dale a place in his heart, had sworn to care for him, had given him a second chance, and Dale... would never think of life without his alpha again.

"Yes. Yes, I'll marry you," he breathed, bending down, about to kneel.

"No, don't do that," Greg said, shuffling forward, holding Dale's belly in his palms. "You're pregnant."

"Just because I'm pregnant, Greg Hastings, doesn't mean I can't kneel." Just to prove his point, Dale held on to the counter and knelt before his alpha, his belly swollen with their son. "Now we're equal."

"Gods, you're so damn stubborn," Greg said, but his eyes shone with love. He took Dale's hand, sliding the smaller band onto Dale's ring finger. "But you're sure about this."

Dale smiled, taking Greg's hand, and the larger ring. Then he slid the ring onto his alpha's finger, pressing a kiss to where metal met skin. "Do you believe it now?"

Greg's eyes lit with joy. Dale cupped his face, kissing him firm on the lips, and Greg slipped his hands around Dale's abdomen, holding their child. Then he kissed down Dale's throat and chest, to his round belly. "Your dad accepted my proposal," Greg whispered, lifting up his shirt to kiss Dale's belly. "We're all gonna be a happy family."

"When I first met you, I had no idea you were going to be this sappy," Dale murmured, a soft smile on his lips. "I just thought you were a reckless young alpha who wanted to get in my pants."

"I still want to get in your pants," Greg said, cupping him between the legs.

Dale purred, his eyes slipping shut. "Gods, I love you, Greg. I guess I'll forgive you for hitting on me."

Greg laughed. "C'mon, the bathroom's probably not the best place to do this."

"It probably isn't. I wouldn't mind a change of scene."

Greg slid his arms around Dale, helping him to his feet. Then he scooped Dale up against his body, and Dale clung to him, his limbs wrapping around Greg with easy familiarity.

Four months ago, when Dale had left, Greg hadn't been sure there was a solution to their differences. Now, with Dale smiling up at him, Greg felt more certain of himself. He would live his life, and continue to convince Dale that Dale was every bit as deserving of his love.

Dale had changed, too, for the stronger. These days, they went to the stores together, and Dale slipped his hand into Greg's, unafraid of others' judgment. On the weekends, they would go to art classes together, and Dale would sit with Greg, touching his arm, or his hand.

This peace had been hard-won; Dale didn't think either of them would forget that. But they had overcome all their hurdles, and they would face the future together from now on, hand in hand, two hearts stronger together than apart.

Epilogue

"MY WATER broke," Dale yelped in the middle of a clay sculpting class, smushing his spinning lump of clay. "Oh, gods, Greg, what do I do?"

Twenty other students looked over.

"Stay calm," Greg said, his own heart pounding against his ribs. They had read up on this. Water breaking was no big deal. They just had to grab their overnight bag and head to the hospital. No need to panic.

"Right, okay. Stay calm." Dale sucked in a deep breath, the lump of clay squeezing long and thin in the grip of his fists. It spun on the pedestal, curving up over his hands, its round tip vaguely phallic. "Oh, gods, this looks like a penis. Is it because it's a boy?"

Greg snorted. "You're the doctor. You tell me."

"I didn't do my dissertation on penis theory!"

The rest of the class was still looking over, and on the other side of the room, June tried to hold back her laughter. Greg sighed. "We're gonna have to stop here," he told their art teacher. "Is it okay if we just leave?"

The beta frowned disapprovingly from behind thick glasses, waving them off. "You're disrupting the energy of this space," she said. "Off with you."

Greg stood, wiping his hands off on his apron. Then he helped Dale to his feet, leading him to the sink. "You're sure your water broke," he murmured.

Dale nodded. "Yeah. It feels a little wet."

"Okay." They rinsed the clay off their hands, drying them on paper towels. They strode—Dale waddled—out of the Meadowfall Art Center, and Greg left his omega on the curb, driving his new car up to him. Then he hurried out, frowning when Dale moved to open the door.

"I can still do things, you know," Dale said, suppressing his smile.

"Your water broke!"

"It's not the end of the world." Dale laughed, and Greg helped him into the passenger seat, making sure the seat belt didn't press on his belly. It was huge now, larger than a basketball. Greg hovered for a moment, smoothing his palm over Dale's abdomen, caressing their child. Their baby kicked against his hand, and Dale beamed. "He likes you!"

"He should like me," Greg said. "I'm his dad."

Dale met his eyes with a soft smile, setting his hands on top of Greg's. "You know, this is amazing. All of this. You and the baby."

"Let's get to the hospital first, and then we'll talk about amazing." The child wasn't born yet, and Greg wasn't going to trust the percentages, not until he had their baby in his arms.

"Fine. Kiss me," Dale said, tipping his face up.

Greg couldn't refuse that. He leaned in, brushing their lips together. Dale purred, his mouth soft and familiar against Greg's, his scent a mix of hibiscus and honey. Together, Dale and the baby were Greg's most precious people, and he couldn't believe he had them so close, that they would get to hold their son soon.

"We're gonna be dads," Greg said, grinning.

Over the past month, they'd done minor changes to the apartment. Dale had wanted to clean everything in preparation for the baby, turn the study into a nursery, add some new decorations to the house before they had their hands full. Greg had wanted to take up a part-time job now that he'd started school again, but Dale disagreed.

I've saved up enough for us, Dale had said. *I'd rather you spend your time with me and the baby. That's more important.*

So Greg had stayed home, helping Dale prepare between his homework. These days, if he had questions about his assignments, he asked Dale instead — the new chemistry professor was nice, but Greg trusted Dale, and some of his favorite moments were snuggling on the couch with his omega, talking about semiconductor synthesis, or the various methods of biosensor production.

When Greg graduated from his chemistry major, he would find a full-time job. For now, he would continue his studies, and help Dale with the baby.

"I feel as though I'm already a dad," Dale

said, cupping Greg's cheeks, holding him close. "Phil's talking to us every time he kicks. I think he can't wait to be out, too."

Greg held Dale's belly, waiting until the baby moved beneath his palm. It was their child in there, and by this time tomorrow, Phil would be in their arms.

"I'm gonna have to start driving," Greg said, dropping a kiss on Dale's belly. "This is a no-parking zone."

Dale laughed, and Greg carefully shut the passenger door, before sliding into the driver's seat. The next stop was home, then the hospital.

THREE HOURS later, Dale had been admitted into the labor ward. His contractions were still minor; the midwife came by to check every half hour, and Greg fought the urge to pace.

"Sit down," Dale said. "Fold your crane."

"I can't just sit!" Greg leaned back into his seat, staring at the thick stack of colored paper they'd brought along for the wait. Their research had said the labor could last twenty-four hours. Greg was certain waiting that long would suck the life out of him. "I'm used to split-second decisions, you know. Snatch the ball, get away, dunk it into the hoop. Not sit still for twenty more hours!"

Dale laughed, making a crease on a sheet with gray grid lines. "I suppose you could chat up every other omega here, if that'll make you feel better."

Greg raised his eyebrows. This was different

from before. "You'd be okay with that? Me talking to other omegas?"

"You do that in school all the time, don't you?"

Greg studied him. Months ago, Dale would have told him to talk to other omegas, on the off-chance that Greg would find someone he liked better. These days, Dale was more confident in himself. He held his belly, smiled and laughed with Greg, and the days he was convinced Greg would leave were far outnumbered by those where he grinned and told Greg to stay.

"I talk to people in school for projects," Greg said. "It's not like I'd decide I'll like someone else better. I've already made my choice."

Dale blushed, looking down at his hands. "Who would've thought?"

"Well, the basketball team did kind of speculate a little. They asked yesterday if they'll be invited to our wedding. I told them I'd ask you first."

Dale opened his mouth. Since the accident last month, news had spread. Greg had brushed off the stares; the attention was like what he'd received when he'd been named MVP—neither event was any of the public's concern. Except he had several friends on the basketball team, and he wasn't sure he wanted Dale to be worried by their presence.

"I don't know. Do you want them around?" Dale asked, his fingers pausing on the paper crane.

Greg shrugged. "It's our wedding. You get a say, too. I just don't want you to be uneasy around them."

"Maybe," Dale said, chewing on his lip. "I'm

still not used to the attention. You know."

"Yeah. I'll tell them you're still deciding, then." Greg reached over, slipping his fingers around Dale's hand. "Don't worry about it."

Dale leaned toward him, and Greg left his seat, settling on the bed beside him.

"How are you feeling?" Greg asked.

"Nervous. Excited. I think he's ready to be born, too." Dale smiled, rubbing his hand over his belly. "He'll be a beautiful child."

"He'll be beautiful like you," Greg murmured, pressing a kiss to his cheek.

Dale nudged him. "You're such a smooth talker."

"I'm not." Greg kissed him again. "Are you sure you really want to call him Phil? I only suggested that because Phil O'Riley was the first name that came up. You could probably find a better name."

"I love Phil," Dale said, snuggling closer, his hair tickling Greg's cheek. "Phil Hastings sounds like a good name."

"Phil it is," Greg said. He leaned in, nuzzling Dale's belly. "Can't wait to meet you, Phil. Your dad and I have been waiting a long time."

Dale stroked his fingers through Greg's hair, smiling.

The idea of being a dad was still alien to him, a little. He was twenty-two. His friends were more concerned about the next basketball game, or their schoolwork, but those had lost their importance now. Greg was looking forward to his baby, and the sleepless nights his friends had joked about.

"I'm glad I'm in this with you," Dale

murmured, squeezing Greg's thigh.

"I'm glad, too," he said.

The bonding marks on their wrists gleamed in the soft light, and Greg leaned in close to his omega, finally content to wait.

PHIL HASTINGS took his time to be born. Dale panted and heaved, his grip so tight on Greg's hand that Greg thought his knuckles might fuse together.

With a cry, Dale *pushed,* and the midwife lifted the baby up, Phil's skin covered in a mess of fluids. The midwife cleared his nostrils, and Phil sucked in a deep breath, wailing.

After all those months of thinking the pregnancy might fail, the sound was only too welcome.

Greg met Dale's relieved gaze. Dale sank back into his pillows, sweat matting his hair, his eyes half-lidded.

"You did great," Greg whispered in his ear, kissing his temple. "I'm proud of you."

"I'm not sure I want another baby," Dale whispered back, his grip loosening around Greg's hand. "This fucking hurt."

"You'll want another one," Greg said, kissing him on the lips. "Maybe not now, but I know you, Dale. You'll love all your babies."

"Fine. But don't you dare try giving me another baby right now," Dale said.

Greg laughed, brushing Dale's hair away from his forehead. The past nine hours had been agonizing for Dale—first the wait, then the contractions, and Dale had been in such pain that Greg felt bad for him, felt helpless for not being able to do anything for his omega. But Dale had held through the pain, birthing their baby.

Greg dropped kisses all over Dale's face, leaning back when the midwife stepped over with Phil.

Dale cradled the bundle, a smile blooming on his face. Greg couldn't believe how tiny their baby was. It would barely fit in his hands, and he was afraid of accidentally hurting it. But Dale pressed a kiss to Phil's little face, and Greg relaxed a little. He'd watch his omega, learn how to do all this. So they could both do the parenting right.

Greg pulled both of them into his arms, protectiveness surging through his chest. Both Dale and their baby had not come easily to him. And as he looked down at his family, he knew he'd do whatever it took to keep them safe.

THEIR WEDDING took place six months later, in the middle of June. When the stress of being new parents had eased a little, and when semester had ended for Greg, they held a little ceremony on the outskirts of Meadowfall, on the edge of the surrounding woods.

Greg had let Dale have the final say on the wedding decorations—from their suits to the forest ceremony, from the hibiscus bouquets to the coffee-and-macarons reception. It was to be a small wedding, with family and friends, and a few of

Dale's ex-students from the lab.

Dale had invited the basketball team along, too. Greg was relieved to see that there was no judgment on his friends' faces when they congratulated him and Dale. Sam Brentwood from the bookshop was there, along with Kade and Felix Brentwood, and their two-year-old daughter.

In the midst of paper cranes hanging from the trees, Greg and Dale stood together, June and Cher in the front row holding on to a beaming Phil. He was dressed in the rabbit onesie, wearing the pink booties Greg had proposed with. It didn't quite match their black-and-white suits, but Dale had grinned when he saw their baby. And that had been all Greg needed to agree on that outfit.

In the last row, Greg's parents sat together, his dad's face austere, his mom's eyes lit with a quiet joy. Greg hoped they wouldn't make a fuss. There would be no asking the audience for objections — not today, not this wedding.

With the birds twittering overhead and a cool breeze rustling through the trees, they exchanged their vows.

Not for the first time, Greg admired his omega, the quiet intelligence sparkling in his eyes, the kindness in his smile, the way he beamed up at Greg, seeing Greg for who he was.

Greg took Dale's hand, brushing his fingers along the silvery scar at his wrist. Strands of gray glinted in Dale's auburn hair, more than there was a year ago. Their relationship and the pregnancy had taken its toll on Dale. But his eyes crinkled when he smiled, and he was beautiful, both inside and out.

Greg didn't care about ages and employment and everything else, when Dale bowed his head and said, "I do."

"Do you, Greg Hastings, take this man to be your lawful omega?" the minister asked.

"I do," Greg said, his throat tightening.

In the privacy of their bedroom, their bonding marks had meant *I will always be there for you*. But here, in front of the audience, their oaths meant a different thing. That they were unafraid of their relationship. That they would no longer apologize for it. And it took a weight off Greg's chest, one he wasn't aware of before.

"You may exchange your rings," the minister said, holding out the two silver bands.

Greg took the smaller ring, Dale's hand slender in his own. He slid the ring onto Dale's finger, watching as Dale blinked back his tears. Then, Dale slid the larger ring onto Greg's finger. It sat warm on Greg's skin, and for a moment, he admired all of this. They were now lawfully wedded. No one could oppose to this bonding. And Dale was his.

Dale looked up at him, his mouth open, wonder and disbelief in his eyes. So Greg leaned in, kissing him softly on the lips. "Love you," he murmured.

"Love you, too," Dale whispered, stepping closer, winding his arms around Greg's neck. Around them, their guests clapped. Greg savored the warmth of Dale's lips, the love in his touch, and hugged him tight.

When they pulled apart, Dale kissed Greg on the cheek, a smile playing on his lips. June stepped up to hand Phil over to Dale, and Greg admired how much their baby had grown over the past six months.

Phil waved at him, making a grab for the red hibiscus in Greg's breast pocket. "Hey," Greg said, catching his hand. "Don't do that."

Phil gurgled, smiling toothlessly.

Greg didn't notice his parents' approach until they were feet away, his mother trailing behind his father with a concerned frown. They were both dressed in black, almost like dark shadows drawing near. Dale gulped, holding Phil tight.

Greg fought the urge to step between Dale and his dad. They were family in name now, but he wasn't going to turn this into a confrontation, not just yet. He straightened his shoulders, stepping closer to Dale, wrapping his arm around Dale's shoulder.

"Congrats," Bernard Hastings said, his solemn gaze darting between Greg and Dale.

Greg hadn't spoken to him since ten months ago, on the night of June's wedding. He hadn't been sure what else he could say to his dad at that point, but in the time since, he'd come up with a few things. Didn't mean he wasn't nervous, though.

"Hey, Dad," Greg said, his pulse thudding. "This is my omega, Dale. I believe you've met before."

Dale gave Bernard a weak smile, and Greg squeezed him, lending him strength.

"This is our son, Phil," Greg said. "I don't know if you'd accept him as your grandson, but that's who he also is. Phil's six months old."

For a taut moment, Bernard looked at Phil, his expression inscrutable. Then he glanced at Dale, and Dale lifted his chin, meeting his gaze.

Pride swelled in Greg's chest. A year ago, Dale had cowered in front of Bernard Hastings, afraid for his job. Now, Bernard had no more control over him, and Dale was happier, freer. And Greg knew his omega would do anything to protect their baby from any danger.

Bernard drew a deep breath, lowering his chin. "Your choices are yours to make, Gregory. I hadn't...considered that the child would be my grandson."

"You've forgotten family," Greg said, his heart squeezing. "That's most important. Status doesn't matter. Neither does age. You can have all the goals you want, but you can't take my family away from me."

"I will not," Bernard said. He extended his hand — the most of a truce he was willing to offer. Greg shook his hand, remembering the better days, back when his father had taught him to play ball and read comic books. When he finally set his college matters aside, Greg was certain that his dad would remember those memories someday.

Bernard nodded at Dale, and looked at their baby again. Then he turned, heading for his car.

Greg's mom stepped up to them with a sheepish smile, pulling Dale and Greg into a hug. "Take care, all of you," she whispered. "I'll bake some casseroles and come visit sometime."

"That'll be delightful," Dale said, breaking into a smile. "I'd love that."

"Dale's favorite is pulled pork," Greg said,

hugging his mom. "Thanks for coming."

She kissed them both on the cheek, then stepped away, waving. "Thank you for the invite. The wedding was all so beautiful."

As she turned to follow Greg's father, Dale stepped in close, leaning into Greg's chest. "That went... better than I expected," he said.

"It'll get better," Greg murmured, hugging him. "Mom was right. He was swayed by Phil."

Dale chuckled, weak with relief. "I hope you're right."

"This time, I think I am."

As the rest of the wedding guests stepped closer to congratulate them, Greg held on to Dale and their baby, pressing a kiss to Dale's forehead. The worst parts of their lives were over with. He was bonded to Dale, married to him, and their baby was happy and healthy. And Greg didn't need to ask for more, when the future ahead was bright and warm, full of hope.

ABOUT THE AUTHOR

A huge fan of angst and bittersweet tension, Anna has been scribbling since she was fourteen. She believes that everyone needs a safe place, and so her dorky guys fall in love, make mistakes, and slowly find their way back into each other's arms.

Anna loves fine lines on her notebook paper, and is especially fond of her tiny glass globe. She is currently living on the west coast of the US with her husband and a menagerie of stuffed animals..

Printed in Great Britain
by Amazon